THE NICOLE PETERSC

Nothing Left to Give

WHEN ALL YOU HAVE IS NOT ENOUGH

Marcus Pomrey Griffin

All scripture quotations are taken from Biblegateway.com, the King James Version of the bible. Public Domain.

Cover and Interior Design by KUHN Design Group | kuhndesigngroup.com
Cover Photo by: Grady Carter Photography

NOTHING LEFT TO GIVE

ISBN: 978-1-7346100-3-1 (paperback)
ISBN: 979-8-9891396-4-4 (eBook)

Published by The Master Communicator's Writing Services— www.mcwritingservices.com

In Memory of My Mother.

A strong God-fearing woman. No fear of any man or woman. Full of faith and conviction. A walking testimony that never cursed. God created the perfect mother for me even choking me once. I don't know where I would have been without her and her determination to raise me the right way. I was such a strong-willed child, and yet she had the attitude, wherever you want to show out, that's where we'll handle it. Because of her, I love strong women.

Thank you, Mama. I love you, my cool Mom!

Perfection is achieved, not when there is nothing more to add,
but when there is nothing left to take away.

ANTOINE DE SAINT-EXUPÉRY

CHAPTER ONE

March 29, 1983 (Tuesday)

I was sixteen, perfect, just like Mother made me, but all I thought about was dying. I wasn't Nicole anymore. I was an attraction designed to make others feel good. I played to the desires of the mayor, governors, and other dignitaries, to piano judges and audiences. I'd played at 307 weddings, events, competitions, and recitals over the past two years, sometimes three or four in a weekend.

The repetition of playing was all the same, note after note, taking me on the same familiar path to nowhere, through another round of a pointless song. The piano was supposed to be beautiful, just like Daddy used to tell me I was. I didn't believe Cristofori had envisioned this when he'd invented the piano, yet I'd learned it didn't matter how I felt. Feelings were a commodity I couldn't afford anymore.

Smile. Hold your head up. Cross your legs just right. Play another song. Play another. Then another. "Composure beyond her age," one interviewer had written.

Mother believed the sacrifices and the small attention to detail would pay off. Keep chasing. Take that extra step. We're almost there. All lies.

Did God even care? Did God listen to my prayers? How had I lost my dream? Was I just a nameless face, a soulless doll? No matter what questions were in my mind, I knew I was nothing more than a container filled and emptied at my mother's whim.

Even my bedroom, once my refuge, now a showroom equipped with a Queen Anne upright piano, plush cream carpet swapped out yearly, walls painted and decorated with images of Beethoven, Chopin, and Bach in oak frames measured and leveled precisely, as Mother demanded. The lamps were centered on the bedside tables; the clothes in the closet were spaced, measured, and hung evenly throughout.

When I was turning twelve, all I wanted was to play in the swimming pool with the friends I once had. I wanted to laugh so hard that my stomach ached. I wanted to get butterflies when a boy I liked spoke and see Daddy's face the day that boy asked me out. I just wanted a simple life, but now I see Mother wanted more.

Daddy's gone now. No one wants me. No one will miss me. No one even cares.

A clear thought to end it all appeared in my mind as I turned to look at the closet: take the t-shirts of the competitions I'd won and tie them together, with one end around the rod in the closet and the other snuggly around my neck. Then I could sit on the soft carpet, and all I had to do was go to sleep. I wouldn't have to go through another day of knowing I was nothing.

I threw the clothes hanging in the closet aside. Would Mother first notice the clothes hanging in disarray or me?

I quickly tied one end of the tied shirts around the wooden clothes rod. I created a slipknot on the other end and placed it around my neck, leaving me just enough room to sit down. The carpet was so soft, almost like thick cotton.

I closed my eyes and let my mind drift, just like clouds.

CHAPTER TWO

March 10, 1979 (Saturday)

The telephone rang in the kitchen. I rushed to answer it, hoping this call was from my best friend, Nadia. I hadn't received my RSVP yet.

"Hello, the Petersons' residence. May I help you?"

"Hi, Nicole. This is Vernon Abrams. Is your father available?"

"Hold on." I put the receiver on my shoulder to muffle the sound. "Daddy, Mr. Abrams is on the phone."

Lately, Daddy's boss seemed to call most days he was off, and today was no different. Daddy sat at our kitchen table, nursing a glass of water. He had his suit pants and shirt on, loose tie, and coat hanging over the chair. He sat seemingly in a trance, tired but almost ready for the wedding, just as he had promised.

"Daddy?"

He sighed and shook his head.

"Daddy, do you want me to tell him you're not here?"

"No. I never want you to lie for any reason. I'll take it." He stood, gently took the phone, put it on his shoulder, raised my chin, and looked deep into my eyes. "Please, Nicole. Never lie for me…or…to me. Please."

"Yes, sir."

He took a deep breath and put the receiver to his ear.

"This is Glen."

I couldn't make out what Daddy's boss was saying, but I saw Daddy intently listening. He was so drained after working so much lately. He never seemed to sleep; if he did, it wouldn't be long.

"Yes," Daddy said, "I left the files on my desk, and I left a copy with Jennifer just in case. I also locked a copy in the safe in my office…Yes, I'll hold."

Daddy sat down.

"What's wrong, Daddy?"

"Nothing's wrong, Sweetheart."

"Nicole," Mama said from behind, "please go out and check the mail and let me know if that letter comes."

"Yes, ma'am." When I walked out, he had his head in his hand.

"Look, Vernon," Daddy said in the receiver, "you know I'm off for the next few days. That's why we hired Clarence to fill in…I'll hold."

Daddy shook his head and closed his eyes.

"Glen," Mama said, "just tell him you can't go in. We have the wedding in a few hours, and Nicole is expecting you to be there, plus we have dinner over at Terrance's house. This is our weekend. You've already worked eighty hours this week. Besides, you need to get some sleep. All these hours aren't good for you."

"I know," he said softly under his breath.,

Mama turned around. "Nicole, hurry up and go check the mailbox."

I stepped outside onto the porch and stood for a moment. Our neighborhood was like a splattering of two-story colonial-style houses built inside a dense forest. All the houses had wooden porches of various colors wrapped around each place, but most of the mailboxes seemed to come from the same store.

Once I walked off our porch, I noticed a chill in the morning air. The clouds were rolling in, and I could almost smell the coming rain. I was looking forward to this wedding. It gave me a chance to finally improvise an entire song instead of regurgitating notes. Also, Daddy would be attending. He had missed most family events, but he'd promised to be at this wedding, so I knew he wouldn't miss it.

I tried not to worry about the call. Once at the mailbox, I pulled it open, and there it was: my RSVP in my favorite color, powder blue. I pulled it out and opened it. My invitation had white lace, the lace that matched my room. Nadia's RSVPs were special. Desiree, my other best friend, would get burnt orange. Karen would get forest green. All the others would get their favorite colors.

I had been waiting almost a year for this party, and it was almost here. It was then I looked up and saw Mama standing on our porch. Now I knew how important this letter was. She never wore house shoes outside. Never.

I quickly checked the other mail in the box. Pushed way in the back was a white business envelope. When I pulled it out, I realized it was the letter Mama was looking for. As soon as she saw the letter, she stepped off the porch and rushed over.

Although the letter was addressed to Daddy, Mama tore it open, which I was sure was a federal offense, but I was also sure she didn't care. She skimmed the letter. With each line, her grin grew into a brilliant, uninhibited smile. She rushed inside the house like a child bursting with news. I slowly followed, immediately losing interest in my RSVP. I knew what the letter meant.

By the time I made it to the kitchen, Daddy was off the phone and sitting at the table reading the letter. Mama stood behind him, grinning, and said, "Glen, look at all those zeroes. I thought you were crazy, but you were right. 'We have not because we ask not.'"

When Daddy finished reading the job offer letter, he sighed and turned to me. I knew what was on his mind. He had told me although he had three productive interviews, he didn't think he would get the job. He had purposely asked for some astronomical amount because it had to be worth it for him to leave me. It had to cover his job and then some, but I had this unshakable feeling he would get it. I just knew.

No matter how many zeroes, if he took the job, he would be gone for a whole year.

"What's wrong, Glen?" Mama asked.

Daddy sat at the table, head in one hand and letter in the other. He slowly shook his head. Although I knew he would have loved the job of engineering, programming, and installing computer networks throughout Europe and Asia, he loved me more.

Mama gently took the letter, pulled a chair close to him, sat and took his hand, and placed it on her cheek. She started reading his job offer letter in a gentle, sultry voice that got his attention. Daddy became lost in her words, her smile, and even the way she caressed his hand. There was no doubt how much he loved everything about Mama, especially that voice.

I imagined that amount of money was the answer to Mama's prayers. She was so worried about bills, the house, and the cars, but it was all material things. I had prayed too. I prayed Daddy would stay. We didn't need any of this stuff, but what did God do when there were opposing prayers like Mama's and mine?

I even went to the altar and was happy Mama's best friend, Ms. Brenda, stood in front of me to pray with me. She had a real connection with God and insight into how God moved in unique situations. I opened up to her and told her my heart. Once the prayer ended, I opened my eyes. I saw her answer in her eyes. The truth hurts sometimes. There were no words left to say.

The silence in the kitchen made me realize Mama had finished reading the letter. Me and Daddy's eyes met.

"Nicole," he said, "how would you feel if I took this job?"

"If," Mama said, "wait. Now you promised me."

"No," he said to Mama, seemingly forgetting to wait for my answer to his question. "I promised if nothing else comes available, then I would leave, but you remember that's what the dinner is for in Valdosta…Terrance's house? You remember?"

Mama closed her eyes and took a deep breath, then exhaled slowly. She, too, was a person of her word. She nodded, opened her eyes, and said, "Yes, I remember, but if it doesn't work out over there, you take this job. Baby, we need it. Okay?"

She placed her hand gently on his cheek and kissed him tenderly. She picked the letter up again and started reading. Without saying anything, I ran upstairs to my room, not wanting to hear Mama read the letter again like it was some romance novel. There was nothing to celebrate. How in the world did it get to this moment?

CHAPTER THREE

March 10, 1979 (Saturday)

My room was my refuge away from everything that happened on the outside. Daddy leaving. Mama's business. The word prodigy. Excessive playing. Pasted on smiles. The list seemed to be endless. I felt like an object on display outside, but I was at home in my room.

My room was the one place I could stay for hours on end. Daddy even created an office in another room in the house where I could do my homework, so my room could truly be my refuge. It had to be the best spot in the entire house to enjoy the weather.

Outside my window, I could see the horizon of homes and trees. The wind blew such fresh air. This time, I saw the black and gray storm clouds rolling in. I sat on my bed and thought about how even the smallest things reminded me of Daddy.

A little over a year ago, Mama wanted the walls in my room to be lavender, her favorite color, because someone wanted to do an article about me, Darlington's Prodigy. She said, "Lavender looks beautiful in pictures," but Daddy said, "So does powder blue."

He even let me choose the powder blue curtains and bedspread, all trimmed in white lace. He told me and Mama if I was going to work so hard for her, then I at least had the right to choose how to decorate my room. Mama definitely didn't like it, but Daddy just kissed her and said, "It is Nicole's room, and she has great taste."

See, I knew how much Daddy loved her. I knew Daddy would do anything for her, so for him standing up for me against her, the one I knew he would die for, made me feel…I couldn't even think of the words, but I knew how I felt—loved.

I knew my place. To Daddy, it was God first, Mama second, then me, but he had such a way of making me feel like I was the only one there. Even after the decision about my room, although Mama got mad trying to reason with him, Daddy didn't budge when it came down to my room.

Distant thunder rolled across the sky. Storms were once my greatest fear, but now one of my greatest loves, all because of Daddy. When I was four, I was scared of the daytime thunderstorms that ripped through our town of Darlington, Georgia, but at night I was terrified. Darkness. Light flashing. Violent thunder. Again, again, and again.

I remember hiding under my bed and covering my ears. The thunder seemed to shake our house like an off-balance washing machine, yet it was Daddy who found me under my bed and turned my biggest fear of storms into my greatest love of music.

He'd pick me up and hold me as the lightning flashed across the sky, and we'd wait for the roll of thunder to shake the house. Then he and I would run to the piano and reproduce the sound of rolling thunder. For as long as I could remember, I just loved sitting down at the same Queen Anne piano that was now in my room, creating feelings and moods, and listening to my father play. He had a way of making chords sound so beautiful, especially during stormy nights. He told me, "There is no sound more calming and beautiful than rain on a tin roof." It was he who tapped into my love of piano, music, improvisation, and all the beauty they could bring.

I got up from the bed, sat at the piano, and played our favorite song, "Silent Night." I closed my eyes and let the music just come to me. It was almost like breathing in. When I exhaled, I was there on that peaceful night, and I let the notes capture the moment. I felt the cool desert air while the wise men walked. The notes of the song rearranged in my mind and took me on a musical journey. I felt the essence of holiness and peace as I played. I saw Jesus sleeping in the manger and thought of the chords that made me feel the beauty of a baby's smile. The warmth of the music and images in my head made me forget about everything that was going on.

It was then I felt someone else in my room. I opened my eyes to see Daddy standing at the door. In his hand, he held the $151.00 fuchsia dress I was to wear to the wedding that was happening in a few hours. Lately, the dresses seemed to get more expensive depending on the importance of the event. This wedding became the talk of the town as it was for Miss Frances Henderson, the Mayor's secretary's daughter.

The mother of the bride was Mama's church friend, Mrs. Louise Henderson, and Mama was doing her a favor by scheduling me to play at the wedding on a day I was supposed to be off. And to top it off, Mama bought that dress when I had so many other dresses, including fuchsia ones, but I guessed they weren't the right shade of fuchsia.

Daddy laid the dress on my bed while I still played, trying to push all of this away, at least for now. He came over and stood beside me, humming "Silent Night" softly while I played. I moved over and gave him room to sit beside me. When he sat down, I stopped playing. He picked up where I'd left off, still engrossed in the song. After a few moments, he asked, "Nicole, how do you feel about me and the job?"

The music played, and I wondered what I could say, but would whatever I said make a difference? I guess he sensed that because he said as he played, "I remember you playing this song during the Christmas program. Oh, Nicole, it was such a beautiful night. I can't believe we didn't record you."

He closed his eyes and tilted his head to the left. Just the way he played those chords and arpeggios took me back. He never rushed me. He wanted me to learn how to express myself, stepping in when he had to. Even that night during the Christmas program two years ago, he stepped in.

Mama wanted me to play some classical song that I just wasn't feeling, but Daddy changed it all in the middle of the program. I was only nine two years ago, and it was hard for me to tell Mama I just didn't feel that song. Although beautiful, I didn't even bother to learn the name, but she didn't care. The show had to go on.

Just before I was about to play, I turned to him and stared. I didn't know what to say, but then he tilted his head as if hearing my heart; he stood up and went to the front of the church and talked to the congregation.

Mama stood off to the side, composed, but I could tell she was mad. When he finished talking to the church, he came up and stood by me, touched me on my shoulder, and smiled. He lifted my chin, then said to the congregation, "Imagine the night when Jesus was born and let Nicole take you there." He smiled and said to me, "Now close your eyes and show us how it felt the night Jesus was born."

He sat in the chair near me. I closed my eyes to his smiling face. I didn't remember what I played, but I knew I felt something that night. All I thought about was the beauty when he used to play "Silent Night" for me when I was a little girl. I pictured how it felt that night as if God himself opened up time and let me in.

Ms. Brenda said she actually felt the calmness in the church and saw Jesus sleeping in the manger. There were other comments, but one quote stuck with me from Ms. Eleanor, a French southerner and owner of Eleanor's Boutique, where so many others and I got our performance dresses. She quoted Antoine de Saint-Exupéry in her French accent: "Perfection is achieved, not when there is nothing more to add, but when there is nothing left to take away."

I really didn't understand exactly what she meant, but her French accent made it sound so good. All I knew were the words made an impression. It was also the night the word prodigy began to spread, and Mama's eyes turned toward me. We had stumbled upon a common ground I didn't know existed.

For the following two years, the word "prodigy" opened up so many doors for Mama's business as a wedding and event planner. She seemed to enjoy every opportunity—piano competitions, weddings, recitals, trips, beautiful hotels, and upscale restaurants. I had hoped for something special between Mama and me as I got older, but over those two years, things didn't turn out the way I had planned, although I tried my best to see things as she did.

I could come up with so many examples, but in reality, we were like east and west, oil and water, and only three things connected us: Daddy, piano, and Charles.

Daddy leaned against me to let me know to come back in my mind.

I leaned against him to show him I was back in the present. Just like that, I thought about him leaving again.

"Nicole," he said, just as he chorded "Silent Night," "you've done such a great job of keeping your word to your mother. I know you were young when you promised her you would help, however she saw fit. I am especially proud of you. You haven't complained about any of the performances during the past two years. Grown people don't even act that mature. You have been exceptional. I know you have another year, but I am so proud of how you handled yourself. To me, there is nothing I wouldn't do for you."

He made a smooth transition to "My Funny Valentine," the song I was supposed to play at the wedding later today, but just the way he played it pulled the truth out of me.

"Then why don't you stay?" I asked.

"I'm trying. After the wedding, we are going over to your Uncle Terrance's house, and he's going to talk about a chance we can start over, and I won't have to leave. Otherwise, there are no other options because we just owe too much money."

"What about my dresses? We can sell them all."

I had a closet with forty pairs of shoes and fifty-two dresses. With that fuchsia one, now fifty-three. I would have been glad to get rid of them all.

"Sweetheart, I wish it were that simple. I know I sound like a broken record by now, but you are almost twelve, and I missed so much about you growing up. Don't get me wrong; I would work tirelessly, but now it's just costing too much."

He stopped playing, and I took over.

"You know," he said, looking down at the keys, "one day I will be walking you down the aisle, and Nicole, I just don't want to miss you growing up anymore. I know people in the military or other jobs do it all the time, but I didn't get married and have you just to watch you grow up in pictures and videos. I just don't want to miss anymore. This is something I need to do.

Although I knew he was right, I had hoped that there was a chance for Valdosta, but no matter how positive or how much I asked God, the answer seemed to be he was leaving, and I needed to prepare. I closed my eyes and tried something new. I tried to ignore my feelings and just believe what I wanted. I chose to hope everything turned out by ignoring my negative thoughts.

I stopped playing, and he picked up where I left off.

"So, let's not miss this moment," he said as he brought the song to an end. "Tell me about the PJs and the Pool party."

I started playing Scott Joplin's "The Entertainer," and we smiled as my words came out like a faucet.

"Daddy, it will be me, Nadia, Desiree, and all the other girls. Can you believe it? Twelve girls over at Nadia's house? Her father built this S-shaped slide that I swear is as tall as the roof of the house. Nadia says you could go so fast that you could even skip like a rock when you hit the water."

"No way."

"Yes. I just want to have fun and laugh so hard that my stomach aches. I want to forget about classical piano for now and be just Nicole. Hey Daddy, what would you say when someone asks me out?"

"I would say when did you turn twenty-one?"

I laughed.

"You know," he said, "You should enjoy your day. I know you've been waiting a while. Yes, I agree. Forget about the piano and just enjoy your friends."

It was then I thought about most of the girls. A lot of them were wearing two-piece bathing suits. "Daddy, when can I wear a two-piece bathing suit?"

"Well…I imagine when you bring that date over—twenty-one? No, twenty-three. Yeah, that's it."

We both laughed.

There was another knock on the door. "Nicole," Mama said, standing at the door with Charles by her side, "I should've known your father was up here when you were playing with all that laughter."

Daddy pulled something from his pocket and placed it on top of the piano. It was the cufflinks Charles needed for the tuxedo he would wear as one of the groomsmen for the wedding. I didn't even know how he found his way into the wedding. I figured it was just an opportunity for him to dress up, but this wedding was an event.

"Hey Nicole," Charles said, "I thought I heard you playing 'My Funny Valentine' earlier."

I knew that was Charles' favorite song, so I switched to playing it for him. Mama closed her eyes. I saw her fingers move as if she were playing. Charles stared at the piano, and Daddy just listened. Even to see Charles at twenty-three, standing beside Mama, the two were still comfortable in silence.

All who knew Charles when he was younger said he was destined for prison, but Mama believed he would be different when he grew up, and she was right. It was like she found the Hope Diamond in a mound of coal. Now, there he stood, 5 foot 9 inches tall, slender, engaging eyes, so much like Mama's eyes. Some people think that he's my brother or cousin, but we are of no relation at all. He's just the son that Mama always dreamed of having.

Nadia, some of the boys called her Redbone, loved that their light complexions and hazel eyes matched. Desiree loved his sense of humor and soothing, sultry voice, a voice he picked up from Mama. Karen loved his curly hair. All my other friends loved something about him, but me, I could use one word to describe Charles—gorgeous. Maybe I shouldn't have called a man gorgeous, but handsome just wasn't good enough.

To think of it, all my friends agreed that he was a light-skinned Billy Dee Williams. Even that day, he wore a royal blue silk shirt just to pick up cufflinks from Daddy.

Charles had his eyes closed, along with Mama. I imagined he was thinking of his fiancée, Joyce. He told me that she was the best thing that ever happened to him. She had beautiful smooth brown skin, a radiant smile, and brown eyes filled with so much love. Charles loved her heart. Just being in her presence brought every good thing out of him.

People talked about what beautiful children they would have, but I didn't think they cared. Charles and Joyce loved each other with their eyes closed. At least that's what Daddy said, and I agreed.

I did a turnaround in the song.

Nadia told me that I was jealous of Charles. Some of the other girls agreed. I understood why they felt that way. Charles was truly a vision of perfection, just like my mother. I knew Mama preferred time with him to time with me. She laughed freely with him and rarely shared anything of any substance with me. I probably should have been jealous, but I really wasn't. How could I be?

Charles gave her things that I couldn't. He loved and appreciated Mama's world, and she needed that, so I didn't mind. He had a way of bringing out the best in anyone, including Mama. Charles had a quiet confidence and a contagious sense of humor, things that she loved and needed from the son she never had. It would have been selfish for me to be jealous of Charles. There was no one like him. Well, no one except Daddy.

It was Daddy who poured his life into mine and opened my heart to the beauty of music. I loved music, the piano, the feel, the sound, just like Daddy loved music. He made me feel beautiful. He made me feel needed and loved. I played the last note and let it linger.

"I love it when you improvise," Charles said.

He wasn't jealous of me either.

"Nicole," Mama said, "you have fifteen minutes to be ready. It's almost time to leave."

"Yes, ma'am."

"Mr. Glen, do you have a few moments? I need to talk with you in private about something."

"About what?" I asked.

"Don't you worry about it, nosey," Charles said.

"I'll meet you in the garage," Daddy said. "Just give me a moment with Nicole."

Mama and Charles left while Daddy stayed seated.

"You know," Daddy said, "leaving is really hard for me. If I have to leave, I would rather sacrifice this year than lose any more time away from you. This is the one final sacrifice, and then you will become my priority. I promise."

"There's still a chance, Daddy."

"Yes, I know."

He got up, kissed me on my cheek, and walked out.

It was then I heard the thunder rolling across the sky.

CHAPTER FOUR

March 10, 1979 (Saturday)

Mama pulled Daddy to the corner near the organ just as the rain started pouring outside. He had gotten another call from work on the way to the wedding, this time about some papers for one of the accounts. Mama was tired of him working so much. This was supposed to be Daddy's time off, but he always seemed to have a problem saying no to work.

He had already been up for twenty-four hours, and she wanted him to stay home and sleep through the wedding, but he wanted to see me improvise. I had a feeling there would be a quiet moment unfolding between Daddy and Mama. Just watching them, it was Mama who tilted her head in such a way that made Daddy nod his head. I guess that wasn't good enough for her because she pulled him farther away from everyone, not wanting to lose her patience. Even from this distance, it was funny because he was listening to the rain now.

Her weddings ran so effortlessly, yet Mama believed Daddy needed a laundry list of dos and don'ts just for sitting down during the wedding. Watching him was like watching a cartoon with words going in one ear and out the other. Mama didn't notice; she was too busy looking around and making sure everything was in place.

"Wow," I whispered to myself, "so that's how Daddy does it. He just goes somewhere else in his mind."

I wouldn't dare try that with Mama, but it sure seemed to work for him.

I went ahead and took my place off to the right and sat in one of the two fuchsia-covered chairs assigned to Daddy and me. He strolled over to me, and as soon as he was by my side, my stomach growled loudly. Mama glanced our way. Daddy placed his hand over his stomach as if he had made the noise. She just closed her eyes. He gave me some candy to settle my stomach.

The church filled quickly, and the ceremony started. Although I had done so many weddings, this was the first time in two years that I would be allowed to improvise and play as freely as I felt.

The church altar was flanked by eleven bridesmaids wearing deep fuchsia tea-length dresses and eleven groomsmen in black tuxedos with fuchsia ties. They were strategically placed on the dais, creating a heart with all eyes on the bride and groom at the bottom.

Mama signaled for me to come and play "My Funny Valentine." Daddy nodded his head. Charles, standing as one of the groomsmen, had his usual warm grin, and he was still somehow getting glimpses from the other bridesmaids. But I knew he was on his best behavior because Joyce was in the congregation.

Once at the piano, I noticed Miss Frances could have been in a magazine wearing this white mermaid floor-length beaded gown with these beautiful, laced sleeves, and yet, in all her beauty, her tears streamed from under her matching veil.

I began playing and praying that this song would comfort her in a way that she wouldn't forget. Daddy said the way I formed chords had a drawing effect, almost like gasping for air, pulling you into your thoughts and enhancing the emotions of the moment.

Mama thought I was too young to understand what all of this really meant to the bride, which was why she would give me my laundry list, too. Still, when I closed my eyes and imagined how it would feel to be standing at the altar with my prince, the one I'd been waiting for my whole life, just like in my fairy tales, I knew it had to be something beyond words.

Thunder ripped across the sky, and the rain poured outside, but those sounds took my mind back to something Daddy said about marriage. The way he explained it, the rain or the storms didn't matter because they came and went. What mattered was to have that one true love standing by your side, ready to go through any storm.

Miss Frances' tears subsided as her fiancé put his arm around her waist. Her expression was different now. Just the way she gazed into the groom's eyes made me wonder about the power of love and how a person could love so deeply. Was love really limitless?

I thought about Daddy and Mama. Even after the many years, they had been married, I knew Daddy just loved Mama. Maybe love was an endless ocean built to weather any storm. Before I could think of anything else, the bride released this radiant smile that could only come from way deep within.

Maybe it was just that simple, adding up to a warm, unexplainable feeling, being there with the one you loved.

I closed my eyes again, took in the good feelings from her, and knitted those feelings into the music that I played. All the way to the end of the song, I wondered: how would my day be? By the time I played the last note, Miss Frances was beaming. I thanked God for His presence and went back to Daddy's side.

I noticed that Mrs. Daily, the mayor's wife, a lady I had never met, was looking my way. She smiled this motherly smile and nodded. Then she turned and watched Mama.

Whenever my mother walked into a room, people would look at her twice. Nadia called it that double-take beauty. She was wearing her fuchsia formal halter-neck gown, but I didn't think that was what caught Mrs. Daily's eye. I believed it was because, at that moment, she looked just like Dorothy Dandridge.

Daddy said that when I was a little girl, I walked around the house with an old March 1966 Ebony magazine because I thought it was Mama on the cover. Mrs. Daily caught Mama's eyes.

Mama had never officially met Mrs. Daily, but somehow there was a connection. Mama matched her smile. She made all of this look easy, but I didn't think anyone knew the late nights she spent on the smallest details. She'd told me a person should walk into any event and feel something special. Looking out over the smiling witnesses, she had done her job well.

My best friends, Nadia and Desiree, wouldn't have missed this wedding for anything either, asking Mama six months ago, then five months. She had finally said yes two months ago. This wedding, the biggest of Mama's to date, was the buzz in Darlington, our small southern town near Valdosta. She always said, "No one knows our town exists, at least for now."

Looking back, I became part of her plan as soon as the word prodigy was uttered. I knew Mama wanted to put Darlington on the map. When I was nine, she had put me in piano competitions and added classical music to her weddings with me as a featured pianist, Darlington's prodigy. Her weddings turned into events, eventually getting Ms. Louise, the mayor's secretary's attention.

While preparing for this wedding late one night, Mama told me, "Besides Jesus, Solomon was the wisest man who ever lived. He said a good name is better than great riches and loving favor better than silver and gold." She would say things like that as we stayed in suites, but even in all her sayings, I saw a deeper longing in her.

In the middle of the ceremony, while Reverend Joseph talked in a commanding bass voice, Charles, or as my friends called him, Mr. Gorgeous, gave me a quick glance and winked at me with his hazel eyes. I winked back. Well, as best as an eleven-year-old could. I had known him my whole life. The winks were all fun. His fiancée, Joyce, sat a few pews away from the front, and she grinned at me.

Charles swore the Commodores' song, "Brick House," had been created with her in mind. My best friends, Nadia and Desiree, sat next to Joyce. Well, Desiree sat next to Joyce. Nadia still couldn't believe Joyce and Charles were still together after almost two years. Nadia wanted twenty-three-year-old Charles all to her twelve-year-old self.

"I'm woman enough for him," she'd say.

I'd tell her, "Somehow, twelve years old and woman shouldn't be used in the same sentence." Nadia would laugh it off, but when I watched her as she stared at Charles, I'd known she wasn't joking.

She winked at Charles, believing she could compete with Joyce. I had to admit that, watching Nadia sit in her lilac dress, her brownish hair up, hazel eyes, she was, in fact, beautiful, too. I also had to admit that if she'd been a little older or within striking distance of eighteen, Joyce would have had to take Nadia seriously. Nadia loved the attention, especially being called Redbone by the boys in school.

Desiree leaned over and whispered in Nadia's ear. Oh, just the expression on Nadia's face. I knew what Desiree had said. "You really could pass for his little sister."

I just put my head down. She hated that, but no matter how we crushed on him, he was too old for all of us. We knew that, but I had to admit it was fun.

I giggled as I watched the bride and groom exchange their vows and their attempt at a kiss. It was a shy peck, unlike the other weddings I'd performed in. Daddy shouted out, "Kiss her again!"

Mama did a slow blink, composing herself, probably thinking he was sleep-deprived. I was sure Daddy wouldn't be attending any more weddings.

The following kiss hushed the church. It was the kind of kiss that made couples think about how they'd met. Charles and Joyce stared at each other. Their eyes told a passionate story. Mrs. Daily maintained a pleasant smile.

Daddy looked at Mama too. She had this glowing smile, but when she and Daddy's eyes met, Mama's smile subsided, and her eyes became intense. She closed her eyes to break their connection and turned away. Even after the bride and groom ended their pledge of love, Daddy's eyes never left Mama.

"Ladies and gentlemen, it is my pleasure to introduce to you Mr. and Mrs. Romero Johnson."

As the bride and groom walked out, followed by the bridesmaids, groomsmen, and the rest of the procession, Nadia came up to me and whispered in my ear, "Nicole, you ever like Charles?"

"Leave it alone," Desiree said, following Nadia. "Charles loves Joyce. And how did you get so boy crazy?"

"I can't help it if my mother has educated me about life."

When we walked out, Desiree and Nadia talked about the upcoming party and bathing suits, but it was Daddy who stopped and watched Mama for a brief moment. Mama was busy going over her checklist and coordinating with the photographer for the wedding party photo shoot.

I took his hand. "Daddy, how will my day be when I get married?"

He pulled himself out of his trance and turned to me. "It will be beautiful, just like you."

As we walked out, I turned to see Mama looking our way. It was that look of something deep on her mind, so deep she stared through me.

CHAPTER FIVE

March 10, 1979 (Saturday)

Daddy was so excited about his solution that he shared it with Mama again on the way to Uncle Terrance's house. That's how they talked everything out. Daddy called it being on the same page.

He stopped at Charles' apartment to pick up Charles and Joyce. I slid over and sat behind Daddy. I'm not sure if anyone spoke to them as they got in. I smiled as Charles and Joyce held hands and watched Mama and Daddy continue their conversation as if they were studying how to talk things out.

Mama sat listening to the details of the potential plan.

"So," Daddy said, "we would move to Jackson Street for a short time. Terrance found someone to buy our house. They love the old colonial-style homes in our neighborhood."

Mama nodded and said, "I understand. Where would we live?"

"You know the yellow house down from Terrance is up for rent. He even said that we could paint it whatever color we wanted."

Mama chuckled. "Lavender?"

Daddy grinned. "Yes, especially Lavender. Terrance already asked."

Mama seemed surprised.

"It's like we would be starting over," he said. "Oh, now I know you remember those days?"

Mama had this girlish grin, seemingly lost in her thoughts. She shook herself and caressed her hands as we turned the corner. We all knew how much she loved our house, but it was something about the way she looked at Daddy. She had this sweet, gentle grin that was deeper than any words.

"Okay," she said softly, "how long would we have to do this?"

"A little over two years," Daddy said, "but we would be free and clear. We can move into the house by Nicole's birthday. You'd have to postpone the Girl's Only Weekend with her, but I'm sure she wouldn't mind."

Mama turned to me.

I nodded. Everyone had to sacrifice, but to me, to have Daddy home was well worth it.

We all waited for Mama to think as we rode down Bemiss Road to Ashley Street. Once Daddy turned right on Hill Avenue, Mama turned toward Daddy. "So," she said, "I would be closer to Eleanor's boutique. She's been wanting me to work with her for some time."

"God is right on time," I said.

Even Mama smiled at me.

~

The close-knit neighborhood where Uncle Terrance lived was on the west side of Valdosta. It was a neighborhood surrounded by a dense forest of oak trees. The two-lane black road with no dividing lines was lined on both sides with various wooden and brick houses of different colors. I could almost hear the sounds of laughter and playing as we got closer to the park across the street from Uncle Terrance's house. On the third right, we saw a small boy riding his bicycle in a circle in the middle of the road. Mama shook her head, almost in disbelief.

"Well," Daddy said, "he's making a perfect circle, his head back, eyes up toward the sky, looking toward God with no care in the world, except for this car."

"Boy," someone yelled, "get out of the road!"

He glanced at our car but kept riding in a circle. Mama turned to Daddy, who had stopped the car. Only then did the boy stop, coming to rest in front of the car. Daddy tilted his head, and the boy did the same, smiled, and then moved.

As we passed by, the boy waved. Daddy and Mama waved back. Mama shook her head as Daddy made a right on the red clay road that ran between Uncle Terrance's house and the large rectangular dirt park filled with kids of all ages.

Large oak trees surrounded the park. To the left, a massive iron swing set almost as tall as a two-story house. To the rear were iron monkey bars and wooden benches. To the right of the park was a large field where men and boys played on a dirt basketball court, also used as a football and softball field. Toward the front of the park closest to Uncle Terrance's house were a metal sliding board and a large red metal merry-go-round with this huge oak tree that was so large you could sit on the merry-go-round while it rained and not get wet. The park was the center of the entire neighborhood.

Uncle Terrance stood on his three-foot L-shaped concrete porch, behind the smoke-covered grill, watching the activity in the park. I saw my cousins on the merry-go-round just as Daddy pulled into Uncle Terrance's yard and parked. Daddy sat with Uncle Terrance while Mama, Charles, and Joyce went inside to find Aunt Gwen.

There were so many kids out playing, unlike in my neighborhood, where only a few played jump rope or tag in the neighbors' yards or the cul-de-sac.

"Daddy," I said, "may I go to the park?"

"Find your cousins," he said.

"Nicole," Uncle Terrance said, "Don't get caught on the merry-go-round, or you'll find out how it feels to fly."

I didn't stop to ask exactly what he meant; I was so anxious to get out to the park before dinner. Some girl was sitting on the monkey bars, plaiting a boy's hair. I couldn't figure out how she was doing it because his hair didn't seem to be that long.

Some other kids were on the swing, flying high, jumping out, and landing. One boy was even riding his bicycle down the sliding board. All I saw were possibilities of what one could be. It was then that I saw the little boy who'd been riding his bike in a circle get on the merry-go-round with some other kids.

I was about to jump on the merry-go-round when my cousin pulled at my hand, grinned, and pointed with her head to some big kids creeping slowly toward the merry-go-round, which was now filled with kids. I stepped back just as the guys rushed up and spun that merry-go-round faster and faster and faster until, one by one, the kids flew off like rocks in a slingshot. The last one, the little circle rider, clung as tightly as he could. It was amazing. The faster it went, the tighter he held, well, until I saw a slip. His hand moved. After that, I started a countdown in my head.

When I reached one, he flew off, rolled, and rested in a puddle of water less than ten feet away. He lay there for a few seconds, then popped up and smiled. Laughter filled the park. He got up and staggered away. It seemed it was best to let go early.

"Time to eat!" Uncle Terrance shouted to us.

When I turned around, the boy fell again, and life continued in the park.

~

The spread in the center of the dining room table was like a Thanksgiving feast: honey-baked ham, barbeque chicken, ribs, hamburgers, collard greens, sweet cornbread, corn on the cob, macaroni and cheese, sweet tea, and even a salad. My stomach growled, and they laughed. I usually didn't eat much before I performed, but at least I had a lot of room.

Uncle Terrance prayed. After he said, "Amen," Daddy smiled at me, and I made my plate.

"Nicole," Uncle Terrance said as I scooped a spoonful of macaroni and cheese casserole, "how was your week in school?"

Before I could answer, the doorbell rang.

"Hey, T," a scraggly man said at the screen door. We could see him through the window in the dining room.

"What's up, Smokey?" Uncle Terrance said from his chair nearest the window.

"PK is out here looking for you. He's running his mouth about Ms. Gwen, saying she needs to stay out of his business."

The scraggly man left.

We all stared out the sliding glass door. At the edge of Uncle Terrance's yard was a man, by definition, but to me, he could have been mistaken for a bear. Everyone in the park stopped and watched as that bear raised his voice.

"T…come on out…and bring that sweet wife of yours out here!"

Uncle Terrance shook his head. "Baby, I told you to stay out of their business. I don't care how many times he beats Candace. Unless she's ready to leave, you stay out of it."

"He put her in the hospital the last time. She asked me for help."

"You the police?"

"T!" the bear said from outside. "You scared? Just send Gwen out to a real man. I'll take good care of her since you can't keep her occupied."

"She ain't got nobody else," Aunt Gwen said.

"She ready to leave him?"

"Baby, I tried to get her to report him, but she's scared it'll get worse. He actually beat their little girl in front of us just to show us. I was going to call the police, but she stopped me."

"Gwen...unless she's ready to leave, and I mean for good...you stay out of it."

Aunt Gwen was about to say something else, but she sucked in her lips and stopped.

"Gwen?"

"Nothing." She bit her bottom lip as her eyes darted back and forth.

Uncle Terrance tilted his head, just like Daddy.

"Terrance. Baby. I know how you can get. I'm fine. Really, I am. She just doesn't have anybody. This will blow over."

Uncle Terrance leaned back and studied Aunt Gwen. "Did he say something to you?"

We all looked at Aunt Gwen. Her eyes stilled as she bit her bottom lip again and then sighed. "He said I was next. But Terrance, I know he didn't mean it. I know Candace is almost ready to deal with him."

"Right."

Uncle Terrance's eyes turned cold. He nodded as if agreeing with himself just as the bear started cursing and challenging anyone in the park. Then the bear took a few steps into Uncle Terrance's yard.

"Boy, don't let me come in there after you."

Daddy and Uncle Terrance's eyes met, and they both went outside, Daddy right by Uncle Terrance's side.

The crowd grew as Uncle Terrance and Daddy strolled toward the bear. The scene reminded me of David and Goliath, but my uncle was empty-handed.

The bear said so many curse words as my uncle came closer, Daddy now slightly hanging back and looking around at the crowd. When Uncle Terrance got near the bear, the bear swung. Uncle Terrance ducked and hit the bear three times, and the bear went down. I heard him fall.

We all ran outside.

By the time we made it near, the bear was lying on his back on the ground—stunned. Uncle Terrance actually let him get up, and when the bear surged, Uncle Terrance swung up once, stopping the bear in his tracks. Then he hit him three more quick times, and the bear was down again. This time, my uncle began hitting him while he lay on the ground. It was weird. Uncle Terrance was like a painter deciding where to place each brushstroke.

There was a lot of shouting, but we all watched.

Daddy covered my eyes as the man's face began bleeding, but I could still hear the solid blows.

"Terrance," Daddy said calmly. "He's had enough."

Above all the shouting, the punches stopped, and Daddy uncovered my eyes.

Uncle Terrance kneeled by the bear, grabbed his chin, and turned his bloodied face toward him.

When the bear opened his eyes, Uncle Terrance stared at him. "You know what this is for?"

He waited for the bear to answer.

The bear nodded.

I heard Uncle Terrance's screen door slam. Mama had gone back into the house.

"The next time," Uncle Terrance said, "my brother won't be here."

Uncle Terrance stood, giving the man room to get up. The bloodied man eventually stumbled to his feet, staggered to his car, and drove away.

We all sat down at the dinner table, quiet at first. Uncle Terrance washed his hands, and when he sat, he turned to me. "Nicole, you didn't get a chance to answer. How was your week in school?"

The park was back to the high noise level. My cousins, Daddy, Charles, and Joyce, filled their plates. I finished piling my plate and started eating just as Aunt Gwen fixed my uncle's plate. She smiled at him. I knew she felt safe around Uncle Terrance.

I told him about my week, and then Uncle Terrance told me and my cousins, "If a man ever hits you, just once, he is capable of hitting you again. Don't ever stay with anyone like that."

"Yes, sir," we said in unison.

Mama ate very little that night, only listening. She stared at Uncle Terrance and then Daddy—twins. Even Drummond dropped by and whispered to Uncle Terrance.

"No," Uncle Terrance said, "leave him alone. We're good."

I stared at Drummond, something people said you don't do. Some people talked about him like he was some type of monster, but for me, I didn't see it. He looked at me, and I couldn't turn away. I couldn't explain it, but it was funny. He was actually just like Daddy and Uncle Terrance. Nothing like what people said about him.

He winked at me and gave me what only could be described as a Mona Lisa smile.

Charles seemed to love what had just happened, asking Uncle Terrance where he'd learned to fight.

"Charles," Uncle Terrance said, "I hate fighting. I hate it with every fabric of my being. I hate killing more. Vietnam. Death. The stench. Even after all of that, the thing I hate more is any man who beats a woman and then blames her for it."

Drummond and Daddy nodded.

"So that's why you and Mr. Glen made that vow?"

The table got quiet. Uncle Terrance and Daddy rarely talked about their childhood, but you could see the cut on the palm of their hands. It seemed to haunt both of them. Daddy was staring at his plate and rubbing the scar on his forearm while Uncle Terrance rubbed the palm of his hand.

"To tell you the truth," Uncle Terrance said, "we never wanted to be like our father caught in that cycle. A man has got to know when to walk away. PK was a good man once, but life got him. Sometimes the things that you see can destroy you, but I think God puts people in your life to help make sense of it all. Don't ever think that you're above it. When you look at another man, don't ever think that can't be you. One choice. Bullet flies. Another choice. Bullet flies."

Mama closed her eyes, trying to gather herself. She slid her hand into Daddy's hand and gently squeezed it.

"Hey, Terrance," Daddy said, "you remember jumping off the garage with trash bags, thinking we could float down."

Uncle Terrance burst out laughing. "Glad we didn't think about trying to get higher."

Even Drummond grinned.

Daddy nodded. "Well, I thought of the roof once, but thank God you wanted to go to the creek."

"The creek?" Charles said.

"Oh man," Uncle Terrance said, "we used to hit the water to get the snakes to get out first, then we would dive in."

While everyone watched Charles, Daddy, Drummond, and Uncle Terrance's animated conversation, I saw Mama's hand shaking. Our eyes met, and she quickly put her hands on her lap.

I would love to say the dinner went well after that, but the silence from Mama pressed its way inside the car on our way home. The only sound was the car radio until Charles gently tapped Daddy on the shoulder.

"Mr. Glen," Charles said, "does Uncle Terrance—"

"Charles!" Mama said. "Is Terrance the type of man you want to be?"

The shock on Charles' face was a surprise to me. Daddy even snapped his head toward Mama. Charles stared at the ceiling, eventually letting time pass. When we got to his apartment, he opened his door, ready to step out; instead, he leaned back in the seat, Joyce's hand in his.

"Ms. Carla," he said softly.

She turned around.

"What kind of man does a woman really want?"

He waited, but she didn't answer.

"You know," he said, his eyes locked in on Mama, "I don't know if you noticed the way Ms. Gwen and his daughters looked at him. You could see in their eyes. Security. Safety. Respect. Who wouldn't want to be a man like that?"

Charles stepped out with Joyce and gently shut the door. Once Daddy pulled away, Mama turned to him.

"And you think, living over there is an option for us?"

When we got home, Mama started painting the kitchen again, something she did to create calmness in our house. Before I went to bed, her hands were still shaking.

CHAPTER SIX

March 11, 1979 (Sunday)

I loved aromas, colognes, perfumes, and flowers, but there was a strange scent that filled my room. I couldn't place it. It was like a mixture of paint, beef, and something spicy. I shook myself and put on a matching fleece sweat suit with matching socks. Mama couldn't stand mix-matched anything, not even to lie around in.

I got up, splashed water on my face to wake up, and went downstairs to find all the windows in the house opened or cracked. I stopped at the kitchen door. Mama was standing by the stove in her apron, seemingly deep in thought.

The source of the aroma was the freshly painted kitchen and the big pot of spicy stew, courtesy of Mama.

The countertops were cluttered with old newspapers. In the corner were folded drop cloths. I didn't think I had ever seen the kitchen that cluttered and messy, at least for Mama.

When she turned my way, her eyes were red and half-closed. Daddy came from the laundry room and headed to the garage with freshly cleaned paintbrushes and rollers. Apparently, Mama had stayed up throughout the night painting. Her hands were still slightly shaking from yesterday, but it could have been because she had been up for almost thirty hours.

Daddy returned and kissed Mama in our newly painted bright yellow kitchen, the second color in three months.

"Wow," I whispered to myself. Watching Daddy kiss Mama was like watching him kiss a mannequin; she had no response at all.

It didn't seem to faze Daddy. When Mama was nervous or had something on her mind, she disappeared into her painting, wanting to create the warm, loving environment she imagined or, as she said, "creating the perfect experience." Her efforts showed in her weddings and events. It showed in the calming colors she wore. It showed in the candles she burned. But looking around the kitchen at the bright yellow, I felt more awake than calm.

She also listened to and talked about classical music, asking questions about anything associated with classical, especially music measures and what was played when and how. Just from the way she glanced at me as I sat at the kitchen table, I prepared myself for her series of questions.

Daddy moved his head back. "Baby, why so cold?"

I guess the room would probably be gold by the summer just by the way Mama looked through Daddy and stared at the wall.

"Nicole," Mama said to me as if Daddy wasn't there, "what is the official name for 'Moonlight Sonata?'"

"Piano Sonata Number Fourteen in C-sharp minor, Opus Number Twenty-Seven, Number Two."

"Carla," Daddy said, "he didn't kill him."

Mama stepped back, breaking the embrace. "You've got to be kidding."

He shrugged his shoulders. "Well, he didn't."

She leaned against the marble countertop next to the stove. "All of what went on over there was normal, right?"

"It's just different. No one frets over little things or holds grudges, and the neighborhood is like one big family. They handle it and move on. I like it over there."

"The place you wanted us to live."

"Yes, it's always an option. Over there, we can relax and live."

"So, let me get this straight. You think I'm going to agree to sell our house, move over there, and get another chance to watch Terrance beat another man senseless in front of the entire neighborhood."

"Baby, did you think he was invincible just because he was that big? Just because he cursed or threatened, we all should cower? PK thought he could do whatever he wanted and try to scare Gwen and the girls."

"It's okay to call the police," Mama said. "Even Terrance told Gwen too."

Daddy frowned. "What if Terrance wasn't home? Then what?"

"Glen…Baby," she said, "you don't get it. It's all in how you handle it. See Glen. Terrance wasn't beating PK. He was beating your father…and he's been dead for years. You didn't see it in his eyes? It's just the way Terrance beat that man. I'm glad Gwen tried to help with Candace, but you have to do it the right way, or one day, Terrance is going to kill somebody. And if we go to live over there, would you get lost in your rage?"

"What?"

"You didn't see your eyes when Terrance was beating him."

"Terrance has never, ever, hit Gwen or the girls, and I've never hit Nicole or you."

"I saw the rage in your eyes when you whipped Charles years ago."

"Has he ever cursed you or even raised his voice at you since that day? Has he? Even last night, when you raised your voice, he remained calm."

"See, Glen, just the way you say that lets me know there's something there. It's like you can't see there are other ways. I know you and your brother had it hard growing up, but Glen, there are other ways."

"No man is to ever treat a woman like that."

"I know. Baby, I know."

"Ever."

"I know," Mama said as she took Daddy's hand, "but do you actually think that vow covers everything between you and Terrance? You think you're helping him, but Glen, if you don't find a way to deal with those feelings about your father, your past, it's only a matter of time."

Daddy took a deep breath, closed his eyes, and then he smiled. When he opened his eyes, he kissed Mama's hand and said, "Carla, the kitchen looks beautiful. I love the colors you chose."

She pulled her hand away. "So, if everything is fine, why are you going to stay with Terrance for a few days?"

He smiled.

"Don't do that, Glen. You know I'm right."

"He's my brother."

"I'm your wife."

"I won't be long."

"How many days will you be gone again, Mr. Fixit? Huh?"

"It's not like that."

"Glen, all you are doing is putting Band-Aids over cancer."

"Carla. Me and Terrance promised that we would be there for each other." Daddy kissed her again and moved to leave.

"Well, Saint Glen," she said, "you go and save your brother and forget about what you have with your own family now."

He turned to her. "You know it's not that way."

"Turn him over to God, and let God heal him."

"I am helping."

"It's funny; I always thought Jesus was the only Savior."

He closed his eyes and took in a deep, cleansing breath. "I love you, Carla." Then Daddy's eyes met mine. "There's nothing wrong with your Uncle Terrance. He would never hit your aunt or your cousins. He's nothing like that other man."

"It's just a matter of time," Mama said.

"No," Daddy said, "I know he's fine."

I would have been scared of Uncle Terrance if I didn't know him. Intense eyes. Hard, calloused knuckles. But when he was around Daddy, he was really a different man. He laughed a lot. Uncle Terrance had never spanked my cousins, but they told me they never wanted to find out how it was to be whipped by him. Daddy had never spanked me either.

Daddy walked over and hugged Mama, but she wasn't in the hugging mood. He kissed her again and then came over to me. "Sweetheart, take good care of your mother while I'm away. Just focus on the upcoming party and the girls-only weekend. I know you're gonna have so much fun."

"Going to," Mama said.

"Going to have so much fun," he said, smiling.

"Glen, she can tell you everything you need to know when you get back. You don't want to keep your first priority waiting."

Daddy closed his eyes. He'd taught me to do that to gather my thoughts. He always said that once you say words, you can't get them back.

"I'll be back late Friday," he said, kissing me on the cheek. "I love you,

Sweetheart. If you need me for anything at all, no matter how small you think it is, don't hesitate to call me."

He was the only one who called me Sweetheart. He called Mama Baby.

"Be careful, Daddy."

"Always."

I listened for the door of his car. From the way his car sped away, I knew he was frustrated, but to see him, I would never have guessed it. I had to admit, Uncle Terrance did have a rage that Daddy seemed to calm. They were twins. Although Uncle Terrance was the oldest, Daddy always remained calm—never raising his voice. Uncle Terrance needed Daddy around to stay calm sometimes.

"Nicole," Mama said, "what notes are played on measure fifty-four of 'Moonlight Sonata?'"

Mama reached for a glass. I could see her hands shaking from where I sat. She hadn't been the same since last night.

"Nicole, the answer?"

"Left hand, C-sharp octave half-note. Right hand, C-sharp octave dotted half five finger, with C-sharp, E-sharp, G-sharp triplet one, two, three finger, or C-sharp major."

"Or C-sharp major? What music are we talking about?"

The C-sharp major is what I saw sometimes when I played. Where people saw notes, I just saw chords, the springboard to improvisation, but she didn't like me playing around that springboard.

"The answer," she said,

"I'm sorry, Mama. C-sharp, accidental…E-sharp, G-sharp triplet."

Mama whispered to herself, "This isn't working." Then she looked at me and said, "Nicole, what if you had an opportunity that could possibly change your life, would you take it?"

I imagined that would have been a question on me and Mama's girls-only weekend on my twelfth birthday. She'd said she would drop her guard, and we would talk about anything I wanted. It didn't matter the subject either. I knew she wasn't asking me for advice, but it was nice to see her ask me questions like she asked Charles.

"Nicole, I really want to know how you feel."

"How important is this life-changing event?"

"It feels like its destiny for our family."

Her eyes were filled with anticipation and hope. I imagined Mama's business opportunities were steadily increasing. I knew she wanted to talk with the mayor's wife, do business for the yearly invitation-only black-tie event, and help with some of the other city events. Still, she hated sounding desperate, so she waited and prayed.

"I'd take the chance," I said.

She breathed in deeply and slowly exhaled. Her hands stopped shaking. She even smiled.

"Thank you." She gave a subtle grin and blinked. "So, in measure forty-nine, how is the left hand played? If you get this right, I'll leave you alone…for now."

I saw the answer in my head and gave it to Mama.

The other night, I'd overheard her telling Daddy she felt she could have been more than what she'd ended up being, but she was something special to me. Even in that floral dress, her hair pulled back, I couldn't see anything wrong. Ms. Eleanor said that when she was a little girl growing up in France, she had seen the appeal of Josephine Baker. Ms. Eleanor said Mama reminded her so much of Ms. Baker, so comfortable in her own skin. When Mama walked into a crowded room, all eyes gravitated toward her, but to look at Mama by the stove, sometimes I really thought she didn't care for any of it. At times, I imagined she felt like an object. I thought that was another reason why she loved classical music. It was calming music that made her feel like she was more than another pretty face.

I knew that was why she loved Daddy. He saw the woman she was on the inside, with all her frailties, and still loved her.

"Nicole," she said, "I need to tell you something. You rely too much on your feelings when you play. I know it's beautiful, but feelings can also take you on a never-ending roller-coaster ride. We're more than that. It's like you go somewhere else in your head, and I wish I could trust you. It takes discipline to reach the highest plateaus. Feelings can deceive you and only get you so far."

I closed my eyes, finding it hard to find the words to respond.

"It's like what you just did, trying to be selective in your words with me, your mother. Am I really that weak to you? That fragile?"

"No, Mama, it's just..."

Before I could finish my response, the phone rang. On the second ring, I answered because that was my job in the house.

"Hello. The Peterson's residence. May I help you?"

"Hi, Nicole. This is Ms. Louise calling on behalf of Mrs. Daily. Oh, you did such a beautiful job at my daughter's wedding."

"Thank you."

"In fact, that's why I'm calling. Mrs. Daily would like to speak to your mother. Is she available?"

"One moment, please." I covered the receiver. "Mama, it's Ms. Louise."

Mama's eyes lit up. She placed the spoon on a saucer, came over, and reached for the phone. Once she got the receiver, she closed her eyes and exhaled, nodding and letting her dimples show. She always thought those dimples were childish—a flaw. She worked hard to get rid of them, but when she relaxed, those dimples shined. I loved them.

"Hi Louise," she said almost in a whisper. She cleared her throat and took a deep breath to calm herself. "I'm sorry...Yes, I'm fine...No, I'm not busy at all."

Mama listened intently, occasionally nodding. "The wedding was our pleasure."

Mama placed her hand over her heart. "Sure, I'd love to talk to Mrs. Daily." Mama straightened her posture. "Hello? Yes...Yes...Thank you so much, Mrs. Daily."

I couldn't believe it. Tears were forming in her eyes.

"Oh, yes," she said. "She knows that song well...A surprise? We've become pretty good at that...When?"

She wiped her eyes, turned to the calendar, picked up the red pen, and started scribbling. She scratched out something and put the pen down.

"Yes, we will be there. I understand, formal...The short notice is just fine... Thank you so much for the opportunity. Thank you. Have a wonderful day."

Mama hugged the phone, smiled, exhaled again, and then gently hung up the phone.

"Mama?"

"Not now, Nicole," she said softly. "Just let me enjoy my moment."

After a few seconds, she picked up the receiver and dialed.

"Hi, Eleanor. You won't believe what just happened. Sorry to call you this Sunday morning, but you just won't believe it. Louise called me from the mayor's office, and Mrs. Daily asked me for a huge favor. She asked Nicole to play at the appreciation dinner. She will be the youngest ever. And would you believe Nicolette Pearson would be there?"

She closed her eyes and smiled at the mention of Nicolette's name. Nicolette was the epitome of perfection on the piano.

"Yes," Mama said, "that's Dr. Rogers's prize student…Yes, he was an upperclassman at Ventura College—extremely talented."

Mama went to the stove, picked up the spoon, and stirred the spicy stew.

"I think he would remember me."

I went over to the calendar and saw the pool and pajama party crossed out and replaced with the mayor's invitation-only black-tie appreciation dinner written in red, which meant it was final, which also meant she skipped a lot of steps.

"Do you have the white chiffon with the sash available?" Mama said in the receiver. "I know the cost, but for something like this, it's worth it. I'll pick it up tomorrow…Oh, you'll open for me?"

"Mama," I said, pointing at the calendar, "what's this?"

"Hold on, Eleanor," she said as she placed the receiver on her shoulder. "Nicole, don't you ever forget who you're talking to."

"Yes, ma'am."

"Sit down and wait until I get off the phone."

"Yes, ma'am."

She waited until I sat and took her time talking to Ms. Eleanor. Although I sat still, my mind raced. Nadia had made that day for me. Desiree had told me to make sure it was okay with Mama. Nadia, Desiree, and I had coordinated everything and asked Mama eleven months ago. Mama had talked with Daddy. They'd agreed, and she'd written it on the calendar in red, which meant Mama and Daddy had to speak before changing anything. She'd even looked at me then and said this was her promise to me no matter what. Nadia's daddy had worked hard on the pool, planning for this day. I didn't have many weekends for myself anymore, but I didn't complain. Just one time with my friends was all I wanted.

They were having so much fun, and all I was doing was playing the piano just because of that stupid word—prodigy.

"Eleanor," Mama said, "I need to call you back. There's something I need to take care of. Yes, we will be there in an hour to get fitted. Thank you."

Mama hung up the phone.

"Nicole, this is what I was talking about earlier. This is that moment you agreed to. This is for your future."

"My future? Mama, I thought you were talking about your business."

"You are my business."

"What about Nadia's party?"

"It's a sacrifice. This is your crossroad."

"But Mama, you promised me no matter what. I'm not trying to be disrespectful, but isn't this no matter what?"

Mama sighed. "See," she said, "you're missing the point. I know how much you admire Nicolette. Nicolette Pearson is representing Piedmont High out of Atlanta. You will get a chance to meet her. Did you know that Piedmont High is like the Juilliard of the South? During her senior year, she will be offered a full scholarship for the piano program at Ventura College, thanks to Dr. Rogers."

"Daddy said to call him if anything comes up. You're supposed to talk to Daddy before changing the calendar."

"Well, he's not here."

I closed my eyes.

"Don't you dare close your eyes on me."

"But Mama?"

"But Mama what? I know what's best for you. I don't need his approval. If you get a scholarship from Ventura College, you're set for life."

I glanced at the calendar. She had been using that red pen system for the past two years to ensure there were no conflicts. I reached for the phone to call Daddy.

She snatched the phone and slammed it down. "Have you lost your mind?"

"No, ma'am. It's just I only promised Nadia that I would be at her party because you promised me almost a year ago."

"This is different. You really don't know how good you are. You have to do the best you can with whatever God gives you, and Nicole, He's given you so much. You have such an incredible gift. For the past two years, I've been trying to show you how good your life can be, how you don't have to struggle like me and your father struggled, but all you think about is your friends and these parties. Why can't you see?"

She continued talking about how good this was for me, but she was the one who'd promised me. For two years, I'd done what she'd asked. "Nothing goes above your word." That was what she told me. So, I did everything I was supposed to do, wedding after wedding, sometimes up to four performances in a day, but I didn't complain because I'd promised her. I'd played every single thing she'd wanted me to play and how she'd wanted me to play it, and on my one day, my only day with my friends, just like that, she'd changed everything over some call.

"Those tears," she said. "Is it wrong to choose what's best for my daughter rather than some party? Is it?"

"But you promised!"

The words just came out. I closed my eyes and heard Mama's quick footsteps. When I opened my eyes, she had disappeared around the corner, toward the back door. Then I heard jingling. She reappeared with a thick black leather belt, two rows of metal holes from one end to the other. I thought of running, but Mama was fast. Once she got to me, she clamped onto my arm and pulled me close.

"Now…say one more word."

I sucked my lips in and held them as tightly as I could.

"Say it!" She tightened her grip, lifted me on my toes, and raised the belt.

I didn't want to move. I lowered my gaze to the floor, but I didn't dare close my eyes.

"Hello." Charles' voice echoed throughout the house. "Ms. Carla? Nicole? I came by to drop off the cufflinks and tell you something."

Mama's grip tightened even more as she lifted me a little higher. I turned towards Charles' voice and then saw him coming around the corner.

"Whoa," he said, looking at Mama.

Mama's eyes burned toward me. I wanted to say I was sorry for raising my voice, but that would have been more words.

"Ms. Carla?"

Mama sucked air in.

"Ms. Carla."

"Would you believe she would rather go to some pool party than the mayor's dinner?"

Charles sighed.

Mama let me go, slammed the belt on the table, and then took the pot off the stove.

"But you did promise her," Charles said, breaking the silence and walking toward her. "She's been waiting for almost a year. I know how you've longed to go to that event, but you promised her."

He took a step closer to Mama.

"You know?" he said. "I do see she's undeniably gifted, but sometimes I think you forget that no matter how mature or composed she may act...she's still only eleven."

Mama turned and studied me. Moments slipped by, and then she said, "True... but when you look closer, she's much more mature than that."

That's when Charles turned to me and stared.

"Nicole," Mama said, "go upstairs, get dressed, and be back in eight minutes."

"Where are you going?" Charles said.

"Eleanor's."

"Can I go? I need to practice my French."

"You know it's 'may I.' Just quit it, Charles. I know what you're doing."

Charles opened up his arms. Like a well-rehearsed dance, I walked up to him, wrapped my arms around him, and laid my head on his chest just as he blanketed his arms around me.

"Charles, stop babying her. Nicole, get upstairs and get dressed. Don't let me have to tell you again."

I rushed to my room, my refuge that Daddy had helped me create. I had filled the clouds with pictures of my friends, piano, encouraging words, Bible verses, and fairy tales, with one large poster-sized picture of me in my princess dress, by the light switch, looking up at all that I loved.

Even then, it took me only seven minutes to get dressed. I rushed downstairs and sat in my waiting chair, letting Mama know I was ready.

Charles was sitting down at the kitchen table. It was unusual to see him so serious.

"I've been saving money for a while," he told Mama, "and we'll see where we end up."

"Do you really think that's responsible?"

"It's time."

"What about your job?"

"I gave them notice a few weeks ago."

"What? And this is the first time I hear of it?"

"I asked Mr. Glen what he thought about it when I picked up the cufflinks, and he agreed."

Mama shook her head.

"I told him not to tell you," he said.

"Well, he definitely kept that secret."

"I wanted to tell you myself when everything was set."

Mama closed her eyes just like Daddy.

"Joyce and I talked about it several times."

Mama gave a deep sigh. "Why the rush? You're only twenty-three, and she's twenty-two. Life can be rough."

"You know I know that. I know the things you wanted for me, but I believe it's just time. We're leaving the day after tomorrow. We're already packed. Joyce is excited. We do have our passports just in case we want to go overseas and try to track down Mr. Glen for his new job. We're going to travel the world. We heard about the island of Crete. We want to visit."

"Passports?"

"Yes, ma'am. Ms. Carla, we're not coming back anytime soon."

Mama turned to the stove.

"You're going to miss such a beautiful event at the dinner. It's something we've both talked about."

"I know what it means to you," Charles said.

"No, this is all for Nicole."

"If it is, then let her decide."

Mama observed Charles.

"What is it really?" she said.

"It's just my cousin. He…umm…is looking for me. He says he just wants to catch up." Charles smirked. "Wishes he would have been a better example for me. But I talked it over with Joyce, and she wants us to just leave now. I agreed."

"So, he's out now."

I hadn't heard much about Charles' cousin besides that he'd gone to prison. I didn't even know his name. I remembered Mama had offered to take Charles to visit him, but Charles hadn't wanted to go. His cousin blamed Charles for the fact that he was in prison, saying Charles had snitched, but Charles claimed he hadn't said anything at all.

"He's been out," Charles said, "for about a week or so, and he says I'm the only family he's got. He said he was just mad when he blamed me, but he knows it wasn't me. He says I can help him like I used to help him years ago, but I'm not that little boy anymore."

"Then tell him face to face."

"Joyce doesn't trust him, and I trust Joyce's judgment. Where's Mr. Glen? Maybe I should tell him and Uncle Terrance, especially Uncle Terrance."

"You don't need that type of help. This is a chance for you to stand and face him like a man."

"But Ms. Carla, you of all people know how hard that is for me, plus I got a chance to leave with a woman who's willing to go wherever I want to go as long as she's with me. We really talked last night after we got out of the car. I've even told her everything, absolutely everything…about me, and she still wants to go with me. Can you believe that—with me? I don't have to be like Uncle Terrance or Mr. Glen. She accepts me just as I am. Isn't that what life is about? Us against the world?"

"You really told her everything?" Mama said, seemingly surprised.

"Absolutely, and she doesn't even care."

"Really?"

"Not at all."

No one really talked much about Charles' past. He'd had a lot of nightmares and night terrors when he was younger. He'd scream out. Other times he'd cry. Mama had always gone to his side. Two years ago, I asked him what made him cry out when he was younger. I could ask him anything, but on that day, he studied me and then said, "Just know not everyone who tells you they love you really does."

What he said didn't make any sense, but after a while, it didn't matter. His nightmares were gone now. It seemed like his past was his past, and Joyce had been his present and his future.

Charles sighed. He and Mama were so much alike.

Then he looked at me and smiled.

"Come here, Nicole." He put his arm around me. "I'm especially going to miss you. Just make sure you send me pictures. And you know, when you improvise on that piano like you did at Frances's wedding, it's…it's…I can't seem to find the words. I mean, I haven't heard you improvise much over the past two years, you know, busy with the weddings and competitions, but when you just play freely, I love it."

"So," Mama said, "just like that, you're leaving after almost eleven years without even a proper goodbye."

"That's why I'm here to let you know what Joyce and I decided."

"Just like that?"

"Ms. Carla, you've done a great job helping Aunt Menzy raise me. I know I wouldn't have made it without you. I have fully learned about you and Ms. Eleanor's business. Mr. Glen taught me a lot about his business too. Joyce just passed her CPA exam, so we'll be fine. We'll even go to France. Ms. Eleanor gave me some contacts."

"It's just so soon. Why not stay until Nicole performs?"

"Don't pull Nicole into this."

"I'm not, but you know going to the dinner is something we've talked about."

"Ms. Carla, I…no. Joyce and I have to leave. That's it."

"That's only a few extra days. Let us just send you two off right."

Charles lowered his head. "It's just I didn't know love could be like this for someone like me. After everything, I found someone like Joyce. You understand, don't you?"

She lifted up his chin. "Yes, I do understand. Please, you have no idea how complete you've made my life. I did something right with you. Helping you helped me. If I had a son, I would want him to be just like you. Eleven years ought to mean something. What if something happened to me? Would you regret it?"

I could see the struggle in his face. Charles loved Joyce, and I didn't think Charles could smile more until he met her.

"If it doesn't mean anything," Mama said, "I understand."

"You know that's not right, Ms. Carla. You know I love you, but Joyce, my fiancée, and I have decided."

"She'll understand. It's only five extra days, and then I'll let you go. I promise."

He looked at me for a brief moment. I shook my head slowly at him and mouthed, "Go" to him. I remembered Mama saying how badly she'd wanted to leave her city, Grandmother, and everything when she was younger.

Charles' desire to break the walls of Darlington radiated from his eyes, but when Mama lifted his chin again, I knew the moment wouldn't last long.

He nodded and said, "Okay." He got up and went to the phone. "Hi, Joyce. Yes, I'm over here. Yes, I talked with Ms. Carla. Hmm. We need to stay five extra days, that's all. Baby, please…"

The conversation between Charles and Joyce didn't seem to go well. I could hear Joyce's voice from where I sat, then silence. Charles looked at the receiver and softly hung up. Then he dialed again.

"She'll be fine," Mama said.

"Hi, Joyce," he said into the receiver. "I'm sorry, but can we just talk?"

Mama was very convincing, but in this case, I felt she was wrong. I didn't know why, but I just felt it. It was his life, just like this was my life, but the puppet master was at her best today.

She turned back to the stove while Charles talked on the phone. I wouldn't have made that promise to break another promise. My mind raced. Charles was leaving, and Mama was the first to break her promise.

What else could go wrong?

CHAPTER SEVEN

March 17, 1979 (Saturday)

"Nicole, Sweetheart, get up," Daddy said, stealing me away from this unexplainable nightmare. I'd been shackled to a piano, playing "Moonlight Sonata" over and over and over again. Mama had watched and smiled through every note.

"Nicole, put some clothes on. We're going by Nadia's."

I looked at the clock.

"Daddy, Mama has my hair appointment at Yolanda's in an hour."

"Just come on. I need to take care of this."

When Daddy left the room, he was still steaming from last night. He'd found out all that had gone on, the pool party cancellation, the last-minute change, Charles not honoring his promise with Joyce, Mama getting him to change his mind. I don't know who he was mad at the most. That was the first time I had seen Mama not say one word while Daddy talked.

Even when we passed by Mama going to Nadia's, Mama only said softly, "Glen, what about Nicole's appointment?"

"Baby," he said, "I suggest you reschedule or cancel since you're so good at both lately."

Then we were in the car. The funny thing about going to Nadia's is that I was also scared because Nadia was still mad at me. No matter what I did or said to make it right, she remained angry, thinking I wanted to find an excuse to go to the mayor's event. I didn't like my friends being mad because of some misunderstanding, especially Nadia. We had been friends for as long as I could remember.

When I asked Daddy what his plan was once we got to Nadia's house, he said, "I don't have any plans. I just want to apologize in person to Nadia's parents and anyone else I made a promise to. Nicole, you always honor your word and hang onto the whole truth or keep your mouth shut. The whole truth is the best you offer your friends if you want their understanding."

At Nadia's parents' house, Daddy told Mr. Jenson, "If you must blame anyone, blame me. I'm just here to make things right."

Nadia's parents and Daddy sat at the kitchen table while I went outside with my friends. I got to see the pool and the longest private slide I had ever seen. Most of my friends were already there. We all loved calling ourselves polar bears, but it didn't take long to warm up in the water. It was then that I saw Nadia.

"I'm so sorry, Nadia," I said.

She ignored me at first, and so did the others, but I kept trying to explain myself. I wanted to give them the whole truth like Daddy had said. I just wouldn't give up. After a bit, Desiree pushed Nadia on the shoulder.

"Come on, girl," Desiree said, "this is Nicole. She's sorry. You know her. This is all we've been talking about. Why would she want to be there when she could be here?"

Nadia stopped at that. She took a slow, deep breath and smiled.

"You got a mean streak," Desiree said.

"I'm sweet on the inside," Nadia said.

Everyone stopped moving at Nadia's statement. Even the birds seemed to stop singing.

"Well, I am."

Desiree laughed. "You got yourself confused with Nicole. Now, you know Nicole wouldn't skip this party for some stuffy event. You know that."

Desiree playfully pushed Nadia again.

When Nadia laughed, my other friends followed.

"I am so sorry, Nadia. I really am."

"It's okay. But Nicole, don't ever do this again. Okay? You really hurt me."

"I'm so sorry. I promise I won't."

We hugged.

"Nicole, it's time to go," Daddy said.

When I turned to leave, I saw Desiree already at the top of the slide and then gliding down. I must have counted five seconds by the time she hit the water. I watched Nadia slide next.

In the car on the way home, Daddy said, "I just scheduled a make-up pizza party at the house. I'll call all the girls' parents. The party will be basically a slumber pizza party. I won't be here because of the job, but I'll make sure absolutely everything is set up before I go. That's the least I could do. Nadia's parents were good with that."

Then Daddy was quiet. I knew he was still steaming from what Mama had done. That was probably the maddest I had ever seen him. Even now, he took the long way home, driving on I-75 and, at times, shaking his head.

"Daddy, let's pray."

He snorted, shook his head, and then glanced at me.

Oh, I knew he was mad, but I wouldn't take my eyes off of him. He prayed about everything, and I knew that was his answer. He took a deep, cleansing breath and grinned.

"My little conscience," he said. Then he took in another cleansing breath. "Okay, Nicole, you pray. I drive."

I took his free hand. "God, it's me and Daddy. I just wanted to thank You for Daddy and all he just did for me. I'm looking forward to the make-up pizza party he just set up for me and my friends. Thank You for using Daddy to make it better with everyone, especially with Nadia. I also want to thank You for my friends. Thank You for Desiree being our friend, too. I didn't realize it until now, but she's…she's so balanced. She doesn't get mad or argue. She's not the typical girl. She keeps us all…together."

I stopped praying and thought about Desiree. Mama had told me that it amazed her that twelve girls could get along so well for so long without all the drama. I think all our parents were amazed. But I knew it was Desiree who did it.

Daddy squeezed my hand. "Why did you stop praying?"

"Oh, sorry, Daddy." I closed my eyes again. "God, you know this wasn't right, what Mama did. It wasn't right at all, but everything was better. Thank You again for all my friends." My mind turned to Desiree again. Then something came over me. Sort of like; I couldn't place it. I just couldn't place it.

"In Jesus' name," Daddy said.

I looked up at his smiling face.

"Amen," I said.

He stopped shaking his head and turned the radio on to catch a slow song.

"Oh," he said under his breath.

I listened closely. The song was about a person going in circles over someone else. The singer and the background singers kept saying. I could tell Daddy was somewhere else. He was mouthing the words. I wondered if he was thinking about Mama because he called her baby, too.

Lately, all Mama had been listening to was classical, and maybe there was some distance between them, but I had to admit, there was something about the music that Daddy listened to.

My mind wandered too—Desiree, tonight's performance, Nadia, Charles, Mama, the pool slide. All the images darted through my mind.

When we turned the corner to our street, I saw the roof of our house through the trees. A little farther around the bend, I saw my window, curtains opened just the way Mama liked it.

Daddy turned in our driveway, and we sat for a few more minutes. He had his eyes closed, listening to another passion-filled song.

"Daddy, what song is that?"

"'Cause I Love You' by Lenny Williams."

Mama rushed out of the house.

"Come on, Nicole," she said, "we have your hair appointment. We don't have much time."

Daddy stayed in the car, listening to the song.

"A grown man acting like this," Mama said. "You know how hard it is to reschedule at the last minute with Yolanda?"

He neither looked up nor said any words.

Mama and I rushed off to my hair appointment. I saw Daddy get out of the car and walk into the house just as we turned the bend.

CHAPTER EIGHT

March 17, 1979 (Saturday)

The black limousine arrived in front of our house as promised. Charles and I spoke to the driver. As Charles and I waited for Daddy and Mama by the limo's back door, a few people came out of their houses, stood out on their porches, and watched. The roar of a jet flying over our neighborhood from Moody Air Force Base filled my ears, so I had to move closer to hear Charles talking.

He really liked my white chiffon dress with the hanging sash and tight white shoes. I had found a better-fitting white pair of shoes in my closet. That change started another argument between Mama and Daddy, with Mama mad for changing what she'd selected and Daddy mad because she'd actually bought the tight shoes in the first place.

"Just because other women do it," he said, "doesn't mean we are going to start with Nicole."

I knew Daddy was frustrated. I was too.

The Clarkson's, the elderly couple who used to babysit me, waved from their porch.

"Charles," I said, waving back and looking at other neighbors staring in our direction. "Have you ever been somewhere you really didn't want to be?"

"Yeah, a long time ago, when I was a little boy hanging around my cousin."

Charles' face lost any expression, sort of like he was deep in thought.

"I was the center of attention then," he said.

"That was good, wasn't it?"

"No, definitely not."

"What did you do?"

"I went somewhere else in my mind."

"How do you know it worked?"

Charles stared off with vacant eyes. Then he quickly blinked, nodded, and said, "I got a lot of practice."

I touched his arm, "You okay?"

He sucked in air, quickly shook his head, and smiled. "Of course. That was a long, long time ago." He turned to me. "We all have days we hate, but you can make it through. Don't get caught up in this. All these people staring; you know they would love to go. Just enjoy yourself, and whatever you play, however you play it, make sure it's from your heart and definitely play it your way. People should learn to love you for who you are. You've got to let them see the real you. I just want to hear you play your way tonight."

"I don't know. The way Mama had me practice, I don't know. But you know Mama better than I do. You think she wouldn't mind?"

"I assure you," he said, "the mayor will love it. And if he loves it, Ms. Carla will love it. Mr. Glen will definitely love it because it would be so refreshing. How many times have we heard 'Moonlight Sonata' played? Our mind could go on autopilot on the first note, but Nicole, if you played it your way, even the servers would love it. God only made one Nicole, and then He shattered the mold. Let us see who Nicole really is. All will love it; you'll see."

"Really?"

The anticipation on his face did the talking.

"Oh yeah. Darlington's own prodigy—that's who they really want to see."

We both laughed at that one, and then I hugged him.

"Joyce is still mad that I let Ms. Carla change my mind about us leaving. She's still feeling apprehensive about everything. I've never really seen her this mad. You know how calm she is."

"I agree with her. You still should have left."

"And miss your performance? I'll definitely be there later. First, I will have to check on Joyce. Then I will be there to see you perform like no other, then I'll meet with my cousin at my apartment, and then I'll have to—"

"Get in your car," I said. "Then you will have to—"

He leaned forward and whispered, "Get married tomorrow morning by Reverend Joseph."

I had to cover my mouth to keep from screaming.

"Shhhh," he said. "Joyce and I are doing a semi-elope tomorrow morning. I know if we told Ms. Carla, she'd want to do the wedding and push everything back more."

"What is this all about?" Mama said, coming up from behind.

"Oh, nothing," Charles said, grinning at me. He gave Mama a long hug.

"Thank you, Charles," Mama said. "These last few days meant the world to me. Here you are." She handed him a thick envelope. "This is a goodbye gift from us to you."

He opened it. All I saw were green bills.

"I can't, and I won't take this."

"Nonsense, it's yours. I've been saving up for years for this moment, and I wanted you to have it now."

"No, Ms. Carla, just use it in your household or on Nicole. Trust me, I've been good with my money."

Mama looked at the money and then at Charles.

"Really, Ms. Carla, I don't want your money."

"I'm so proud of you, a man now," she said as she placed her hand on his cheek.

He grinned like a little boy.

"Joyce still angry with you?"

"Yes," Charles said, "but I have a feeling she'll be over it soon. Will Mr. Glen be okay?"

"Don't you worry about that," Mama said.

I shook my head slowly. Charles had been at the house late last night. Daddy told Mama she should have respected Charles' decision and let him go without the guilt trip. "He's grown." Then he'd told Charles, "If you promised Joyce that you were leaving, then you should have ridden out the disappointment of Carla."

Charles would have left last night, but Mama had said that he had already promised his cousin he would meet with him. Daddy said that he or Uncle Terrance would go with him to meet with his cousin last night.

Charles smiled and said, "Now, I didn't say I was scared. I got this."

Daddy came out toward the limo and shook Charles' hand. "Are you sure you don't want my help? I can still call Terrance to go with you. Terrance said he and Drummond could visit or go with you while you talked to him."

Now, Drummond—there was something in his eyes. Charles even hesitated at the thought.

"Charles," Daddy said, "I'd feel better if you took him."

He looked at Mama and laughed. "And scare my cousin?"

"Well," Daddy said, "it was just the way you acted at first."

"Hey, Mr. Glen, do you see any concern on my face? We're just gonna talk and clear up some old stuff, that's all. Don't you think some of you or Uncle Terrance has rubbed off on me by now? I was making a big deal out of nothing, you know."

Daddy studied Charles and then nodded his head.

Mama, then Daddy, got in the limo. I watched Charles drive off. We could have used him in the limo because the mounting tension between Mama and Daddy escalated fast.

CHAPTER NINE

March 17, 1979 (Saturday)

I loved the way the black leather seats in the limousine wrapped around me. Even my seat felt comfortable, like our old upstairs couch. Daddy sat to my left, and Mama sat in front of Daddy, her ankles crossed, hands neatly placed on her lap. Her hair was up, not one strand out of place. I tried to sit like her. She made it seem so easy.

The limo ride was everything she had talked about. Even the way people in our neighborhood stood and watched as we got into the limo made me feel important, just like she said it would.

"Nicole," Mama said, "what are you smiling about?"

"Nothing."

I really wanted our first time riding together in a limousine to be special. Mama and I had reserved a limo in Atlanta for our girls-only weekend a week from now. That weekend was supposed to be our first time, but tonight's ride had stolen its place, and the feeling of experiencing the moment together just wasn't there.

This night was for her. I was a key she used to get in the door. Now inside, where she wanted to be, I was just along for the ride. I knew Charles was her favorite. She also kept talking about Nicolette. Dr. Rogers had even sent Mama a videotape of Nicolette's performances, which we'd watched many times, yet my videos collected dust. Mama constantly showed me pictures of Nicolette, who was probably becoming another favorite. I could see why. Nicolette was breathtaking and talented.

Although people said I looked just like Mama when she smiled, I didn't see it. No matter how long I stared in the mirror, I just didn't see it. Maybe it was because she didn't smile at me much anymore, not even in my new white chiffon dress from Ms. Eleanor's. Thinking about it now, we should have ridden in a limo two years ago, when all of this was fun, and none of this really mattered.

It hadn't always been this way. Playing the piano used to be different—full of possibilities. I used to play anything just the way I wanted, improvising, fills, trills, you name it, but then Ms. Eleanor mentioned and then emphasized the word "prodigy" while referring to me. Shortly after that, Mama came home with the news that she had entered me in a classical piano competition in Atlanta. I was reluctant at first, but she said it would be fun. She even let me pick out my first competition dress at Ms. Eleanor's. She smiled at me and said I had impeccable taste.

Stepping through the door at the competition, I knew I didn't want any part of that world Mama seemed to love. I felt the tension in the air. And to top it off, at that competition, people were just uptight—so many people compared to others. I saw one girl crying in the bathroom because she had actually made a mistake. Mama told me what I saw would never happen to us. "Just play from your heart and create a unique experience."

So that's what I did that day. I played from my heart and found a deep closeness in the music Mama had given me to play. I began understanding the composer's story through the music and attempted to bring it out through the piano. Through those efforts in classical music, a bond formed between Mama and me, something we'd never really had until then.

I even found that she had this laughter that made my stomach fill up with the giggles that had to escape. Mama called them "joy bubbles," and the cure was tickling. She didn't care what the onlookers thought at the first competition. She had said, "We'd always have fun."

I won, but I didn't understand the big deal. Who could play freely with that much pressure? When we returned home, word spread throughout the city, and people treated me differently like I was some sideshow holding the sign, "Come See the Prodigy." I didn't understand all the attention. I was still the same Nicole. I was a girl who loved the piano, the sound, the touch, the feel—everything. I loved recreating the music in my head, but what if I didn't have the gift? Would someone love me less?

In Valdosta, many people loved playing football. They lived and breathed football. Daddy would take me by the Death Valley stadium Friday nights in Valdosta, and it would be packed, especially during the Lowndes-Valdosta high school football game, but to me, they were regular people. I even knew some of the people who played for Valdosta. They lived in Uncle Terrance's neighborhood. They had real friends.

Looking back, I didn't exactly know when things changed. It could have been the time I ended up on the cover of Darlington's Society Magazine. I had on one of Ms. Eleanor's expensive dresses. Under the photo was Darlington's child prodigy, Nicole Renee Peterson. After that photo, Mama's demand as a wedding coordinator picked up, and more upscale weddings came to be.

Mama didn't tickle me anymore. That wasn't ladylike. We didn't laugh aloud anymore. Smiles really didn't come anymore. Now we were just like everyone else at the piano competitions, tense and afraid to make mistakes.

We passed by Jenson's Pool Supplies, Nadia's father's store. I almost asked Mama about the party, but before I conjured up the courage, she said, "Nicole, just get over it."

I lowered my eyes.

She tilted her head and stared at me. To my mother, that meant to straighten up, and I did just that. Eventually, Mama turned the classical music up and stared out the window. It felt like we were in a funeral procession. I moved slightly in the seat to find a more comfortable position. She didn't like it when I squirmed.

The air thickened with each note. Dull, steady notes from the cello tightened around my neck. I felt like I could hardly breathe. I reached for the door, felt the silver lever marked WINDOW, and pushed. The cool air burst through, and the sun lit the car.

My mind escaped and raced along the winding road, rushing past the signal lights, stop signs, and the large lake near Nadia's house. Even before I reached the backyard, I heard Karen's scream, so high my friends believed she could shatter glass.

I could see my friends standing around the pool, splashing in the water, floating on loungers, or sitting by the side of the pool. The scent of mesquite from the barbeque pit lingered in the air. Nadia's daddy made some of the best barbeque hot dogs and hamburgers. Out of the corner of my eye, I saw the S-shaped slide.

I was at the bottom of its steps, looking up. I was scared of heights, but I wasn't going to miss out because of fear. When I touched the metal handle, a chill ran through my hands and up my arm. I lifted my foot and placed it on the cold, wet bottom rung. Looking up, it seemed like I was climbing a mountain. Each step had my heart racing as I realized how high I was going.

Desiree ran toward the slide, laughing.

I kept stepping up, counting: "twelve, thirteen, fourteen, fifteen." At the top, I was higher than I could have imagined, almost able to see the roof of their house. Water sprayed down the slide like the log ride at Six Flags over Georgia. As all the girls watched me, I sat down and held on tight.

"You can do it!" Desiree said.

The other girls waited.

I took a deep breath, closed my eyes, let go of the handrails, and glided down the slide, shooting toward the water. Swoosh. I was airborne.

"Nicole. Nicole!" Mama's voice pierced through my thoughts. "Stop that daydreaming and put that window up. It's messing up your hair."

"She's fine," Daddy said in a worn voice.

Mama's glare shifted.

I thought, Oh no. Not another one.

Daddy sighed.

Mama closed the sliding window between the driver and us.

I pulled the WINDOW button. It couldn't go up fast enough. Daddy had taken a stand against all of this. The only reason he'd agreed for me to play was because of some technicality, but he didn't like it when anyone sought an excuse to bypass their word.

"So, you want to do this here?" Mama asked.

"Carla, no more."

"Then when?"

"Please, leave it alone."

"So, you think all of that daydreaming is good? You think she knows what's best for her? But no, you're always gone lately, and you were not here this time either."

When there was no response, I looked up at Daddy. His chest rose and fell slowly. Then he closed his eyes.

"Glen, don't do that to me?"

"I'm sorry. Please, just let it go."

"You really don't care, do you?"

"Why so tense? We're here…all going where you wanted to go. It'll be over in a few hours."

"Don't avoid the question. Do you even care?"

"You know I do. I care about you. I care about Nicole. I care about this family. I just think—"

"You think?"

"Yeah. Times like these, these moments, right now, are to be enjoyed. She's already missed the pool party. She'll miss the pajama party too, something you knew was important to her, but as soon as the mayor's office called, you broke your promise, dropped everything, and here we are. She practiced that song more than Beethoven would have. For what?"

"So, it doesn't matter what she does and even how she does it?"

"I didn't say that."

"See, that's the problem I have with you. You didn't say this, or you didn't say that. Sometimes I wonder…"

He shook his head slowly but kept eye contact. I remembered how he'd told me, "Never stop looking into the eyes of the one you love."

With his shoulders slightly slumped, I wondered how long he would last.

My mind went back to the time I had gotten out of bed to get some water. That was when I'd heard Mama's voice from down the hall.

"I'm tired of this," she'd said. "I know you've been searching for just the right job. You know that job is it. Just at least apply. I know you'll get it. It will solve all our money problems."

"There's more to life than money."

"What planet do you live on? Do you think these people are just going to let us slide because you say, 'There's more to life than money?' If one more thing happens, then I don't know."

"Baby, it takes time. Your business just broke even this year, and you should be able to have more time to strategize. You can cut back on the weddings you choose. I could find something stateside. Besides, that job will send me away for a long time. I don't want to be away from you or Nicole for—"

"Go."

Silence.

I crept closer and leaned against the door, cupping my hand around my ear. When Daddy spoke, his voice cracked.

"Carla? You would…you would want me…gone for a year?"

"Go."

Again, silence.

Suddenly, my parent's bedroom door opened, and Daddy almost tripped over me as he stepped out. Mama stood by the dresser with her arms folded.

"What are you doing up?" Daddy said as he closed the door behind him. He tried to smile, but he wasn't good at pretending.

"I wanted to get some water. Daddy?"

His eyes stopped me from asking more.

"Sweetheart, everything's fine."

I'd climbed on his back and laid my head on his shoulder as he'd carried me back to bed. He'd tucked me in, got me some water, and waited for me to finish. While drinking, I noticed the tired expression on his face.

Now, in the car, I saw that same look.

CHAPTER TEN

March 17, 1979 (Saturday)

The limousine came to a halt just as the one-sided argument finished. A tall, dark-skinned man wearing an inviting smile opened the door. I placed my hand in his as he helped me out of the gloom of the limo.

"You make us proud," he whispered.

"Thank you," I whispered back.

When my mother stepped out, she smiled as if nothing had happened. Daddy, on the other hand, had no real expression. Mama gently took Daddy's hand and squeezed it hard.

They were missing the beauty and grandeur of the front of Darlington Convention Hall. I tried to imagine what could actually fill that building. I thought about Noah's ark, not remembering the specific cubits but knowing that the ark was massive, just like the building. The white columns reminded me of Roman colosseums. Lights from the ground lined the walls of the building from one end to the other, all shooting beams of white toward the sky.

We made our way down the wide red carpet that ran from the carport to the broad glass entrance. I recognized the faces of those who attended from billboards, bank walls, bus stop benches, and even from the back of the telephone book, all clamoring to enter the building. Then I saw her, Nicolette Pearson. I had seen her from afar, but up close, I could see that the pictures Mama had of her did her no justice. She was absolutely stunning in her gown. I couldn't believe how nervous I was, as if I had seen a celebrity. Mama left me and made her way over to Nicolette and Dr. Rogers.

Nicolette seemed to be pleasant and composed, just like Mama. Mr. and Mrs. Winthrop, editors of the Darlington Society Magazine and the society column in the Darlington Daily News, stood off to the side, holding hands as if appreciating a slow, steady stream of people passing by. Their eyes glistened, yet their faces had what seemed to be permanent smiles.

Mr. and Mrs. Winthrop stepped away from their spot, went over to Mama, Nicolette, and Dr. Rogers, and started taking pictures of them. Then I wondered if Mama wished Nicolette were her daughter instead of me. All the things Mama had shown me, Nicolette had mastered—the stance, the pose, and the smile. Sometimes it hurt seeing Mama smile so warmly for others. I turned away, looked at Daddy, and smiled to myself as I realized that his mind was already somewhere else, probably out fishing with Uncle Terrance.

In a matter of moments, Daddy found our contact, Lori Henderson. Lori made sure my parents were settled before ushering me backstage. Tonight was everything Mama wanted. She sat behind the mayor while I stood backstage, waiting to perform.

Lori and I made our way through the organized chaos backstage. All the workers were dressed as though they were going to a ball. We reached an energetic, balding man no taller than Lori.

"I got her," he said to Lori. Then he turned to me and introduced himself. "I'm Carl, Carl Landers. Just hang out here and make yourself comfortable. I'll be back in a moment. The refreshments and water are on the table over there." He pointed to a beautiful buffet Mama would have been proud of.

"Excuse me." He turned toward the chaos. "Jack! Don't put that there." He rushed off toward the misplaced flower arrangement.

I saw a comfortable-looking chair off in the corner and out of the way, and as soon as I could get through the stream of workers, I went over to that quiet spot and plopped down. I wasn't supposed to plop, so I stood back up and sat down again.

"Nicole," Mr. Carl said, coming up to me, "you'll be on right after Nicolette Pearson. You will enter from the right of the stage. Lori will help you." Then he rushed off again.

In the corner was a full-length floor mirror. I stood in front of it and thought about Mama as I checked myself. I slid those tight shoes off, the only pair that matched, or so Mama said. Everything else was fine. I found my chair again and thought about the performance and exactly how I would walk out on stage and sit. It was then that I saw the curtain to the right move, and Mama appeared. I hurried to put my shoes back on. A sudden rush of butterflies stirred in my stomach. I stood and smiled.

"Remember," Mama said almost in a whisper as the stream of people parted for her, "it's an honor to be selected. You're going on after Nicolette."

Why was I on behind what I considered to be the encore?

"You are the youngest of those asked to entertain tonight, and I expect you to be on your best behavior."

She raised her eyebrows, and her eyes focused on my hair. "I paid too much for this."

In such a short time, the steady stream of busy people had dwindled to a trickle.

I showed her the full-length mirror in the corner, and she rushed me over to it. I felt the frustration in her tug. Even when she was like this, Mama was still elegant. Her hair, dress, and makeup were flawless, and her shoes were breathtaking, unlike mine, which were still tight. I winced.

Looking at her and then at myself, it was no wonder why it was so easy for Mama to see what was wrong with me.

The tugging on my hair stopped when I sighed; I caught her eyes in the mirror. I had made a definite infraction, although I didn't know exactly what.

"Excuse me," she said to a blond man in a tuxedo passing by. "Is there anywhere I can go to have a private moment with my daughter?"

"Use the blue dressing room in the corner, over there," he said, pointing to our left. "No one's in it."

Mama gently took my hand and led me to the room, speaking to some as we passed by. Others backstage watched, some smiling. As soon as she softly closed the door behind us, she grabbed both my arms, yanked me close to her face, and whispered, "Listen, little girl, I'm sick of that attitude. You need to check that nonsense at the door and grow up. You will be playing for the mayor tonight, and I don't want to see any attitude in the way you walk, talk, or even stand. Do you understand me?"

I was afraid to answer. She grabbed my chin and shook it hard.

"Do you understand me?"

"Yes, ma'am."

"Now, when you go out there, you smile and act like you got some sense."

"Yes, ma'am."

"And stop those tears."

"Yes, ma'am."

"I'll give you one minute to get yourself together. When I knock on this door, that attitude had better be long gone."

"Yes, ma'am."

She closed her eyes, breathed in and out deeply, and smiled just as she walked out, softly closing the door behind her. I stared at myself in the mirror inside the room. The sash on the dress that hung from my waist was beautiful and soft. I remembered the first time we'd gone shopping for a dress together. We'd made a day of it, and she'd let me pick out my dress and shoes. When we'd gotten back to the car, she'd said, "You have such good taste."

I wiped my tears, stood by the door, and waited.

It was almost five minutes before I heard the knock. I pasted on my smile and stood by the door.

"Excuse me, is this room occupied?"

"I'm sorry, yes. We shouldn't be long."

The doorknob turned, the door opened, and Charles stood at the entrance.

"Charles," I whispered as I smiled, "where's Mama?"

"Hanging out with the mayor and his wife. I told her I'd finish your hair."

He stepped in, closed the door behind him, and then we turned toward the mirror. Charles had a much gentler touch than Mama. Even the way he pulled the stray hairs was done with so much care, allowing my mind to wander.

I thought about the song for the mayor. How could I play it better? Could I sit any more erect? Could I slow the song down? What tempo did Mayor Daily like? I heard Charles say something just as I decided to watch the mayor as I played.

When I sighed, Charles stopped.

I forced a smile but didn't look up.

"It's just us, Nicole," he said.

When he touched me on my shoulder, I felt a tear almost escape.

"Have a seat," he said, pointing at the burgundy cloth chair by the mirror. He then kneeled in front of me. "Not that good of a day, huh?"

I shook my head, too afraid to talk because he had a way of pulling out what was wrong. We were in public, and I had to be ready to smile, but when he touched me on my shoulder again, all that was real came forth.

"Everything I do is wrong now, even if it's only subtle. The way I sit. The way I stand. Even the way I breathe. She used to like how I played, but now nothing seems good enough. I missed when it used to be fun. She even says I have an attitude now."

"Why don't you talk to her like you talk to me?"

"Yeah, I'll paint the sky while I'm at it."

He shook his head slowly. "I know your mother can be demanding."

"Really?"

He pressed his lips together. "You know," he said, "It could be worse. Way worse. There are far worse families than this one."

I shook my head.

"Yeah, Nicole, there are," he said. "I know that for a fact. Nicole, like I said at the limo, we all have days we hate, but you can make it through this. You know how much these tickets cost?"

I didn't care about the cost. They could have given my ticket to someone else.

"I'll tell you this," he said, "and it's guaranteed to work. As I said earlier, you play from your heart and let yourself go. Everyone will love it. I know I will."

"Mama too?"

"Yeah, definitely her, too. Now, let's see what we have here."

He turned me to the mirror. Charles was so much better at hair than Mama was.

"Well," he said, "let me get to my seat and rub shoulders with the mayor."

He escorted me back to my chair outside the room. Once he left, the women backstage seemed to follow Charles out with their eyes. After the curtain closed behind him, they whispered amongst themselves, and one woman shook as if a chill had run down her spine.

I sat down again and thought, Play it my way.

~

When they called Nicolette to go on, I watched perfection in motion. Hearing Nicolette play from backstage filled my stomach with butterflies. Her perfect posture, her movements, and even the way she used the pedal were remarkable. Everyone, especially Mama, was so enamored with Nicolette. I had to admit, I was too.

When she played her last note, she received a standing ovation.

Nicolette passed by me, touched me on my shoulder, smiled, and said, "Nicole, you'll be fine."

"Thank you," I said. She was so nice.

Lori stood at the edge of the curtain as my name was announced and received applause. "Nicole, the stage is yours." She gave me a wink and grinned.

Once I was on stage, I looked out at the audience, seeing the sea of tuxedoes and dark, shimmering gowns, and even in all that, I saw Charles' turquoise bow tie. He was truly his own man.

I saw Mama's countenance, which could have brightened the entire room, especially when the mayor turned around, nodded, and shook her hand.

When I sat on the black leather bench, the lights were like a warmer for food in a restaurant. Charles had taken Nadia, Desiree, and me to Jimbo's Burgers and let us put our hands under the heat lamps. It wasn't that warm at first, but eventually, we felt just how hot it could get.

I closed my eyes, letting the sheet music that had been burned into my memory appear. I positioned my hands and pressed down, and the sound filled the hall. The sonata was so beautiful on that Steinway. It was so automatic. I was programmed to do this, but then a cool breeze of air brushed past my neck. I thought of Charles. Out of me arose a harmony that added to the C-sharp minor. I realized that the new combination of notes created a sound even fuller than the original, a sound that Charles loved. Another harmony came, so I played it too.

Note after note, chord after chord followed, creating another version of Beethoven's sonata that I knew Charles loved. Then, I pictured myself in a faraway place on a moonlit night, looking over a field of daisies and dandelions. Sitting down in the field, I plucked a dandelion, blew it, and let the notes form and carry the white seeds to the moonlit sky until the original piece reappeared in my mind, and I played the last few measures as written.

As soon as the final note sounded, I opened my eyes to jubilant faces. Charles was right. Even Nicolette was standing. Dr. Rogers nodded his head to Mama. Daddy, of course, clapped louder than anyone else. The mayor had an expression of awe while clapping vigorously, almost competing with Daddy. I saw Charles smile and wave as he left to elope with Joyce. I stepped away from the piano and took a bow.

When I raised myself up, at the sight of Mama's eyes, a chill engulfed me. Her gaze was like an eagle, and I was her prey. I tried a smile, but her head moved, so subtle, from side to side.

I could see the clapping hands, but the sound slowly faded. I made it off stage, found my chair, and watched and waited for the curtains to move.

"I have never heard the piece played that way," Mayor Daily said backstage with his wife beside him. "She said it would be a surprise, but I had no idea."

Mrs. Daily gave me a warm, affectionate hug.

Mayor Daily shook my hand. "I absolutely loved it. I would like you to play for us next year."

Mama was surprised, but she recovered.

Mayor Daily looked at Mama as he let my hand go. "You have a bold daughter. Others I know would love to hear Darlington's prodigy play. I can make sure of that. She is so amazing—and just eleven! My office will contact you with the details for next year and hopefully throughout the year. Thank you again for my refreshing gift and agreeing to come tonight on such short notice. My wife told me how gracious you were. I will never forget that. Have a good night."

Outside the convention hall, my parents and I stood with Dr. Rogers and Nicolette. "Carla," Dr. Rogers said, "you got me on that one. I agree with the mayor. That was a bold move to improvise Beethoven." He had a hearty laugh. "You improvised Beethoven. If you ever choose to leave Darlington, come to Atlanta.

We'd love to have you in our program. It's a new school, a new program, turning into one of the best in the nation thanks to talent like Nicolette."

"It was beautiful, Nicole," Nicolette said.

"You really think so?"

"Of course," Nicolette said.

"It was," Daddy said.

Dr. Rogers and Nicolette left. Shortly after, our limo pulled up, and Mama stepped around me and got in. I followed, and then Daddy climbed in after me.

Mama sat in front of me, looking out of her darkened window.

"Mama, what did you think? I mean, it turned out great, didn't it?"

"Do you really want to know the truth?"

"Yes, ma'am."

Daddy, who was sitting beside Mama, watched her as she stared out the window and talked.

"I was thinking how hard I'd been on you and how I did you with the party. For the past two years, you've done everything I asked for. I admit your father was right about taking you to Nadia's house to clear things up. I was sorry I broke my promise. It's just that you don't realize how many doors your talent can open. Your gift will have you playing before mayors, governors, or senators."

She shifted in her seat, still looking out the window.

"I had planned on us leaving early and dropping you off at Nadia's. I thought it was even unfair to put you behind Nicolette, yet the way you played tonight was…phenomenal. I even tried to imagine playing like you, and even after all the years I practiced, I couldn't have done what you did."

She shook her head.

"I couldn't even come close. Nicole, you are so talented." She looked directly into my eyes. "But…this was not your night. I thought I had taught you discipline. Over and over, asking question after question. What do you think these past two years have been for?"

She closed her eyes and shook her head.

"Talent can only take you so far. You have to learn your craft. This was not a night for improvisation. The mayor loved the original sonata just the way it was. That's what Mrs. Daily told me. I'd assumed you'd play it straight. I had never heard you improvise that piece in my whole life, let alone over the last few days. Why would I believe you'd do it tonight?"

"But he loved it," I said. "He invited us back next year."

Mama shook her head. "You're not Beethoven. Mozart. You are Nicole Renee Peterson, a child prodigy who is learning…to develop her gift to the fullest. And so now you think you are better than Beethoven. You think you know so much more."

"No, ma'am."

"Carla."

"I don't want to hear it, Glen. This is your undisciplined creation," she said, pointing at me. "She thinks she can drop her gift off like some trash, jump in a pool, play around, and pick it right back up. How do you think I feel, spending two years showing her what life could be, and then when she's on the verge of everything we've worked for, she just throws everything I taught her back in my face?"

"But Mama, Charles probably loved it."

"So, the truth finally comes out. You played it for Charles. I knew it." She tilted her head. "I actually thought this night was supposed to be for the mayor. So, to clear this up, you're grounded. I don't want to ever hear you blame anything else on Charles, even…if…he asked you."

"But Mama, the mayor loved it."

"What else is he going to tell a little girl who has just ruined the most precious sonata? You tell me, what is he going to say? He's a politician."

She motioned with her hands, "Headline…'Mayor Makes Darlington's Prodigy Cry at His Gala.' You are more than just some whim of improvisation, like some jazz pianist trouncing around the keyboard, playing whatever you feel."

"But Mama?"

"One month grounded," she said. "No phone. No visitors. Just homework, chores, and school."

I sighed.

"Two months."

"Carla," Daddy said.

"Three."

Daddy reached for her hand, but she moved it away from his, laid it on her lap, and stared out the window.

"Four."

CHAPTER ELEVEN

March 17, 1979 (Saturday)

Silence had a way of crying out in our house. No one went to bed early. Mama sat at the kitchen table alone. Her expression meant she didn't want to be bothered. Even Daddy took heed as he sat on the patio in his favorite chair.

The phone rang, cutting through the thick cloud of silence in our house.

Mama got up and answered. "Hello…Joyce…Calm down. What's wrong?"

Joyce was supposed to be eloping with Charles tonight.

"We saw him leave after Nicole played around a quarter to nine. Have you heard from him at all? How long was he supposed to be with his cousin?"

"Mama, what's wrong?"

"We'll go check on him for you. Make sure you're by the phone."

Mama hung up and dialed.

"Mama, what's wrong?"

"No one has heard from Charles," Mama said. She dialed. "Charles, if you get this message, we need to hear from you. Please call on Glen's car phone or the home phone. Nicole will be here to answer. Just call us. I want to make sure you're okay. We're heading right over to your apartment."

Mama went to the back patio. "Glen, we need to go to Charles' apartment. Call Terrance. He's closer."

Mama and I went to get dressed.

"What's wrong, Mama?"

"Everything's fine. Just stay here, keep the doors locked, and do not answer that door for anyone except Charles. Keep the phone with you. If he comes over, call your father's car phone."

"May I go?"

"What did I just tell you?"

"Stay by the phone and answer the door only for Charles."

They rushed out of the house. Time just ticked by. I was sure he was okay. He'd probably forgotten something for when he and Joyce were going to elope. He loved giving surprises, especially to Joyce. This was probably Joyce's way to get Mama and Daddy over to the house to surprise them just before they left. I should have told Mama he was going to elope, but that was me and Charles' secret.

At around eleven, I turned the TV on to breaking news.

Jarvis Collins was on. Nadia always thought he was so cute.

"At approximately 10:30 pm, a Lowndes County sheriff's deputy stopped a 1969 Chevy Camaro on a speeding violation. When the officer asked for his license and registration, the driver opened fire on him, hitting him in the shoulder. The officer returned fire. The driver led sheriff's deputies and Valdosta police officers on a high-speed chase that ended on Highway 84 in the Levi's parking lot. The driver continued firing, forcing the officers to return fire. The driver, thirty-five-year-old Devin King, was pronounced dead at the scene."

When they showed the photo on the screen of Devin King, he favored an older Charles but was more muscular, with light skin, hazel eyes, and wavy hair.

"Devin King was paroled after serving ten years in prison after one of Georgia's largest drug busts. The driver…"

I wondered where Charles was and if he was even watching TV. I wanted to call Mama, but I didn't want to tie up the line. I peeped out of the window and watched for Mama and Daddy.

"Also, in the news, twenty-three-year-old Charles King was found brutally beaten at the Timberland Apartments…"

I ran to the TV.

"A witness told police he heard noises like an altercation but nothing else. Thirty minutes later, he saw a light-skinned male, about six foot two, 260 pounds, hurriedly leaving Charles King's apartment and driving off in what appeared to be Mr. King's Chevy Camaro. It is believed the man wanted for questioning fits the description of Devin King, who was recently killed by police in a shootout in the Levi's parking lot on Highway 84. In other news tonight, the following…"

I called Mama, but there was no answer on Daddy's phone. It couldn't be Charles; he was supposed to get married. He'd told Daddy everything was okay. His cousin wouldn't hurt him like that. I sat in the chair, waiting for Charles or Mama to call. I changed the channel from the news and later watched an "I Love Lucy" episode.

I really liked Lucy.

When I heard the front door, I jumped up to let Charles in, but it was Daddy and Uncle Terrance. They both had this solemn look on their face.

"Don't believe what you hear on the news," I said, shaking my head. "I wasn't supposed to tell you this, but Charles was supposed to elope with Joyce, so that person couldn't be Charles."

"Nicole," Daddy said, "sit down. I have something to tell you."

"Daddy, would you like some water?"

"No, Sweetheart."

"What about you, Uncle Terrance?" I said, turning toward the kitchen.

He didn't answer, but I knew they had to be thirsty. I would hear Daddy late at night getting water. I'd even started getting water, too. I remembered Daddy would always want four ice cubes. I didn't know why, though.

"Uncle Terrance, how many cubes do you want?" When he still didn't answer, I figured he was just like Daddy.

"Nicole," Daddy said behind me. "It's Charles."

"Daddy, he just eloped, that's all. He told me himself. He's probably with Joyce right now."

"We have to go to the hospital."

"For what?"

Daddy stared at me, and Uncle Terrance turned away. Uncle Terrance never turned away from anything. The room began spinning. All I remember was Daddy rushing over to me.

CHAPTER TWELVE

Spring Break

I was lying down on the couch. I had a cool rag on my forehead. Daddy and Uncle Terrance were by my side. I thought it was all a dream until Daddy spoke.

"Nicole," Daddy said, "at least he's still alive."

On the way to South Georgia Medical Center in Valdosta, so many thoughts and fears ran through my mind. The closer we got, the main thing I tried to do was prepare myself for what I wasn't ready to see. I remembered how the blood dripped from the face of the man Uncle Terrance had beaten. I asked Uncle Terrance how Charles looked, and he even winced.

Daddy remained calm. It was hard to gauge what to expect. The only words I held onto were "at least he's still alive." I didn't remember much of the walk toward the intensive care unit. The hospital had this clean, sterile smell, bright walls, fluorescent lights, and matching bright floors—all cold and impersonal. I didn't know why I paid attention.

"Sir," the nurse said, "how old is she?"

"Eleven," Daddy said.

"She must be twelve to visit the intensive care unit."

"I'll be twelve in a week," I said.

"Twelve is the rule. I'm sorry."

It seemed the world started when you turned twelve, so I was resigned to the waiting room to entertain my thoughts and fears.

There seemed to be a ritual in the waiting room. Groups of people were standing or sitting in sections of chairs throughout the room, waiting for a doctor or a nurse to come through the door.

Our little section was filled with friends of Charles and our family: Joyce, Uncle Terrance, Aunt Menzy, and others I didn't know. I watched the parade of visitors come and go. It seemed everyone saw him except me.

For the next few days, Mama and Daddy didn't say much. It was spring break, and I just lay in bed until the third day. Then the hospital transferred him to a regular private room, and I could finally visit Charles. I peeped around the corner, and he wasn't as bad as I had imagined. Just to see his healing bruises, his split lip, and the bandages that ran down the length of his face, I sighed and kept myself from crying.

Joyce and Aunt Menzy were by his side. From them, I found out that his cousin had cut his face. Daddy was right; at least he was still alive.

I sat on the chair beside his bed, not really knowing what to say. He mostly slept. Sometimes I heard him cry. Other times he stared at the ceiling, but he didn't talk to me. He just hid his face.

The hospital gave permission for me to stay one night before I went back to school. That night, a storm came through Valdosta. The pine trees swayed, and the rain beat hard against the window. The lightning off in the distance and the rolling thunder vibrated the windows, but I loved it. I lay down and watched, hoping the storm would calm Charles. It wasn't long before I went to sleep, eventually waking up to hear Joyce and Charles talking.

"She sleeps hard during storms," he said to her.

"I know," Joyce said. "She sleeps peacefully, something you don't do."

I kept my eyes closed. I probably should have gotten up, but the rain sounded so good, and it was nice to hear his voice.

"Thank God you weren't there," Charles said. "But everything is behind us now. He's dead now. After I get out, we can leave, get married, and just travel. No running. Just start anew."

Joyce was silent. I rolled over and kept my eyes shut.

"I'm already packed," he said. "I got everything. Reverend Joseph said he's still ready anytime we are."

"Charles?" Joyce said.

"Yeah, Baby?"

"You act like nothing happened to you."

"Joyce, what does it matter? It's over. You already know everything about me. This is nothing new."

I could hear Joyce breathing deeply. "All the stuff you told me about him, about everything," she said. "How did you overcome that?"

"Ms. Carla. You learn not to spend time digging up the past. It's dead, buried, never to resurface. You just bury it in an unmarked grave and move on."

"I don't think that's correct. Eventually, all that hurt comes out no matter who you are and no matter how deep you bury it."

"God forgives completely."

"But He still acknowledges and accepts the truth, something you're not doing."

"Well, it works. Ms. Carla showed me that."

Joyce took a deep breath and then another. "So," she said, "you owe her your life."

Charles sat up in bed. "What's really wrong?"

"I could have been there that night. Just think of what he would have done to me had I been there."

"But you weren't. God kept you from that. It's over now."

"That's not the point. The funny thing about it is that a part of me wishes I had been there to help as best as possible, but now, at least until now and over the past week, I finally see you for who you are."

"What are you talking about?"

"What do you want me to say?" Joyce said.

"The truth. I thought I was the man you fell in love with."

"I thought you were too, but I finally see you're the man who can put a smile on your face, bury everything else so deep, and never deal with it. I thought you were the man who opened up to me before all this. You told me everything about you, your fears, your vulnerabilities, and I loved you for that. The things he did to you. I was ready to run away with you when you admitted you weren't strong enough to stand against him. I loved that about you."

"But."

She shook her head. "You let another woman talk you into suicide. You promised me a week ago we would leave, but you led me to believe a lie."

"No, I told you everything. That's why we were leaving. I knew something like this could happen."

"Yeah," Joyce said, "if you knew something like this could happen, then why on earth did you let Ms. Carla talk you into staying? We…decided as a couple to leave. We…made a decision as future husband and wife to get on with our lives—our lives, not hers. There are other ways to face a monster besides—" Joyce sighed deeply.

"You know," she said, "we made that decision together, but you let Ms. Carla change everything. I should have known it. Ms. Carla this. Ms. Carla that."

"But I see now. I was wrong. I admit it. I was. Give me a chance. I promise I will make it right."

"Really. You couldn't even tell Ms. Carla we were getting married? Why?"

Charles was quiet.

"You could have told her the whole truth and that we were leaving. I told you to tell Mr. Glen or at least Uncle Terrance. You even could have gotten Drummond, and you know nothing would have happened to you then. All you had to do was tell them you were in over your head, but you let her lead you like some little boy. You let her talk you into making light of this."

She placed her hand on the side of his face. "You can't put a smile over all of your secrets, over all your pain. You just can't. As long as Ms. Carla is here, we will never have a life together. I know you will have to get her approval again."

"But we're leaving, so she won't be there."

"No, Charles. She's right here." Joyce placed her hand on Charles' heart.

"I can't lose you," he said.

"I love you so much." She kissed him. "I can't be second to another woman."

"But she's like my mom."

"I know…I know…You are like a mama's boy and yet so gentle with women. So kind. Joyce stood up and shook her head. "I can't…and I won't…be second to no other woman. I deserve better."

"Please don't leave me. Please, Joyce. Just listen. Please."

Joyce took her ring off and laid it on Charles' chest. "Bye, Baby." Then she walked out of the room without looking back.

After a few minutes, I stood up to the backdrop of hard rain.

Charles turned his head away from me.

I went around to the other side so that he could see me and kissed him next to his bandaged scar.

"I don't care about your scars, your secrets. I love you no matter what."

"Really?"

"No matter what."

Shortly after that, Mama sent me home and stayed at the hospital with Charles until he got out.

CHAPTER THIRTEEN

March 23, 1979 (Friday)

My first day back to school wasn't good. Darlington Elementary had been closed for a week at the beginning of the school year. Although we'd been happy about it then, we'd known we would have to pay back the days. One of the replacement school days was the last Friday during spring break. Going to school on that day was hard enough, but thankfully, we didn't do much. Even the teachers didn't want to be there.

The lunchroom reminded me of the hospital waiting room. Groups of people gathered in their own sections focusing on their own conversations, and my friends and I were just the same. Some groups were sitting at rectangular tables and some round tables. My friends and I sat near the exit doors at two round tables that held eight chairs each. I sat closest to the door between Desiree and Nadia.

"How's Charles?" Desiree asked.

Other girls waited to hear.

Even the surrounding tables got quiet. Charles' story and his cousin were big news, yet none of them had visited him. None of them seemed to know what to say, just like me.

"I don't know," I said.

"What do you mean, you don't know?" Nadia asked.

"He's talking and everything, but I mean, how would you feel if your cousin tried to kill you?"

Nadia leaned back.

I didn't want to tell them he'd cried. I didn't want to tell them that Joyce had left him, and he'd begged her to stay. They really thought Charles was perfect. How do you mess up someone's image? I didn't want to do that.

"I never knew anybody like what happened to Charles," Karen said.

I nodded in agreement. There were other nods, some staring at the table, others closing their eyes. It's like we all appreciated the silence.

"Well," Nadia said, "somebody said he was…you know…when they found him."

"What?" Karen said.

"Naked," Nadia whispered. "You know what I mean?"

I stared at Nadia, then got up and excused myself. I went out to the edge of the school's campus. At least I didn't have to hear rumors or anything like that. It was peaceful out there. Ducks played in the pond. I even saw a hummingbird.

"Nicole," Desiree said, coming up from behind, "you okay?"

"No, I'm not."

Desiree sat down beside me.

"I really don't know how he's doing," I said, "how he's dealing with it. How would you feel if somebody in your family tried to kill you? I don't know what to feel. I mean, have you ever known anybody who got beat like that?"

I turned to Desiree, who had a tear rolling down her cheek. When more tears followed, I didn't want to say anything else to upset her. I knew she had to be close to Charles. In fact, we all were.

"It happened to my mother," Desiree said.

"I'm sorry. Did they know who did it?"

"My father."

"Did they catch him?"

She shook her head. "We never reported it. The only people who knew were me, my mother, and now you. Not even Jeremy knew. I was four then. I remember the thuds when he hit her. I remember my mother's screams, and I remember the silence. Daddy just left after that. I went into the room. I covered her naked body and waited by her side until she woke up. I never told her what I saw and heard. I believe she thinks I was too young to remember."

"I'm sorry," I said.

"We ran all over the country trying to get away from him, but he found us because he said he owned Mama. I later found out it was Jeremy who kept calling him and telling him where we were. Daddy got killed by some woman's husband, and that's when Mama burned our emergency bags we used when we ran from him. We eventually settled in Darlington, and that's when I met you in school. You invited me to your birthday party. I had never been to one. You were my first real friend."

Desiree and I sat at the edge of campus, watching the ducks.

CHAPTER FOURTEEN

March 23, 1979 (Friday)

They released Charles from South Georgia Medical Center on Friday afternoon. He didn't look like the Charles we knew, not physically. It was like someone had cut the Mona Lisa just to do it. He stared at the passenger side vanity mirror, touching the healing scar on his face, and then he slowly dropped his hands to his lap. Mama touched him on his shoulder, but he pulled away.

"I'm not a baby," he said. Then I heard him whisper, "From Billy Dee to Scarface in one jagged cut."

"Charles," Mama said softly.

"I'm leaving tonight."

"Where are you going?" she asked.

"I don't know yet, but I'll know when I get there."

"Don't you think you should be a little more responsible and have a plan?"

"I had a plan," he said, "but that's gone. I've had enough of being responsible. I just want to live now."

"What's wrong?"

"You know what Joyce did? She went to the movies with my best friend. I get it. I get it. I see the message loud and clear. I don't blame you, Ms. Carla. You saved my life when I was young. You taught me to bury my past in unmarked graves. What Joyce did, that's life. Something else I'll bury. I don't even regret facing my cousin. You can't run from your past, no matter how hard you try. I showed him I wasn't that little boy anymore. I slashed him four times before he got me."

"But Charles."

"No. No buts. I know who I am, who I will always be."

"Damn it!" Mama said. She pulled the car over to the side of the road.

"What?" he said.

"Everything has tried to destroy you," Mama said, "but I'm not going to let it. Charles, don't you ever forget how strong you are. Don't you dare forget! That black-hearted bastard deserves to be dead. I'm so sorry you had to go through all you experienced in your life, but you are a beacon of hope for me. I have never met anyone as strong as you, not even Glen or Terrance."

She grabbed his chin. "You are a strong, powerful black man who deserves the best of life."

"And just put a smile on it, right?"

"You're damn right!"

"Mama!" I said.

He smiled his golden smile, and then he started laughing. Mama burst out laughing.

He said, "Aren't you the one who taught me there are too many words in the English dictionary to curse?"

Mama laughed so hard that she started crying.

"Remember Florida on 'Good Times,'" he said. "Damn! Damn! Damn!"

My ears were burning from all the "damns" I heard.

"Ms. Carla, I'm really good. I really do know who I am. I know it will take time. For now, it is what it is." He hugged Mama and kissed her on the cheek.

The word damn was running through my mind. As Mama pulled back on the road, I whispered, "Damn, damn, damn."

I heard the pop from Mama before I felt the lick on my leg.

"Nicole," Mama said, "until you learn all the words in the dictionary, don't ever say damn again."

"Next time," Charles said, "say, Darn! Darn! Darn!" He laughed and said, "But Ms. Carla, you have to admit. 'Damn' sure captures the mood."

They both started laughing again, but I was the one who'd gotten popped.

CHAPTER FIFTEEN

March 23, 1979 (Friday)

Charles dropped by the house before he was to leave town for good. He wanted to hear me improvise "My Funny Valentine," his favorite song. I was reluctant at first, but Mama said, "Have at it and play with all your heart."

Daddy and Mama sat next to Charles while I played.

Halfway through the song, Charles' smile returned. His eyes closed, and his tears flowed past his smile. After I played, I stood by the piano and took my bow, and as I rose, I thanked God for this moment with Charles. It was as if I witnessed the sun rising over snowcapped mountains, its rays bursting forth to embrace a misty valley of lakes and trees. Mama's smile, which had been absent all week, had finally come out of hiding, and I basked in its warmth, feeling loved and, more than that, wanted.

"Charles."

Hearing my voice utter his name brought an unexpected reaction in me. I took in a deep breath and slowly exhaled. In the word association games we had played at school, the words sunny, smile, or even baby all brought automatic responses. This time, the name Charles produced the tears that welled up.

I didn't know what to do now. Trying to imagine our family without him was like trying to breathe without air. I didn't know how we would survive. The more I thought, the more I realized I didn't know how to exist without him. He was always there.

I lifted my head up a little higher. "It's funny, but I never thought this day would come." All other words eluded me. My lips quivered. All of my memories of Charles flooded in, threatening to overwhelm me. I searched for different expressions and sayings. Volumes of thoughts raced through my mind, but there was nothing else to say, so I finally resigned myself to release him with two words.

"Bye, Charles."

There were no words to take away the dull ache in my heart. I walked into his arms and listened to his heartbeat. Then I released him.

We were all smiling until Charles got in his car and drove away. When his car disappeared around the bend, Mother's smile dissipated. She went into the house and locked herself in their bedroom just as thunder rolled across the sky.

A little later, I lay in bed, listening to the pouring rain playing steady rhythms on the tin roof of the carport below my bedroom window. The lightning flashed bright lights across the darkened sky. The brilliant white lights of electricity tore through the air like a jet breaking the sound barrier.

One…Two…Three—boom!

The thunder continued to rattle our house in my normally quiet neighborhood. I watched the millions upon millions of drops splashing as if tiny feet were running through the water. The stream that had already formed rushed down the street and disappeared into the darkness, only to be seen clearly by the next brilliant flash that lit up the sky.

During storms, Daddy had slept on the floor in my room. Mama would also come, but not tonight. She needed time. I had already packed for our weekend getaway. I wouldn't ask her a lot of questions. It would be nice just to spend time alone with her.

Daddy had fallen asleep on the floor, and I watched the rain and thought of Charles.

CHAPTER SIXTEEN

March 24, 1979 (Saturday)

Daddy got up early and sang Happy Birthday to me. Imagine hearing that song when you're half-sleep, but I woke up when he gave me an envelope. Inside was a rain check for "almost anything" for a later date.

"Almost anything?" I asked.

"John the Baptist lost his head when a king promised a young girl anything. I wasn't sure if your mother or grandmother would try to influence your request."

I know he didn't think Mama would do anything like that. Now, Grandmother was different.

"It's just," he said, "our family isn't in the right state of mind for birthdays, so I want you to think about what you really want when you feel better about all that has gone on, including Charles, the mayor's event, and even the pool party. When you know, then redeem the rain check."

He smiled as he got ready to leave. "Uncle Terrance and I are going fishing early this morning. I saw your suitcase for the girls' only weekend, so you won't be here. Tell me all about your weekend when you get back."

After he left, I thought about where Mama and I would stay. Mama gave me a choice, so I chose this new hotel called the Westin Peachtree Plaza Hotel in Atlanta. They finished building it a little over two years ago during our bicentennial. I'd picked it because I wanted to finally get over my fear of heights. Daddy and Uncle Terrance told me the best way to overcome fear was to face it head-on. What better way than to choose the tallest hotel in Atlanta and look out the window of one of the highest rooms in the hotel?

Even thinking about it, I got excited. I was going to stare out the window for ten seconds first, but by the time we left, I would be able to sit and see the view. I didn't want fear stealing any more beauty from my life.

I imagined the check-in would be 3 p.m., but I wasn't sure. I was packed and ready. I got up, made breakfast, ate, and cleaned up. Then I waited in my waiting chair for Mama to come down. It usually took about four hours to get to Atlanta from where we lived. When I heard Mama's footsteps, I got up to ask her what time she thought we'd get there.

When Mama appeared, she had her hair pulled back and was wearing a lavender sweat suit and carrying her Bible and notebook.

"I need to go to Bible study. I really need some time alone."

"When will you be back?"

"Around noon."

"Do I need to call and let the hotel know we're going to be late or something like that?"

She just stared at me, and then her eyes tightened, but I didn't know why. She'd taught me to be courteous and communicate in business, especially with a reservation like that.

She closed her eyes and shook her head as if disappointed in me. "One day," she said, "you'll find the world doesn't revolve around you." She opened her eyes. "All I see is one big silver spoon sticking out of your mouth. Are you paying for the room or driving or anything like that?"

"No, ma'am."

"All I got to say is that plans change. Ask Charles, or have you already forgotten about him? The way I feel, I don't want to go anywhere with you."

She turned around, walked out, and locked the door behind her.

A minute must have passed before I moved. Things were already different. I wondered what was wrong with Mama. All of this was new because there was no Charles to buffer anything between Mama and me. Come to think about it, the only things we had in common were the competitions and weddings, but even that had changed. I really thought things had been different after we'd picked Charles up from the hospital. Still, the common denominator was Charles.

I thought of things that would make me feel better. I thought of the chiffon dress. Even the name was elegant. I put my performance dress on, loving the way chiffon felt. I stood in front of the full-length mirror in my room. The reflection showed a growing girl, but the closer I looked in the mirror, there was something so familiar about my face. I moved in even closer.

I took my hair and quickly put it up the same way Mama wore hers during the mayor's black-tie event. I rushed to my photo album on my desk, opened it quickly, found Mama's junior high school pictures, and just stared. Even then, she'd been so beautiful and elegant. I went back to the mirror and stared.

Was that really me? I looked like Mama. As I stared, I ventured to say aloud, "Maybe I'm beautiful too."

I stepped back, let my hair down, and smiled.

"Maybe I am."

The melody of the doorbell rang throughout the house. I took a deep breath, breathed in the light perfume on the chiffon dress, and smiled at my first test as a responsible guardian of the house. I went through my mental checklist.

One. I could just stay in my room or sit at my desk. I remembered those rules Mama told me. The only person to let in was Charles, and Charles was gone now. It was too early for the mailman or any package to be delivered.

Two. I could check who was at the door, but I knew no one else. It couldn't have been Mama; she told me she had a key. She'd said to only open the door for Charles, so I hoped it wasn't Grandmother because she wasn't getting in. I knew Daddy would laugh at that one.

I kind of laughed aloud as the doorbell rang again.

The second ring piqued my interest. Could it be an emergency or someone needing help? Mama would be proud if I saved someone's life. I smiled and decided to check. While I made my way downstairs to answer the door, I rehearsed the house's number one rule: never let strangers in under any circumstance. Mama and Daddy didn't joke about that one.

When I drew nearer, I saw the silhouette of a man through the frosted glass on the front door. My heart jumped. I thought about the church's number on the refrigerator, but if I called, it would show I couldn't handle one simple matter. I didn't have to answer the door.

The silhouette moved, and the doorbell rang again.

I wiped my sweaty palms against my dress. "Can't do that again."

Inching closer, I stared at the image that stood patiently at the door.

Charles?

The silhouette moved.

"Charles!"

I flung the door open. "What are you doing here? I thought you were gone?"

He stepped back. "Wow," he said under his breath. His eyes wandered.

"You okay?" I asked.

He rubbed his head. "I just wanted to drop by one last time to tell your parents…tell them thanks, I love them, and I'll miss them."

"I got a number for Mama. I'm sure she would love to hear from you. I don't know exactly where Daddy is."

"When did they leave?"

"Daddy, early this morning. Mama about twenty to thirty minutes ago."

Charles stared at me. He looked over his shoulder and then back at me.

"Would you like something to drink?" I asked.

He rubbed his head again. "No, I'm good."

He just stood there. It wasn't like him to be without words. At any party or gathering, he was the center of attention even without trying, but to see him, shirt wrinkled, shoes scuffed, and hair uncombed, was just not Charles.

"I'm sorry, Nicole, for not standing up for you. You know."

"What do you mean?"

"I'm the one who put it in your head to improvise."

"Daddy always said we are responsible for our own actions. When you stand before God, he's going to be looking at what you did, so you might as well start now. So, Charles, I don't blame you at all."

"You forgive me just like that."

"Of course."

Relief came over him. "You know, Joyce wasn't as forgiving as I thought, but you've always been forgiving to me." He grinned. "Is that the dress you wore the other night and last night?"

"Yes. Mama told me to be very careful with it because it cost a fortune. I actually wiped my hands on it. Can you believe that?"

"Your hair. I've never seen it like that. It looks nice." He leaned against the doorframe.

"You serious?"

"Yeah."

"Thank you," I said. "You okay? Because I've never seen your hair like that either. I mean, really, are you okay?"

"I was ready to get on the plane, but I couldn't. Then I wouldn't. Everybody kept staring at my scar. I ran out, drove around town for a couple of hours, and even passed by the end of your street twice. I didn't know it would be this hard to leave."

Charles was definitely different now. I'd noticed before, but I couldn't talk to Mama about it. He just seemed burdened. He was still a handsome man to me. If the people at the airport had known him, they wouldn't have cared about his scar.

"You mind if I come in?"

I stood aside and let him in. It was strange. Charles had this musky smell covered with heavy cologne, so unlike him. It was like he hadn't showered today. He also smelled like he had been drinking, something he never did.

The birds kept singing in the trees, seemingly happy about today. My friends playing in the big front yard next door seemed happy, too. Even Bubbles and Snowflake, the two little Shih Tzu's playing with my friends, seemed happy.

I turned at what sounded like Charles falling down on the sofa. He, on the other hand, wasn't happy. I closed the door and walked over to the loveseat to the left and adjacent to where he sat. He fidgeted with his hands, focused on the coasters stacked on the coffee table in front of him, and then he focused on the TV that wasn't on.

"Are you okay?" I asked again.

"Hmmm, I thought I'd try something new last night. I went to the Fifth Inn in Valdosta. Guess what they call me now?"

"What's that?"

"Scarface. You know, like Al Capone."

I didn't know what to tell him.

"You know," he said, "the more I think about it. I'm sorry, Nicole. I…I know you don't like it, but I should go."

"What's wrong?"

He shook his head and leaned back. "You know, I do understand why people mention things but change their mind when it's time to say more. Some things are better left unsaid. At least, that's what I read."

With all he had gone through, I could have only imagined the things running through his mind, and yeah, he had been drinking, but he didn't seem to be drunk. It was weird, though. In a split second, his mind seemed to be elsewhere again. He stared at the coasters he'd bought for our family. He shifted, sat up, straightened his coat and tie, and tried to rub the wrinkles out of his shirt. When he finished, he stared into my eyes.

"I can see you're not a little girl anymore," he said. "Ever since Ms. Carla had me look at you again before we went to Eleanor's, I've seen you differently. I didn't even notice until now. And this past week, with everything I've been through and how you handled the hospital, I'm impressed with how you're talking now. So much more mature than Joyce, even most women I've known. They play too many games."

He sighed and continued talking.

"I thought for sure Joyce was the one, but for her to actually go out with Reggie, my best friend, she didn't have to do that. But it takes two, and for all I know, they may have been seeing each other all along, and she was just looking for an excuse to break up. After everything, you were stable and consistent. Even my scar didn't bother you."

When Charles stopped talking again, I had a chance to be like Mama with him and share quiet moments. The light by the baby grand reflected off the beveled glass, making it seem peaceful over there.

"You may not know," Charles said, "but your mother told me that when you find someone, you least expect, be willing to give it a chance. I don't know why I didn't believe her until now. You..." His voice trailed off as he mumbled something and went back to staring at the coasters.

"Nicole," he said, "I can't do this. I can't make time stand still. I do think God is so unfair at times. I do. Here I am. I didn't pick my life, all the things I've gone through, and now I'm faced with another dilemma. It ain't right."

He took a massive breath and exhaled slowly.

"I've been searching for someone like—"

"Joyce?"

"No, someone else, for what it seems like my whole life, and just when I was about to leave, I see…she…was always right there in front of me."

He lifted his chin and said, "I understand your fairy tales now. I understand why the prince would search an entire kingdom to find the love of his life."

I closed my eyes and almost melted at the thought. So, this is how finding love is.

"Do you mind playing something for me?" he said.

"What do you want to hear?"

"My Funny Valentine."

I got up and went to the piano. His voice behind me. "I like the line 'Your looks are laughable…unphotographable…yet you're my favorite work of art.'"

When I sat down, I heard him sigh again.

"I hope the woman of my dreams will love me just like that song."

He stood beside me.

I closed my eyes, and as I played, I thought about Charles finding his bride and standing at the altar, her loving him just the way he was even after all he had been through. Just like the birds, my friends, even Bubbles and Snowflake, he would be happy too. I wanted to watch them ride off into the sunset and disappear into their new future with all the bad behind him.

It was then that I felt an awkwardness in the room. When I opened my eyes, he stood behind me while I played his song.

"I've always loved the texture of your hair," he said. "May I one last time?"

I nodded. His touch was different, nothing like anything he had ever done before, more like when Daddy used to gently run his hand through Mama's hair.

"What's her name?" I asked.

He stayed preoccupied with my hair.

"Charles?"

I stopped playing, but it was like he didn't notice.

"What do you really think about me?" he asked, and he stopped with my hair, moved to stand by the piano, and stared into my eyes—no smile.

"Y-you already know," I stuttered. Hearing my voice tremble made no sense until I saw how he was looking at me. I had never seen him that way. I just couldn't explain it. I got up from the piano and moved to go toward the kitchen. "You want anything to drink?"

"You already asked me that."

Suddenly, Charles walked toward the door. Each step away from me brought relief until he stopped and stood at the door with his hand frozen on the doorknob.

"I thought," he said softly, "you'd always tell me the truth no matter what. At least, that's what you told me years ago, that you would just say whatever was on your mind. Have you changed toward me just like everybody else?"

I struggled not to say anything. I wanted to stay quiet, not knowing why.

"Nicole, have you changed too?"

I tightened my lips, battling the urge to answer. I just knew that once he left, this strange feeling would go away.

"I see now," he said, nodding his head. "I'll tell you, just like Ms. Carla told me when I was trying to leave with Joyce. What if something happened to me, and this was the last time you ever saw me alive? Will you long and pray for the words to tell me?"

I kept quiet. I don't know how much time passed, but he broke the silence.

"I see now," he said. "I really mean nothing to you. It's fine."

Before I knew it, I heard myself say, "I don't care about your scar. You've always been special to me. The one who'd always protect and love me."

Once the words escaped my lips, I felt something dark enter the room.

CHAPTER SEVENTEEN

March 24, 1979 (Saturday)

"Carla, what's wrong?" Brenda Solomon, the Bible study teacher, whispered. "You've just been sitting there staring out the window."

Carla scanned the faces of the other women sitting in the Sunday school room, hurriedly grabbed her things, and quickly left Bible study. Once she was in the parking lot, she pulled her keys from her purse and then paused by her car. Her thoughts were uncontrollable, taking her to a place she didn't like, driven by her emotions.

"God," she said, "I'm tired of jumping every time I think something's wrong with Nicole. I'm tired."

She shook her head.

"God, why can't You just tell me straight what's going on? I'm tired of this struggle. I'm tired of praying and begging You for answers that never seem to come. I'm tired of being wrong. And God, I am so tired of feeling like I'm not a good mother. You know I try. All You have to do is just tell me. Am I Your daughter too?"

"Carla," Brenda said at Carla's passenger door. "What's wrong? You haven't been the same for a couple of weeks, and I can understand why, but you walked out of Bible study without a word."

"It doesn't matter how I feel," Carla said.

"Why?"

"Because I have one daughter who really doesn't need me. I can't have any more children, and Charles, oh, how I wish he were my son. I had a chance to adopt him, but I didn't because I was on bed rest, pregnant with Nicole. He was the one bright spot that made me feel like I was worth something. Now he's gone."

Carla thumbed through her keys and then opened her door.

Brenda hesitated for a second, opened the passenger side door, and jumped in just as Carla cranked up. Before Brenda could close her door, Carla sped out of the parking lot, chasing another bad feeling.

~

After a long silence in the house, Charles said, almost whispering, "I went out to watch you during a field day about a month ago. I just showed up, and there you were, the leader of all those girls. Then, my heart jumped when I saw you perform in that dress for me last night. The way you played for me, it was like I had been away for years, and I was back, and you had grown up."

He turned to me.

"I was at the airport, knowing I needed to leave, but I just couldn't. All the things your mother said made me want to protect you more. I knew I would regret this if I didn't tell you. I believe you are the one for me, the one I've been looking for. Jacob waited for Rachel for fourteen years. I can wait six years for you. I just wanted you to know."

He started walking toward me. His eyes were different. "Have you ever dreamed or thought about me late at night? Have you ever dreamed of kissing me? Have you ever…"

The way he asked the questions, it was like he didn't want answers. I took a step back. Then he opened his arms.

~

Carla sped through the yellow light just as it turned red.

"I never get it right, at least with Nicole," she said to Brenda, who clutched the armrest. "About a month ago, I had a feeling like this. I was home early one morning, and Nicole was at the same park with her school—a field day. This feeling came over me, this horrible feeling. I got in my car, half out of my mind, and sped away, but I was stopped by a police officer. I convinced him something was wrong with my daughter. He escorted me there, sirens blaring, but Nicole was fine."

She hit the steering wheel.

"I still had curlers in my hair, my housecoat, and house shoes on. Glen thought I was having a nervous breakdown."

Carla sped past another car.

"It's getting worse. Every day, I deal with these dark thoughts that something is wrong with her, but I get no clear answers. Then we found Charles badly beaten. I was terrified. If Charles can't protect himself, then what can Nicole do? I even promised her that when she turned twelve, I'd talk with her about everything from boys to growing up into a woman on our girls-only weekend but look at me—like I really know something. What am I going to tell her? What do I really know? Besides, she's smart."

A horn blared as Carla sped through another red light.

Charles stood there, his arms still open in the silence, waiting patiently. He smiled at me; he was now the way he'd always been before saying goodbye. I was still uneasy, but I didn't really have a reason to be. This was Charles.

When I walked into his arms and wrapped my arms around him, he just held me like he always did before he left. I felt safe again. My breathing slowed, and a smile formed. It was then his hands slowly moved down my back.

Daddy had told me, "No one except your husband is to touch you below your waist."

I had never felt any fear of Charles until today.

I pushed him away, not knowing what to say. I took a few steps back. His eyes slowly moved down past my waist. I put my hands and arms in front of me, trying to block his stare.

Speak up, Nicole. Tell him to leave.

He took a few steps toward me, reached out his hand, and almost touched my arm.

"Nicole," he said, his voice eerily calm, "why are you so nervous?"

My hands shook.

"Charles, I-I…want…to make sure you arrive safely, s-so…y-you probably want to…get on your plane."

"That's what I love about you. So caring about me. Nobody else is like you."

My legs buckled as I took a step toward the door. When I passed him, he touched my hand, but I jerked back. He just smiled as sweat ran down my back.

All I had to do was make it to the door.

I glanced back at Charles and saw him standing several feet away. My hand moved slowly to the handle.

Push down, pull, and run. Push down, pull…

The second I touched the metal handle, Charles was there. He slapped my hand away. He blocked the door and locked it behind him. My legs gave way, and I staggered back. He stood in front of the door, his eyes cold, just like his cousin's eyes on the news.

I heard voices outside. They sounded as if they were in my front yard.

I shut my eyes tightly, wishing he would disappear.

What?

His lips pressed against mine. I shoved him and backed away until the corner of the wall blocked me.

"Stop!"

Charles grinned. "Stop what?"

This time, I couldn't answer.

He moved closer.

I slapped him with all I had in me and then pushed myself deeper into the corner. In movies, sometimes a slap would bring a person to their senses, but it didn't this time. He just smiled, his eyes empty.

Then he grabbed me. Each time I exhaled; he squeezed tighter like a python. I managed a word. "Why?" He wouldn't answer.

It was hard to breathe. I smelled the mixture of day-old sweat, strong cologne, and alcohol. I hit him one last time on his scar. He didn't even flinch. Instead, he pinned my hands against my sides and started carrying me upstairs. I stared at the door, praying that Mama would show up, and then we disappeared around the corner as he carried me toward my room.

~

Carla heard Nicole's voice in her head just as she barreled around the corner and headed down her street. Suddenly she slammed on her brakes.

"God, I'm not doing this anymore," she said, still hearing Nicole's voice in her mind. She shook her head. "I'm not going to go crazy over this."

"Just go," Brenda said, grabbing Carla's hand. "Go!"

Carla began to press on the accelerator to move forward, knowing she needed to hurry, but she stopped again.

"No," she told the voice in her head. "No, God. I'm not gonna be Your fool anymore."

"What are you talking about?" Brenda said.

"Glen is good at these strong feelings, and so is Nicole. If this is how it is with God, this guessing game, then I don't want it. I don't want these feelings anymore. We'll get to the house. Nicole will be just fine, and that will be something else that I was wrong about. I'm tired of looking stupid. No. I'm not doing this anymore."

"Carla, please! Let's go. It's right around the bend."

Carla could see the roof of her house, and Nicole's bedroom window curtains were open like they were supposed to be.

"No, Brenda," she said, shaking her head. "No. Why do I have to beg God? Why? I'm the one who carried her, lying on my back for months, bedridden. I did it. Now, Nicole, she has everything I ever wanted, but it's like God just gave all of my dreams to her. It's not supposed to be like this. It's not fair. I always knew life was hard. I didn't complain. I learned to stop crying and whining about how bad life could be. You have to work and work and work to earn everything you get, but I look at her every day, and life is just laid at her feet for her to just reach down and pick up. All the things I worked so hard trying, doing, and practicing, she gets effortlessly. She's a free spirit. She's smart, sometimes brilliant. She even has a loving relationship with her father—something I desperately wanted with mine.

"What do I get? What could I possibly teach her? That's why I don't want another reminder of the cruel joke that God has played on me. Now the one person who really looked up to me is gone. Sometimes I wish it were the other way around. Now I have to go home every day and have God just laugh at me and show me what a failure I really am."

"Carla, don't say that. You're not a failure."

"Yeah," Carla said as she turned the car around and began to drive back toward the church, "that's what I try to tell myself, but I'm tired of lying."

~

My last finger gave way after holding onto the door frame of my room. My hand slid past my poster by the light switch. I heard the poster tear, and then I saw it was the picture of me ripped at the waist. I backed away, staring at all the pictures of my friends smiling on the wall.

He shut the door behind him. The lock clicked.

I ran to the window, but he caught me, threw me to the bed, and closed the curtains. I ran to the door, but he pulled me away, and then he let me stand in the middle of the room.

This isn't happening. This isn't real.

"Charles, please don't do this. Just let me go. I won't tell anybody. I promise I won't. Please, Charles."

He stepped closer.

"No. Don't." All of my words had fallen on deaf ears. I closed my eyes as he tore my dress. Then there was the muffled sound of my own voice and then another tear.

~

Carla ignored Nicole's muffled cries, and they eventually grew quiet, giving Carla a silent ride back.

Soon they were back at the church. Carla brought the car to a stop and parked by Brenda's station wagon. Most of the women were already gone.

Brenda sighed and turned to Carla. "There will come a time when Nicole will really need you," she said, being selective in her words. "She's going to always be a daddy's girl, you know that, but there is something about a mother's love that no matter how you feel, you can't deny. Carla, you have a wonderful daughter, but now I realize you are so caught up in Charles that I don't think you even see her. You need to open up your eyes and see how much she admires you. Please, just listen to her when that time comes. Don't react. Just listen."

"Listen? And then what?" Carla shook her head. "Brenda, I've tried. I really have. See, I was so good with Charles. If she could—"

"No," Brenda said, interrupting, "I'm sorry. I hope you don't take this the wrong way, but Carla, you can't put a smile on everything and make this go away. After what he went through, you can't just shove that down on top of all that other stuff and expect him to be okay. Every person, no matter who they are or how strong you think they are, has a breaking point. We all have them, and so does Charles.

"Just listen to Nicole when that time comes. If you don't, you'll miss out on one of the most precious blessings of being a mother." Brenda stepped out of the car and turned around. "I hope you heard me."

Brenda closed the door behind her, and Carla headed home.

I stood at the barbeque pit on the back patio, not knowing how I'd gotten out there. The torn dress and everything else were lying on the grill. For a moment, I thought of the chiffon and how much I'd looked like Mama in the dress. I'd actually been beautiful. The wind blew, capturing his musky scent from my clothes on the grill. I took the can of lighter fluid and poured and poured. The can was almost empty by the time I realized I had soaked everything, but then I saw his eyes. I felt his grip, his lips. I struck the match and dropped it.

I sat down on Daddy's favorite chair. The bonfire blazed as I heard my friends laughing and playing. The birds continued singing, the dogs barking. A cool breeze wrapped around me. It wasn't long before the sound of my friends began to disappear, along with the singing birds and the barking dogs. Even the breeze that brought me comfort began to fade as I went to a place of emptiness, numbness, but safety.

All I wanted now was to see Mama and have her tell me everything was going to be okay.

CHAPTER EIGHTEEN

March 24, 1979 (Saturday)

Carla drove around town for a while before going home to face Nicole's endless barrage of questions, especially about Atlanta. She made a right into her neighborhood with Brenda's words still on her mind. She knew Brenda couldn't understand that it was the smiles that helped Charles stand up to his past. Even her mentioning he needed counseling was absurd.

Counseling had done nothing for her, and it especially wouldn't do anything for Charles to have someone tell him how messed up his life had been until she'd come along. All of them were wrong, even about the way he'd bounced back after all his cousin had done to him. No one was ever going to know him better, not even Joyce.

Carla told herself she was the one who'd stepped in when Aunt Menzy hadn't been able to handle Charles. She was the one who could reach him better than anyone else. Charles had worked hard to quiet the voices in his head, something she'd learned to do when she was a little girl. She'd even taught him to overcome his abuse from his own family and now his cousin.

She knew Charles struggled. Who wouldn't? But when she saw his beautiful smile, she knew he was alright. He was still the beautiful young man she knew best.

Carla almost missed her turn down her street. Once headed to her house, she noticed a light stream of smoke in front of the backdrop of the blue sky. The closer she got to their house, she saw smoke streaming from the rear. They had told Nicole not to cook anything while they were away, let alone barbeque. Carla sped up, whipped her car into the driveway, and slammed on the brakes.

"That girl," she mumbled under her breath.

Once in the house, she closed the door.

"Nicole!"

No answer. A slight trace of smoke led her to the opened back door. She'd told Glen that the pit was in a bad spot because the wind could blow the smoke through the back door. Still, as far as cooking, Nicole knew better.

Once through the door, Carla stopped as if she had run into an invisible wall. It wasn't hot dogs or hamburgers that lay on the grill. There was a blackened mound of clothes, with one strip of a smoldering white cloth hanging over the edge. When she touched the strip, she knew immediately what the pile was. Nicole had even burned the shoes.

Out of Carla's left eye, she saw something move. She turned to see Nicole dressed like some thrown-away rag doll. Her hair was all over the place, and she had gray and blue sweats on and pink and purple socks.

Carla thought, *she knows I can't stand mismatched clothes, especially socks. She's not color blind. All of this over the mayor's event and her punishment?*

A burning rage grew in Carla's chest. She had told Glen that Nicole was becoming defiant.

"What is this," Carla said, "some challenge?"

Nicole turned her head slowly toward her mother. She had no expression on her face as if she were in some creepy horror movie. Did Nicole think she was going to scare her?

"Why did you burn this?"

No response.

This child thinks I'm playing. "Nicole! Nicole!"

~

"Nicole!"

It was like Mama had just appeared, standing by the pit as she held the burned sash. I didn't know how long she'd been there or how much time had passed. A thin layer of smoke from the pit headed through the screen door. Mama fanned the smoke smoldering in the pit.

My mouth moved, but nothing came out.

"Oh, it's like that?" Mama said.

She came toward me and yanked me up. Daddy's chair clanked as it turned over. Just inside, she slammed the door behind us. Then she grabbed the belt hanging on the wall and swung it, hitting my thigh.

My mouth opened, but nothing came out.

"Why did you burn that dress?"

I tried to answer, but before I could say anything, she swung again and didn't stop. The belt felt like a repeated drumbeat of searing pain.

Mama shouted each word in sync with the lash of the belt. "Why...did... you...do...that? Answer me!"

I could hear the scream inside me, but nothing was coming out. Each time the words formed, I felt another lash, and then another, and then another across my legs, thighs, back, and arms. Then, as quickly as the beating had started, it stopped. She grabbed me and swung me over to the kitchen table toward a chair. Once I landed, I heard the chair crack.

"We've given you everything you have ever wanted, and now you do this to me. That was the most expensive dress I'd ever bought, and this is how you repay me?"

She held up the belt again. I knew she wanted to swing, but she just stood there snorting as she exhaled. She eventually lowered the belt.

"Get out of my face before I do something I regret."

I got up and walked out of the kitchen toward the staircase. All I could think of was climbing into my closet and closing the door.

"I wish Charles was my son," Mama said from behind me. "There, I said it. Now you know. At least I would have been successful in raising one grateful child."

She didn't have to say it. I already knew. I felt something in my throat and coughed. Mama's words weighed heavier than I thought, but I kept walking. I couldn't say I was choking back tears, but with each step, her words hurt. It was then that I heard footsteps behind me.

"What did you say?" Mama said. "Nicole! What did you say?"

I turned around, and she slapped me so hard that I didn't remember falling or landing against the wall at the bottom of the steps. My ear had this high-pitched sound. Once I looked up, Mama towered over me—her eyes filled with rage.

"Don't you ever...say anything about Charles."

"But Mama, I didn't say—"

She picked me up as if I were some rag doll and slammed me against the wall. I couldn't breathe. My head throbbed. She pinned me against the wall.

"I'm sick of you and your wasted talent. I gave you everything, but all you do is live in a fantasy world and belittle Charles."

"But Mama, Charles—"

She slapped me so hard that my head hit the wall. My left ear rang louder. My jaw stung. She pulled me within inches of her face with one arm. Her fist tightened on my collar and pressed against my throat.

"His life's been hard enough," she said, her voice eerily calm, "and do you think for one moment I will let some spoiled brat tear him down? Oh, little girl, that's not going to happen. Don't you ever say anything bad about Charles…as long as you are living in my house. Do you understand me?"

She added to the grip around my collar, tightening it slowly. It was hard to breathe. The room was quiet. Her eyes glazed over when she tilted her head. I stood still as she put her free hand slowly around my neck and began tightening, her thumb pressed against my windpipe.

"Mama?"

She slapped me harder.

"Do you…understand…me?"

Her head slowly tilted as she put her hand back around my neck. Before she could tighten, I answered, "Yes, ma'am."

"Yes, ma'am…what?"

"I…I understand. Mama. I understand."

She slowly let go, and then she released me.

"Get out of my face."

Mama stared at me, her face contorted.

I ran upstairs. Once at the top, I turned to see her staring at me. A few seconds passed, and then she turned toward the kitchen.

I went to my room, missed the light switch, and hit the poster of me instead, making the half that was hanging fall to the floor. I picked up the torn piece, stared at it for a moment, and then let it go.

I stood in the middle of the room, remembering everything. The full-length mirror was shattered, with pieces lying all around it. Mama didn't like my room, feeling it was like a little girl's room. I got a couple of cardboard boxes from Daddy's closet, but the welts on my back hurt as my clothes rubbed against them. I took a long, hot shower, eventually easing the pain.

I put my long-sleeve matching sweats and white socks on and continued what I had set out to do. I took the other piece of my poster down and neatly rolled up the torn piece from the floor. Soon, my room was free of all dreams and fantasies. I lay down on the floor, away from the glass, watched the sky turn dark, and longed for another day. Another chance.

CHAPTER NINETEEN

March 24, 1979 (Saturday)

I reluctantly opened my eyes, expecting to see an empty room, a continuation of yesterday, but what I saw startled me. All of my posters were hanging. Even my princess poster was on the wall, intact. The morning sun peeped around the edges of my drapes, hinting at the beauty and promise of a new day.

I rubbed my eyes, barely believing it had all been just a long bad dream. It all seemed so real. I could hardly believe it. I flung the curtains open and then slowly turned around in my room, taking in everything until my eyes rested on my closet. There was a distinct creaking sound when I opened my closet door.

I reached forward and glided the back of my hand over the soft white chiffon fabric of my dress with the sash, breathing in the light perfume Mama had sprayed. I felt my smile and tuned my ears to what was going on downstairs.

"Glen, do you know where my keys are?"

"No, we'll just take my car."

I hurried downstairs to my parents.

"Hi, birthday girl," Mama said.

"Mama!" I ran into her arms. "I'm sorry I improvised the 'Moonlight Sonata.' It's all my fault."

She rubbed my back.

"I'm so sorry, Mama. I'm sorry about everything."

"Nicole," she said, "look at me."

"Yes, ma'am."

She smiled and shook her head. "Nicole, I'm the one who should be sorry.

I have been getting so many calls about your performance. Then, after Charles left and last night, I had a lot of time to think, and I now see God has blessed me with you. I have a beautiful, wonderful daughter. You're all I've ever wanted in a child, but I've been so blind."

"You really mean it?"

"Of course I do."

"Carla," Daddy said, "go ahead and tell her."

"You couldn't even wait one moment." Mama laughed. "Nicole, your father also came to me last night."

Daddy posed like Superman with his chest out and his fists on his waist.

"Stop that, Glen," Mama said, smiling. "Anyway, he came to talk with me last night while you were asleep. I can't ground you. It took me time to realize that creativity is just a part of you. This weekend is for us—our girls-only weekend. Your father will chauffeur us to Atlanta. Then, on Monday, we're going to Six Flags. It shouldn't be crowded because others will be in school."

"So, I can miss school?"

"We all really need it. We're going to get a fresh new start. It'll take me a little time, but I'll loosen up. I really wanted you to know that I love you, and I am so proud of you. Do you forgive me?"

"You really love me?"

"Oh Nicole, yes," she said as she touched my face the way she would touch Charles' face. "Things will be different from now on between us. Okay?"

I watched the dimples in her cheeks as she smiled. She didn't even try to hide them. I hugged Mama, not wanting to let go.

"Nicole," she said, "your father and I are going to Valdosta to see Uncle Terrance and Aunt Gwen for about an hour, but we'll be right back. They are family, and I want to do better with them, too."

I took my parents' hands and escorted them to Daddy's car.

"Hurry back. Mama, while you're gone, I'll look for your keys."

"No need. I found them in my purse."

"Interesting place," Daddy said.

"That man," she said, shaking her head. "Nicole, we'll be right back."

I stepped back and waved bye to them as I watched them drive away. The rocker on the front porch caught my attention. The cool breeze whisked around my ears and neck. I felt more alive. I sat on the porch for a few moments. Then got up and ran upstairs. At my desk, out of the corner of my eye, I caught a glimpse of myself in the mirror and stopped and stared, still remembering the realness of my nightmare.

That was when the doorbell rang, but this time, I didn't dare answer. It rang several more times, but I refused to answer. I headed to the back porch and sat in Daddy's chair for a while, listening to the birds singing and the dogs barking. The same gentle breeze from earlier played in my hair, and then I turned my face toward the sun as I thanked God again for this day. If I had shown any signs of being spoiled, I wasn't going to be that way anymore.

After a little while, I got up and went to my room upstairs. While I walked, I noticed the house getting darker with each step. I checked the front door and saw it was still locked.

"Mama! Daddy!"

There was no other sound. I clapped my hand. Not even an echo. Deadness. I walked to my room and stood at the entrance. My posters were all in place, but it seemed to get dark as if a storm had suddenly breezed in.

Once I walked past the threshold of my room, I heard a distinctive tearing sound. I turned and almost screamed as my poster slowly tore in half. The other posters and pictures on the walls fell off and disappeared. My closet door creaked open, revealing my white chiffon dress, which moved. The sleeve slowly tore, and then the sash fell to the floor. The dress began to blacken.

I turned around and ran out of the room, down the stairs, and flung the front door open only to see Charles standing there.

"Charles," I said as I ran into his arms, "something's wrong."

He didn't respond. It took me a bit to gain the courage to open my eyes. Once I did, we were in my bedroom. The door closed behind us and locked. I stepped away from him. My bedspread slowly pulled back, and my curtains closed. In the dim light, I watched Charles' eyes turn cold and harsh.

Something picked me up and placed me on my bed. Cologne filled my nostrils. I felt a hand on my shoulder and lips press against my cheek. My body stiffened when I heard footsteps leaving my room.

It was then that Charles approached from the dark corner. I could hardly move. I was restrained. I fought harder, but his weight was heavy. I struggled, opened my eyes, looked up at the ceiling in the darkness, and somehow found the strength to throw him off. I heard a thump as he hit the floor. In the darkness, I grew still. Something touched my foot.

I jumped up from my bed. The boxes I had packed were in the middle of the floor.

Then I heard footsteps and saw a silhouette of a man at my bedroom door.

"No!" I said. Lights blinded me.

"Nicole?"

I covered my eyes and screamed again. "No!"

"Nicole, it's me. Daddy. You fell asleep on the floor, and I just put you in the bed."

I don't know how long I cried, but by the time I stopped, we were standing in the middle of the floor, his arms placed snuggly around me. My boxes were still in the middle of the floor. There was nothing on my wall.

"What happened today?" he asked, lifting my chin.

Once our eyes connected, words began to form.

"Glen!" Mama's voice preceded her.

She stood at my doorway, her eyes frigid.

I shook, but Daddy held me securely.

"Carla, what in the world happened here today?"

"Whatever I say or do won't be right. You'll just take her side, anyway."

"This right here doesn't get any better until you—"

"Forgive? Is that what you were going to say?"

I shook my head.

Daddy looked at me. "Nicole, it's okay. What happened today?"

"She's probably mad because I punished her," Mama said.

I saw the frustration in his eyes—eyes that were now distracted.

"Daddy, I was—"

Mama rushed toward me. "I was what? Frustrated? Tired? What?"

Whatever words I had found left. Daddy stared at Mama, seemingly shocked. Mama's eyes burned through me. Then Daddy said, "Wait a minute, Carla. What's wrong with you? She's your daughter too."

"Don't remind me."

"Hold up," he said. "Are you serious?"

"Ah," Mama said, "what's the use? You don't want to know the truth."

Daddy breathed in deeply. I saw his lips counting down from ten. He made it to seven before Mama interrupted.

"Six, five, four, three, two, one, zero. Now what?" she said. "The truth is, earlier, she just stared at me like, 'what are you gonna do?' This was after she burned everything and the shoes. You are so blind by her supposed innocence, but I know how young girls can be. The things they can hide."

We both stared at Mama, who was looking through us.

"What is wrong with you?" Daddy said.

"Nothing at all."

"Nicole," Daddy said, turning back to me, "just come and find me when you want to talk. I'll stop whatever I'm doing." He kissed me on my forehead.

"Oh," Mama said as Daddy was leaving, "so you'll talk anytime she wants, but I have to wait?"

"You know it's best I don't talk to you right now. I'll be on the back porch."

Mama followed him out and slammed the door behind her.

I walked to my piano, sat down, and let my hand hit a note. The sound voiced my pain. I started playing a series of notes and chords that eased more pain. The more music I played, the more my mind settled. Eventually, I found words to send up to God, yet my thoughts kept telling me that God won't answer me. While I played, I prayed, waiting, hoping that God would hear my heart above my head.

CHAPTER TWENTY

March 24, 1979 (Saturday)

Glen sat on the back patio, looking out over the horizon of the large two-story houses peppered along the country hillside. The night sky was clear, the stars bright, and a breeze rustled the leaves in the trees, but he didn't focus on any of that.

"This doesn't make any sense at all," he said to himself as he stared at the barbeque pit. Sometimes when he heard himself speak, it helped him figure things out. He thought of Nicole and knew this wasn't her. He thought of Carla, but no real answers came. Then he thought of Charles.

"Hmmm."

He went to use the unlisted phone in his home office to page Charles. It was about a minute before his phone rang back.

"Hello," Charles said in a frantic voice. "I just got this page."

"It's me. Charles, where are you?"

"Why? What's wrong?"

"It's Nicole."

"What?" Charles said. "Um, what…did…what did she say?"

"It's what she did. She burned that white dress. I was trying to figure out… why?" Glen heard in the background what sounded like boarding announcements at an airport. "Where are you?"

"I should have left when I was supposed to, but it was Ms. Carla who insisted I stay. It's my fault Nicole burned her dress. It's me."

"What do you mean?" Glen asked, concerned at the tone of Charles' voice. "Charles, what did you do?"

"I'm the one who told her to just go somewhere else in her mind because she didn't want to be there."

"Where?"

"At the limo before the mayor's thing. I should have stayed out of it, always trying to fix something, but it didn't help. I was the one who suggested Nicole play freely, not her, but I didn't say anything to Ms. Carla. If Nicole hadn't listened to me, then Ms. Carla wouldn't have gotten so mad. And to think, not once did I stand up for Nicole. I just should have left when I planned. I'm sorry that I caused all of this."

"There's more to this than what you're saying."

"I'm sorry, Mr. Glen. All I know is that if Ms. Carla had taken Nicole to the party like she had promised, Nicole wouldn't have burnt her dress. I'm sorry. I already said too much."

"Where're you going?"

"Around the world to see where it takes me. To go where no one knows me or will find me. I hope everything works out. I gotta catch my flight."

Charles hung up.

Glen went back to the patio and thought about Carla and Nicole. His train of thought changed a small degree as he stared at the burned remains and wondered how his family had gotten to this point. He didn't think he was giving Nicole any special treatment. She'd been a great daughter. Straight-A student, honor roll, with no issues at all, so there was no reason to be hard on her. She wasn't spoiled. Carla was wrong, so his mind ventured elsewhere for answers.

He rechecked the pit, but he found nothing there. He took everything off the grill, put it in a trash bag, and cleaned it. There was definitely tension, especially over the past few weeks between Carla and Nicole, or rather, Carla toward Nicole, but it could have been all because of Charles, too.

He took the trash bag with the rest of the residue and put it in the can outside. Once he closed the top, a thought occurred to him.

"Carla."

He came in through the back and noticed the black belt was missing. He went up to their bedroom, but he paused in the hallway and listened to Nicole playing the piano.

Definitely not like her.

He walked into their bedroom and closed the door behind him. Carla was reclining in the bed, reading a book. While selecting his words, he tried to fill the gaps between now and Charles' hospitalization and his leaving. Charles wasn't telling him everything, but Carla wasn't either. As he thought about the way Carla had been acting since he'd gotten back, he realized he wouldn't find out why Nicole had burned the dress, at least not tonight. The more important issue was to get Nicole and Carla back on track. He was leaving in three days, so he decided to forget about the dress for now and everything associated with it and work on Carla and Nicole instead.

"What are you doing?" Carla said, looking up from her book.

There was a sharpness in her tone. Glen knew she was right to be mad about the dress, but there was something else.

"Glen!"

"Okay, Carla…I don't care about the dress, at least now. I know something happened, but it doesn't matter right now. Just go talk to her. She's not herself."

"So, just like that, you let her off the hook."

"No. It's just not important right now."

"Then when?"

"What's wrong with you? You know this is not her."

"Why does it always have to be me, my fault? What if I burned the car up? What would you say?"

"Carla, I'm not trying to blame you or anything like that. All I know is this is way out of Nicole's character. Something is wrong."

"Really."

"The way she's acting doesn't add up to Charles leaving, some punishment, or anything like that. Just go talk to her and listen. Please. That's all."

Carla put her book down. "When did you turn into a doormat? You're so ready to forgive and ignore consequences, but nothing changes. Nicole burned a $422 dress, and the only thing you think, it's out of her character? What is your problem?"

Glen took a massive breath and nodded his head.

"All right, if you want to go that route. Why did you beat her?"

~

Carla's arms twitched, and her heart skipped a beat as Glen stepped toward her. She wasn't worried about him hitting her. That wasn't her husband, thanks to a vow he and Terrance had made to be different from their father and never hit a woman. Thank God for that vow because Glen favored their father the most. It was times like now she found comfort in the vow, but the thoughts were always in the back of her mind.

"That belt," he said, "is not hanging where it normally hangs. I know it didn't fall off, and I definitely didn't use it. So…Carla, did you beat Nicole?"

He took another step.

"And no," he said, "I'm not talking about a spanking or a whipping. I'm talking about a beating."

"Where did that come from?" she said.

"Answer me. You did say you punished her. So, how was it?"

"What do you want me to say? Your perfect little princess never does anything wrong."

"Don't change the subject."

"She burned the dress!"

"She wouldn't just burn the dress unless she had a reason."

"A reason?" Carla slammed her book down and stared at him. "Everything has to be a reason for you."

"You got that right."

I'm so tired of this. It's no use. You'll only take her side, anyway. Can't have precious Nicole be wrong about anything. Oh, it's okay, Sweetheart. It's just your self-expression. Next time, just burn the damn house down. "I don't believe this."

"Well, Carla," Glen said, "since the dress is all you want to talk about, what would make her burn a dress?"

"Glen, I…do…not…know."

"Then you…need to…figure…it…out."

Carla thought that Nicole was just being rebellious and believed that if Nicole had burned the dress to send a signal, she was done playing, but Glen couldn't see it. Glen would have let her waste the opportunity. Nicole wanted to rely solely on her talent and not work, so pushing her a little more aggressively to participate in more piano recitals and competitions was too much for her.

Come to think of it, Nicole could have burned it because she'd missed the party. She even could have burned it because she didn't like the toothpaste or the cereal. But Carla knew it definitely could have been because of her first real punishment in her entire life for her improvisation.

Glen went to the bedroom door. "Well?" he said as he opened the door.

Looking at me like I got answers.

"Carla…you need to go and make sure she's fine."

"What's that supposed to mean?"

"It means get up, get out of that bed, and go see about our daughter."

I hate this. "Okay, okay," she said. She snatched her housecoat and stormed out, slamming the bedroom door behind her and rushing toward Nicole's room. Then she stopped.

It took her several moments to calm down. Just as she was about to knock on Nicole's door, Carla heard several piano runs from the other side of the door being played with more passion than she'd ever heard anyone play.

Carla whispered to herself, "Even Nicolette never sounded like that."

Suddenly, she felt a force physically pulling her hand to the doorknob. It was even stronger than the impulse at Bible study, but just as she was about to turn the doorknob, she heard Nicole play another run so clean that a stranger would have thought it was Beethoven himself. Carla pulled her hand away from the knob and listened closer.

Nicole played with more passion than Carla had ever heard, and even more importantly, she played far beyond her age. This was the Nicole Carla knew she could be. Carla felt she was right about all the hidden potential that she had imagined about Nicole. She thought about all the accolades Nicolette and Dr. Rogers were getting and how easily they could be Nicole's. Her mind was filled with endless possibilities of the success Nicole could reach.

Carla sat down on the floor outside Nicole's door and listened, amazed at the concert her daughter was playing on the other side of that door.

Just think, if she were to practice, I mean really practice, imagine how good she could be. I'm really finally right about something.

The urge to open the door came over Carla, so much so that she stood and touched the knob again. She remained frozen, struggling with the feeling that if she opened the door, her own dreams for Nicole would dissipate.

She heard another run and then pulled her hand away again. At that very second, Carla decided she wasn't going to listen to those urges from God anymore. Those urges made a fool of her, made her feel like a failure, and even worse—made her feel vulnerable. It was time for her to push Nicole to new heights as a pianist that only hard work and discipline could accomplish.

Listening to run after run outside the door became easier. She smiled, nodded, and whispered to herself, "Nicole will be the best, and then Mother will see."

~

Glen looked over at Carla's book lying on the bed. She had been gone for some time now. The urge to check on Nicole came again, and this time he sat up, got out of bed, and walked toward the door. Just as he pulled it open, Carla appeared.

She was calm as she stepped past him into the room and closed the door behind her.

"How's Nicole doing?" he asked.

"Oh, she's fine, just like I thought. She's practicing the piano for the first time this late, finally listening to me and my directions." Carla smiled to herself, took her housecoat off, hung it on the bedpost, and lay down on the bed.

Glen's heart nearly jumped out of his chest as the feeling of urgency to check on Nicole grew within him. His hand sprang toward the doorknob, his feet already positioned to walk down the hall.

"You don't believe me?" Carla said. "She's fine. I know you have all the answers, but I'm tired of you second-guessing me. So, go ahead and check."

He stared at Carla. He watched her head tilt to the side, waiting, and then he glanced toward Nicole's room. He knew something was wrong. His hand found the coolness of the knob.

"Glen, you told me to go. I submitted myself to you as your wife and went like you said. What am I supposed to do when you don't even trust me on some little thing like checking on my own daughter? Tell me, then, why did I go?"

The tugging from Nicole's room prodded him to move.

"She's fine," Carla said as she began to cry. "She's fine. Why can't you let me be right this time? Please, Glen, this one time, please trust me. I know you may have a feeling that's way better than mine, and maybe it's just because of the way I've been acting, but start tonight. Please start tonight."

There was a deep groan in his chest. He took a full breath, turned away from his wife, and opened the door.

"You promised me you'd never turn your back on me. I'm begging you, Glen, please listen to me. Please. Let me be right for once. Just once."

He couldn't take his eyes off Nicole's room; he could hear the sounds of pain in her music, and he knew things weren't right. He shook his head and went to check on Nicole.

"Glen?" Carla appeared right next to him, taking his head and pulling him back. She coddled his chin and turned his head away from Nicole's room until their eyes met. "Please, Glen. Just this once, please." She moved her lips to his ear and whispered, "Please, just tonight."

He shook his head.

"I promise she's fine. She really is."

Carla's voice was chloroform to his will. He fought, trying to reason with himself, but his heart sank. No matter how he struggled, he could tell what he was going to do. Carla slowly closed the door and shut out the sounds of Nicole's piano.

"Glen, trust me."

He stared at Carla.

"Please trust me."

He took a deep sigh. "Okay."

She kissed him tenderly on his lips. "It's better than okay. It really is. Thank you. Thank you."

Carla walked back across the room and got in bed, with Glen following behind.

"Good night, Glen."

Glen lay in bed with his wife in his arms. He knew he should have gone to check on Nicole, but tears had always been his weakness. He'd watched his mother's endless river of tears over his father, a bitter drunk who'd regularly beaten her.

His mother had always pleaded with him to stay when Glen had fought his father, trying to keep balance in the family. His weakness could have been from holding Carla through her crying spells after her third and fourth miscarriage when she'd been afraid that he would abandon her because she couldn't give him a child. No matter what the reason, he had ignored his conscious and turned his back on his daughter—something unforgivable.

~

The doorknob to my room never moved. I told God I would tell them everything no matter what happened to me, but as I looked at the closed door, I realized maybe God didn't answer people like me, anyway.

I stopped playing and praying. In a few seconds, the dark presence in the room would descend on me again. The music was the only thing that kept it away, so I started playing again. I shouldn't have opened the door to let Charles in. I should have just stayed in my room.

"God, I'm sorry. I'm sorry, God. I'm sorry."

CHAPTER TWENTY-ONE

March 30, 1979 (Friday)

Money was the reason my daddy was leaving. We had expenses: a Mercedes, Cadillac, and an old Corvette he didn't even drive. Mama's closet alone was an endless rainbow of dresses, just like my closet.

Daddy had already pushed his job report day back one week. For that week, I pleaded with him to stay. I didn't care about money or what we had. I didn't care about any of that. We could move to Valdosta and stay near Uncle Terrance in his neighborhood. I knew Mama wouldn't want it, but at least I would be with Daddy. The people there were like a family, and there was a park nearby. I had my cousins.

I had a feeling that if he left, things would go bad for our family. Mama was acting strange too—a quiet calm. Nothing rattled her. She kept up with Dr. Rogers in Atlanta, constantly asking about Nicolette. She talked even more with Grandmother. I could tell because each time she got off the phone, Mama would look at me as if I was an object.

Each night, Daddy and I would talk on the back patio, but it was Mama who had her way with him when their bedroom door closed. Two days before Daddy was to leave, I watched him stand by the phone. I could only imagine what was going through his mind. Daddy hadn't even packed yet, so I was hoping he would stay. Mama's eyes were on him too. Her gaze remained on his still body for at least two minutes. When he reached for his wallet and picked up the phone, Mama sprang from her chair and rushed to his side.

"What are you doing?" she asked.

I got up and left the room. Then I changed my mind, turned around, and moved closer, making sure they didn't see me.

Daddy put the receiver down.

"She looks so tired," he said. "So depressed. I can hear it in her voice. Something is wrong with her. Can't you see it? She's never been this way. She doesn't want to dress up, wearing dark colors all the time now. I don't need this job. Tell me, why should I leave?"

"I know Nicole's been different," Mama said. "You ever think it's because of what happened to Charles and his leaving? You know they were so close. You're about to leave. Punishment? It's too much change, and she acted out, that's all. I'll be here to take good care of her and help her through. She'll be fine."

"Come on, Carla. Is this job really worth it?"

"Worth it? Do you remember how much debt we're in?"

Mama stalked over to a drawer, pulled out a stack of papers, walked back to the kitchen table, and slammed them down.

"Let me see," she said, rifling through the stack. "Hospital bills, credit card bills for medicine, house note, car note. Creditors keep calling, and we keep making arrangements. We can barely make ends meet."

"We can sell the house."

"And live where? No one will give us another loan."

"But we'll find a way. We're making it. Just have faith."

"Yeah, I know your favorite saying, 'God will provide,' but I'm tired of just getting by. Aren't you the one who quoted, 'Owe no man but to love him?' This is a chance to finally get rid of all that debt. We're almost there. I thought I could finally get some sleep and not worry about losing our house. And you want to throw this job…God's answer…away just because she's been depressed?"

Daddy lifted Mama's hand. "What good is all the money if our family isn't together?"

"The money?" She snatched her hand away. "We don't have any money. The creditors have it. Period. The only way we're going to have money is to pay them off and never owe them again. Every dime I made in weddings over the last two years went to business expenses and creditors. Not one dime of my dream did

I take home. We've already spent the money I meant to give Charles, but even that was only a small percentage of what we owed."

"You don't get it," Daddy said. "One day, we're going to be free of this debt. What state will our family be in when that happens?"

Mama touched her stomach and whispered, "I'm sorry I couldn't carry a child full-term until Nicole. After the second miscarriage and my medical bills kept mounting, I was ready to adopt, to give you the child you longed for, but you said God was going to give you a daughter. Years ago, you wanted to keep trying to have children. I wanted to wait because we were struggling financially, but I agreed. After five pregnancies—five and more hospitalizations—we have only one daughter and tens of thousands of dollars of debt."

"Don't start with that selective memory. We both agreed to keep trying—both of us. Not once have I complained about the hospital bills or loans. We were both happy the day Nicole was born. And you say, 'only one daughter'?"

"You know I didn't mean it like that."

"Then what in the hell did you mean?"

"It's just—"

"Nicole is precious," Daddy said, "sweet, talented, and ours. I gladly worked long hours, overtime, double shifts, two to three jobs over the past several years to pay for those medical bills, the loans and to finance your wedding consultant business. I was glad when you found something you loved, and your business has finally taken off because of that one daughter. That miracle is a godsend to enjoy." Daddy shook his head. "I'm sorry for the setbacks," he said. "I'm sorry that the bills kept mounting. We had to take the second mortgage to keep up, but I didn't do that for money. I did it for my family."

Mama stood in front of Daddy and took his hands.

"I am your wife, and I need this. You claim you sacrifice for your family, so sacrifice for me. We have an opportunity to be free of this debt, but unless you take this job, I don't think we'll make it." Mama stared into Daddy's eyes. "Why are you hesitating?"

Daddy stared at the refrigerator for a few moments. I almost stepped in, but then he spoke. "It's Nicole. She's my biggest concern. Really, my only concern."

Mama squeezed his hands and kissed him on his cheek.

"Glen, it's just one year. You can do this."

"Promise me that you'll pay extra attention to her. Look me in my eyes and promise me that you'll take great care of her."

Mama took both of his hands, pulled them to her mouth, and kissed them. "I promise I will. When you get back, you'll see. Things will be so much better."

Daddy sighed, sat down at the table, and lowered his head. Mama pulled his head to her stomach and rubbed the back of his neck. In a few moments, her gaze slowly turned toward me, and a soft grin formed just as our eyes met.

CHAPTER TWENTY-TWO

April 1–2, 1979 (Sunday–Monday)

Daddy's old tan soft leather carry-on bag was light, so I helped him carry it while we walked out to the car hand in hand. It would be a year before I held his hand again. Unfortunately, we caught all the green lights on the way to the airport and even found a close parking space. He checked his bags, and then we walked together to his gate and waited. Finally, he gave me one final hug and one final kiss before boarding. Mama and I watched him enter the plane, and then the door closed. The plane taxied away, took off, and disappeared into the sky. That was it. He was gone.

I lingered by the window, watching the sky. Then I turned to Mama, who had no tears.

"Come on, Nicole."

We rode home in silence. Once in the house, Mama and I went our separate ways. Mama walked to the kitchen while I went upstairs to Daddy's closet and found his tan overcoat. I slipped my arms into the sleeves and rolled myself up into a tight ball in the corner of his closet. The coat smelled like him.

Then I heard Daddy's voice. "Sweetheart, give it a chance."

I took his coat off, neatly hung it up, and went downstairs to a kitchen filled with the aroma of honey-baked ham. Mama was leaning against the counter, watching the water boil. I sat at the table thinking of making the best of our year.

"Mama, what do you want to do this afternoon? We can go to a movie or take a walk around the neighborhood. Maybe we can start out by sitting on the back patio like Daddy and I did?"

She took a big scoop of rice from the glass container on the counter. Then she poured and stirred several times, turned the heat down, and covered the pot.

"Nicole," she said, staring at the pot, "I only have one question for you." She turned to face me, leaned against the counter, wiped her hands on her apron, and then folded her arms. "Why did you burn that dress?"

The question echoed in my mind. I searched the grooves on the table as if searching for answers. Mama's index finger was tapping a steady beat. It was like watching a countdown.

What could I say? She'd made it clear about Charles. Everything about the dress was Charles. Forty-five long seconds passed.

"Until you are ready to tell me about that dress, we have nothing to talk about. Do you understand?"

"Yes, ma'am."

She turned back to the stove. "Now, go upstairs and practice until I tell you to come down for dinner. Start with the "Moonlight Sonata" and then go on to something else. After dinner, get your clothes ready for school tomorrow."

I dragged myself upstairs and practiced. After dinner, I pulled out my dark-blue winter dress with a long-sleeve gray blouse, made sure I got all the wrinkles out, and hung them up.

The next morning, I found a soft powder-blue dress with spaghetti straps and a white sweater hanging on my door, with white sandals underneath. I took the powder-blue dress and neatly put it in the closet. I used to love dresses like that, especially that one, but now I felt naked. Come to think of it, I didn't like the way some of the boys stared at me like I was some piece of meat. I didn't like the way some of the men looked at me either when I was out with Daddy or Mama.

After school, I went upstairs to hang my dress up and prepare for school the next day, only to find my powder-blue dress, white sweater, and all the rest of my clothes missing. In their place were some old clothes—five multicolored dresses that were more like clothes with explosions of faded colors, sprinkled flowers on some, and big butterflies on the others. The price tags on the dresses, fifty cents, twenty-five cents, and three for one dollar, were still attached. I rushed out of the room and found Mama at the kitchen table.

"Mama, where are all of my clothes?"

She looked up at me.

"Why didn't you wear the dress I put out for you? It was your favorite color."

"You told me to get my clothes ready for school. I didn't know you wanted me to wear it."

She placed her pen down next to what looked like a grocery list labeled "Nicole's rules." "Who else do you think put that dress out? Hmm?"

I lowered my eyes, not making eye contact.

"All that money," Mama said, "we spent on those dresses, and you don't care. You burn one and disregard the others."

"I really didn't know, Mama."

"Sure, but don't worry about it. It's all my fault anyway, like everything else around here. I've spoiled you, but I'm about to take care of that, too. I took all your dresses for your performances and put them in my closet. The rest of your clothes are in your father's closet. I will put out the dress you are to wear to school each day, and you will wear exactly what I give you and exactly how I say to wear it.

"I bought a few old dresses and old nightgowns for you to wear in the house just in case you get the urge to burn another one. It's time you learn to appreciate even the smallest things you have. You will finish out the school year in exactly what I tell you to wear. If you have any complaints, I will buy you uniforms. Not just any uniforms, but the classy ones like I wore at Brighton School for Girls. Don't you ever let me catch you outside looking thrown away or trying to show me up."

"Why are you doing this?" I said, surprised at myself for even speaking.

"You remember I grounded you for four months? Just for that, your punishment will be through the entire summer now. At the end of the summer, if you don't mess up, you'll be free to go back to your friends and your life, but for now, you'll be working for me. No telephone, no TV, no visitors. I'll also be entering you into a lot of piano competitions this summer—all classical. You will listen to nothing else. And if I ever catch you improvising anything, even "Mary Had a Little Lamb," without my permission, I haven't even come up with that punishment yet."

"But Mama—"

"Listen, little girl, don't 'but Mama' me. Your father allowed you to question our decisions too many times. Since he's not here, there will be no more questioning. You will wear what I tell you to wear and do what I tell you to do. Do you understand me?"

"Mama? May I please ask something?"

"No, Nicole, you may not. When I want your input, I will ask for it, but for now, you will do as I say."

"Mama?"

She stood up and headed toward the back door, returning with the belt dangling from her hand. "Nicole…Renee…Peterson, don't let me have to ask you again. What did I tell you?"

I never took my eyes off that belt as I said, "You told me no more questioning. When you want my opinion, you'll ask for it."

"Ah, I see you are very smart. And your answer to me will be either 'Yes ma'am' or 'No ma'am.' You have no other options."

"Yes, ma'am."

The telephone rang.

My heart jumped, but I didn't move.

Mama laid the belt on the table, its buckle pointing toward me. By the fourth ring, she picked up the receiver.

"Hello. Oh, hi Glen. Yes. Yes. Hold on." Mama put the receiver over her shoulder. "Nicole, your father would like to speak to you."

I walked over and reached for the receiver. Mama picked the belt up and put it over her shoulder. Then she gave me the phone.

"Hi, Daddy."

"Hi, Sweetheart. I already miss you, and I love you so much. I'll be traveling a lot in Europe and even Asia, building and installing networks and computer systems. I even picked up a part-time job writing computer programs. Time's going to fly by, but I'll miss you every day. I love you."

"I miss you and love you too, Daddy."

I listened for a few moments to Daddy talk, all the while staring at Mama.

"Nicole," he said, "are you still there?"

"Yes, sir, I'm still here."

"How's your mother?"

"She's…she's taking care of me."

"Everything's okay?"

"I'm just missing you."

"Okay," he said, "let me speak to your mother."

I gave the telephone back to Mama and stood by her. She took the belt off of her shoulder and put it back on the table.

"Oh," she said, "Nicole and I will accomplish so much, especially with the business. Everything is fine. She won't have time to sit around and mope…Yes. That's fine. I know I promised. Don't worry about us. Just focus on what you have to do there. Uh-huh…Bye."

She hung up the phone, picked up the appointment calendar, laid it on the table in front of me, and drew four black lines through the makeup pizza party Daddy had written in crimson red.

"Now," Mama said, "you call all those girls your father invited and tell them your party has been canceled. I never agreed to that party. And the first one to call is Nadia."

My breathing deepened, and my tears welled up. I shook my head slowly.

She picked the belt up. "I don't think you understand. I wasn't asking. And just for that, I'll go ahead and start purchasing your uniforms. Now…call Nadia."

The tears started rolling down my cheeks.

Mama started her countdown: "Ten, nine, eight…"

I picked up the telephone and hesitated, trying to remember Nadia's number.

"Nicole!" Mama said, slapping the belt on the table. "Stop wasting time and dial."

I started dialing, hoping I'd hit the right numbers. I was relieved when I heard Nadia's voice, but only for a short time.

"Hi, Nadia. It's me, Nicole."

"I can't wait for your party. Just make sure you have pepperoni."

"I'm sorry, Nadia."

"Don't tell me," Nadia said just as her end went silent.

"Nadia?"

"What is it this time? We're not good enough for you? You need a better group of friends?"

"No. I'm on punishment until the end of the summer."

"You're kidding! But your dad came by. Where is he?"

"He's gone for a year, working in Europe and Asia."

Nadia got quiet again.

"Nadia, please, it's hard enough."

"Wait a minute," Nadia said, "you tell me. So, you won't be in any competitions or anything like that?"

That's when I got quiet.

"Nicole, tell me. I know when I'm on punishment, it's only school and chores. Definitely no extracurricular activity."

"Nadia…I—"

"I get it. You're nothing but a liar," Nadia said calmly. "I knew it when you started playing those weddings and competitions. I always knew you were special, but…I thought we were too."

"I'm not lying."

"What is it this time? The mayor's daughter wants you to come over to play?"

"Nadia, I didn't lie to you."

"Yeah, I see now. You're all to yourself lately, cutting the ties with all the trash. You're all quiet sitting alone in the corner out at lunch. You don't want to talk. Not hungry at lunch, but it's just we're not good enough for you now. You've made your choice for this summer. You think you're all that because you're Darlington's prodigy. I saw your picture on Ms. Eleanor's wall, right next to a signed copy of Josephine Baker. Yeah, you're all that."

"Please don't be mad at me."

"Some friend you are. Then be like that. I don't need you, anyway."

I heard the click on the other end.

"Nadia! Nadia. Nadia?"

Before I could say anything, Mama said, "You have three minutes to get yourself together and keep calling."

I waited the three minutes, then called the other girls as Mama watched. It was all the same. I shouldn't have waited the three minutes. Nadia had already called most of them. By the time I got to Desiree, I had almost hung up before I heard her voice.

"Hello, Nicole?" Desiree said.

"Desiree." That was all I could say. I didn't want to repeat everything anymore.

"Nadia called me," she said.

I waited to hear her curse me out, just like some of the others had. I'd found it went better if I didn't defend myself.

"Nicole, you okay?"

I felt my eyes widen and my tears stop.

"Desiree, are you mad at me?"

"Over something like this? That's nothing. At least you're still here. This too will pass."

I smiled.

Mama stood up, belt in hand.

"I've got to go," I said, stepping back. "I'll talk with you at school tomorrow. See you later, Desiree."

"Now that you're finished making calls," Mama said as she walked over to the stove, "go upstairs, take that dress off, and change into one of those work dresses. Bring that dress you had on back downstairs. You have one minute."

She put the belt around the back of her neck and let it hang.

"If you are one second late, I'll be upstairs to help you." She glanced down at her watch and started counting. "Fifty-nine, fifty-eight…"

I ran upstairs, grabbed one of the dresses, and threw it on the bed. I rushed to take my dress off, but the zipper stuck. I pulled and tugged, but the zipper wouldn't budge.

"Twenty-eight, twenty-seven…"

The zipper finally gave way. I changed and put the other dress on, grabbed my old dress, and ran back downstairs. My heart was racing as I handed the dress to my mother.

She looked at her watch. "Two seconds to spare," she said, holding the dress up. "This was a beautiful dress." She shook her head, walked over to the trash, and threw it in.

My eyes welled up again.

"Now, go upstairs and practice piano and then do your homework. Your grades better not slip just because you're grounded. I'll call you down when dinner is ready."

I stood still, wondering what was going on.

She stared at me. "Do you want me to give you something to cry about?"

"No, ma'am."

"Then straighten that face-up."

"Yes, ma'am."

I went upstairs and sat at the piano. The flowered dress carried a tinge of musk, dust, and some other foreign smell that only time could create. I tried to wipe my tears away, but it was like trying to stop a flood. At the sound of the sharp, quick footsteps in the hallway, I sat up straight and started playing "Moonlight Sonata."

The steps stopped and then went in the opposite direction. I practiced for a few hours and then worked on my homework. Later, we had a quiet dinner. As the night wore on, I prepared for bed. I glanced at the picture of my family on my bedside table, knelt to pray, and then lay down on the bed. I had left the ceiling light and my bedside lamp on. Turning toward the wall, I pulled my blanket over my head. I didn't like the dark anymore, and I hated going to sleep because, most times, Charles was waiting for me in that same recurring nightmare, but I had figured out how to keep him out of the house in the dream. If I locked all the doors and windows, then no matter what, he couldn't get in. I turned the night light on. Multiplication tables helped me stay up as long as I could. One time, I got up to thirty-two times twelve equals 384.

"One times one is one. One times two is two. One times three is three. One times four is four... seven times seven is forty-nine. Seven times eight is fifty-six... eleven times eleven is one hundred...twenty-one." I shook myself and rubbed my tired eyes. "Eleven times twelve is one hundred thirty-two...twelve times one is..."

~

I stood on my porch, watching the neighborhood kids play next door.

"Hi, Nicole!" Desiree yelled, playing double Dutch in slow motion. The other girls were all laughing and smiling. The sky was dark and overcast. The wind blew stronger, but everyone played like it was a sunny summer day. Out of the corner of my eye, I saw Charles' car creeping toward my house.

I rushed inside, locking the door behind me. Running throughout the house, I made sure all the doors and windows were locked. The squeal of his brakes stopping burst through my windows.

"Hi, Desiree," Charles said, "Could you come here, please?"

I ran to the window and saw Desiree heading toward Charles while the other girls continued playing double Dutch. He turned around and smiled at me. Then he turned back to Desiree. Desiree waved at me.

"Nicole doesn't want to play with me anymore. Would you like to?"

I yelled through the window, "No, Desiree! Run away! Run!"

Desiree waved at me and walked toward Charles' car.

"No, Desiree! Don't go! Don't go." My voice gave way.

I heard Charles' car door open. I walked to the front door and unlocked it. When I cracked it open, I heard him say, "Desiree, you need to go back to your friends. She's changed her mind."

"Bye, Charles," Desiree said, and she went back to jumping rope with the others. Then I heard his footsteps.

Charles pushed the door open and stepped in. "Awe, look, she's concerned about her friend. How sweet."

The door closed behind him and locked by itself.

~

I woke suddenly just as he reached for me. It took me a moment to realize I was back in my room—no Charles anywhere nearby. I took a deep breath and went to my piano. I knew I would be up for the rest of the night.

CHAPTER TWENTY-THREE

April 3 – 9, 1979 (Tuesday – Monday)

Nadia eventually calmed down, and so did my other friends. Desiree seemed to be the happiest. Over the days at school, they talked about long punishments, and before we knew it, we were all laughing. I was even laughing at some of the creative stories. Karen's story was something else.

Karen said her mother had made her jump on one foot while saying repeatedly, "I will not scream at my little brother anymore."

That one made no sense to any of us, but apparently, it happened about two more times, and it was then that Karen had noticed her calf had gotten bigger.

She showed us her calves, and it seemed like one was just a tad bit larger than the other. "I don't scream at my brother anymore," Karen said, "but he's still a pain."

School was good, and memories of Charles were slowly being pushed down.

On the Saturday of the canceled pizza party, I looked at the time. Everyone would have been over here. I imagined the laughter would have filled the house. It was then Mama came into my room and gently laid one of my performance dresses with matching tights on my bed and placed the matching shoes on the floor. Then, she walked out.

I put the clothes on, hoping the outfit was something she wanted to try on me. I checked myself in the mirror. Once finished, I found Mama in her bedroom, getting dressed as if she were going out with some of her friends to a dinner party.

"Nicole, we'll be leaving in thirty minutes. The mayor needed a last-minute pianist at his dinner party, and he asked for you. The Winthrop's will be there taking pictures.

"Mama, I'm on punishment. Nadia will think this is the reason I canceled."

"Well, the mayor needs a pianist at his dinner party, and the governor wants to see the local celebrity play."

"But Mama."

Mama opened up her purse and pulled out the belt. "Now, I don't remember asking your opinion. Do we have a problem here?"

"Mama?"

She dropped her purse, swung the belt, and hit my left thigh. That lick hurt so bad I didn't even make a sound. It was stuck in my throat. Mama stood patiently, belt hanging but ready to fly again.

"Nicole, do we have a problem?"

"No, ma'am."

~

In the mayor's mansion, I don't know how many times I went to the bathroom that night, hiding from every photo op. They may have gotten me on the piano, but I thought I would be safe if I didn't take a picture with the governor or the mayor.

"Nicole," Mama said from across the room, smiling with Mrs. Winthrop, "she's been looking for you all night. The governor wants to get a picture with you and Mayor Daily."

"This will be a perfect cover," Mrs. Winthrop said.

"Mama," I whispered, "I have to go to the bathroom."

"You can hold it for a few moments. Mrs. Winthrop, she's ready."

~

On the way home, I prayed, "God, please don't let them find out."

~

Throughout the day at school on Monday, no one said anything about the dinner party. Some of the girls spoke to me, and by lunchtime, I thought I could breathe. I went to sit down at the table with all my friends, but before I could sit down, Nadia spoke.

"I take it you had a quiet Saturday on punishment and everything, right?"

They all stared at me, including Desiree.

"Let me explain," I said.

Nadia threw the society magazine on the table in front of me. On the cover was a picture of the governor, the mayor, and me. "Some punishment, huh?" Nadia said. "I see you had caviar with your pizza."

Nadia got up. "Come on, girls, we can find another table. The little princess needs her space."

"I didn't want to go," I said.

"Right," Nadia said, "then you need to be an actress because that smile looks real to me." She looked at Desiree. "You coming?"

Desiree remained seated.

"You believe me, Desiree, don't you?"

Nadia stood on the other side of Desiree and waited a few seconds.

"Desiree," Nadia said, "just know you can't go back and forth. You gotta pick."

"Desiree," I said, "please stay."

"You know what this means," Nadia said. "Especially with the other girls."

"I think I'll stay," Desiree said.

"Like a loyal pet," Nadia said. "You'll find she won't treat you any better, giving you lame excuse after excuse, and you, of all people, know that."

CHAPTER TWENTY-FOUR

April 25, 1979 (Wednesday)

I answered the phone the first time Desiree had called and thanked her for staying. The second time, I shortened the call when I heard Mama at the door. We talked and laughed the third time. The fourth time, after I hung up, I heard the belt jingling before Mama appeared at the door to the room.

She stopped, the belt hanging in one hand and a sheet of paper in the other. She stared at me. The longer she stood in silence, the more fear crept into my heart.

"There is an interesting thing about deceit, which is?" she said and paused, wanting me to give her the definition of the word.

"The action or practice," I said, staring at the belt, "of deceiving someone by concealing or misrepresenting the truth." Then I looked at her. Her eyes didn't seem stable.

"So," she said, "let's get to the truth. No. Better yet, let me tell you a story. Since you and your father enjoyed so many stories, let me tell you one. The twenty-fifth chapter of Deuteronomy, the third verse, talks about forty stripes. 'Forty stripes may be given him, but not more, lest, if one should go on to beat him with more stripes than these, your brother be degraded in your sight.'"

Mama gave me the sheet of paper she held. It was the phone bill, and Desiree's number was highlighted.

"Come on," she said as she walked to the closet. "Just wait by the bed."

I heard her in the closet. She returned with one of my dresses, picked up a pillow, and draped the dress over it.

"In Second Corinthians, though, the number is thirty-nine—an interesting number. Why thirty-nine and not forty? Hmmm. The number, at least to me, is out of compassion."

She laid the pillow on the bed. "Oh, I'm sorry." She turned the pillow with the front of the dress facing down. "Do you realize that thirty-nine is an important number? Come on, it's almost perfect. They would flog according to the punishment. 'Five times I received at the hands of the Jews the forty lashes less one,' and it was not to belittle the person; it was more of a correction. At least, that's how I took it. But the interesting thing, why not forty? I don't know how true this is, but I read somewhere that flogging was thirty-nine times because forty was enough to kill a man. Now…I need you to count."

Mama swung the belt with such force that it sounded like it cut through the air and hit and wrapped around the pillow, and then she snatched the belt back.

"One."

As I counted, I began to see the imprint of the belt against the dress. Like a baseball pitcher, she took her time, ensuring she hit her mark as if throwing strike after strike. I listened, watched, and counted. As she continued, the sound grew louder, and after thirty-nine, she stared at me and swung one more time. That was the loudest lick of them all.

"One small caveat," she said. "Know this number—eighteen. That's the number used if a person cannot bear forty. Then they receive eighteen." She tilted her head. "But that one is strange…because how do you know what anyone can bear unless you take them to that level?"

"Now," she said, "since you obviously think of me as some fool, let this fool be very clear in my meaning. If you ever…do anything else behind my back again, that pillow will be you. Do you understand what I mean?"

"Yes, ma'am."

For the rest of the summer, I didn't answer the phone for anyone.

CHAPTER TWENTY-FIVE

Summer 1979

I wondered about Desiree. How was she doing? Sometimes I'd pass by the window to see people playing outside, but then I saw a dirty window, and I had to clean it. I didn't like windows. I understood why others didn't like them either. Cleaning glass without leaving streaks was an achievement.

Our house was 4,522 square feet filled with corners, walls, and baseboards; it felt like several miles of surfaces to be cleaned every day.

The summer had come and gone, and just like Mama had said, I worked. I took no calls, and I had no visitors. My waking hours were dominated by chores, exhibitions, competitions, weddings, and piano practices.

Mama posted the individual measurements of the towels, washcloths, and dishrags on the refrigerator daily at 3:45 every morning. She had even created a set of rules that reached 172 and was still climbing. The rules had to be studied, memorized, and recited at any given moment. The frequency of the competitions, exhibitions, and weddings increased. On top of that, every day, I vacuumed and swept the entire house, dusted everything from top to bottom, cleaned the bathrooms, scrubbed the kitchen floor, and washed and folded clothes to the specifications she had posted. Every weekend, I did the yard work, washed and detailed the cars, and scrubbed the garage floor.

Over the summer, I learned flexibility. I also learned Mama didn't care about my feelings. She accepted no excuse—how tired, how unfair, how nothing. She called it all whining; everything I said was whining. Eventually, she just gave her demands, and I'd comply. She felt that the military had a positive effect on many other people, and she figured the discipline they used was exactly what I needed.

"Just like in the military, I'll strip you of everything and build you into a vision of perfection." She said that statement more than once.

One day, I accidentally brushed up against Mama, and the contact alone made me want to be held, but as she kept walking, I realized that even my desire for a touch would have to pass. That was when my epiphany occurred.

I would just do what I was told—period.

I didn't need any affection. Once that realization settled in, everything else over the summer became smoother.

Three weeks before school began and the end of my punishment was near, Mama took me on a shopping spree in Valdosta for school clothes. I was surprised to see that she bought me pants, jeans, shirts, shorts, blouses, and tennis shoes—all the latest styles.

The adventure was so relaxing. She didn't even rush me.

I finally wrote the first letter to Daddy and gave it to Mama. She edited it with red and gave it back. I corrected it and gave it to her. She corrected it and deleted more and gave it back. By the time my letter was ready to go, it read:

> Hi Daddy,
>
> How are you? I've been busy, and I know you have too.
>
> Love,
> Nicole

After all that, I figured I would go ahead and wait until my punishment was over to freely write Daddy.

CHAPTER TWENTY-SIX

August 13 – October 19, 1979

Two weeks before school started, it didn't take long for me to finish all my chores, practices, and every other demand Mama had. I was able to stay up and look out the window and enjoy the night air for the first time that summer.

Unfortunately, Mama held her first white-glove inspection at 4:30 the following morning. I didn't get up at 3:45 to check the refrigerator. My flowered dresses weren't evenly spaced, plus the towels, washcloths, and hand towels in the linen closet were all off by one inch. Measurements she had changed that morning.

She took some new clothes out of my closet and added one week to my punishment. Once the inspections began, if there was even the slightest infraction, Mama would take another new article of clothing and add another week to my punishment.

In five days, Mama had replaced all my new clothes with uniforms: twelve dresses, four plaid, two black, two dark blue, two dark grey, and two light grey; five white long-sleeved button-up blouses; five white short-sleeved shirts; and five plaid jackets. She added nine pairs of stockings: three white, three black, and three neutral, with two pairs of black shoes. She also found some more old musky, flowered dresses. I stayed up late washing them and getting the smell out of the clothes. Just before leaving the house, I saw a spot on the refrigerator, rushed and grabbed the vinegar cleaning solution, and hurriedly cleaned it. While scrubbing, I spilled some of the vinegar on my leg.

I went to Mama and told her I had spilled the vinegar and wanted to change my stockings, but she said she didn't want to be late.

The first day of school was different from the previous years. Instead of being surrounded by my friends, I was on an island where only Desiree spoke to me. Nadia and the other girls had stopped talking with me over the summer. I really didn't blame them.

Nadia had the girls surround me that morning by the lockers. She took a deep breath and then pinched her nose with her fingers. "What's that smell?" she said.

It was the vinegar, but once I was identified as stinking, it didn't matter what I said or that it would never happen again.

That was strange to me. Some of the girls I didn't even know held their noses as they passed me by. After a while, I gave up. They had their minds made up about me.

Every morning, Mama would post on the refrigerator my "Uniform of the Day." There were no exceptions to what she said. She had already talked to the principal and my teachers, explaining to them the need for uniforms and her plans to have me wear them to school. She showed them the catalog, the quality of the clothes, and even the best boarding schools in the world. She told them she wanted to make sure I focused on school and did not get caught up in the latest fashion craze. No one said anything; all accepted my mother's point of view.

A month later, I made the mistake of asking to wear a dress instead of a uniform. Mama brought her sewing machine out, bought some material, and said I could make a dress. She gave me one hour. Sewing was something she'd tried to teach me when I was younger, but I wasn't that good at it. I gave it my best shot, though.

When the time was up, Mama had me put my creation on. One sleeve was about a half-inch longer. The dress was bunched up on the right side, and the hem was jagged and crooked. The only thing I liked was the material. I moved to take my best efforts off.

"Oh no," she said. "Since you're the fashion designer, you will wear that original to school tomorrow. We shall call your creation a Nicole original."

"I'm sorry I complained. I won't ask again, Mama."

"I know you won't. You will wear this Nicole original, and you will wear it with dignity and make no excuses. If I hear any complaints, I will take care of it."

"But Mama?"

"And another thing, calling me Mama. It sounds so childish. You will start calling me Mother."

"Yes, ma'am."

She tilted her head.

"Yes, Mother."

That next day at school, in homeroom, all it took was for Nadia to say, "Guess who she looks like?"

As the names flew, Nadia observed me. I just stared forward.

"Cindy...No...Cinderella."

I looked up at Nadia. That was when she smiled and took a snapshot with her Polaroid camera. I should have never let on that it bothered me, but laughter spread once she passed the picture around to all the girls. Once she got the picture back, she gave the picture to me with "Cinderella" written on the bottom.

"Just blow it up and hang it on your wall like you did the other one."

After that day in my homeroom, Desiree was the only girl who still called me Nicole; the rest called me Cinderella.

"Where's your fairy tale now?" Nadia said, her raspy voice echoing in my ears.

At first, I held my head up. I told myself, "Sticks and stones may break my bones, but names will never harm me." They were only names, and I knew my name, but as the weeks went by, Mother seemed to get worse, plus the nightmares with Charles increased. The names began to hurt. I couldn't ignore the girls or the names anymore. Several nights in a row, I sat in the corner of my closet and cried.

Mother didn't ask me about my day, school, or how I felt. She just went through my folder, and if I missed any questions, she'd make me write the questions and answers repeatedly until she got tired. Her point: It is better to do it right the first time instead of unlearning and relearning.

And my answer was, "Yes, Mother." That was all I'd said lately. "Yes, Mother." "No, Mother." And when I made mistakes, I became well acquainted with that belt. I was now grounded for over twenty-eight weeks—over two times longer than the Marines Bootcamp.

CHAPTER TWENTY-SEVEN

October 21, 1979 (Sunday)

God," I said, but no more words followed. My mind was really blank. I wanted to pray. I tried to find the words.

"Nicole," Mother said at my door, "We are going to church this morning. Brenda said the pastor has been waiting for us to go for some time. We've missed too many Sundays, so we're going, and you will be on your best behavior. Be ready in fifteen minutes."

I hurried, got ready, and put on the clothes she'd set aside for me. Church was one of the few places where I felt at peace. We rarely attended anymore. Most weekends were spent practicing, cleaning, or participating in some obscure competition.

Once we arrived at church, Mother changed right before my eyes. Her frown was replaced by a pleasant smile. She greeted others with warmth, some with a kiss on the cheek, and a few with a loving hug. She even listened intently while Mrs. Larson cried about her daughter, Naomi, and said, "I just wish she were more like Nicole."

"Patricia," Mother said, "please be patient with your child. Your daughter is probably doing the best she can."

Mother smiled at me. I smiled back, just as I was trained to do. We entered the front door and walked across the carpeted foyer through the arched wooden doors that opened into the sanctuary. In the front was a raised platform with three chairs, one like a throne for the pastor, and two smaller versions on the right and left sides. The elevated choir stand behind the pastor had the forty-five choir members. Off to the right were the piano and organ.

We found our seats on the right side of the sanctuary. Mother talked with those around us while we waited for the service to start. My mind was elsewhere during the announcement, offering, and the choir's A and B selections; church was different to me this time.

Ms. Brenda and Mrs. Joseph, the church's first lady, stood in front of the congregation.

"God is good!" Ms. Brenda said.

"All the time!" the congregation said.

"All the time!"

"God is good!"

"Praise the Lord!" said Mrs. Joseph. "I've wanted to do this for some time. Every time I walk through the back and look at all the redesigned parts of the church, it is because of this woman who has become a pillar of our community. The colors, the style, the grace, and she did all of this, even helping us pay for it. Her grace and giving out of her abundance are commendable. In the Bible, it talks about giving honor to those whom honor is due, and so we would like Mrs. Carla Peterson to come up so that we can give her a token of our appreciation."

There was applause throughout the congregation as Mother joined Mrs. Joseph and Ms. Brenda.

"Say a few words."

"What is there to say but thank you," Mother said. "I considered it an honor for you to even ask me. I want to tell you I love you and am so thankful to be a part of this church body. Just keep us in prayer as we fulfill our obligations. Thank you so much for all you do for us."

Oh, they loved her. The humility she portrayed. Mother had perfected her part. It was all about a well-fabricated image. When she smiled in my direction, I knew what she wanted. She wanted me to smile and honor her like everyone else did. So, I played my part and smiled, but it all felt like deceit. As I stared at Mother, I realized it didn't matter how I felt. It didn't matter at all.

I thought about my life and wondered why we even went to church. Going was so much like a ritual for my family, and as the makeshift ceremony ended, our pastor shifted in his seat, preparing to step into the pulpit. I even knew Reverend Joseph would talk about something that would get everyone excited, like a sermon on Shadrach, Meshach, and Abednego, Daniel in the lion's den, or some other well-known Bible stories. Then he would get tuned up and start shouting. People would get happy, and well, there had to be more to church than that. There had to be. I hoped Mother and I would just tip out, but that would have been rude.

"God," I whispered, "do You even hear me?"

Reverend Joseph stepped behind the pulpit, grabbed the edges, and said, "Good morning, Church," in his deep bass voice that I imagined shook the windows.

"Good morning," the congregation responded.

"Oh, you don't hear me. Good morning, Church!"

A resounding "Good morning!" echoed throughout the building.

"This is a good day, a blessed day, a great day!"

"Amen!" rang out.

"But you know, some in here are in need. Oh, don't get me wrong. The ones I'm talking about believe in the power of God, but their world is like a living hell."

People nodded in agreement.

"We can put on our Sunday best, paint on our smiles, and come into the house of God, but deep down on the inside, our souls are crying out. Praying. Asking God, when will my time come?

"They want to experience love, not the love of this world, but the unconditional love that God freely gives. They want to know if God is going to answer their cry. I'm talking about that one who is tormented in her dreams. Who hates to sleep?"

I almost jumped out of my seat.

"God had me up last night until the early morning, making me feel the burdens of the souls who were up last night as well. Some are crying out to God for change, and others have almost given up believing God even cares. I'm here today to tell you that God has not forgotten you. He knows you by name. He saw what happened to you in the dark. He's here today to heal you from all that was done to you. All you have to do is come and lay your burdens down on the altar. God has set aside this time, this Sunday morning, to bring about a miraculous healing to all those who desire it. I say again, God has not forgotten you. Don't ever believe that He doesn't love you or feel your pain, your suffering, your needs. You're never alone."

Reverend Joseph continued in his deep booming voice, "If anyone wants peace, if anyone wants joy, God is here. No matter what you've been through, God can, and God will restore you. God will make you whole again. God will bring back the joy and peace you so desperately desire. Just come to the altar and give your burdens to Jesus. While the choir sings, come."

The choir softly started singing:

Pass me not, oh gentle Savior,
Hear my humble cry,
While on others Thou art calling
Do not pass me by.

There was almost a flood of people going forward. Even those around me got up and went, leaving me and Mother watching. Others got up, and I began to stand to go forward. I just had to get to the altar.

When I moved, I felt a sharp pain above my left knee. Mother had clamped down with her nails and squeezed. She leaned over and whispered to me, "Don't you dare…embarrass me. You…sit…here."

"Please, Mother, may I go?"

All those around us had already gone.

"Nicole…don't you dare move."

"Mother, please," I whispered.

Her nails dug in.

Something told me to go, get up and run to the altar, but the more I moved, the deeper she dug until I stopped moving. Pressure released. I looked around, and no one saw. Mother only looked forward, nails still in place.

Only after my body had relaxed and I'd leaned back in the pew did Mother release my leg, and the pain subsided. I watched Mrs. Larson and Naomi go hand in hand to the altar.

"Is there anyone else?" Reverend Joseph said as he scanned the congregation. "God has told me there is someone else. Please don't let this chance pass you by. Come just as you are. Please."

"Mother?"

She kept her head straight and gently placed her hand on my thigh. Someone else got up, and the congregation clapped.

"Come on down for your healing."

I saw an elderly lady going toward the front. Two motherly ladies wrapped their arms around her when she made it down. Then she wailed out, and the women held her securely.

I felt my mother's nail tap on my leg. I bowed my head and cried silently as I listened to the choir sing:

Savior, oh Savior,
Hear my humble cry,
While on others Thou art calling.

I whispered, "Please, God…don't pass me by.

CHAPTER TWENTY-EIGHT

November 6–9, 1979 (Tuesday–Friday)

The pond at the edge of campus was my favorite spot because it was so far away from everyone. The ducks just floated around, and the fountain had such a soothing sound, almost like rain. In my solitude, I had to accept I didn't know what else to do. It seemed that everywhere I turned, there was no help, not even in church. I'd never know what God had intended for me at the altar. My fear had consumed me. I was so afraid of Mother. It was like I was numb as I walked through the campus.

Even inside the school, I realized I wanted to do some of the things I saw others doing, but if I couldn't even go to the altar at church, what made me think I could try anything else? I was like a doormat available for anyone to wipe their feet on.

One girl knocked my books down, and all I did was pick them up. Another pushed past me, and I just stood there. Over the past two weeks, I'd realized that maintaining and holding on to what I had left was all I could do for now.

"Nicole," Desiree said from behind me, "we need to talk."

I stood and turned to see her walking toward me with a purpose. Desiree was my friend, and I just listened each time I was with her. I was afraid of saying the wrong thing, so I was happy that she freely talked.

"Please sit down for a moment," she said, "and let me get this off my chest."

I quickly sat down, and she came around in front of me, blocking the fountain.

"The first thing I want to say is this is nonsense, this thing between you and Nadia."

"Desiree, I—"

"No," she interrupted, "hear me out."

I nodded.

"It breaks my heart to see that Nadia can hold such a grudge and to watch all the girls blindly follow. It would have been different had you been mean, but you're so nice. I just don't get it. I chose to stick with you at the table, and I don't regret it. You're my friend." She looked down as if thinking about her words. Then she nodded and stared into my eyes. "You're my best friend."

I smiled because Desiree never lied. A few moments passed.

"Nicole, there are several things I just don't understand. I purposely watched you at school and kept track of your performances away from school. I found you were lovely and all smiles on stage. You're focused and the perfect student at school, but when you're out here, you're always staring off and alone at the edge of campus."

Desiree took a deep breath. I just felt she was right about it all, but something changed as I gazed into her eyes. I couldn't explain it.

"I have called you at least twenty times over the past few weeks," she said, "and you never called me back, so I talked with my mother about you. I told her everything, and she opened my eyes about us, and what she said made me question whether we were friends."

"What? We are friends, Desiree. I just don't want to be a bother. I know it's hard—"

She shook her head, and I stopped talking.

"No," she said. "I don't want to hear excuses. I just want you to hear me, to hear my heart. My mother told me that when people don't call you back, no matter the reason they give, there comes a point you have to accept their actions above their words. Reality is…they may not want to be your friend anymore."

"But I do," I said. "You know I do."

"I always believed your words, but that hurt when my mother said that. That really hurt. I guess I can be blind. I still hold out, believing that my brother Jeremy will change one day. I guess that's just me. I honestly believe there is something else, some feasible explanation you're acting the way you're acting. Still, my mama told me that sooner or later, I'll have to admit that you and your family travel in different circles now."

She sat and touched my hand.

"When I watched you over the past few weeks, I saw someone who wanted no part of anything else. You didn't audition for a pianist for the school choir, although you are the best pianist I've ever seen. I mean, the way you improvise and play is so moving, but it's like it's beneath you now."

Then she sat back.

"And when did you start calling your mother 'Mother'?"

"This year," I said.

"Why didn't you try out for cheerleader?"

"Do you honestly think anyone would have voted for me? Besides, I would need Mother's permission. I almost forged her name but eventually tore up the form, not wanting to be tempted anymore. I remembered."

"Remembered what?"

"Nothing."

"See," Desiree said, "I'm your best friend, and I get the word 'nothing' from you. It's like it's so one-sided, and I know it's hard for you. I know what Nadia did about the locker assignments, moving all the girls away. I even confronted her, but she plays the innocent part so well, and yet I stood by you. I stood by you every step of the way. I know Nadia and the other girls can be so…so…much like plain ol' mean, and the thing that amazes me about you, you never complain. You never lash out. You never do anything. You take 'turning the other cheek' to another level, but Nicole, even after all that, I just don't know what you want."

I thought about the word want. For me, it didn't matter what I wanted.

"I'm talking about us now," Desiree said, taking me out of my thoughts. "Forget Nadia and all the other girls. I don't care what they think or do, but what I do care about is our friendship, or is there an illusion of a friendship on my part?"

She leaned forward.

"So," she said, "when my mother asked me how I knew you were a true friend, I had no answer."

She pressed her lips together.

"I thought about it. I actually called you on my birthday, but you didn't call back. That hurt…really hurt, but like I said, I even still long for my brother to change. I get it. I'm loyal to a fault. It feels like you just tolerate me. I get it. I imagine being you, in the mayor's mansion and seeing yourself in the society paper. That has to feel good. Admired. Even seeing your photo hung right next to a Josephine Baker photo in Ms. Eleanor's boutique. I get it."

"But," I said, "Desiree, there is more to the story like you thought, but—"

"No. There are no buts in this. No excuses. I know you can tell me whatever you want to, and the sad thing about it is I'll believe it because I want to, so I can't afford to listen to any more excuses."

I stood. "Desiree, you've gotta believe me when I tell you—"

"Better yet," she said as she stood, "I don't want to hear any excuse right now. Just hear me out before you say anything else."

There was a seriousness in her eyes as she tried to find the words to say something.

"I'll tell you again," she said, "I really want to believe all you say, but nobody is on punishment for that long—nobody. Even Jeremy's punishment lasted no more than a month, and that's from him taking the car without permission and without a license. I mean, are we really friends?"

"Yes," I said, "you know we're friends. You are my only friend."

"You don't come to any of my track meets, and I'm not talking about hanging out by the fence. I ask you to come and sit in the stands, and you come up with an excuse, but then I see you in another photo shoot smiling. I get it; either we're friends, or we're not. You need to let me know—soon. If you are my friend, call me at least once every one or two weeks. That's all I ask. That's not much at all for a friend. You just call. We don't even have to talk long. I'm tired of feeling like a fool for you. I promise you; I'm done with you if you don't call. I just can't do this anymore unless I know you're all in."

I watched Desiree walk away, and some of her friends joined her. I didn't say anything much around her because I didn't want to be a burden. I saw all she went through. I did go to her meets at school, but I watched from the fence like she'd said. I knew she wouldn't be able to focus if I was there, but I did go.

I needed to call Desiree before the week was out. The next morning, I got up early, and I made sure I finished all my chores. I planned to have a lighter attitude around her and just talk. I understood how she must have felt with a person only listening. I made her a present congratulating her on her victory in another cross-country meet, but she didn't show up at our lockers over the next few days. She didn't come out to the edge of the campus. I finally found her in the lunchroom, but when I walked over, she put her hand down to stop me from sitting down.

"I still haven't gotten my call yet."

From the look in Desiree's eyes, I didn't have long to prove I was still her friend.

CHAPTER TWENTY-NINE

November 15, 1979 (Thursday)

The house was far from a home, and it was worse now, knowing I could lose my only friend. I was tired of crying in the closet. I needed to say something more to Mother than "Yes, Mother" and "No, Mother."

On Mondays, it seemed Mother woke up on the wrong side of the bed. Tuesdays and Wednesdays were her days set aside for business and planning for the weekend. Thursday was the earliest best day.

I finished my homework and piano practice early on Thursday, wanting to make sure that day would be different. I checked myself thoroughly in the mirror. My hair was combed, all strands in place. My shoes were gleaming. My nails were clean, and my glasses were spotless. I had spent an extra twenty minutes ironing my dress, and I was ready to go and talk. Breathing in and out deeply helped slow my racing pulse. With one last glance at the mirror, I headed downstairs.

Once in the kitchen, at the sight of Mother at the stove, I could hear my heartbeat in my ears. I wanted to turn back, but to what? I took a few more cleansing breaths, and then I walked up and stopped at my designated place—three paces away from her.

"Mother," I said softly, "may I have permission to speak?"

She turned around and inspected my appearance for about twenty seconds, then nodded her head.

"Speak," she said.

"It's been over seven months since my punishment began."

"Your point?"

"I…I…have been working really hard. I mean really hard. I…I…was just hoping that I…could…"

She turned and slammed the spoon down on the stove. "Stop that stuttering and get to the point!"

I had forgotten what I'd gone to her for. I looked down at my dress and said, "May I have something different to wear to school?"

"Do you want to make another dress?"

"No, Mother."

"Still ungrateful?"

"No, Mother. I'm just not good at sewing."

"I don't want to hear another excuse from you, not from the one who burned a four-hundred-dollar dress."

"Mother, I've learned."

"Listen and listen good," Mother said, "Just as I said before, and it hasn't changed, you wear what I tell you to wear, when I tell you, and the way I tell you to wear it. You need to know that clothes don't make a person. You need to get that into your head. Besides, these years of your life don't matter much anyway."

I sat down at the kitchen table. That wasn't what I'd wanted to say. I was tired, and it didn't make sense anymore. I shook my head slowly and just let it out.

"Mother," I said, "all the girls at school call me Cinderella mainly because of that dress I made and how I smelled when the vinegar got on me, and some call me names I can't repeat. They think I'm stuck up, and I chose this life over them. I probably would have been mad, too. Nadia's still mad at me. She thinks I'm lying about my punishment and doesn't like me anymore. She turned all the girls in the school against me, all except Desiree.

"Mother, it hurts so bad when they call me Cinderella now. Nobody talks to me or even smiles at me. Mother, I only have one friend left, Desiree, and I'm about to lose her.

"I can tell she's even getting tired of me. All she wants me to do is call her once a week; that's it. Just tell me what you want me to do, and I'll do it. If you want to give me more chores, I'll do them, but I just need to call her. I promise I won't stay on long. Please. Please, Mother, help me. I just can't lose her."

For the first time in months, I saw compassion in her eyes, eyes that blinked quickly. She turned away and took several deep breaths. She started to turn her head to me but then snapped it back toward the stove. To see her struggle to gain her composure brought an inkling of hope. She walked over to the pot on the stove, bowed her head for about ten seconds, and took a quick breath. I sat back in my chair and waited. After a few moments, she spoke in a slow, methodical voice.

"All…that you are going through…will…make you stronger. You will find out if Desiree is a true friend, so one call won't make a difference…but…you need to learn to stand alone if necessary and get control of your emotions. No… matter…what."

There was a pause in her words, and when she spoke again, her voice had strengthened.

"And I mean no matter what."

She took a long, deep breath and exhaled slowly. When she turned around, her cold demeanor had returned.

"Always…be…in control." She came closer and said, "Remember this: the day you lose control at that school is the day you will regret walking across the threshold of this house."

I sank in my chair and thought about the night before Daddy had left, the night I'd listened to Mother and Daddy talk about bills. Then my thoughts turned into words.

"I overheard the promise you made to Daddy." Even as I listened to myself, I didn't know why I spoke. I could have let it go and tried another day, but there was no other time. Maybe I was just plain stupid.

It was like she glided to me as she mimicked my words: "You told him you'd take great care of me? Do you remember?"

When she stopped in front of me, I saw her hand coming. As the force struck my left jaw, I let out a groan.

"Don't you ever question me again."

A tear rolled down my cheek.

"Stop that crying! Those tears only show how weak you really are."

I dropped my hand to my side and tightened my lips, but I couldn't stop the tears.

"What did crying ever do for you? You've got to learn that life will eat you up and spit you out. You won't survive if all you do is cry. Friends come and go. To be the best, you have got to quit letting those feelings rule you."

"But Mother."

"Go to your room. Now!"

On the way upstairs, I couldn't get Desiree off my mind. I thought about the last words she had said: "I still haven't gotten my call yet." I saw the telephone. In a moment, I was dialing. I knew I didn't have much time at all.

"May I speak to Desiree?"

"Nicole?"

"Desiree, we're friends; please know that. Please believe me. I don't have much time, but please meet with me at my locker tomorrow morning. Please be there. I'll tell you everything."

"Okay."

I looked up and saw Mother standing there with the belt.

"See you later, Desiree."

I hung up and stood.

Mother just pointed to her room.

I lay on her bed and held onto a pillow. The belt cut through the air. Searing pain.

"One!" I said, thinking of Desiree. "Two! Three!"

The last number I remembered was twenty-four.

CHAPTER THIRTY

November 16, 1979 (Friday)

Going through the front metal tan doors at Darlington Junior High was like walking on the road to hell, and my destination was the seventh-grade girls' wing of the school. One of only two safe havens at the school was my locker there. I was hoping Desiree would be there. I was going to tell her everything, show her my back, and tell her about Charles, Mother, and absolutely everything. I wasn't going to lose my only friend.

I was even sick of the assortment of colors that segregated the boys from the girls. The teal green represented Nadia's domain of the seventh-grade girls' locker hall. I passed by rows A through F and stood at the entrance of row G, where my locker number 210 was buried deep in the little cave six feet wide and eight feet high. I usually found my area's lighting peaceful, especially since there were very few girls on that row, but this morning, I was afraid to go in without Desiree.

Nadia, with five other girls who used to be my friends, stood on the other side of the hall behind me. I would have waited at the end of the locker, not wanting to be trapped without Desiree, but I needed my Science and English books. I closed my eyes and rushed to my locker. I was sure Desiree would show.

I opened my locker and quickly swapped out my books.

"Nicole." Nadia's raspy voice echoed in the hallway.

I quickly gathered my books, closed my locker, and tried to rush out of the little cave, but Nadia and the girls blocked my exit.

Desiree was nowhere to be found. My hands trembled, but I held my books tightly against my chest to still them.

“Why are you rushing away?” Nadia said calmly. “I just want to talk.”

I didn’t say anything.

“Oh, come on, Nicole,” she said, the other girls smiling, “we’ve known each other for far too long, and I was hoping that you would consider sitting with us at lunch.”

I turned my head a little, trying to read her intentions. I really didn’t trust her.

“I’m serious,” she said.

I studied her, and it seemed like she was genuine. Maybe God was answering my prayer in another way. There was a strange relief in seeing Nadia’s smile form. I let a few seconds pass, and then I smiled back.

Then her right hand moved.

I felt a sting on my left cheek.

My books and purse fell from my arms.

It was like time slowed.

I could barely see my glasses lying by my books on the floor. When I inspected Nadia’s face, she had a smirk that made my stomach turn. My teeth were clenched. I was sick of her, of all that she continued to do to me. I pictured myself hitting her square in the nose with all my might, wanting to break it. Just before I was about to swing, I thought about Mother and her belt.

No matter what, I would have to face Mother again. My lower back was still tender from yesterday. Before I knew it, I was crawling on the floor, hands outstretched, feeling for my glasses. Once they were back in place, I stood up slowly, turned toward Nadia, and waited.

All the girls watched me as if I were some sideshow act.

“Wow,” Karen said, “you were right.”

“Nothing,” Nadia said, looking around at the girls. “I told you she wouldn’t do a thing. Pay up.”

Nadia shoved me. My head hit the lockers. She kicked my books, sending them flying back toward my locker. More girls poured into my once peaceful refuge.

“Now, what’re you gonna do?” Nadia said.

I straightened my glasses again.

“See, I knew it,” Nadia said. “I knew you wouldn’t do a thing. You’re just a freak. You should at least fight back or something, but you’re thinking you’re better than everybody else just standing there trying to be this perfect little concert piano player. What do you want to do now—cry? Go ahead and cry!" She leaned in closer.

"Nadia!" Desiree yelled from behind the crowd. "What are you doing?"

Without turning around, Nadia said, "This ain't about you."

Girls quickly jumped aside like a parting sea. Then Desiree stepped between them and me. "Oh, yes, it is. Why are you bothering Nicole again? Did she do anything to you? Did she even say anything to you?"

"Why are you helping her nasty behind? She don't even treat you right. She definitely thinks she's better than you. Can you even see that?"

"What's it to you anyway? She's my friend. Something you don't know nothing about."

The girls pressed closer as a larger crowd formed.

"Friend!" Nadia said. "When was the last time she called you? When?"

"Last night!"

Nadia was shocked.

"Yeah," Desiree said, "So if you want to fight somebody, fight me." Desiree shoved Nadia. "All right, come on! I'm sick of all y'all anyway."

Many of the girls backed away.

"She used to be your best friend," Desiree said.

"You don't understand," Nadia said.

"Oh, yes, I do. Just because she changed, you want to treat her like this? Now you just want to beat her down for nothing? Nicole doesn't mess with one person in this school."

"Come on, are you that blind? Look at Cinderella, Miss High and Mighty. Look at her now with her old stank self."

"What has she done to you?" Desiree asked. "What?"

Nadia was silent.

I looked around at all the girls. Some had their heads down, and none met my eyes.

"Yeah," Desiree said, "I figured."

Whispers started, and a lot of the girls left. Someone whispered to Nadia, "It's Mrs. Carter."

Mrs. Carter towered over most men, but it wasn't so much her height that intimidated, but her arms, which were bigger than most of the girls' thighs.

"Girls, what's going on over here? What's the problem?" Her voice was a deep alto that commanded answers.

More girls cleared out.

Mrs. Carter stared at us. Desiree and Nadia were within inches of each other. She glanced down at my books on the floor.

"Nadia, Nicole, and Desiree, come with me, and the rest of you girls clear the hall and go to your homerooms."

My heart jumped as I imagined my mother's face when she showed up at school. She might lay me on her bed again and strip me down this time. I couldn't take that belt again.

"Mrs. Carter," I said, "nothing's going on. Everything's fine."

Nadia beamed and said innocently, "Nothing is going on, Mrs. Carter. We were just talking."

Mrs. Carter focused on me. "Nicole, is that correct?"

I nodded, not looking into her eyes.

"Look at me."

I did.

"Are you sure?"

"Yes, ma'am, I'm sure."

Some students stood nearby, lingering.

"Girls! I told you to clear the hall and go to your homerooms! I don't have time for this."

The girls scattered.

Mrs. Carter gazed at us and then focused on me again. "Okay, Nicole, if that's what you say."

A pale, slender girl with a squeaky voice spoke up. "Mrs. Carter, you're needed in the lunchroom."

Mrs. Carter followed the young messenger, careful not to run her over. When they were out of sight, Nadia turned to me, shaking her head.

"See Desiree. Yeah, she called you, but how long did you talk?"

Desiree looked at me.

Nadia smirked. "See how easy it is for her to play you. To do just enough to string you along so you can keep fighting for her. You're wasting your time. Just like I said. She's a freak. A robot. It don't matter what you do to her. She keeps that stupid blank stare and stands there trying to act all innocent. Some friend. Plain sorry if you ask me."

Nadia strolled off, kicking my papers one last time. She walked down the center of the hallway and then made a left.

As soon as the hallway cleared, Desiree whipped her head around to me. "Why don't you fight back?" Desiree said, her voice sharp. "Why?"

"I can't."

"I'm sick of that word. Can't do this. Can't do that. Then tell me, what in the world can you do?" she said, her teeth clenched, her muscles in her jaws pulsated, her fists balled up.

I wanted to say so much, but I realized I was too late to explain. She didn't want to hear anything else from me. As I thought about opening up, I realized: what could Desiree do, anyway? Really, what could anyone do for me? Everyone in this city loved Mother and believed she was an angel. Everyone in the school admired Nadia—her beauty, her leadership, and her confidence.

I shook my head slowly. "I'm sorry. I can't do anything."

"Nadia was right about one thing," Desiree said. "Some friend. Why did you call me anyway, to just string me along like she said? Not once have you called me back this summer. Ever since school started, I've been there for you. I stand up for you, but it's hard to always step in, especially when you won't fight back." Desiree sighed. "If you would just fight back once…just once…I know you'd end all of this. I'll be there, and I promise I won't leave you. The worst thing that could happen is your mother would be called to the school, but then we could tell your side, and I'd be there to back you up."

I wondered if Mother would slap me in front of Desiree.

"No," I said, "so much more could happen."

"Like what!" she said. She surged toward me but stopped short. I didn't move. I found it better to just take it, but she didn't slap me, push me, or anything like that. I didn't know why I'd thought I could hold on to a friend. I knew I wouldn't be able to call Desiree anymore. I could tell Desiree all that had happened to me, and then what? No one would believe me. And besides, I really wasn't a good friend to her. I was only trouble for her. I found myself just staring at her.

"I just don't understand," Desiree said, her voice softening.

Just to see her. It just wasn't fair to her. I saw then how selfish I was, trying to hold on and just take from her, knowing I had nothing to give back. It was then I decided to let her go. She deserved better than me.

"You don't have to stick up for me anymore," I said. "I'll be fine. And Desiree, even if you join in, it's okay. I won't hold it against you. I promise I won't. Besides, this time in my life doesn't matter much, anyway."

Desiree's mouth dropped open. "So, you expect me to just stand by and let them beat you down?"

I'd seen Desiree laughing with the other girls at the beginning of the school year. I hadn't seen her laugh since then, and I wanted to see my friend laugh again—I mean, really laugh. Without me in her life, she would be happy. They would willingly follow her over Nadia.

Desiree's voice pulled me back into reality. "Do you expect me to just stand by and let this happen?"

She gently touched my arm.

I put my hand on top of hers and softly smiled and said, "Yes."

I actually smiled as the seconds ticked by. We stared into each other's eyes. I had finally done something good. I knew she would be fine. "Bye, Desiree."

I kneeled down and started picking up my books and papers.

Desiree turned and walked down the quiet hallway.

Desiree squeezed her eyes tight, not believing how evasive Nicole was being. Can't help anybody who acts like some doormat. Almost at the end of the hallway, Desiree had a familiar nagging feeling at the core of her stomach. It was like a God-given connection between her and Nicole that wouldn't let her go. She turned around to see Nicole slowly picking up her schoolbooks.

Desiree decided to go back to Nicole. As she got closer, Nicole's blouse slipped up. Desiree slowed at the sight of something dark on Nicole's lower back. Desiree softly walked toward Nicole. She knew the dark discolorations were bruises, the same welts she used to see on her mother. No one had come to the aid of her mother, but Desiree knew she needed to stay. It was then that she thought it was God who had given Nicole to her as a friend. It was a divine connection, and she knew God would never want her to turn her back on her friend. Never. No matter what the cost.

Nicole slid her blouse over the bruises and continued picking up and stacking her papers.

The bell rang—time for homeroom. The sound made Nicole drop her head, stop, and sit on the floor, not moving and staring at the exit sign.

After a moment, Nicole quickly began to pick up her papers and pencils, throwing them in her purse while glancing at the exit sign. Desiree kneeled beside Nicole and reached to pick up what appeared to be Nicole's science homework just as her friend reached for it.

"I got it, Nicole."

Nicole pulled at her blouse again to cover her back. Desiree smiled kindly and patted her friend on the back of her hand.

Nicole shook her head. "No, Desiree. Nadia's right. I'm not a good friend at all. I'm sorry. So, don't fool yourself. You need to go. Please."

"No. I got it." Desiree said, remembering when her mother had been alone and abused, and no one had helped.

"No more Desiree. No more. You just go now, please. You get a chance to have real friends now."

Desiree touched her hand and stared into Nicole's eyes. Nicole closed her eyes and shook her head.

"Nicole, I'm your friend no matter what."

"You don't get it, do you? When I go to my homeroom, all I hear are insults. The teacher never does anything to stop it. How many more times will I be slapped, pushed, and shoved? How many? And my mother…" Nicole shook her head quickly. "No. Please leave. Just leave me. Let me do one good thing. Okay? Just leave me. It's okay."

Desiree gently placed her hands on Nicole's cheeks, stopping her from shaking her head. "I promise…I won't ever leave you."

Nicole opened her eyes.

"Nicole. No matter what."

"Are you sure?" Nicole said.

"Yes," Desiree said, and then she began to pick up what was left of Nicole's scattered belongings.

Nicole reached out to help.

"No, Nicole." Desiree gently took her friend by her arms and positioned her to sit. "Just rest. I'll get them."

As Desiree stacked Nicole's Science and English books, the bracelet Nicole had given her when she was six slid down her arm. Desiree remembered how sweet Nicole had been; she had invited Desiree to her sixth birthday party in kindergarten, telling all the girls that someone special would be there. Even Desiree couldn't wait to see this special guest. When Desiree heard Nicole single her out as the special guest, Nadia thought it was some joke.

Desiree still remembered how it felt for Nicole to stand up for her in front of all her friends and place her arm around her. Nicole had told Nadia, "This is my friend who has traveled around many states. She's even been to California." It had been funny to Desiree because she had only told Nicole once about all the places she had been to, but Nicole had listened and remembered.

It had taken Nadia a bit to warm up to the new girl; it had been Nicole who'd shared all of her friends with Desiree.

Desiree's bracelet jingled as she picked up pens and pencils. She remembered staring at all Nicole's gifts at the party. Nicole had asked her mother if she could give Desiree her bracelet. As Nicole had wrapped the bracelet around Desiree's wrist, she'd said, "Mama said when she gave this to me, 'Anytime you feel lonely or like you need a friend, just touch this bracelet and know how special you are, and that God always loves you.' See, it reads 'You're never alone.'"

Desiree could still feel the love from the hug Nicole had given her that day—her first real friend.

Desiree picked up one last sheet of paper with vocabulary words listed on it and placed it in Nicole's English book. Before they stood, Desiree unclasped her bracelet and put it on Nicole's wrist.

"Did you change your mind?" Nicole said.

"No, just hold on to it for me. Remember, anytime you feel lonely or like you need a friend, just touch this bracelet and know how special you are to me and that God always loves you, and I love you too."

Desiree helped Nicole up and put the books and papers in her arms. Side by side, they walked silently to Nicole's homeroom class. As Desiree opened the door for Nicole, Nadia said, "Oh, there she is. It's Cinderella modeling her new line of fashion today."

"Quiet girls. Nicole, take your seat," Mrs. Primrose said.

Nicole looked back at Desiree and mouthed, "Thank you." She walked to her desk, sat down, crossed her legs at her ankles, and sat up straight in her chair.

Desiree heard another voice in the room say, "Look at her, the freak."

Nicole touched the bracelet and lifted her chin a little higher.

"Karen," Mrs. Primrose said, "Do you want to go to the office?"

"No, ma'am."

Desiree turned and walked toward her own homeroom. She realized that no matter what, she could never turn her back on her friend.

CHAPTER THIRTY-ONE

March 6 – 8, 1980 (Thursday – Saturday)

Nicolette Pearson was the pride of Atlanta's Piedmont High. Mother had become more engrossed with her. During dinner, Nicolette was all she talked about, but the drawback for me was that she made my work even more challenging. Whatever exercises Nicolette did, I did three times as many. Mother discovered and studied everything Nicolette was learning and made me do them too, eventually believing that I could beat Nicolette now. If I beat her, I would become nationally recognized immediately; I would automatically be catapulted into the spotlight, a spotlight I hated.

A few weeks before my thirteenth birthday, storms were building up in Georgia, and for a moment, I thought of Daddy. I watched the rain from my window, but I didn't have time to really pay attention to it. Mother had given me a list of questions that she knew Daddy would ask me when he returned home, questions like how I felt about the competitions, the weddings, and so many other events. The questions covered all the things Mother believed he would be interested in. I was to study and memorize the answer to those questions every day, and eventually, it would seem like the answers came from me.

Mother also told me I was ready for what she said was the first of the three events, the mayor's annual black-tie event. It didn't make matters at school any better once the girls at school saw the society column.

After that, I had two of the most important piano competitions of my life, according to Mother. If I won both, the victory would almost certainly ensure a scholarship to Ventura College. Although Mother had attended Ventura College, she'd never been accepted into the concert piano program. Mother was really good, but I guess they must have had outstanding pianists back then.

Two days before the first of the two competitions, I had the music down that I was to play. I had learned all the questions Daddy would ask. I was happy about that because I had pop quizzes and a few tests to take. At around 9 p.m. Thursday, Mother came to my door with some sheet music.

"Nicole," she said, "I had your piece changed for Saturday's competition. I'm sure this piece will be good enough to beat Nicolette."

I closed my history book and looked at the music. I didn't care about the titles anymore. I wasn't judged on titles; I was judged on the music played. Playing had become measure-to-measure, and this one was filled with more notes and chords than usual.

I sighed and shook my head. Why would she do this? I wanted to ask, but when Mother tilted her head, I had five seconds to get my attitude together. It took me two seconds to gather the music sheets together, and I was seated at the piano by the fifth.

"I'll be back at three to see what you have."

"Three in the morning?"

"Is there a problem?"

"No, ma'am."

She went back to her room.

I skimmed through the music. I had never heard or seen this piece before, and yet when Mother said three, she meant to have the piece down. I slowly began to sight-read the music, paying close attention to the crescendo, decrescendo, and all the other signs I couldn't even think of the terms for. My mind was filled with history. I knew we would have a quiz, and I couldn't miss any questions. I nodded for a moment, lost my place in the music, and had to start over.

The struggle to fight through learning the music went on until midnight. I shook my head, not believing how tired I had gotten. All the mistakes I made were setting me back because, whatever I heard, I remembered, even if it was wrong. Correcting errors took even longer.

I decided to set my alarm clock for 12:20 and take a quick nap. As soon as my head hit the pillow and I closed my eyes, I felt pain across my leg.

"Get up," Mother said.

I jumped up out of bed.

"Oh, you must have the piece down."

I looked at the clock. "3:01" I rushed to the clock. I had set the alarm for p.m. instead of a.m.

"Get back to the piano, and don't you stop until you have it down."

This time, when she returned at 5 a.m., I could play the piece without making mistakes. I played it two more times for her. Then I took my shower and got ready for school.

When it came time for the history quiz, I missed an answer. The question: "Who was known as the 'Swamp Fox'?" I knew the answer, but I guess I nodded off and put Frances Henderson. When I got the graded quiz back, I couldn't believe it. She'd been the bride at the wedding where I'd played "My Funny Valentine." The real answer was Francis Marion.

The rest of the day at school wasn't good because I knew Mother. So many things ran across my mind. When I got to the car, I gave her the quiz because even being slow to answer was deceitful, at least to her. When she saw ninety-five, she whipped her head around and stared at me. Then she flipped through the quiz. Daddy would have laughed, but Mother only nodded her head and said, "What's this, some type of joke?"

"I'm tired, Mother."

"You don't know what tired is, but I'll show you."

When we got home, she quizzed me for several hours on Daddy's questions again and on all my subjects in school, asking an obscure question from the corner of the book. I took a break to eat dinner. Then, she gave me the sheet music and told me to practice. She told me the tempo and how she wanted it played. Saturday morning, Mother had me do a dress rehearsal and play the piece until she was comfortable with my performance. It was 2 a.m. by the time we finished, but I had the piece down.

At the event, I stood backstage and listened to Nicolette perform. She was brilliant. Her interpretation, her fingering, everything was immaculate. She smiled as she passed by. The announcer called my name, and I went to the piano. I turned the dial on the bench to raise it and give myself some time. The keys were blurry. After a few seconds, the piano finally came into focus.

The notes in my head were jumbled, and I missed the timing on the first measure and played a flat instead of a natural on another measure. I took several deep breaths just as the notes in my head cleared up. It was almost like I was on autopilot. I followed every note and chord in the sheet music in my head. I closed my eyes once and then opened them quickly. I was in another section of the piece, still playing. I had fallen asleep. I pressed my lips together, not knowing exactly how I had played the music. I knew Mother had noticed.

I focused as hard as I could and made it to the last notes. I stood, smiled and bowed, and hurried off stage. I rushed to the restroom, trying to remember what I had just done, but I just couldn't remember. It was blank.

When all the contestants lined up, my heart was beating so fast. There were only two places left. If they didn't call my name, then I had really messed up.

When they called my name for second place overall, I smiled, took the trophy, relieved, and later congratulated Nicolette on first place. The distance between first and second, though, was like the distance between the moon and the earth.

"Nicole," she said, "I was worried when you played. That's a difficult piece. I've been practicing that piece for the past two months, but I wouldn't dare play it yet. What do you do to get through the middle of the music, more specifically around measure ninety-nine?"

"Oh," I said, "I pray."

We both laughed. I didn't tell her that was one of the measures I had fallen asleep on.

"You know," she said, "I do a lot of praying too. I actually have a sister and a cousin your age."

Dr. Rogers stood off to the side, talking with Mother. He signaled for Nicolette.

"Well," Nicolette said, "I have to go, but again, Nicole, your piece was so beautiful."

I slowly walked toward Mother. Just as I was within arm's reach, a judge said, "Mrs. Peterson, it is a pleasure to see Nicole's poise, grace, and composure at such a young age. It was a very close second."

"Really?" Mother said.

"Oh yes," he said, "she stumbled at the beginning, but after that, it was amazing to see her make it through the most difficult part of the music. Just get that beginning down. Regardless, you should be proud of her."

"Oh, I am," Mother said.

As soon as he left, Mother turned to me, and the solemnness on her face let me know she had just lied to the judge. She wasn't proud of me. Even staring into her eyes, I could see the flicker of anger ignite. When we got to the car afterward, Mother stopped at the driver's door and stared at me. I could always tell the hurricanes that formed in Mother's eyes. Just like the weather, all I could do was ride out her storm. After a few seconds, she unlocked the door.

I got in the car and gently closed the door behind me. I wouldn't look back anymore. She fumbled with her keys and slammed the car in reverse. She slammed on the brakes and threw the car in drive.

Mother could have given me the music earlier, but it was like she wanted to have something to be mad at me about. Once we left the parking lot, she spoke.

"Nicole, how could you make such blatant mistakes? I had you practice that piece forty times last night, and still, you mess up? What's wrong with you?

"Mother, I was exhausted."

"I don't want to hear another one of your sorry excuses. There are no excuses for mistakes."

"Mother, people make mistakes."

"Like falling asleep in the middle of the music?"

I stared at her.

"Just because I gave you that music late, you thought it was okay to fail. You spent so much time fighting against how unfair or focusing on your perceived shortcomings that you wasted so much time. And I'm supposed to just accept any old mistake because you're exhausted? You want me to be one of those parents who'd say, 'Oh, you did the best you could.'" Mother grimaced. "You must be crazy. You will play with perfection at all times, no matter what. Period. You will be perfect. You will not fail.

"When we get home, put your work clothes on. Scrub the kitchen floor, and it had better be spotless. Then take the pots, pans, silverware, and glasses out of the cabinets, wash them, and dry them. Pull out all the cans and containers from the pantry, dust them, and put them back, ensuring the labels are all lined up perfectly. You better get a ruler for that one. If you can't focus through practice, I'll make you focus through long, tedious work until you get what I demand. There is no excuse for anything less than perfection. Your lack of concentration is repulsive."

I held my head down. I was always holding my head down.

Mother popped my chin.

"Look at me when I'm talking to you, acting like you're some cowardly dog."

Her eyes went back to the road and then at me.

"People would die for your talent," she said. "You're much better than Nicolette. You bought into this mystique of Nicolette like everybody else."

I wiped away my tears. Maybe I was giving up too easily. She wouldn't correct me if she didn't love me. Even God corrects those he loves.

"Mother…is the only reason you love me…because I play the piano?"

I could almost see her withdraw, her tone, her attention, almost like I was disappearing. She turned the classical music up and went silent.

"Mother?"

Her gaze remained forward. I thought about what Charles had told me several years ago when I asked about his nightmares. He had told me, "Just know not everyone who tells you they love you really does." I stared at Mother.

It couldn't be.

"Mother…do you…even love me?"

She remained quiet.

I slowly reached to touch the back of her hand. As soon as my finger touched her skin, she jerked her hand away as if some insect had touched her. I just stared at her, but she didn't even look my way.

Just imagining how she may have felt towards me hurt, but I pushed the thought out of my mind and just stared out the window and watched the trees.

CHAPTER THIRTY-TWO

March 23, 1980 (Sunday)

I've been thinking," she said calmly, "if you want all of this to end, then in the next competition, you give me your all and show me that you can play the perfect piece. If you do that, then that will show me that none of this training was in vain."

She left the room and went to bed.

Early Sunday morning, the day before my thirteenth birthday, the day of the finals of the piano competition held in the Darlington Convention Hall, I performed my first chore of the day by picking up the newspaper in the front yard. I laid it neatly on the table six inches from the corner. After removing the rubber band that held the paper, I washed it and put it in the drawer marked 'Miscellaneous.' I made sure the additional rubber band didn't disturb the paper clips, pencils, erasers, and correction type already in there.

I got comfortable on the stool in front of my piano and played the piece I was to perform later that day for the competition. Every run through the piece took me exactly the same amount of time. I practiced walking on stage, sitting, standing, and smiling. Mother came into my room and listened to the piece three more times. After the third time, her subtle nod of approval brought me hope that tonight, when they announced the winner, I would hear my name.

Two hours before we were to leave, I stood in Mother's closet, watching her rifle through the seventy-five performance dresses. The closet seemed to contain colors beyond the rainbow, neatly blending from shades of white to yellow to green to pink to blue. I hoped she'd choose blue, sapphire, or even lavender, but her final selection was a white lace chiffon dress. I didn't like wearing white at all, but I was too close to let even that mess me up, so I prayed that God would help me focus even more.

This competition was pivotal for people who sought music scholarships. Winning was a guarantee to attending any musical college, and for me, it would bring me one step closer to Ventura College. The competition drew the best talent from across the nation, including Nicolette. She had won the competition for the past two years.

After I was dressed and groomed to my mother's standards, we left. At the hall, I saw the school music teacher, newspaper reporters, Mayor Daily, Mrs. Winthrop, Dr. Rogers, and, more importantly, Mr. Tomlinson, a recruiter from Ventura College. He and Nicolette were talking.

Ventura College was one of the most prestigious schools in the country for concert pianists, and it was the program my mother had once dreamed of being a part of but had never been accepted—a deep disappointment.

The stage was adorned beautifully and contained a table displaying all of the trophies, including the most coveted prize for competitors of all ages, "Best in Show."

Standing backstage, everything whirled around me until it was time for me to go onstage.

"Nicole Peterson," the announcer said, "will be playing…"

I stepped out. Every moment on stage counted with my mother, not just the act of playing perfectly. "Acknowledge the audience"—Rule #32. "Touch the bench, sit erect, and ensure correct distance away from the keyboard"—Rule #45. I had practiced those fifty times last week.

I began to play. Every note and every musical symbol were memorized. Even my fingering had to be perfect. I had practiced every fortissimo, pianissimo, and glissando until they were so familiar that even if I were to play in my sleep, I couldn't fail—not this time. I rode along with the music as if on a wild ride, note after note, and phrase after phrase at the exact time. I did not let my mind wander or improvise even the slightest emotion. I was the robot playing just as I was designed to do: over and over, repeat, recycle, repeat, and recycle. I had finally figured it out. Do not question; just do.

Halfway through the song, my heart began to well up, feeling everything would go right. I slammed that thought down and focused. Next note. Next phrase. Next. Next. It wasn't about emotion. It was about imitation, and I realized I was that replica that would finally do something right. As I focused on the sheet music, my mind turned the page to the last measures. I played with the same intensity that I'd started with, and the countdown began, measure seven, measure six, measure five, measure four, measure three, measure two, measure one.

I exhaled as I played the last note and lifted my hands off the keys. I breathed deeply. The playing was complete, but my performance was not over, at least not for Mother.

"Exit appropriately"—Rule #82. "Walk with perfect posture"—Rule #76. I had worked on those two rules alone for a week. As I left the stage, I felt the tears well up. If I won today, all I had to do was accept the trophy perfectly.

The contest wore on. I found a corner away from everyone backstage and practiced shaking imaginary hands because of Rule #175— "Shake hands firmly." The handshake had to look natural, so to me, this rule was the hardest because I had to gauge the actions and emotions of others.

In the middle of my thoughts, I heard deafening silence. I stepped into the area with everyone. No one moved as if in a trance. It was then that I heard someone playing on stage. It wasn't the regular playing, but as if Mozart himself had graced the stage. I gingerly went to the edge of the curtains backstage to see Nicolette.

From backstage, I watched and listened to her play with such grace, such emotion, and such perfection. The more she played, the more I realized that even at my best, even after all I had done, all my praying and focusing, Nicolette was just Nicolette. Watching her made me realize I couldn't be the one thing I was sure Mother longed for. I couldn't be Nicolette. I peeped from behind the curtain and saw Mother with her eyes closed, no doubt imagining how it felt to play like Nicolette.

I closed my eyes and felt her performance. I didn't try to analyze the whys or hows; I just listened like everyone else. When her last note sounded, a long-standing ovation followed. For some crazy reason, I actually believed I still had a sliver of a chance until I saw her in her navy-blue gown—absolute perfection—displaying royal grace as she walked offstage.

I went off to the corner, away from everyone, and started practicing congratulating Nicolette on her victory. I had to pull back to keep from crying, but I prayed that God would give me the strength to mean what I'd said to Nicolette. I would clap for her, shake her hand, and exit the stage with dignity.

The finalists stood to receive their awards, and as I expected, Nicolette won in her age category, and I won in mine. At the end of the evening, I stood next to Nicolette. She had a light fragrance of some perfume I had never smelled. The edges of her hair were soft, and her smile was warm. This close, she was even more beautiful than the first time I'd seen her.

"And the best in show is..."

There was a long pause as the announcer fumbled with the paper. I rehearsed the whole congratulations process one last time. As soon as I heard "Nicolette Pearson," I clapped my hands for her. She turned to me, and I stuck my hand out to shake hers. She shook perfectly.

People started staring my way. I thought I was standing correctly. Maybe we were supposed to back up. I scanned my dress to see if I had a spot on it. I thought it was strange when Nicolette kept clapping and smiling at me, but then I saw her lips move.

"Nicole," she said, "it's you."

"Me?"

She nodded. I turned to the smiling announcer. He nodded and said, "Best in show...Nicole...Peterson."

When I heard my name, my mouth gaped open. Pull it together, Nicole. I prayed that I wouldn't trip on the way to the announcer. I walked up and accepted the trophy and shook hands—perfectly. I whispered, "God, thank you. Thank you."

As I turned to walk to my spot, I heard the announcer call my name again. "Nicole."

I turned around and walked back, making sure I stood erect and smiled.

"I wanted to say on behalf of the judges that your performance today was a vision of perfection. Your poise and grace at twelve years of age predict a bright future. It has been an honor to see you play. Your parents should be exceptionally proud of you."

"Accept compliments with grace and poise"—Rule #42.

Once off stage, Nicolette was the first to congratulate me.

"Nicole, it took me everything to gain my composure after hearing you play. It has been an honor to me as well. Enjoy your moment."

She had such a beautiful smile.

The rest of the contestants were gracious toward me, as were so many others. Mayor Daily came backstage with his entourage and told me he was proud of my representation of our community. When the mayor left, Dr. Rogers and Mr. Tomlinson shook my hand.

After everyone had gone their separate ways, I finally saw Mother a few feet away from me, off to the side, away from everyone else. I calmly walked up to her, knowing that in only a few moments, all of this would be behind me; no, it would be behind us. I couldn't contain myself and rushed over to Mother, and my mouth opened, and words flew out.

"See Mother, I didn't make any mistakes. I played perfectly. Mother, you heard what the announcer said to me. I received the trophy and shook his hands exactly how you taught me. See Mother. Did you see? Did you see?"

The flood of words stopped just after my mind began to comprehend everything I saw. No smile. No sparkle in Mother's eyes. No emotions. It was as if I were invisible, and she was waiting for someone else.

"I'm sorry, Mother. I was just—" I thought, *happy*. Her eyes focused on me. I couldn't tell where she was, but I knew her look of disappointment.

"No crying in public"—Rule #201. That was the hardest rule to keep.

I had done all she'd asked. I had done everything perfectly.

"Nicole," Mother whispered calmly, "why does it always have to be about you? The only reason you pushed was because I pushed you. You didn't do it yourself. I did it. See, you wanted something and got it, but you had no personal pride. It's like you would do anything to go back to that fantasy world, but I'll be damned if I let that happen."

She took a deep breath and nodded her head. "Well, at least I know now that you are capable of far…more…than I ever imagined. You can reach perfection at all times if…you put your mind to it—your mind. So, from now on, I will expect nothing less."

Rule #201 was about to be broken.

Out of the corner of my eye, I saw Nicolette's parents and two girls my age hugging and kissing her. They were all smiles. They were all so beautiful. Nicolette's mother put her arm around her, held her close, and kissed her on the head. Her father smiled and hugged them both. They all walked together, enjoying each other.

That must be nice.

"Come on, Nicole."

"Yes, Mother."

I watched Nicolette and her family as I walked behind Mother, pretending I was with them.

"Nicole," Mother said, "you're moving too slow."

"Yes, Mother."

CHAPTER THIRTY-THREE

March 23, 1980 (Sunday)

We rode home, taking what seemed to be the longest possible route. We even stopped by Ms. Eleanor's boutique, where Mother picked something up. Ms. Eleanor took another picture of me with the trophy. I smiled as I'd been taught.

Mother and I rode back to the house quietly. While I sat in the car, my mind searched for answers. What would it take for Mother to be like Nicolette's mom, or even be like she was at church?

A vision came to me of a ship in the middle of a storm. There was one rescue boat left to take a little girl to safety, but the captain insisted that she lighten her load. She threw her doll collection, papers, books, posters, and clothes overboard. As the storm raged on, the girl disappeared and reappeared with a small chest. It was all she had left. She wanted to take her chest box of dreams, but the captain yelled, "No!" She would have to trust the captain, but that meant leaving the box behind. Otherwise, she'd be stranded on a sinking ship.

I saw a familiar figure as we turned the corner to our house and then came around the bend.

"Daddy?" I said under my breath.

We got closer. Yes.

Before the car stopped, I jumped out.

"Daddy!"

I ran. It had been a year since I'd seen him. His arms opened wider with each step I took. I couldn't run fast enough.

"Nicole! Nicole! Control yourself!" Mother shouted.

I immediately stopped running a few feet away from Daddy and walked up to him. Once I stood in front of him, I said, "Hi, Daddy."

He snatched me up and squeezed me tight. "Oh, I missed you so much."

I could always feel when Mother was staring. I turned my head to see her piercing eyes. I restrained myself and didn't squeeze back. Daddy didn't know Rule #114 — "No excessive public displays of affection." Hug but not too tight and not too long; we were in public.

It was as if he heard my thoughts and stopped squeezing me. His release of me was slow and steady. When my feet met the ground, Mother had parked the car correctly and was standing beside us. He searched my eyes and then pulled his head back an inch, puzzled.

"Nicole," she said as she stepped forward and took my hand, "get the trophies out of the car, take them inside, and put them in the place I cleared on the trophy shelf. Your father and I need to talk."

I turned back to Daddy.

"Nicole," she said, "now go."

"Yes, Mother."

As I stepped toward the car and heard Mother's voice fade, each step took me back to the little girl on the sinking ship standing with the captain of the rescue boat. A wave from the violent seas almost blew the little girl off the ship, but the captain grabbed her hand.

The little girl held on to her box with all her might, and her other hand began to slip from the captain's hand.

"Let it go," the captain said, "and grab my hand!"

Her hand still slipping, he shouted, "Let it go!"

At that moment, the young girl decided to let go of the last thing she'd been dearly holding on to. The captain grabbed her free hand and pulled her to safety. Then he studied her as the two climbed into the boat, with no life jackets, shivering from the cold and receiving no warmth. She and the captain watched the ship sink into the deep black ocean, and the two drifted off into the night.

"Glen, you won't believe how much I've guided Nicole to success since you've been gone. Even today, you should have heard what the announcer said about her. He said…"

Inside the living room, Mother talked nonstop about today, showing Daddy all my trophies. She also showed him that she had paid all the bills with the money he had sent home, plus she said, "With the competition Nicole just won, it won't be long before Ventura will be calling, and that means there is no further need for a college fund. That money can be used for something else."

"Carla, don't jump the gun."

"Oh, you'll see what I've done."

Daddy sat back on the sofa. "So, things really have changed. I was concerned when I got only two letters from Nicole, but I see you were right. You did keep her busy. I'm so proud of both of you."

He jumped off the sofa. "How about we celebrate? I'm gonna make a special dinner, something I learned to cook while traveling."

In about an hour and a half, he had finished cooking the meal, and we sat down to eat.

"So, Nicole," he said, "I see you've won a lot of competitions."

I looked at Mother, sat up, and put my fork down on my plate. It took me five seconds to lay it down exactly right. I hadn't practiced that like I should have.

"Oh yes, Glen," Mother said, "as I told you before, she's a vision of perfection on stage. She needs a little more work off stage, though."

"Carla, she can answer." He looked at me. "Nicole?"

"Yes, sir?"

"Do you like the competitions?"

"Glen," Mother said, "I've already let you know how she's doing in piano. Besides, she has yet to reach her full potential."

"Carla, I was talking to Nicole."

"Fine," Mother snapped. "Go ahead, Nicole. Answer him."

"Daddy, the competitions are exhilarating. I work exceptionally hard to be ready at any time. Mother has taught me how to prepare, and I will reach my full potential."

"Do you enjoy it?"

"It's not so much about the joy as it is about becoming the best that I can be."

"When did you start calling Carla, 'Mother'?"

"The decision was made because I'm getting older, and how I address Mother is important for those around us."

I'd almost dropped that question. Mother had told me he would ask about why I'd started calling her 'Mother.' I had done pretty good up to that point. At least Mother was smiling.

Daddy sat back in his chair and sighed. "Nicole," he said, "I saw in the news a couple of weeks ago that a line of thunderstorms came through here. Did you listen to the storm?"

"No, sir. I had to prepare for the competitions and an important test."

"But you noticed the storm?"

"Yes, sir."

Daddy kept asking me specific questions, and I could answer all of them just the way she had prepared me, but then Daddy asked a question Mother had missed.

"What's your favorite color?"

I thought for a moment. "Hmm," I said, looking at Mother, "lavender?"

"So, it's changed from powder blue?"

"Huh." I hadn't remembered. It had been a year, and I just hadn't remembered.

"Glen, are you finished? That was a stupid question. Maybe her favorite color has changed?"

"But," he said to Mother, "I thought your favorite color was lavender, or has that changed too?"

"You're not making sense. Are you finished?"

Daddy nodded, and I got up to do the dishes.

"I got them, Nicole," Daddy said.

Mother got up and went upstairs. I went to the sofa to do my homework.

Daddy remained seated at the table in silence as if he were a model posing for a sculpture. I went through my reading assignments, and even after about an hour, he was still there. I thought of going to him and asking him about his trip, but I had so much work to do. Then he got up and started doing the dishes, but it was like he was in another world.

~

With his hands in the hot sudsy water, Glen thought about 'perfection,' the term Carla had used most of the night. The fact was, yes, Nicole had learned etiquette. That was obvious by the way she raised her fork, the way she sat, and the way she held her head. She had even turned into a conversationalist, aware of current events. Almost on cue, she knew when to speak and when to listen. She even knew when to laugh. Yes, she'd developed a vocabulary far beyond her age. Her articulation was superb. But even with all the external show, he could see that emotionally she was almost gone—almost. It seemed to him that only he saw the emptiness in her smile.

"Nicole, could you please come here?" he asked, not even knowing why he called her.

She stopped three paces away from him as if there was an invisible barrier between them. He reached his hand out. "Nicole, you can come closer."

She moved within a foot of him. He wanted to see for himself the condition of his house through his daughter's eyes. The longer he searched, the more his heart ached. All he saw was emptiness. Deadness. Finally, he admitted to himself that his financial venture was the worst mistake he had made in his life.

"You can go back to the sofa now."

After a few seconds, Glen marched upstairs, slamming the bedroom door behind him. Carla lay in bed, watching TV.

"Carla, what went on while I was gone?"

"What do you mean?" she said calmly.

"Nicole. She's not the same. In fact, she's worse."

"Glen, you're going to have to explain that one to me. What do you mean?"

"What do I mean? You can't see that she's different?"

"Don't even start. You're not making any sense at all. You've been gone for a full year, and all of a sudden, you think you're going to cook one dinner and then walk up in here and expect everything to just change back."

She sat up in bed and turned the TV off.

"Well," Carla said, "let me make sure we're on the same page before we take another step. I commend you for your hard work and wise investments that cleared up our debt. I thank you for getting the loan to start my business and especially all the other financial support you have given, but let me make sure we understand each other."

She got up, walked over, and stared directly into his eyes.

"I…was the one who pushed for the financial freedom of this household. I know you are the man of this house who worked to provide for his family but don't think you run anything inside this house anymore. I…purchase everything that crosses this threshold, from toothpaste to paper towels. I have already gotten rid of your toothbrush and toothpaste. We don't use those brands in this house.

"Yes, while you were gone, I pushed my daughter to a level of excellence in school and at the piano that no one thought possible, but I…did it. Because of me, Nicole is highly successful, and I am not finished yet. So, if you think for one moment, you'll come here and tell me how to be her mother after I sacrificed my body giving birth, you're sadly mistaken."

"Hold up, Carla."

"No, Glen. No. If you don't like the rules, you can leave anytime, but not with my daughter. See, while you were away, I discovered I was way stronger than I knew. Just do what you're supposed to do. Go out and get a job. You take care of everything outside the house, and I'll take care of everything inside like I've been doing for the past year while you were away."

She stepped within inches of his face. "Now, Glen…you read my eyes and tell me what you see."

The woman standing in front of him was a total stranger. Her eyes, once beautiful, were now cold and callous. All the things he'd feared were coming true, and still, he found himself hoping and praying something would turn around.

Carla returned to her side of the bed and turned the TV back on. He left, went downstairs to the kitchen, and stood staring out the bay windows. Before his thoughts could wander further, the telephone rang in the kitchen.

I heard the telephone ring again, but Daddy didn't move from the bay windows. I knew he would need some time to adjust, but I knew that since he would have a lot of time home, he would be able to change some things around the house.

After the fifth ring, I put my science book down and rushed to the phone.

"Hello?"

"Hi, Nicole. This is Vernon Abrams from your father's old job. How have you been?"

"I've been fine. And you?"

"Oh, doing well…How old are you now?"

"Twelve."

"Wow, time is sure flying. Has your father made it back yet?"

"He just got back today."

"May I speak to him?"

"Hold on."

I gave the receiver to Daddy, who definitely wasn't himself.

"Who is it?"

"Mr. Abrams."

It was obvious to me that Daddy didn't want to take any calls at this moment. Mr. Abrams had been Daddy's old boss before he'd gone overseas. The only time he called was for business, never just to see how Daddy was doing.

Daddy placed the receiver to his ear while I stood for a moment and listened to his responses to Mr. Abrams.

"Hello…Yes, adjusting…I'm glad I could help your company throughout the year…Yes, I'm listening."

I went back to studying. I would have stayed in, but I was getting tired, and my teacher told us we might be having a pop quiz. After this week, Daddy and I could start going for walks, part of a promise he'd made before he'd left.

"Hold on for a moment."

I heard him lay the telephone down, and then he came into the living room and watched me. I had a fortress of science, math, and English books, stacks of papers, two dictionaries, and a thesaurus between us. I knew he wanted to talk, so I was trying to hurry to cover the material. I didn't even have time to look up long.

I knew we were supposed to have time together, but I also knew what that call was about. I wasn't worried, though. I was going to be his priority.

He turned away and went back into the kitchen. I thought for a moment, then put my books down and rushed in after him. I could at least meet him half-way and make him my priority, too.

"What are we talking about?" he asked into the receiver. He sighed.

"Daddy?"

"Then double the salary I had this past year…Done?…But you haven't heard what I made…Am I hearing this right? You're willing to give me a signing bonus too?…No, I don't mind the traveling anymore. Yes…When do you need me to start?"

Our eyes met, but I knew what had just happened. I knew I wouldn't see him much anymore. He was supposed to spend time with me, but I knew the term for him—workaholic. I turned away just as I heard him say into the receiver, "Tomorrow is fine."

I was back behind the fortress, knowing I had to focus. I now had more time to study. I heard him hang the phone up and go outside to the back patio.

I remembered when Daddy and I used to sit out on the patio late at night. Most nights, the skies had been clear, and the only thing we'd heard were leaves rustling in the trees and the occasional car that passed by.

Several hours had passed, and I had one more subject to cover. I heard the back door and then his footsteps. He seemed surprised that I was still studying.

"Nicole," he said, "how much more work do you have to do?"

"Maybe another hour?"

"Go ahead and put your books away and go to bed."

"But Daddy, I may have a pop quiz." He didn't understand I couldn't miss any more questions. I'd heard the way Mother had spoken to him upstairs. What was he going to do?

"You're very smart. I'm sure you'll do well if you have a quiz."

I laid my book on my lap and shook my head. "Daddy, I can't miss any more questions. I just can't."

I prayed he understood. Changes in this house wouldn't happen overnight.

He stood looking at me for a minute; I stared back, my eyes pleading with him to let me stay up. I didn't want to hear any more arguments.

He exhaled, and I was instantly relieved he would let it go. He came over, kissed me on my cheek, and said, "Please don't stay up much longer. Okay?"

"Okay, Daddy."

I watched him go upstairs and heard the bedroom door close softly.

~

Glen quietly slid into bed and then turned the bedside table lamp on. Carla slept with an innocent smile. He looked at her hands resting on top of the blanket.

He gently took her hand and placed it in his. She pulled it away and rolled over in bed. The only thing he had lived for was his family, and now it was slipping away. He just didn't want to admit it was already gone.

CHAPTER THIRTY-FOUR

March 28, 1980 (Friday)

Glen's stomach burned each day he came to work, with Friday being the worst. He remembered another meeting scheduled for Friday afternoon and then another on Saturday. He reached into his pocket and pulled out his wallet. Inside was his small note to himself.

"All of this will be worth it when you return home and look into Nicole's eyes."

It was a note he'd written to himself while on the plane. When they taxied and took off, he could still see Nicole staring out the airport window. What he now saw on his desk was all the stuff he'd put before her. He read the note again.

He had promised Nicole that he would make her a priority when he returned from his overseas job. He didn't need the job or the money. He hadn't expected the boss to pay double the salary he'd had over the past year plus the bonus, but up until then, he knew he'd gone along with things like a lazy river, but now he was determined to fulfill his promise to Nicole.

He left work early and canceled his afternoon meetings. He wasn't afraid to get fired. Depending on his plans with Nicole, he would most likely quit his job and find something else to do.

Glen made it home to an empty house and decided to check the place out. The house was cleaner than the day they'd first moved in. He ventured into Nicole's room, which was more like Nicole's lavender-colored showroom. He opened her closet to find expensive school uniforms and old flowered dresses neatly hanging, evenly spread apart. Her shoes were all evenly spaced. Her closet could have passed any military inspection.

Nothing resembled the Nicole he'd left a year ago. As he scanned the room, he saw no pictures of her friends or anything like it used to be. He went to check the calendar. It was filled with weddings, competitions, and recitals through the end of the year. He found the old calendar and saw his make-up pizza party crossed out. He didn't find the girls-only weekend that Carla and Nicole had planned.

The stroll around the house revealed a cold detachment to him. They all seemed to be so busy doing things from day to day, but no one was living. He actually smiled to himself at the thought of creating a weekend with Nicole like the one she was supposed to have had with her mother.

Glen called his job and told them he wouldn't be available for the Saturday meeting or any travel next week. The job didn't give him any flack, although he had hoped they would.

Glen went to the back patio. His mind ran with possibilities of things to do. He knew his taste in clothes couldn't compare to Carla's. He knew nothing about pedicures, manicures, or facials, but he was ready to find out. Whatever Nicole needed, he would make sure he gave everything to learn.

He heard the front door. Just as he entered the house, he heard Carla and Nicole go upstairs. He went to Nicole's room and knocked on the door.

"Nicole, may I come in?"

I was taking my dress off and measuring the distance it had to be from other clothes in the closet.

"Hold on, Daddy," I said, wondering what he was doing home. Since he'd been back, he wasn't home until late at night, and I hardly saw him anymore. It seemed the more money a person made, the less they saw their family. I scanned my room and had to straighten my shoes in the closet. I took one last look around just in case Mother came in.

"Okay, Daddy, you can come in."

He opened the door slowly and stepped in almost apologetically. I was wearing one of my flowered work dresses I had gotten used to, and he just stood there. From his expression and his tired eyes, I knew he was trying to find words.

"Daddy, what are you doing home?"

He smiled, almost embarrassed. "I wanted to see you."

"How was your day?"

"It was okay. How was yours?"

"It was fine."

Although it was all just small talk, I found that I was smiling too. He walked over to the piano and started playing something. It was unlike anything I'd heard over the past year. For me, it was just classical, no more improvisation. Then he stopped playing, but I didn't go over and sit down. I didn't try to think of any chords. I didn't think he understood how things were now.

He nodded his head, which used to mean he was acknowledging reality.

"You know," he said, looking into my eyes, "I umm…I was wrong, Nicole."

I said nothing. I just wanted to listen.

He nodded his head again. "You know…taking this job. It backfired on me." He stood up from the bench. "I promised you, and I just needed more time, but I should have told my boss no. I should have been more straightforward. I was surprised when he doubled my salary without hesitation. He even gave me a signing bonus. I could have asked for the raise before I left. I never figured he would give me that much of a raise."

"But Daddy, you would have still been traveling."

"I know, but I don't think things would be like they are in the house right now."

His words weighed heavy on my heart. We didn't have a home anymore, and I just couldn't come up with words. I plopped down on my bed.

"Nicole," Daddy said, "Uniforms? We never had you wear uniforms. And even these flowered dresses, almost like a garage sale from Woodstock. I don't want to hurt your feelings, but I got to ask; do you even like your clothes?"

I rubbed the fabric I had gotten used to. It had taken me a long time to get the old musky smell out. Daddy didn't know that it wasn't whether I liked the dresses; it was just my life. I wasn't going to lie to Daddy, not today, so I said nothing.

He nodded his head again.

He sat on the bed next to me. "Nicole…did you and your mother ever go on the girls-only weekend, or did you ever have the pizza and pajama party?"

I shook my head.

"Let me fill in."

I turned to him. "What are you talking about?"

"Tomorrow morning," he said. "I want to do whatever you want to do. I canceled my meetings, and I will be off next week. I want to make you a priority. I don't care about my job. All I care about is you. So, what do you say we start out and go clothes shopping?"

I could already see where this was going. I saw his heart, but he just didn't understand.

"Nicole, would you like that?"

"That's okay, Daddy. My clothes are fine."

"What about the hair salon?"

"No, Daddy. Everything is fine."

I had to admit that just watching him try made me smile. That would have to be enough.

He sighed. "Nicole, I just want to spend some time with you, that's all. I know how much you wanted to go on that weekend with your mother. I would love to try. We can get a room in Atlanta. We can go to Six Flags. We can even go to a movie or to a park. Nicole, this is your weekend. I just want you to at least try to ask me whatever you want. I mean, if you don't mind."

I shook my head.

"Nicole," he said, "I'm sure I'm nothing compared to your mother. I mean I…I just want to find out what you like again. We don't have to shop or anything like that, but I want to do whatever you want. It's just that I remember the girl I sacrificed everything for, and although I made a mistake, I just want to make it right. I just ask that you give me a chance. What do you think about that?"

I watched his pleading eyes.

"My tastes have changed some."

"As long as it's you."

"Daddy…what about Mother?"

"This is our day. I don't have to spend a dime. If you don't want to buy clothes, I'm good with that. I just want time. Better yet, it's our weekend to do whatever you want, and you can ask me anything, just like you were going to ask your mother. I'll do my best to answer. But if I don't know, I can find out. I'm in no hurry at all. If this weekend turns out well, I can leave this job. This is just where we are, and that's enough for me."

I hugged him and squeezed him as tightly as I could. Things were going to be different around here.

"Tomorrow morning," he said, "I will cook an exquisite breakfast before we leave. Something I learned overseas."

Later that night, I heard Daddy tell Mother about our plans, and Mother said nothing. Daddy sat in his favorite chair on the back patio, smiling as he stared at the sky.

CHAPTER THIRTY-FIVE

March 29, 1980 (Saturday)

It had been a long time since I had been excited about anything. I didn't even have any nightmares about Charles or playing the piano. Nothing. I got up early and put on one of my school uniforms. I realized I didn't have anything casual to wear besides those flowered dresses. They were only for inside and yard-work, definitely not for outside. I went downstairs to see Daddy in the kitchen, already cooking breakfast.

He was such a messy cook. There was batter on the countertop from the waffles and eggs dripping from the bowl for the scrambled eggs. I even saw the grease from the bacon. I wished I had a camera. Our house actually looked like a home.

I went upstairs and changed into my flowered dress because I knew I would have to do some cleaning. When I got back downstairs, he said, "Nicole, why did you change? You looked so professional."

"Daddy, I love you, but you know that stove is a mess."

He giggled as he glanced back. "Yeah, you're right, but this is nothing compared to some of the big breakfasts we had in Germany. I tell you, I sure learned how to cook over there, or as I look at this kitchen, maybe we were just hungry."

From the looks of things, I thought they'd probably been hungry.

"Just sit down," he said. "We need a good breakfast. I learned to make eggs Benedict while I was away. Just try them."

I stared at what he'd made.

Daddy looked at the concoction again.

"Well," he said, "I probably need to practice a little more."

I picked up a fork and took a bite. "Hmmm. This is actually good."

Daddy took a fork and tried it. "Wow, it sure is." He patted himself on the back. "I told you I knew how to cook."

As we ate, I listened to Daddy tell stories of what it was like being overseas, like driving in England on the left side of the road.

"I tell you, Nicole, you gotta pay attention to which side you are on, but on the M1 and the A1, I was flying, but it's nothing like driving on the Autobahn, though."

He talked about getting in the passing lane once, and when he looked up again, a Ferrari was flashing its lights, which meant get out of the way.

"We think we drive fast in America," he said, laughing. "Oh, and Nicole, I want us to take a trip to the island of Crete in Greece. I mean, Nicole, the water is so clear, and the weather, oh, so beautiful. I also spent time there during the rainy season. The rain poured. I just opened my bungalow doors that let out on the Mediterranean Sea. Oh, it was so peaceful."

He showed me pictures that were like postcards.

"Oh, you'll love it when we go there."

"Are you sure you were working?" I asked.

"Of course. Most times, I just took the long way to work. I made sure every day mattered."

The breakfast lasted an hour, and I admitted I was looking forward to Atlanta. We cleaned up and got the kitchen back to an immaculate condition so that Mother wouldn't complain. Just before we walked out to change for Atlanta, he put his arm around me, and we looked at the kitchen.

"See Nicole," he said, "this is how life is. Sometimes, in our messes, these are the most precious times. All the messes in our lives can be cleaned up, and the experience through it all makes life so much sweeter. This is probably the best breakfast I ever had."

I didn't think I would ever look at the kitchen or breakfast the same.

We both got ready to go. I got back in my school uniform and considered what to pack. Daddy came to my bedroom door. I kept looking around and didn't want to carry my other school uniforms.

"Daddy, do you mind if we go by the Valdosta Mall?"

"Where else?"

"Atlanta?"

"Sure, you don't even have to pack. We'll buy some things at the mall, and we'll be on our way."

On the way downstairs, my smile went away on seeing Mother standing at the door for the first time this morning.

"Carla," Daddy said, not noticing Mother's eyes, "Nicole and I are going to the mall, and then we're going to Atlanta to stay overnight."

"Really?"

"I told you last night. Remember?"

I didn't want to say she had an evil grin, but the only other term that came to mind was a sinister grin.

"Carla, I just want to spend time with Nicole, that's all. That shouldn't be a problem."

"But there is," she said with an eerie voice. "I determine what Nicole wears, not you, and definitely not her."

"I'm not here to change her wardrobe. This weekend is to spend time with her."

"No, I think you're mistaken. Nothing's changing in this house."

"You know I'm not arguing with you," Daddy said. "Come on, Nicole." He reached for the doorknob, and Mother slapped his hand away.

"How far are you willing to go?" she asked.

"Carla, please move."

He reached for the door again. Mother slapped his hand harder.

"Mother, don't," I whispered. "Please."

"Carla, don't hit me again."

"Or what?" Suddenly Carla shoved him. "You remember your vow?"

Daddy breathed harder. He stared at the scar in the palm of his hand, the reminder of his vow with Uncle Terrance to never beat a woman or be anything like their father even if they had to die.

I couldn't believe it. Did Mother want Daddy to die?

She shoved Daddy again.

Daddy sprang forward, picked Mother up, and pinned her against the door.

"What are you going to do," she asked, "beat me in front of your own daughter? Then what? Turn into your Daddy?"

"No!" The word just burst out of me. Daddy turned toward me. My hands were over my ears. "No, Daddy. No!"

He released Mother and then reached for me.

"Nicole," he said softly, "we don't have to stay here. We can leave right now. Just you and me."

I backed away, knowing Mother would rather die than lose. "I don't want to go anymore. It's okay. It's okay, Daddy."

Daddy turned toward Mother, tapping his fist against his leg. She still had that sinister grin, and I knew she would gladly take this beating.

Daddy looked like Uncle Terrance just before he'd beaten that bear of a man.

I walked over to Daddy, took his fist, and pulled his fingers loose.

"My Daddy is a kind man, and he won't ever hit a woman…no matter what. Daddy, I'm fine. I'm fine with what I wear. It was my fault. I'm responsible for all my actions. I knew better than to want something different."

"Don't say that," Daddy said.

"Really, Daddy. I'm fine. Thank you for breakfast. I will always remember it."

Daddy groaned and walked toward the kitchen.

The telephone rang. The sound must have been strumming his last nerve to see Daddy's reaction. I rushed to answer the phone to stop the sound.

Mother grabbed my arm. "You stand right here."

Another ring.

Mother came into the kitchen. "Aren't you going to get that? Probably your job."

Another ring.

She stood with folded arms.

Another ring

"Glen!"

He snatched the phone, ripped the cord out of the wall, and threw it against the pantry door. The phone shattered into pieces, landing everywhere on the kitchen floor.

He walked past Mother, then me, to the front door.

As he walked out, Mother said, "Don't forget to buy a new phone."

He yanked the front door open and almost slammed it behind him. Then our eyes met. I just stared back. He shook his head and softly closed the door.

CHAPTER THIRTY-SIX

March 29, 1980 – March 26, 1981

Glen stood staring at the closed door. Nicole had the same eyes his mother had the day Terrance left home for good—eyes filled with fear and worry. He even saw Carla's grin as she stood behind Nicole.

He got into his car and drove around town. He knew he still loved Carla; maybe he was even blinded by his love for her, just like he was blinded by his love and duty for his mother. At fourteen, Glen had known he was tired of fighting his own father. He'd known he was tired of the cycle of the empty remorse of his drunken father each time he'd beaten their mother and the certainty that his mother would never leave his father, no matter how bad it had gotten.

Eventually, Glen drove out toward the edge of town, still hoping for something different for his family this time around. Nicole's eyes of fear and worry burned in his mind.

He turned up a winding hill and drove under a canopy of trees to a plateau called Bluffington's Point, the hidden view that peered over the city of Darlington, where, in the morning dew, a person could get rid of all his thoughts. As he parked, he rubbed the scar in the palm of his hand.

Glen knew killing or fighting was not the answer because, when he was nineteen, he'd beaten his father senseless. He'd been ready to kill him and free his mother, but she stopped him. At that point, he knew she would never leave, so Glen was forced to leave, knowing he would kill his father one day. That was the same reason Terrance left at fourteen. In his case, Terrance pointed a .357 magnum at their father's head, and it was only a remembered Bible verse that stopped him.

Glen remembered the first hug he and Terrance had given each other that day, the day of the vow, the day Terrance had left home for good. Afterward, Glen hoped for the best for himself, his mother, and his father, but all the fighting only prolonged the agony of the inevitable—standing at the gravesite of a wasted life.

Glen wondered if he could really change things around his own house with Carla. He'd pray to find another way to co-exist with Carla and possibly avert his family from turning into everything he'd seen growing up. Glen knew there had to be another way. He remembered the vow and the words, "even if it costs him his life." It was then that Glen knew the answer. There were many ways to give your life for your family. He just had to endure until things got better.

I changed into my flowered dress and practiced piano for about two hours, but there was still no sign of Daddy. I went to the kitchen, got the broom and the dustpan, and swept up the pieces of the phone.

"Let him clean up his own mess," Mother said from behind me.

I went back upstairs and waited for him.

Daddy returned to the house by noon. He was different. He had a placid expression pasted on his face. He cleaned up the shattered pieces of the phone and installed the new one. Mother came in. "You missed a spot."

"Yes, dear."

After that blowup, Daddy never argued or fought. He didn't count anymore when trying to stay calm because, when he reached zero, he knew he would do what she said. I imagined he stopped wasting his breath.

No matter what Mother said or did to him, he only answered, "Yes dear" or "No dear." At that point, Mother started talking about sending me to Brighton School for Girls. Daddy didn't say anything. Even when Grandmother started coming around more often, he kept the same placid expression.

Daddy went back to work and poured himself into his job. Daddy and I also grew further apart. We didn't talk much, but I guess it was for the best. Mother continued to become stronger. She was even invited to the mayor's house to just sit and have tea. After a while, the days and nights all became the same. School was the same. I was the same, and Daddy was the same.

I remembered Daddy's fear of time passing by. I understood now because a year had gone by, and I was fourteen. He made no plans for me and deferred everything to Mother. He actually asked permission to buy a cake, but she said no, and he complied. On my fourteenth birthday, I spent time onstage at the mayor's black-tie event.

Mother actually had a seat at the table of honor. Daddy was away on a business trip. For once, I was sure he was happy not to pretend and smile, but honestly, I didn't think he was pretending anymore. He just existed. After the black-tie event, Mother dropped me off at the house to spend the rest of my birthday home alone.

Daddy returned from a business trip two days after my fourteenth birthday. I heard the dishes in the kitchen and then heard Mother telling him to make sure he didn't leave a mess like he had three weeks ago. I rushed downstairs.

"Yes, dear" was all he said while sliding the cup of water and saucer with a half-eaten slice of toast to the middle of the table, and then he headed outside, leaving his Bible and notes on the table. Mother went upstairs to their room. When I heard her door close, I skimmed his notes and discovered he had written a prayer about wanting to be a better father and a better man and, more than anything, to have a whole family. That was also when I really paid attention to how much weight he had lost since he'd returned a year ago. I decided to make sure that he ate and that I cleaned up for him to Mother's specifications.

I warmed him some food and took it outside, to his surprise. I watched him eat. He gave me a heartfelt thank you and went to do the dishes, but I told him I would take care of them.

He fell asleep on the couch in less than two minutes. I covered him with a blanket and finished the kitchen.

The only thing out of the ordinary was the upcoming eighth-grade dance at school.

CHAPTER THIRTY-SEVEN

March 27 – April 10, 1981

The eighth-grade dance was an event at Darlington Junior High where all eighth-graders dressed up and went to a dance in the gym during school. I planned to sit in my homeroom the entire day and read Gone with the Wind.

All of that changed when a new transfer from California, Kevin Taylor, asked me for the last dance and to attend the Students vs. Faculty Basketball Game in front of the school. When I realized he wasn't joking, I knew I had to ask permission. I asked my mother, and surprisingly, she said yes.

I told him, yes, but later, I saw him talking with Nadia, and I realized it was only a matter of time before he made an excuse to get out of it. Nadia was probably the most beautiful girl in the school, and she'd started developing before all of us. I was also sure Nadia explained to him that I was a pariah and that he shouldn't risk his reputation.

I was ready to stay away from the dance, which was in April, but I decided to at least go to the game because I'd promised him. I would tell him it was okay to change his mind about the dance later. There were so many other girls in this school, and I knew that it would be better for him, anyway.

It was fun watching the basketball game in front of the school. Kevin was really good. He made the science teacher, Mr. Ulrich, fall. He even dunked the ball when another teacher jumped up. The ball bounced off the teacher's head. I tried not to laugh, but when the teacher laughed, I gave in.

Kevin smiled a lot and trotted effortlessly. It was like he truly loved basketball and running. I was so impressed with how well he played, but I wasn't the only one. He was getting attention from most of the other girls. I didn't know if it was his Michael Jackson Afro, his smile, or even his body, but there was something about him.

By halftime, he had twenty-seven points. I had counted. I figured I could wait until later to tell him about the dance. At halftime, I got up to leave. As the students' team headed into the locker room, I heard someone call my name.

"Nicole!"

I turned around to see Kevin coming my way.

"Nicole!" echoed throughout the gym again.

Everyone got quiet as if they were witnessing a stage play.

"Hey," he said, "where are you going?"

I looked around at everyone looking at me.

"You have enough fans."

"Don't forget about our last dance."

He just stood there waiting for an answer like it was just me and him in the gym. No one said anything. I actually went on the court.

"Kevin," I whispered, "There are so many better choices. It's best you choose someone else. Maybe even Nadia?"

"No. I like you."

"You're still serious about that?"

Nadia, my former friend, and everyone else were engrossed in our conversation.

"Taylor!" the coach yelled. "Come on!"

"I'm not leaving until you say yes," he said.

"Taylor!"

"Okay," I said, "yes. Now, go."

"Pinky swear?"

I laughed and did a pinky swear. He ran off with the coach still yelling at him, but before he turned into the locker room, he looked back at me and smiled. I felt special.

~

During lunch, I headed to the edge of campus and smiled when I saw Desiree waiting for me.

"What was all that about at the game with you and the new guy?"

"Kevin? He asked me for the last dance on eighth-grade day."

"What about your mother?"

"She said yes."

"Really? Did you drug her?"

I knew she was joking, but I had a problem. I'd never learned how to dance. I mean, I'd danced with my daddy when I was way younger. I'd stood on his feet, but I was sure Kevin didn't want me standing on his.

"Do you know how to dance?" I asked.

"No, but if it means that much to you, I know…I know someone who does." Desiree closed her eyes and shook her head. "How important is this dance to you?"

"Now," I said, "look at me. Do you think there is anything else worthwhile in my life?"

She actually grimaced. "Now you're going to owe me. I'll ask Jeremy. I can ask him to show me, and then I can show you. Ugh."

She never talked much about her brother, but I'd heard girls and women talk about him. They all seemed to be enamored with him. He was handsome.

"Nicole," she said, "you owe me. You know I love you to do that but let me tell you something about my brother. I love him, but he's a straight-up dog. Never trust Jeremy. He's devious. You know, like that serpent in the Garden of Eden. I swear they were related."

"He can't be that bad, can he?"

"Let's just say I'm thankful he's my brother because, even if I were his third cousin, I would have to watch it."

"When I went over when you were sick, he didn't bother me."

"I told him to leave you alone. Keep his hands off you. So…you owe me big.

~

She was an excellent teacher, and she made me feel comfortable.

"Most likely," she said, "the last song will be slow, so all you have to do is place your left arm around his waist and your right hand in his left and follow him like this."

To get the picture, I imagined how it would feel to be in his arms and hear his heartbeat.

"You're a fast learner, Nicole. Just enjoy the dance. He already likes you, and that alone is the biggest part."

A few weeks later, I anxiously waited at the gym for my one dance. I really felt stupid, but Kevin had reminded me of his promise. During the dance, the gym had banners and balloons hanging from the ceiling. The dance was actually filled with eighth-graders who could dance and some who seemed like they were dancing to a different beat of music. I sat off in the corner, in a chair, watching the dance and remembering what Desiree had taught me. I watched others feeling out of place, but I liked my world. I even liked the music, especially the song "'Cause I Love You." I almost cried as I listened to the words.

At the dance, Kevin escorted Nadia in. I wasn't surprised. I believed he had changed his mind for real, but I was determined to at least keep my promise, so I waited, not really expecting him to follow through.

When the last song was introduced, Kevin got up and walked toward me. I couldn't believe it; he was actually going to keep his promise. It was then that I saw Nadia head toward Kevin, and I decided that the thought of the last dance was good enough.

I shook my head, and he nodded his head and mouthed, "You promised."

I got up, trying to remember what Desiree had taught me, stepped on the floor, and headed toward him. Nadia stopped him, and they had a quick exchange that grew so heated that a teacher came over. They both nodded to the teacher, and Nadia stole my last dance.

He mouthed to me, "I'm sorry."

I went and sat back down and watched Kevin and Nadia.

Desiree stopped her dance, came over to me, and said, "Nadia had sex with Kevin to get him to be her boyfriend. You know her by now. She will do anything to get what she wants."

I watched Nadia's head on Kevin's shoulder and his arms around her waist, imagining how it would have felt to be in her place.

I caught a tear and rushed to the bathroom, but I couldn't stop the tears. My heart ached, and then I saw myself in the mirror. I actually saw what Mother saw.

I slammed the mirror with my hand.

"Stop that crying!"

I put water on my face until I felt the tears subside. I thought I could finally leave with my head up, but that was short-lived as I heard the last note of the last song when I passed the gym.

While waiting for Mother outside, I decided to submit wholeheartedly to Mother without any reservations. I wiped the fresh tears away. It made it impossible to do all I now knew I had to do. I finally understood the Antoine de Saint-Exupéry quote. "Perfection is achieved, not when there is nothing more to add, but when there is nothing left to take away."

The only thing I was determined to do for myself was to study for the SAT and take it by my sophomore year because Ventura College had a low acceptance rate.

CHAPTER THIRTY-EIGHT

April 10 – 18, 1981 (Friday – Saturday)

I was pleasantly surprised by how a simple change of pursuit affected my actions. I sat up straight and stayed conscious of the small things: seat posture, hand placement, head tilt, and much more. Even with the random questions Mother asked, I listened with the intent of supplying the perfect words.

When we got home from the dance, the phone rang. Daddy answered it.

"Calm down, Gwen. What's wrong?"

He listened quietly for about a minute and then said, "I'll be right there... The Sanctuary off of 84? I know where it is." Then he hung up.

"So, you're running again?" Mother asked. "When is this going to stop?"

"I've got to go check on Terrance. He keeps saying there's no other way."

"Let me guess, he hit her again?"

"It's more to the story."

"Call the police," Mother said. "That's what you do for a wife beater."

"I've got to go. If I can talk with him, we can get this worked out."

"So, he's that volatile. Then you definitely need to talk to me right now. I need you here."

"No, you don't."

"What do you mean I don't?"

The argument went on between Mother and Daddy for ten minutes. Daddy knew Uncle Terrance didn't need to talk to the police right then. He wasn't in the right frame of mind. Daddy eventually picked up his keys and rushed out of the house, leaving Mother to argue with herself.

~

Glen sped along I-75 and turned on Highway 84. The Sanctuary was a club deep in the woods on Highway 84, between Valdosta and Quitman. It was called the Sanctuary because it was a refuge, and no one bothered anyone out there. The owner, Midnight, a dark-skinned, six-foot-five, solid, 320-pound man, made sure it was that way. Even the roughest could go there to relax and think, something Terrance needed to do.

When Glen made a right by the massive oak tree, he was relieved to see Terrance's car in the crowded parking lot. Once in the club, he looked over at the people sitting at the scattered tables throughout the floor and caught the eye of Midnight behind the bar. Midnight gestured with his head for Glen to go to the back of the club, through a double door, to the room where they played poker or any other card games. Glen heard Terrance's voice rise above the crowd.

"Think you all that, sitting there. Think somebody scared of you."

Glen saw a couple of people hurry out through the double door.

As soon as he got to the door at the club's rear, near the exit sign, he saw why the people had moved.

Terrance was sitting at a large card table with six chairs around it. Across from him sat Drummond, who had a serious and sobering expression on his face. The other four chairs were empty, and people moved away from the table. No one messed with Drummond, but Terrance wasn't afraid of anyone.

Glen pushed through as he heard his brother tell Drummond, "You turned out just like your sorry daddy." Glen saw Terrance stare at something in his hand, but before he could say anything, he saw Terrance pull out his gun and point it toward Drummond. Then he saw Drummond move faster than he could follow and heard two shots. Terrance hit the floor.

When Glen finally got to Terrance, he saw that Drummond had shot Terrance twice in the chest.

Terrance was still alive. In his right hand was his .45, and in his left hand was a picture of Gwen and the girls. At that point, Glen realized that Terrance had been talking about himself.

Drummond came over. "Man, why you do that?"

Terrance whispered to Glen, "I'm just like that bastard."

It was then that Drummond's head went back as if remembering. "Damn."

~

Around 2:35 in the morning, I heard Daddy's car door open and close. I got up and went to the kitchen to warm up his dinner. He made it in and closed the door.

"Daddy," I said, "I'm in the kitchen."

His footsteps were slow, way slower than usual. When he came from around the corner, I screamed when I saw all the blood on his shirt and pants.

"Sweetheart," he said calmly, "it's not mine."

Mama rushed downstairs. She took in the sight of Daddy and put her hands on her hips.

"When are you going to let go of that fool?" she said to him, then she looked at me. "See, Nicole, what he won't tell you is that his older twin brother, the one he looks up to, the one he swore wouldn't hit Gwen, beat Gwen in front of the girls just because she was trying to help him get off his sorry behind and get another job. And that's who your father wants to be like."

She pointed at a picture of Uncle Terrance on the wall. "Gwen was only trying to help him. Then he actually divorced her, leaving her to raise her girls by herself."

Daddy picked up the phone book and slowly scanned the yellow pages, ignoring Mother, but she wasn't one to be ignored.

"Look at him. Now your father is neglecting his family because his brother has him running up and down the road to Valdosta on any given whim because of some childhood vow. I can only imagine the hospital bills this time. Maybe he should have moved in with him. I'm sure he would have been happier."

"Carla," Daddy said, "I got to change and go back and help Gwen. I'd like for Nicole to come with me, if you don't mind."

"She can visit him at the hospital on the weekend."

Daddy flipped through the pages.

"What in the world are you looking for? You know the number to the hospital by heart."

Daddy stopped and turned to Mother. "I'm looking for Harrington's Funeral Home."

I saw it was hard for Mother to say she was sorry, but when she uttered the words, Daddy had gotten up and was already turning the corner to head out to the back patio with the phone book.

At the funeral, I found Uncle Terrance had been a really good man, nothing like Mother had said. I even found out what had happened in both fights with Aunt Gwen in front of the girls.

The first time, it had been Aunt Gwen who'd hit him with a lamp when he'd been walking away. She didn't mean to hit him, but when he'd turned in shock and anger and hit her in front of my cousins, it had broken his heart. He'd turned himself into the police that first time. Up until that point, he'd never thought he would hit a woman, let alone in front of his daughters.

He'd divorced Aunt Gwen, telling his daughters a man should never hit a woman but should always walk away.

The second time, when he'd agreed to reconcile with Aunt Gwen, another heated exchange had occurred, and after he'd hit her again, he'd said, "There's no other way."

People in their neighborhood loved him. He'd made the same vow as my daddy and believed the only way to protect his family from himself was to ensure he was dead— "even if it cost him his life."

Even Drummond came to the cemetery, standing off to the rear. Daddy went to talk with him.

Drummond took his shades off.

"Terrance never carried a gun. I should have known he wasn't going to use it from the way he held it. It's just my reaction. All those years over in that damn jungle, I knew how he held his gun when he meant business. I liked Terrance. I just wish he wouldn't have pulled his gun."

He shook his head, put his shades back on, and left.

When Daddy returned home from the funeral, he moved into the spare bedroom.

Mother didn't even ask why.

CHAPTER THIRTY-NINE

April 18, 1981 – March 21, 1983

Over the next twenty-three months, the relationship between Daddy and Mama waned to almost nothing. They managed to replace their verbal communication with notes and lists. Emergencies were placed on the left corner of the kitchen table, marked according to urgency. Grocery lists and shopping lists were posted on the refrigerator. The agenda that kept the house running smoothly was posted on the pantry door, telling essential details of who, what, when, and where. The whys were no longer important. Nothing was discussed anymore. Words were a commodity treated like water during a drought—used only when necessary.

Daddy and Mother were like strangers. I was the only thing they had in common. Daddy finally accepted that his voice counted for nothing, even when it came to me in the house. He had become a silent partner where he existed only to finance all the things Mother needed—or now all the things she wanted. He didn't have to tell me; I could see it in his eyes.

Mother had finally gained the control she desired. Daddy and I didn't go against Mother anymore. She had completely conquered our wills, emotions, and our desires—all lined up with what she believed. She ran the household with precision. Everything was always immaculate and in its place. The shoes throughout the house had their place. The dishes had their place. The videotapes, photo albums, and curtains all had their place. Daddy and I had our places. Nothing would stop Mother from achieving her goal for me, complete perfection.

I consistently won every competition she entered me in, and many colleges had already sent letters offering full scholarships, even though I was just a sophomore in high school. I was now nationally recognized for my excellence in concert piano.

With the success came interviews that were printed in local newspapers and national magazines. According to the stories, my family lived a picture-perfect life. The articles that originally focused on me soon gave way to Mother, crediting her as the catalyst for my excellence and success. The photographs told the whole story: Mother sitting in the center while Daddy and I stood behind.

I had no words to express how Mother felt about the past several months. She loved the admiration the others in the church and community poured on her. She was even on a first-name basis with Mayor Daily and his wife. Mother was invited to speak on how to raise a successful daughter at women's meetings and parenting conferences throughout the surrounding counties. Mother figured Grandmother would be the proudest.

I knew that she had imagined Grandmother reading the articles and telling her friends about her. She imagined receiving Grandmother's expressions of approval. I didn't understand why she needed such things, but I definitely didn't linger on that because it didn't matter what I thought.

The pinnacle of the achievements was soon to come. She scheduled my interview with Ventura College on my sixteenth birthday, the same day Daddy and I were going to celebrate, but I didn't question her decision—another lesson Mother had taught me well.

After that interview, Mother could sit back and enjoy the success of all of her hard work. She told me once, "I knew I was right about your talent, and I'm proud of myself for the resolve to let nothing get in my way."

Daddy also told me, "Make no mistake; there's a consequence to every action we choose."

I understood why Mother wanted perfection. She wanted my future to be secure, and she wanted to win Woman of the Year. She would prove to Grandmother she was something. After her achievement, our house would become a home. Daddy would see Mother differently, and she would also find satisfaction in me. Daddy just hadn't seen it yet.

CHAPTER FORTY

March 21 – 22, 1983 (Monday – Tuesday)

Something happened at Darlington High School, something I had never imagined. A boy started looking my way—and not just any boy, but a senior, Desiree's older brother, Jeremy. When I thought of Jeremy, I thought of Solomon in the Bible, not because of wisdom but because of women. Solomon had 700 wives and 300 concubines. It was almost impossible to imagine one man having that many women, well, until I heard of Jeremy. He had the worst reputation for how he treated girls and also women. There were rumors he actually had girlfriends at Valdosta State College and girls as far away as Atlanta.

I knew his reputation. He'd slept with most of the girls in the school, and I guess I was all that was left. I knew how other girls felt about him, especially Nadia. They all talked bad about him, but they smiled from ear to ear when he sat near them.

Monday after school, several days before my sixteenth birthday, I stood alone outside, waiting for Mother, and he spoke to me.

"Nicole?"

I turned around, and there stood Jeremy. I'd never paid much attention to him before, but with him, that close to me, saying Jeremy was attractive was an understatement.

"Nicole, you have a beautiful smile."

His voice was like a blanket on a cold night. It was then that I realized those were the first kind words I had heard in several years from someone other than Daddy or Desiree. I could hardly believe he was talking to me, but then I also knew who I was talking to. I often wondered how woman number one thousand felt about Solomon. She'd probably been like me.

"What's wrong?" Jeremy asked as he walked closer. "You have nothing to say?"

"I don't need to be talking to you," I said sharply, trying to get him to go away.

"Why not?"

"You know why."

"Oh, Nicole." He touched my hand, and I snatched it back. I knew Jeremy, and I wasn't stupid.

"Let me start over. Hi, my name is Jeremy, and what's yours?"

I closed my eyes and whispered to myself, "These games."

"You're not going to tell me your name?" he said.

"You know my name."

"I understand you're going by what other people say. I understand. See, Nicole, I know what people say about you too, and I think they're wrong."

I turned to him.

"I know it's hard to overcome a reputation," Jeremy said. "Oh yeah, I heard all the things that people say about you. I know you've heard about me. I have women in Atlanta. Show them to me. So, Nicole, I'm willing to ignore what everyone says about you and find out for myself all about you if you are willing to ignore what they say about me. Will you let me do that, find out for myself all about you?"

I was torn. If I said no, then I would be alone, which was okay, but if I said yes, I wouldn't be alone, but I would definitely be a fool.

"Tell you what," he said, "you think about it and tell me tomorrow."

He moved in close, breathed in deeply, and then smiled.

I took a step back. "What was that for?"

He shook his head. "All those girls are stupid. You smell wonderful."

I smiled.

"You have a beautiful smile, too."

I covered my mouth and shook my head.

"Who have you been listening to?" he said. "Wait a minute. You're moving too fast for me. Think about letting me get to know you. I mean, I'm talking about the you that you've always wanted someone to know, and I promise…I won't hurt you."

He slowly reached and touched my hand. I did all I could to let him. His touch did something to me that I couldn't explain. His hand was so gentle.

"You do have a beautiful smile."

I thought I was dreaming. All the girls in school loved Jeremy. Boys wanted to be like him, and girls would do anything to be with him, but now he was right in front of me.

"Thank you," I said, pulling my hand from his and squeezing my books closer to me.

He reached out and touched my chin. I tensed up at first, and once I relaxed, he caressed my cheek.

"You have beautiful, soft skin."

My eyes closed. I breathed in and then slowly opened my eyes. "I need to go." I pivoted to walk away.

He took my hand again. "Nicole…I'll stop only when you want me to. Just turn around, look me in my eyes, and tell me you want me to stop."

This can't be real. Nadia stood off at the edge of campus, looking our way.

"Aren't you afraid?" I asked.

"Of what, words?"

"To be seen with me?"

He kissed the back of my hand. His lips were soft and warm.

"Do you want me to stop?" he asked, gliding his hand over mine.

My eyes darted around, but he guided my face back to his.

"Nicole…do you want me to stop?"

I shook my head.

"Would you like to have a friend…or boyfriend? I can be either one. Think about it and let me know tomorrow. Same time, same place."

He let my hand go and walked away. My hand was cold, and I was not only alone. I was lonely. A new car pulled up to the curb and idled in front of me. Then the window rolled down.

Daddy was smiling.

I rushed over and jumped in.

"Daddy, when did you get this?"

"This afternoon. Hey, I have to leave tonight to go on a last-minute business trip."

"How long will you be gone?"

"Thursday night."

All that meant to me was late Friday or early Saturday morning. He was hardly ever back in time from those trips. I was used to that, but Thursday was my birthday.

I turned away.

"I'll be back Thursday night in time for us to celebrate your birthday. Just you and me."

"Don't say that if you don't mean it."

He raised his right hand. "I vow to you right now I will be home for your birthday."

"Daddy, you know your trips. Don't say anything you don't mean."

"I don't care what's happening; I'll be here."

I looked into his eyes, eyes that wanted me to believe him. I had to admit, this was the first time he had ever vowed to me. I found myself smiling. I exhaled and relaxed in the leather seat of the Cadillac as he pulled away from the curb. I rubbed the wood grain dash and breathed in the new-car smell. For a minute, I played with the power window, shifting the switch, powering it up and down, and then I finally left it down, letting the wind mess up my hair.

I closed my eyes and thought about Jeremy's caress.

The next day after school, Jeremy was actually waiting for me.

"Hi, beautiful."

I shook my head.

"You don't think you're beautiful?"

"No."

"Why?"

"Don't pretend you don't know," I said.

As he took my hand, he said, "Let me tell you what I see. I see a beautiful smile you don't use enough. It's so sweet and innocent, almost like the Mona

Lisa, with so much depth. Your hair, it's obvious you take great care of your hair. And your eyes—I love your eyes, full of desire and hope. Just let me be your mirror for now and capture the vision of what I'm blessed to reflect back to you."

"You're just saying that."

He whispered in my ear, "Just because you can't see gravity doesn't mean it's not real." He breathed in deeply and whispered, "I love the way you smell."

I wanted to believe him, but I looked around and saw people looking our way. He didn't back away or anything. I pulled my hand away.

"Jeremy, this can't be true. I know something's up. As long as I've known you, you've never spoken to me."

"That's because of Desiree."

"I have a feeling this isn't real. Am I some kind of game to you? I mean, look at me."

"Okay, what do you want, Nicole? All these people around here acting like they're all that, and the reason they pick on you is because they are all afraid they could be next. Why should they let you believe in yourself and find you have so much more than them?"

He gently took my hand. "Your hand is beautiful. I'm serious, Nicole. You go home tonight and think for yourself and decide if you want to take a chance with me or not. Decide, and I will respect either decision."

He lightly touched my lips with his fingers and walked away.

CHAPTER FORTY-ONE

March 23, 1983 (Wednesday)

I knew I should have prayed about Jeremy, but for the first time in a long time, I wanted something of my own. I wanted Jeremy. I had to pay attention to all the girls I knew who'd been dogged by Jeremy, but they all had so much passion when they thought of him. They felt so deeply.

I would have kneeled to pray, but why, to have God say no and leave me in oblivion? I thought I had buried my emotions, but they came back strong, awakened by him. As the night wore on, I knelt and prayed anyway.

"God, take away all of my emotions so I can't feel anymore. Make me numb to any pain and sorrow. Make me never hurt again..." The more I prayed, the more I realized God wasn't going to answer that prayer.

Jeremy was right. My dilemma was a simple question with a simple answer. Either give Jeremy a chance or don't. The more I thought of it, I knew he could use me badly and toss me aside like so many others. Many girls had left school because of Jeremy. He could lie to me and break my heart, but I also realized he could really like me. He knew me through Desiree's eyes.

That night and the next day went by in a blur. Homeroom, first, second, and third through sixth periods. I looked up, and school day was over. I grabbed my books and strolled outside, thinking about a simple answer. Jeremy was already waiting for me.

I walked closer, wanting him to hold my hand. He met me and didn't disappoint. Then he whispered in my ear, "Have you decided?"

I shook my head.

"What's wrong?"

"Be honest," I said, staring into his eyes. "Do you really want me the way I am? Just the way I am. And before you answer, please don't lie to me. Just take a good look at me and tell me the truth."

My smile disappeared.

"What happened to you?" he asked.

"You didn't answer my question," I said. "Do you want me just as I am or not?"

He took my books and laid them on the sidewalk, took both my hands, and said, "I want you just as you are. You don't have to change your clothes, your hairstyle, your glasses, or anything you don't want to. I can pull out the best you have and give you an experience you've only dreamed of."

"So confident."

"You would be too if you found what I found. I don't care what these people think. I have found a priceless diamond, and though I admit it's rough, it's way more valuable than all the polished cubic zirconia running around here."

I scanned the campus, and it appeared so many were looking our way. I saw Nadia again, watching us like a movie. She and Kevin were still together, but she couldn't take her eyes off us.

"Why are you so concerned about Nadia?" he asked.

I didn't say anything. I didn't tell him we used to be friends. That was something he already knew. I'm sure he heard a lot from Desiree, anyway.

"Nicole, I want you to believe me. I really want to get to know you, and I want you to give me your all. Do you know what I mean when I say give me your all?"

"No."

"That's the difference between a friend and boyfriend. Desiree is your friend. I can be your boyfriend, physical benefits and all."

He rubbed the back of his hand down my neck.

"I can't."

"I don't believe in the word can't. You either will or won't. Tell me honestly, which is it for you?"

"I won't."

"Thank you," he said as he kissed my hands. "Then we're friends. If you change your mind and want a boyfriend, call me Friday night and let me know. Desiree and my mother will be home."

"I don't even know if I can talk on the phone."

He smiled. "It doesn't matter what time. Just call me, and I'll come by and pick you up."

"Did you even hear me?"

"Of course I did." He took my hand and kissed it. "I promise if I'm your boyfriend, I will make you feel things you never thought possible. It will be well worth your while."

His hand slid away from mine as he walked away.

~

That night, I dreamt of Jeremy and being in his arms. I woke suddenly, panting.

CHAPTER FORTY-TWO

March 24, 1983 (Thursday)

6:32 p.m. I stood in my front yard, anxious for Daddy's return from his business trip. I had to admit that I felt alive. The flowerbed was clean; the yard was mowed, and the shrubs were trimmed just the way Daddy liked it.

My sweet sixteenth birthday was special, mainly because Daddy would be here, and this time, there was much more to be thankful for. I wished Desiree could have been here, too.

If I get accepted into Ventura College—no, when I am accepted—Mother will be happiest, and then we will be a family again. Mother and Daddy will talk to each other, something they hadn't done for some time. To top everything off, I will be sixteen, able to drive, and I'm sure Daddy will buy me a car and let me have my first boyfriend.

I couldn't believe I had already made up my mind about Jeremy. As I stood outside, I took one last look at the yard. In the corner of the flowerbed, three defiant blades of grass stood out. I went over, plucked them, and glanced at my watch. It was time to go into the house to prepare for my eight o'clock interview.

Once I entered the door, the telephone rang.

"Hi, Sweetheart," Daddy said.

"Hi, Daddy! Where are you?"

"I'm sorry, Nicole. I stayed later, but I got a late flight. I'm really sorry."

"Then what time will you be home?"

"Eleven thirty."

"Well, it'll still be my birthday. I'll wait up for you so we can sing 'Happy Birthday.'"

"Oh, Nicole, I couldn't have asked for a better daughter. I love you."

"I love you too. See you tonight."

I rushed to get ready and waited patiently for my interview.

The doorbell rang at 7:57. I headed downstairs.

Mother opened the door to a distinguished older gentleman, briefcase in hand, with a suede trench coat hanging over his arm. The smile on his face was warm but tired.

"Hi, I'm Gary Tomlinson, Ventura College."

"Come on in," Mother said in her new cream-colored outfit. "I don't know if you remember me?"

"Yes, of course, from the competitions."

"No. My maiden name is Robinson. Carla Robinson."

His eyes tightened as he studied her and then softened.

"Yes," he said, "Carla Robinson. Yes, I remember you well. You were extremely diligent. You had more drive than any student I had ever met. I admired that about you."

"I saw Eric Rogers at a few of the competitions."

"Oh, yes, he's Dr. Rogers now. Doing an exceptional job with that classical program at Piedmont High. He really pushed for Miss Pearson's acceptance. Now, back to you. I hated the fact the school didn't accept you. No one ever matched your drive. It made little sense. I fought for you, but the dean said no. No one came close to you as far as work ethic, but I had to admit there were so many talented people back then. Maybe they saw something I didn't see. I'm sorry."

"Don't be. I'm just glad you remembered me. Please, come in," Mother said, taking his trench coat and hanging it on the entryway coat rack.

Mr. Tomlinson peered through his designer frames, skimming the house. He leaned closer to the painting Mother had purchased just for this occasion.

"Beautiful," he said.

"Thank you."

"The delays at the airport were tough," he said. "I thought for sure I would be late, but I am absolutely thrilled to be here." He turned to where I was patiently standing on the steps. "Hi, Nicole."

"Hi, Mr. Tomlinson."

I was dressed in an A-line ivory-colored satin dress with matching shoes. Ms. Eleanor felt I would look better in a mermaid style, but Mother wanted the dress to be subtler. I'd just stood on the platform and let them decide.

"It is nice seeing you again," I said as I stepped forward and reached out my hand to shake his. "Would you like to have a seat?"

"Thank you, yes."

After we all sat down in the living room, he began talking.

"I would like to go ahead and get to the interview if you don't mind. This interview may be a little different from what you may be used to or what you may have heard."

"Yes, sir," I said, sitting with my legs crossed at the ankles and my hands gently lying on my lap, something I had perfected watching Mother.

He pulled a notepad from his briefcase, picked up a gold-colored pen, and glanced over his glasses at his first question.

"What or who would you credit for the passion you display while playing?"

"The music itself. Music has become my lifeblood. When I play, I become connected to the sounds, the touch of the piano, and the textures of the chords. I have studied the history of the pieces that I play, and I immerse myself in the meaning. You may call it passion, but for me, it's inhaling and exhaling all the notes on the pages to tell the composer's story. Although many composers are gone, their remaining stories and written pieces have enabled me to interpret and communicate their hearts to you."

Mr. Tomlinson looked at Mother, slowly nodding. He turned back to me. "This is not one of the questions, but how old are you?"

"I am sixteen as of today."

He sat back in his chair, took his glasses off, and smiled.

"Nicole, I could go on with the questions, but after that first answer, all of this is now a formality. You're amazing. Just amazing. I want you to know each year, we budget for one exceptional student regardless of their grade. The selection must go before a board, and the competition is fierce.

What I'm about to do rarely happens in the history of our school, especially for sophomores. We usually wait until senior year, but as I said, on rare occasions, this happens. And what pushed you over the top is that we received your SAT scores."

"And?" Mother said.

"Perfect score."

I was waiting to surprise Mother, but at least the score had fulfilled its intended purpose.

"Nicole," Mr. Tomlinson said, "we're offering a full scholarship with one hundred percent coverage of all tuition, board, food, books, and materials. All you have to do is come. We have rarely seen a talent as developed as yours. Each performance has been spectacular. I will give all the forms to your mother to fill out. Once the forms are completed and accepted, you will be on your way to Ventura College, after you finish high school, of course. That's it."

I stood with him.

"Mr. Tomlinson," I said, "thank you for the opportunity to sit down with you. Again, it was a pleasure."

"The pleasure has been all mine," he said, shaking my hand. "Have a good night."

On the way upstairs, I overheard him tell Mother, "She is a wonderful young lady and exactly what Ventura College is looking for…Hmm."

I went up to the top of the stairs, around the corner, and listened.

"Thank you," Mother said while slowly handing him his coat. "Please forgive me, but what was the 'hmm' for?"

"I was wrong about everything I thought about her. Absolutely everything."

Mother paused. "Meaning?"

"Over the past few years, I have attended most of her competitions. To hear her play has been breathtaking, to say the least, but I started watching her closely during one performance. It was like she…I don't know. Something was missing. It was almost a void, an emptiness. You see, I was supposed to retire earlier this year; I stayed because I wanted to recruit Nicole myself. She intrigued me. How could someone be that good and not love what she was doing? As you know, there's no way she would survive the rigors of Ventura if she didn't have her own passion for classical music. I wanted to be wrong."

"What do you mean?"

"These interviews are sometimes heartbreaking. The candidates look at their parents, hoping their response is correct. It's unfortunate when the parents want the accolades more than the child, but Nicole is different. She seems…alive. There is something that has changed about her—something different. Seeing her today, I realized I had to open my own eyes. In this case, I am so happy I did. She's such a rare find. There is something about her. You can see it in her eyes. I'm glad an old dog like me opened mine. How could anyone be able to answer the way she answered without passion? All my questions are unique, and I have to accept one simple fact. She's just in another league. Well, Mrs. Peterson, I better go. You have a great night."

I peeped from around the corner.

After Mother closed the front door, she stood for a moment in the hallway, thinking about something. I heard her put in a videotape. In a few seconds, I heard one of my old recitals.

I crept to my room, changed, and started practicing piano.

~

11:16 p.m. After I finished practicing, I went downstairs. Mother had left some of the videos on the floor. I put them back in their places and pulled out leftovers to warm up for Daddy. I set the table with all the dishes, plates, and saucers with teacups, cloth napkins, and the silver cutlery only used on special occasions. I cut the cake, set out the ice cream, and waited.

11:31 p.m. I stood by the door, looking outside and waiting for the car to come. My heart jumped when a Cadillac pulled into the driveway. It was only my neighbor, Mr. Claiborne, turning around.

11:35 p.m. I returned to the kitchen and sat at the table.

11:51 p.m. Looked at the telephone, wanting to hear it ring.

11:59 p.m. I walked to the front door and looked outside.

12:01 a.m. Went in the kitchen, wrapped his plate, and put it in the refrigerator. I poured the melted ice cream down the sink and covered the birthday cake.

12:15 a.m. Knelt and prayed, "God, something must be wrong because Daddy wouldn't break his vow to me, so please get him home safely."

I pulled the telephone book out and started calling.

"Hello, my name is Nicole Peterson, and I was wondering if any accident victims arrived tonight...His name? Glendale Peterson Jr.... Please check?"

I called all the surrounding hospital emergency rooms. There were no accidents. I called the police department, but he hadn't been gone long enough to be considered missing. It was then that I felt peace on the inside and just knew he was okay. But then my heart sank.

"If he's fine, then why did he miss my birthday?"

CHAPTER FORTY-THREE

March 25, 1983 (Friday)

At 2:17 a.m., I heard the front door open and close. Daddy stood at the door for several seconds before his steps came toward the kitchen. When he saw me sitting at the table, he shook his head. He wearily put his briefcase down, took his coat off, and laid it over the back of the chair. He hugged me and kissed me on my forehead.

Without a word, I got up, warmed his dinner plate, and gave him a slice of birthday cake.

"Thanks, Nicole. I'm so sorry I missed your birthday. I can't believe I did that. My flight got canceled."

"Your original flight that was supposed to have you here by 6:30?"

He took a deep breath.

"No," he said, "something came up at the meeting, so I changed flights to leave a little later. I actually paid two thousand dollars for the seat, but that second flight got canceled, and they got me on another flight. I'm really sorry."

"They, the airline?"

"Yes," he said.

He reached into his pocket and handed me a wrapped gift. I neatly removed the silver wrapping paper to reveal a long black velvet box that held a diamond-studded tennis bracelet.

Up until this point, everything had been so automatic. I was supposed to smile, say thank you, and say how glad I was to have him home. I was supposed to sit down and listen to him talk endlessly about his trip. I was supposed to do some other things, but when I attempted a smile, the smile was gone before it formed. I just sat there, numb, wanting to ask what had happened to the vow he'd given me. I wanted to ask why he'd changed flights, but really, he was home. I'd prayed for that. Maybe that was all I should have ever expected from him.

"Daddy, I know you would have been here if you could have, but it's okay. My sixteenth birthday is not that important. The most important thing is that you got home safely."

Daddy sighed.

I knew why. Normally, I excused everything he did, but I guess I was just tired, tired of disappointment. I got up, pushed my chair back under the table, took the gift, and kissed him on his cheek. He was still my father.

"Before you go," he said, "may I ask you something?"

I nodded.

"Do you ever think about leaving and wanting to start over?"

A whimsical smile formed on his cheeks. He could have been talking to himself then.

"When me and your mother first got married," he said, "we didn't have much of anything, but we were so happy. I made $2.85 an hour and worked sixty hours weekly, but I felt like I had everything. Having someone who loves you for who you are is priceless.

"I really miss that. All this money I've made, and look at us now. Money truly can't buy happiness. I'm beyond tired of flying and business trips. I'm tired of missing important dates. I have another trip scheduled the day after tomorrow."

He slumped in his chair.

"You know, Nicole, I remember the first time I held you. I remember your first steps. The first song you played on the piano, 'Mary Had a Little Lamb.' I remember those things so clearly, but now…I don't remember much of the last few years."

He lifted his chin.

"So, Nicole, if you had a chance to leave, would you?"

I knew he was probably exhausted. He would probably feel different after a good night's sleep.

"Nicole?"

"Daddy," I said, "after the mayor's awards ceremony tomorrow, things will be different, and then we will have a fresh start where we are. Daddy, I love you. Have a good night."

I was about to leave, but then I remembered.

"Oh, that's right, I almost forgot. I was offered a scholarship to Ventura College. Mother has the paperwork. At least Mother will finally be happy. Maybe you can start with her."

~

Glen watched his daughter walk out of the kitchen. Her normally perfect posture was slumped. He thought about what was important in his life. He ate a couple of bites of cake, but he soon put his fork down and pushed the plate away. He stared at the cake and then the table and thought back to when he'd been growing up—how he had longed to have a close, loving family. He rolled his left sleeve up, revealing a four-inch scar on his forearm resulting from the family he'd grown up with.

Instinctively, his right hand reached over to stroke the raised skin. He thought about his father, who had thrown him against the fireplace when he was eleven. He remembered how the cut had bled, and Terrance had jumped on Glendale Sr.'s back, choking his neck. Glen jumped back into the fight by throwing a lamp, missing his father's head by inches. The spray of blood on his father's face stopped the fight.

The cut had been worth it because it ended the fight. He remembered the pride he and Terrance felt from going the distance in protecting their mother from their father, Glendale Sr. He remembered his father leaving, but he knew his father would soon be back, continuing the same cycle of empty excuses. Glen believed he was truly becoming his father.

His mother had told Glen and Terrance the same laundry list of recycled excuses. "Your daddy is just having a bad time. He lost another job, plus, you know, football season. It's almost over with. He didn't mean to do what he did. He's a good man, but we've run into some bad times, and we have to stick together to help him find his way. You have to always honor your father."

Terrance refused to accept her words. "No, we don't. He don't deserve honor.

Why do you let him beat you like that? Let's just leave. We can make it without him."

"A boy needs a man around to show him how to be a man."

"I don't want to be a man like that," Terrance had said.

Glen had always admired his brother's ability to see and accept the cold truth. As Glen looked at the cake, he thought of his father's words after his father had returned.

"Glen, Terrance," Glendale Sr. said as he embraced their mother, "one thing you will eventually discover is life happens. Sometimes you become a man you hate and despise. You don't know when it happens, but somehow it does, and you don't know how to change."

Was there a chance to be different from his father? He wanted to find out and start by accepting the cold truth. Glen finished his slice of cake. He cleaned up after himself and went upstairs to see Nicole.

I lay in bed, counting, wondering if there was any purpose in repeating the multiplication tables. I always fell asleep, prolonging the nightmares that seemed to follow. There was also nothing to give my mind a break from my room. My walls were filled with composers and Mother's to-do list. I didn't even want to touch the lamps because, every morning, I had to measure to ensure the lamp was perfectly centered.

"Nicole," Daddy said, "you got a moment?"

I opened my eyes to see Daddy's distraught face.

I sat up in my bed and asked, "what's wrong?"

"I want to apologize for the last…I can't believe it, four years," he said as he lowered himself to the floor. "I broke promise after promise to you. I shouldn't have even taken this job because I was supposed to spend time with you once I got back. I even broke my vow tonight, acting like I was doing something when I made that vow to you. I don't want us to be in this cycle anymore. I don't want to stay this way.

"I always put everyone else in front of you. I guess it was always okay because you forgave me so easily. I was wrong about everything. I just wanted to say I'm sorry. And when I think about it, you've taken care of me. I know I didn't deserve it, but I just wanted to thank you for everything."

I watched him rub his hand over my carpet, his face unreadable in the cast of shadows from the hall lamp.

Smiling down at him, I said, "You know, Daddy, you were up one night, and I saw you in the kitchen. You wrote something on a notepad and then put your pen down. After you left the room, I read what you wrote: 'God, please help me to be a better man and a better father.' That's why I started staying up late, waiting for you."

He cracked a grin and got up to leave.

"Daddy?"

He stopped.

"I know it's stupid, but you got any stories to tell?"

He gasped. "Really?"

I nodded.

"Well, I do have one."

"You don't mind, even with me being sixteen now?"

"I'm just thankful you would ask me to do anything for you after all my broken promises."

He leaned against the wall, and I lay down and peered over the edge of my bed.

"Who are you tonight?" he said.

"Nicole."

"Princess Nicole?"

"No, she's gone. I'm simply Nicole. Could you make a story up—one with a happy ending?"

I still loved hearing Daddy's voice, especially as he began: "Once upon a time, in a place not so far away, lived a beautiful young lady with a forgiving heart…"

I listened to him take me on a journey filled with hope, dreams, and, more importantly, a promise of love. The way he told this story was different from the stories from my childhood, though. At times, he'd stare off as if he was gathering his will to ensure all he said would come true.

~

Glen continued telling their story. As he spoke, Nicole's eyes grew heavy in the shadows. The longer he told her story, the more he longed for his family's fairy tale to come true. Even though he said his words of hope, he wondered if there could be a happy ending for him, too.

When her eyes closed, he allowed his voice to trail off. He watched her sleep for a moment. All the memories of his daughter flooded his mind until his heart was filled. He kissed her cheek and gently walked out of her room, went downstairs, lay down on the couch, and watched the night sky.

He found himself praying, "God, how did I get here? I don't want to lie to Nicole or myself anymore. What am I supposed to do when I don't even trust myself anymore?"

He watched a shadow fly by the window.

"You know what, God? Just do whatever you have to do to make our story come true. Now, I'm willing. I put it all in your hands. I don't care how bad it gets; I just need the next step, then the next. You made a promise to all of us, 'Delight yourself also in the Lord, and He will give you the desires of your heart.' You know what's in there. For now, just tell me the next step."

No more words came, and he soon fell asleep and woke up at 4:47 a.m., knowing what he had to do. He called his boss, resigned over the phone, and before he could battle the next step, words dropped in his heart, "Trust me." He took the step of faith and walked into Carla's bedroom to tell her fully what he had just done.

CHAPTER FORTY-FOUR

March 25, 1983 (Friday)

I woke suddenly to the sound of breaking glass and Mother shouting. It was 4:57 a.m. I rushed out of bed to Mother's room and burst through the door to find her pacing the floor. A broken mirror covered the floor next to Daddy, who was leaning against the wall.

"Glen, how can you be so stupid to quit your job? Quitting without even a two-week notice, just an early morning phone call? This is not like you; irresponsible and leaving the company hanging like that. Just take a vacation. I know you got more than enough time."

"Claude Thomas died a few weeks ago, and all they did was bury him. We signed a card and sent flowers. They've already found a replacement. It's like he was never there."

"So, this is some mid-life crisis?"

"Come on, Carla, let's not pretend anymore. Look at us, sleeping in separate rooms. This is no marriage. Let's just leave town and start fresh. I got Charles and Joyce's point. They should have left. We can leave…now." He stepped away from the wall toward Mother. "I know you loved Atlanta."

Mother shook her head. "No. No. No! Atlanta has nothing to do with this."

"Come on, Carla, let's give it a shot. I was a sorry man before. I failed you and made so many mistakes, but I'm willing to start all over again. You can be a wedding planner in Atlanta. I can help. We can make it a family affair. Anything you want."

"You're delirious," Mother said. "You've lost too much sleep. I am not going to leave and start anywhere else, and Nicole isn't either."

"Carla, this is not you. I know you. You're not this hard, this cold and callous. I take the blame on that. Blame me, but I'm ready to start again. Let's just give it another chance. I know with all my heart that if we leave now, right now, we will be like we were when we first got married. Simple."

Mother sat down. "So, you think demanding success from your child is wrong? You think I want to give up everything I've worked for to just start over? Why are you threatened by my success?"

"I know you did everything you set out to do, but the way you did it was way wrong. You don't realize the price you're going to have to pay. There is nothing in this world for free."

"Yeah, but I'll tell you this much. Right or wrong, I'm not leaving, and Nicole isn't either."

"She's sixteen, and she can choose." He turned to me. "I was serious when we talked earlier. Let's just start over. We can leave right now. I know I messed up, but I see clearly now. You can finally choose, and there is nothing your mother can do."

I thought about Jeremy, my first boyfriend, his touch. He had awakened something I had never felt. I know that's what Mr. Tomlinson had seen when he'd said I was alive. Jeremy was the reason I'd gotten the scholarship.

I shook my head.

Mother came over and put her arm around me.

"Nicole," Daddy said, "you really want to stay?"

I remembered Jeremy's lips on the back of my hand. All I could say was "yes."

Daddy closed his eyes for what seemed like an eternity. His lips moved, and then he slowly nodded his head.

"But Daddy, we're almost there. The award ceremony, after that, everything will be fine."

He opened his eyes and stared at me as if puzzled. Then he pursed his lips together, took a long, deep breath, and nodded his head.

"No, Daddy. We are really almost there."

He nodded his head again and came up to me. "I know you believe that." He kissed me on my forehead, turned, went into his closet, pulled out a travel bag, and packed it. Both Mother and I followed.

"So, just like that," Mother said. "You leave your family again. You're always running. Mother was right about you."

He stopped, stood, and looked at Mother. He almost said something but caught himself. Then he closed his suitcase with what little he had and left.

I listened as Daddy's car gently pulled away. It was different from any other time. This time, it was like he was saying goodbye. Mother even listened.

When the sound disappeared, Mother said, "Go ahead and go back to bed. You have school in a few hours."

While in bed, I wondered, why now? Why the desperation to leave? After all these years, and in just one more day, it would all be okay. Mother would win her award. She would be able to celebrate. They could meet Jeremy, and everything would be just fine.

~

Carla slowly cleaned up the glass in her room, and a passing thought occurred. Is all of this really worth it? She was sure the thought had come from Glen's words, but the thought opened another thought from Glen. You don't realize the price you're going to have to pay.

While she cleaned the shards of glass, another thought hit. Is this really my family?

Carla looked at the multiple reflections in the mirror and tried not to succumb to the thoughts that lingered. She hurriedly put the broken mirror in a brown paper bag, and just as she got a wet hand towel to clean the hardwood floor of the remaining pieces, Glen's words pierced her mind: "You don't realize the price you're going to have to pay."

CHAPTER FORTY-FIVE

March 25, 1983 (Friday)

Gladys sat on the porch in her favorite white rocker. "Carla, you've been a good girl. You've done everything I've trained you to do. Fetch the paper for me?"

"Yes, ma'am."

Carla went to the edge of the yard where all the papers had piled up and brought each paper, one by one, to her mother. Headlines read, "Nicole Peterson Wins Best in Show." Another headline read, "Nicole Peterson Receives Scholarship from Ventura College. Each time Carla dropped a paper off, Gladys patted her on her head and said, "Good girl."

When the last paper lay at Gladys' feet, Carla turned to go home.

"Where are you going?" Gladys asked.

"I'm going home to Glen and Nicole."

"You don't have a family anymore. Every day we go through this. They're gone."

"Where did they go?"

"I don't know, but it's been years. You're here with me. Get me a cup of coffee?"

"But my family?"

"I'm your family now."

~

Carla woke up reaching for Glen. All she felt were the cold sheets on Glen's side of the bed. She knew she should have been used to it by now. He had stopped sleeping in their bed almost a year ago, but she found herself missing him. She glanced at the clock—6:45 a.m. Nicole would already be up and waiting for her.

While she hurried and brushed her teeth, it dawned on her that she and Glen rarely talked anymore. She got dressed, hurried downstairs, and saw Nicole waiting on the sofa with her books perched on her lap. Carla walked into the kitchen and got a cup of water. While she stood and drank, she watched Nicole sit as if she were in a trance.

Carla put her cup down and walked in to see what Nicole was staring at. The only thing she could have been watching was a blank screen on the TV. Carla went back into the kitchen and finished her cup of water; just as another thought hit her.

"Nicole, please come here."

Nicole put her books down, walked quickly over, and stopped three feet away.

"Yes, ma'am," Nicole said plainly.

"Have you eaten?"

"Yes, ma'am."

"Alright, I'll be ready in a moment."

"Yes, ma'am."

Nicole went back to the sofa and sat in the same position, void of emotions, sitting as if she had never moved.

Carla put the glass in the sink and drove Nicole to school. For the first time, Carla paid attention to the early morning ride. Only classical music played, but no talking. Nicole only stared out of the window. Such a quiet ride until they reached the campus to let Nicole out. The door opened.

"Bye, Mother," Nicole said and rushed out of the door before Carla could respond.

Did I ever respond?

Carla stayed parked, watching Nicole walk through the crowd of children as if she were invisible, without one person acknowledging her. Once Nicole disappeared into the school, Carla thought about the recruiter's words.

Had he actually been right about her?

On the way home, she thought about Nicole's performances again. She hadn't paid attention to any of her expressions, really at all, admitting that she had been so accustomed to listening with her eyes closed to better detect errors. She hadn't really listened for her daughter. Another strange thing seemed to happen. Carla was seeing the real Nicole.

She thought about the performance tapes again. She didn't see or understand much from last night's viewing, but she knew there had to be something in those tapes. Carla sped up, hurrying to get home, making it to the driveway, rushing in the house, and heading directly to the performance videotapes that were all neatly titled and organized by dates.

She grabbed Nicole's first recital at four years old and dropped the video box on the floor, taking the tape and sliding it into the player. Almost immediately, Carla laughed when she saw Nicole in her cute pink and white ruffled dress, her hair pulled neatly back into a bun. Her skin tone blended nicely with that dress. Even at that age, Nicole loved girly stuff.

Nicole smiled as she bowed and proceeded to play well beyond her age. Her bounce and laughter became more animated when she hit a bad note, but the imperfections only added to the joy of her performance. When she finished, she stood, took her bow, and waved bye.

Each tape that Carla pulled out revealed Nicole's love of music and captured the vibrancy she exuded. Tape after tape, Carla smiled and laughed at seeing her little girl so full of life. Ages seven, eight, and nine showed her growth in style and grace, and her beautiful grin always brought smiles.

As Nicole grew year after year, her personality shone through in how she walked, dressed, and laughed. Her sweet, bright outlook poured into her piano playing, where she excelled and stood out from all the other pianists. She was in a class of her own.

Then, at nine, Carla remembered hearing the word prodigy several times. At first, she ignored it, but finally, she really listened to Nicole. That's when she decided to enter Nicole into the competitions. Nicole really didn't want to at first, but Carla remembered she'd promised her it would all be fun, something they could share together.

Carla remembered all the promises she had made to Nicole and the look of her trusting eyes, probably agreeing, mainly wanting to spend more time together. The beginning tapes marked the times that Nicole picked her own clothes and did her own hair. She was independent and had impeccable taste. A week before her twelfth birthday, the tape of the mayor's function showed her maturity as she wore the white dress she had burned. Nicole smiled before she began to play, in spite of Carla's broken promise. Even that disappointment couldn't hide Nicole's natural beauty.

Carla listened to the way Nicole played "Moonlight Sonata." Effortlessly done, but for the first time, Carla really listened to Nicole's improvisation. Rather than condemning it from the first altered note, she listened.

By the sonata's end, she paused the tape, rewound it, and listened again. After the fourth time, Carla shook her head. Nicole's performance was masterful, graceful, and really a breath of fresh air.

How could I have punished her for that?

A little later, on the same tape, Carla had recorded Nicole's birthday performance for Charles. That night, Nicole wore the same white dress from the mayor's function.

Wait a minute.

Carla stopped the tape.

She loved that dress. Why would she burn it? Was it really because I punished her?

Carla removed the tape and picked up the video titled 'May 29th,' a little over two months after Nicole's birthday. Carla immediately noticed a difference—no smile and something else.

Carla looked closer. *A tear?*

She paused the tape and stood closer to the TV.

Yes, a tear. She's never done that before.

Nicole's entire countenance had changed. She was nothing like a few months before. She started going through all the tapes after her birth date.

July 24, 1978: no smile, technically excellent.

August 17, 1978; August 24, 1978; October 11, 1978: All showed increases in skill level, all superior performances, but no more personality, no more laughter, and no more smiles.

March 6, 1981: Flawless.

Eventually, she compared the tapes to the earlier ones. Everything was done to perfection, but there were no smiles. The more she looked, the more she realized Nicole had truly changed, yet not for the better as she initially thought.

I can't even remember the last time I saw her smile.

Carla studied Nicole's expressions.

I caused that. I did that.

Carla realized the Nicole she had known, the one she had given birth to, was gone. Slowly and methodically, Carla thought of the changes she had sought for her daughter, but what she created was an empty, hollow performance machine. After the age of twelve, there was no more joy in her child. Nicole didn't object to anything she said or did to her anymore.

Hindsight was a strange thing. Even Nicole's last performance, Carla didn't see it then, but the parents and children talked to each other. Some laughed. Some parents were encouraging, yet Carla sat imagining they all needed discipline to be like Nicole.

Carla liked the attention of the other parents asking her questions and tips. They even asked Nicole, who stayed focused and answered questions, sitting erect and poised.

But now that she thought about the attention, even the way Nicole dressed was all Carla, with Nicole doing exactly as she was told. Come to think about it, the last time Nicole had objected to anything was over three years ago when Carla slapped Nicole for reminding her of the promise she made to Glen of taking great care of her.

Carla's mind was clear, bringing her thoughts back to the exact moment that happened.

No. No. "No!"

Nicole had pleaded for help about the school bullying, but all Carla did was turn her back on her, then slap her. Since that day, Nicole didn't even ask her to pass the salt or margarine on the table. Come to think of it, Nicole did without before asking her anything, yet her daughter was now compliant in everything. She displayed no personality of her own—at least with Carla. Carla wanted the perfect daughter. She thought she was doing this for Nicole, but that answer didn't settle in her heart.

Carla decided to go to church to clear her mind, but once she entered the sanctuary, her mind was flooded with the truth. Nicole, her daughter, had truly become a perfect young lady—externally. Yes, Nicole could eat correctly, clean correctly, sit, respond, and do everything correctly, but the truth was clear now. She stole her life to fulfill her own dreams, and Carla got exactly what she wanted.

She realized she had also destroyed the most precious gift God had given Nicole, her spark of life.

Sitting in the pew, thoughts of her creation swirled around in her mind, showing her a girl she didn't know anymore. She didn't know her favorite color, her favorite food, or even what made her smile. She saw herself as a puppeteer pulling Nicole's strings, eventually raising the perfect little puppet.

That's when the smell of the burnt dress overtook her, bringing her back to that day and now remembering what Brenda Solomon said. "Listen to your daughter."

Carla bowed her head in shame because she didn't listen. Just then, the church went completely silent. Carla stood still, listening and waiting. Then, suddenly, images of everything she had done wrong flooded her mind again and wouldn't stop. One after the other, like clips of a movie, ran through her mind. Image after image came until she could hardly breathe. It was then she remembered choking Nicole.

She closed her eyes as picture after picture kept playing. Then she heard Nicole's voice from the corner of the rear of the church.

"Mother, please help me." Nicole's voice wouldn't stop. No matter what, the images and cries from Nicole played continuously in her mind. The dress, the tears, and the slap eventually began to speed faster and faster.

Carla could hardly see. She got up to leave and, as she hurried down the aisle, she saw Nicole sitting in the corner of the church.

"Nicole," Carla said, "what are you doing here?"

The choir began singing, "Pass me not, oh gentle savior," and then Carla heard Nicole ask, "Mother, please, may I go?"

"Yes, you can go."

Just as Nicole was about to stand, Carla saw herself appear by Nicole and squeeze her leg. Nicole winced.

"Let her go," Carla shouted. "Please, let her go."

Nicole just sat asking again. "Mother, please, may I go?"

Carla ran out of the church to her car and rushed home. She didn't remember how she had gotten home, but she was able to get to the telephone. Her hands were shaking so badly, but she dialed, hoping to call Glen.

The phone rang. Carla anxiously waited for anyone to answer. As soon as someone picked the phone up, Carla shouted, "Glen! You were right to quit your job. I can't do this anymore."

"No," Gladys said calmly, "this is your mother, and I see your call was an accident."

Carla realized she had dialed the wrong number and remained silent at first, then she tried to hurry off the phone.

"Mother," Carla said, "I've got to call Glen."

"Why?"

"He was right. He finally left. You just don't know what I've done. I went through all Nicole's tapes, and Mother, I've destroyed—"

"So," Gladys said, interrupting and taking her time, "let me get this straight. You're afraid to lose some man…going through a midlife crisis?"

"No, ma'am. It's Nicole."

"Nicole is much stronger than you could ever imagine. How much work have you put into your household, making it the perfect home?"

Carla didn't answer, knowing there was no conversation to be had with her mother.

"So," Gladys said, "all that beauty wasted on you. I'm still cleaning up your messes. Sending you to the best school this country has to offer, Brighton School for Girls. That school made you strong."

Carla winced at the name Brighton School for Girls. The haunting images plagued her thoughts.

"Carla," Gladys said, "steady your mind. You still have an issue with that school, but that school saved your life. You thought after that pregnancy and abortion, I was supposed to coddle you and keep you around to let you get pregnant again? You needed to be cleaned up completely of your little fairy tale dreams, and that school was the perfect answer. I don't care what hell you believe you went through; no more tears and crying about fairness. The only thing this world understands is to fight and stand and don't you dare back down from anyone. You should have closed your legs and used your brains if you wanted freedom, but I took care of that. I changed your course. Do you think you would have been anything different without that school?

Carla wanted to speak, but this was Gladys, and there was no winning or no reasoning.

"And to show how foolish you were, out of all the potential suitors in the world, you go to the gutter and choose Glendale Peterson. Hmmm. You called me wanting my advice about Nicole, and I gave it to you. I still can't believe you bore an actual prodigy. I told you this road wouldn't be easy because she was too much like her father to ever become what she is today. I saw the gift in her years ago, and just as I predicted, you were almost there, and now you come crying to me, losing your resolve because Glendale Peterson quit his job and wanted to start over?"

"How did you know?"

"You two are so predictable. And that's the man that you want, the one who moved out of your bedroom. He's the one who just chose to exist. So weak… and you want to tell me that Nicole would have beaten Dr. Rogers' prize pupil, Nicolette Pearson, if she was at all like Glendale?"

Carla remained quiet.

"Carla," Gladys said, "I want an answer. Would Nicole beat Nicolette on that day when she was twelve had she done it Glendale's way?"

"No, ma'am."

"Your little family would have moved over to Valdosta next to Terrance, and you would have lived far beneath your means. You look at your closet, car, bank account, and tell me you're willing to give all that up for some fantasy?"

"But—"

"No. You lack the resolve to follow through. If you want that, if you want to go off and ruin your life, do it, but you owe Nicole the best life she deserves. Life for a black woman is nothing but resolve. See, Carla, you were always weak, and for the first time in my life, over these past years, I've seen how strong you've become. It only takes a strong man to not wither, just like Glendale. He's nothing more than a puppet. Once you stop pulling his strings, he goes off searching for the elusive vision from God."

"It brought him this far."

"Shut up and get yourself together! All of this is well worth it. Who knows the mayor in their city? How much power do you have when he knows you by your first name? The governor? The police chief? You will be the first black woman to win Woman of the Year. Look how that sounds, and you are whining about some husband walking out on you?"

"But Mother?"

"Don't 'but Mother' me. I've told you many times; women have been doormats for far too long in this society. The church teaches how to be that doormat. Raise the children, submit to the man. Where in the hell is the love from the man who is willing to die for me like Christ died for the church? God, in all His wonder, wants you to submit to what? A man who would walk out on you? A man who would beat you down over half of a verse because he can't get his act together? Betray you? Toss you aside when things aren't going his way? Please.

"So that man you call your husband leaves, quits his job like he's in high school with no explanation, and instead of sticking it out, he just packs, trying to take the one good thing in your life?

"I told you about that man when you married him, and here we are, years later, ready to go back in time, to get those goosebumps and live on love.

"Now get yourself together, dry those wasted tears, and see what that man says about you after you win the Woman of the Year. Listen to me and listen to me good. You tell me, who wouldn't want the first black woman who won that coveted award in the South? You talk about power? Clout? Authority? You tell me if it's worth it?"

"Yes, Mother."

"Clean that room, put those tapes up, and get yourself ready for your award. Suck it up, and call me afterward. Otherwise, if you don't think you can do this, pass Nicole to me. Let me take over, and I will show everyone who Nicole can really become. With my means, Darlington is only the beginning. Imagine Nicole written in history books. Little girls longing to be Nicole. That would be one legacy you can have in your pathetic life."

"Yes, Mother."

"Now," Gladys said, "you may hang up."

"Yes, Mother."

Carla gently hung up the phone, wiped her face, and cleaned up just as she was told.

CHAPTER FORTY-SIX

March 25, 1983 (Friday)

The school day rushed by. I focused on my performance tonight. I couldn't get caught up in whatever was going on between Mother and Daddy. We were just too close. Mother and I had to attend the mayor's black-tie event tonight. I had planned on calling Daddy's car phone after Mother won Woman of the Year. I'm sure Mother would want to see him then. Daddy would finally see that things would change in the house, and then he would come back. After this evening, I was going to ask Mother about going out with Jeremy. If I couldn't go out tonight, I would ask for Saturday, but I wanted to see him tonight.

Today felt different. Daddy had apologized to me, but it wasn't his usual apology to make himself feel better; he was really sorry, not blaming anyone for his failure. Plus, he really wanted to make sure I was okay. Maybe that was how I always felt: hoping he would keep his word like he used to. Last night had been really special. Then there was Mother, acting strangely, asking about Daddy. I honestly hadn't thought she even cared anymore. I wondered what she would say tonight to explain Daddy not being there.

I had to admit this past week with Jeremy had been nice. He showed me he was a person far different from his reputation, and I believed I was showing him I was different from mine. He was kind to me and made me feel alive. I even liked the thought of feeling different.

"Hi, beautiful," Jeremy whispered in my ear.

I took in the fragrance of Jeremy's cologne as he stood in front of me. People stared at us as they passed by, but Jeremy never took his eyes off of me.

"What are you doing here?" I asked.

"Disappointed?"

"No."

I watched Nadia pass by with her entourage. They all stared.

"Nicole," he said, pulling my focus away from Nadia. Then he leaned forward and whispered, "See you after school in our spot."

He turned and walked away.

The words "our spot" brought a glowing smile that warmed me, a smile that wouldn't be denied.

When I got to my desk, Nadia wouldn't stop looking my way. She wasn't going to take away my smile. I knew she hated me, but knowing her, she probably wanted Jeremy, too. Then it occurred to me: I didn't care what she thought or even what she wanted.

I had pop quizzes in my first and second-period classes. I didn't miss anything. By sixth period, my mind was filled with introducing Jeremy to Mother.

"Nicole, where's your mind?" Mrs. Jordan asked me in my sixth-period U.S. history class.

That's how my day went. With all the things happening, I thought about Daddy. He talked so much about his vision for our family, a vision that was so far from what we had. I'd seen the changes in him some time ago. I knew his heart was breaking. He had shut down emotionally, and maybe this morning was his last act of desperation, believing that at least things for our family would get better if we left. Was leaving really the answer? The school bell rang before my thoughts could finish.

After class, I went to a payphone and called Daddy's car phone a couple of times, but there was no answer. I should have told him I loved him before he'd left.

I had to hurry outside to the spot Mother had assigned to me. She didn't want to look for me. I had hoped I would see Jeremy in my spot, but when I went outside, he wasn't there. I was like a prisoner in Mother's imaginary cell, watching people walk around the campus with so much freedom.

"Hi, beautiful."

Jeremy stood close to me. When he touched me on the cheek, I felt a tremor in my body.

"What's wrong?"

His voice was warm and gentle. *Please don't let this be fake.*

He caressed my face and wiped the sides next to my eyes. I could have stayed there forever in our spot. Maybe finding someone to share your spot, no matter how small, was what life was all about.

"Nicole, why the tears?"

I backed toward the edge of my imaginary wall. He came even closer.

I hated these emotions. I hated being vulnerable.

"Nothing to say?" he said.

I looked over and saw Nadia and the others staring again. I was tired of the stares always being on display. What had I done that was so wrong?

"Nicole, everything is going to be okay." He lifted my chin and kissed my cheek. "See, I'm here. I'm your boyfriend, right?"

"Yes, but are you really interested…you know…in me? Nicole."

"To me, you're a chance of a lifetime."

I watched him and laughed. "Sure," I said, "until the next chance of a lifetime comes along."

"You have a beautiful laugh. You need to do that more often."

I covered my mouth.

He pulled my hand away. "Why don't you believe me?"

That was an interesting question. Why didn't I believe him? It was what I wanted. In fact, it was everything I wanted, but he was Jeremy.

I shook my head.

He smiled. "Still unsure, still believing everything you hear?"

"Do you?"

"I've already heard what people in this school say about you, and I don't care. I've always made up my own mind. What I see in you is something so different from any of those other girls or women I've ever met. You stand alone, like an island. You're very thoughtful, and Desiree thinks the world of you."

I raised an eyebrow.

"You know that," he said. "Just call me tonight."

"I have to go to this thing tonight. Afterward?"

"No matter what time."

Before he could walk away, I saw a beautiful girl standing by his car. I squinted.

I took his hand. "Jeremy, who is that?"

"Oh, that's Gloria. She just needs a ride home, that's all."

"Right."

"Whoa," he said. "You have a little jealous streak?"

"No."

"Baby, it's all in your face."

He called me Baby.

"Gloria!" he said, turning to the girl, "come here!"

She started walking our way.

"Let me introduce you to her."

When she passed by a couple, her smile to them was bright, like the flash of a camera. Boys just stared at her as she walked our way. She was built like a woman. Daddy had told me not to compare myself with anyone, but I wished I had asked him how to stop. Just seeing her move towards us was like watching someone walk in slow motion in a movie. Seeing her made me wonder what Jeremy wanted with me. My heart beat harder the closer she got. Jeremy watched me.

"Gloria, this is my girlfriend, Nicole."

"Hi," she said.

"Nicole," Jeremy said, grinning, "This is Gloria."

I said nothing. I wanted to leave.

"You okay?" Gloria asked.

I nodded.

"Baby, just call me tonight." He took my hand and kissed it.

Gloria's smile reappeared just as she left to go back toward the car. I felt like I was in a dream world. I really had a boyfriend. One who wasn't ashamed of me. These walls I had raised for so long were now crumbling because of Jeremy. I did something I knew I shouldn't have done. I whispered in his ear.

"I know you won't wait by the phone."

He whispered back. "Two rings. If I don't answer by two, then everything they said about me is true."

"Sure."

"You're going to have to call to find out. Bring something special tonight."

Jeremy walked back toward his car as Gloria waited by the door. He opened her door, and he waved goodbye just before he closed the door. And just like that, I was alone. I picked my books up, ensuring they were neatly stacked in my arms, straightened my purse strap over my shoulder, and made sure my posture was straight. As I looked around the school, I felt different. I felt lonely.

Car after car left, but there was no Mother. I imagined she was probably anxious and nervous about tonight. I couldn't believe I was trying to figure Mother out. We were so close to her goal, and I couldn't afford to fall apart.

Off to the left, I saw Mother's Mercedes coming my way. Even from this distance, I could tell it would be another quiet ride to the house.

I'd stopped calling our house a home some time ago. I'd noticed Daddy had too. Our house was nothing more than four painted walls with a roof—a place for laying our heads and eating; for Mother, a piece of property to impress others. I really believed Daddy and I were like the furniture or the knick-knacks used for decoration.

I thought of Daddy just as I opened the rear driver-side door.

"Mother, did you talk to Daddy today?"

"No."

There was no elaboration with Mother, at least with me. That was the mother I knew. My questions had to be straightforward and direct, which showed that I knew what I was asking for. Come to think about it, it must have meant I only got what I deserved. I shut the door and tried to make the least amount of noise.

I put my books down beside me and stacked them in a pile from largest to smallest.

Once Mother drove out of the parking lot, the stack tumbled. I quickly picked the books up and stacked them again. I didn't want to hear about my failure to properly stack books.

"Nicole, why do you stack your books like that?"

It's all in how you respond to her. I always told myself that.

"How do you want me to stack them?"

"Your books are fine the way they are. How was your day?"

"Fine." I guess I was a lot like Mother in answering questions. Another mile of the familiar silence went by.

"Nicole," Mother said, "if you are concerned about the books falling, maybe just put them on the floor. What do you think?"

I reached over to do something new and put the books on the floor. Mother turned a corner, and the books fell over. I continued stacking them as quickly as I could.

"Nicole, please stop for a moment."

I resisted a sigh. I sat up, placed my hands on my lap, and focused on her eyes in the rearview mirror.

"Yes, Mother."

"I wasn't trying to tell you how to stack books. I thought the first way you had them was fine."

I started stacking them the original way. I learned with Mother not to question, just do, no matter how menial or how long. Once I finished stacking my books back in the original position, I laid my right arm over the books and laid my left hand on my lap.

"Nicole?"

"Yes, Mother?"

I looked at her eyes in the rearview mirror, waiting for her next command. A few moments passed, and then she shook her head and said, "Never mind."

Neither one of us spoke afterward.

CHAPTER FORTY-SEVEN

March 25, 1983 (Friday)

The mirror in the room showed a young girl growing up and looking so much like her mother. I remember when I was twelve, I'd felt special because I almost looked like Mother's picture in her old yearbook, but after Charles, I'd stopped looking in the mirror altogether. I guess I still felt like that twelve-year-old girl, but today, I saw a different Nicole.

I was a sixteen-year-old girl who allowed herself to be dwindled to measurements for Ms. Eleanor, measurements that changed over the years and ones I'd never paid attention to until now. I was five foot two and three quarters. I wore a size four dress, shoe size six and a half, but the reflection in the mirror somehow showed more. I saw it in my own eyes.

I saw things I never noticed because I had stopped pretending my appearance mattered to me. Until now, I'd been just a walking, talking mannequin who'd modeled Ms. Eleanor's dresses. I was sure her mannequins never looked in the mirror and wondered if they were beautiful or wondered if anyone would love them.

Maybe that was what life was about. Maybe we survive, and something or someone wakes us up, and then, for the first time, we begin to see what others may see. For years, I guessed all I'd seen was the little twelve-year-old girl, and I'd never taken the time to realize I'd been growing up. I'd been so driven in the pursuit of perfection that I'd never thought about how I felt until Jeremy breathed life into me.

I had been on an emotional roller coaster ride this past week alone. I even thought about the interview with Ventura College. Mr. Tomlinson would have been right about me had it not been for Jeremy. As I looked in the mirror, I saw the spark of life instead of that deadness Mr. Tomlinson had once seen. I felt so alive, and I knew we were close. This time, I knew we were near the end.

I was not under any illusion that this journey was about me. It was all Mother's quest. Every breath, every performance was all for Mother. I didn't know what else to say. I used to pray a lot, believing God would somehow make everything okay and make my nightmares go away, but God only seemed to answer enough for me to just get by, and maybe all of this had always been for Mother.

I knew now why I held onto faith in God. Daddy held onto faith. Daddy always seemed to believe the best would happen in our family, eventually. He believed Mother would change. He believed our family would be whole one day. Now he was done with Mother, and possibly with God and me. If Daddy had given up, I knew it was only a matter of time for me, but at least Mother would get all she wanted. Maybe after that, God would turn his attention toward me.

"Nicole," Mother said, "you need to be ready in—"

She stopped her words and came into the room. She stood behind my right shoulder and stared at my reflection in the mirror. I wanted her to say something. I guess I was still that little girl longing for her affirmation.

"We'll be leaving in five minutes."

She turned and walked out.

I took a deep breath and exhaled the disappointment away. I should have paid attention to her eyes. Maybe that's what I was supposed to see.

I looked around the sparsely covered walls of my room. All the things I loved were gone.

The walls of my bedroom, once powder blue, the white billowing clouds, pictures of my mother, father, and the friends I'd once had were all gone, replaced with a now sterile, white backdrop.

I watched myself in the mirror with no real smile and no real joy. But then I thought about Jeremy. No, I'm not going to lose this feeling. No, I'm going to hope again.

The gala Mother so loved was just like so many others. I could have taken a picture year after year, and I wouldn't have been able to tell anything different about them. But this night was not for me; it was for Mother. She painted a smile on her face and mingled with the powerful crowd, waiting for the event to start. She laughed with Mrs. Daily, Ms. Eleanor, Ms. Brenda, Ms. Louise, and others. Occasionally, Mother would look my way, but after the fourth time, she stopped. She knew I would be everything she taught me to be.

I resisted boredom and other detrimental feelings and remained focused until my moment to perform on stage. As soon as I sat down at the piano, an unexpected flood of emotions came over me. I tried to stop them, but my heart took over, and I began to pray as I played. Thoughts of Daddy poured out, forming my words, asking God to bring him home. While I played, my heart asked for God to bring healing to my relationship with Daddy. I wanted God to hear me. I didn't want to be an afterthought. I wanted Daddy to come home. I just wanted.

I played each note as written, but somehow the emotion brought the concerto alive, and for the first time, I saw what Mother saw in classical music. I saw the same longings that transcended time. I saw the tears, the loss, and the despair. I felt it all. Not once did I look up to manipulate the moment. I was in the moment, and I felt free. I played the last note. Unexpected tears ran down my cheeks. A standing ovation filled the room.

I gathered myself and went to the powder room to put water on my face just like Mother would have done to compose herself. I made it back in time to see Mayor Daily standing at the podium, ready to announce Darlington's 1983 Woman of the Year. Mother pulled out a slip of paper.

"It is my pleasure," Mayor Daily said, "to introduce a lady my wife and I believe to be the picture of elegance and grace. The weddings that she has organized for many of you and your families in the audience kept bringing attention to our community, either in published papers or national magazines. Any event or fundraiser she has led has brought honor to our city. I have never met anyone with such an eye for attention to detail. I had the pleasure of discovering this when the governor came to visit in December. She saved my behind that night."

Laughter spread throughout.

"Yes, she remembered every person's name on his staff. I have tried on several occasions to get her to work on my own staff, but to think about it, I don't need to give the voters another option for mayor."

More laughter spread.

"We are on the map because of Mrs. Peterson. She is the ultimate example of a business owner becoming one of the most successful wedding and event planners in South Georgia.

"Her business has brought many jobs into our community, as Darlington Convention Hall has become one of the preferred venues for events throughout the surrounding area. The businesses she has helped in some form or fashion, be it marketing or promotions, are too many to mention. Her success and elegance have even been passed down to her daughter, Nicole, an outstanding performer and nationally recognized concert pianist with a full scholarship to prestigious Ventura College.

"So, please stand and give honor to the 1983 Woman of the Year for Darlington, Georgia, Mrs. Carla Peterson!"

The ovation was filled with smiling faces, showing the closeness of our community. I let myself experience the woman everyone else saw that night. I probably would have enjoyed getting to know that woman.

Mother stood at the microphone. "Thank you, Mayor Daily, Mrs. Daily, and everyone here. I won't be long. For a woman like me to receive an honor like this on this day is all I've ever dreamed of. To even be mentioned and nominated—"

Mother paused. That was the first time I'd ever seen her lose her composure, yet she closed her eyes, took a deep breath, and exhaled to reclaim her composure.

"I'm sorry," she said. "I didn't know it would hit me so hard."

Mother thanked Reverend Joseph, Ms. Louise, Ms. Brenda, Ms. Eleanor, the mayor and his wife, and all of those who were significant in encouraging her to follow her dream.

"I'd also like to thank my husband, who isn't here right now. He has freely given me the means to do what I love. And more than that, I'd love to thank my daughter, Nicole."

She stared into my eyes. "Words cannot express what I feel. To all, thank you for the honor and this moment in my life."

Her words were followed by another standing ovation. She even let a tear roll down her cheek.

I listened while all those around spoke highly of her after the program was over. I found myself hoping that now that she had gotten what she wanted, I would experience the woman she had been for everyone else.

There were many photo opportunities with all those present, and seeing her graciousness, I thought she could have rivaled any actress in Hollywood.

~

We had a quiet ride home, her hand on the passenger seat, reaching for a hand that wasn't there. She eventually took the award and placed it in the seat next to her. I just observed because we were there at that place after all those years, and it was over. She had everything she wanted. I should have been excited, but all I could do was watch her. Was she overwhelmed? Overjoyed? Was she just numb, almost like a doctor would feel after finishing her internship?

Even when we walked into the house, she went to the kitchen table and just sat down. I sat across from her, anxious to hear how it felt to finally get what she'd wanted.

Mother kept looking at her award. She placed it in the center of the table as the object of her affection, above all else. She'd finally gotten it.

"Nicole," she said, staring at her award, "I always thought all of this would feel different. You know, after all my sacrificing and long hours pushing and pulling, you name it, I really thought it would be different."

Mother picked up her award, studied it, and then gently placed it on the table.

"I spent a lot of time praying today," she said. "First time in a while. It was so clear. It was as if God had told me to choose. It was almost as clear as it was four years ago when I was outside your door. I see now that was my crossroad, and I didn't even know it."

There was silence again; she now stared through the award like she was staring through time. She nodded her head and then looked at me with sorrowful eyes.

"Nicole," she said, "I should have opened your door. I should have. And today, again, I made the wrong choice. Glen was right. We should have left with him. But Nicole, I just had to see how it felt to win, just once."

"What are you talking about, Mother?"

"Four years ago, that Saturday night after Charles left, the day we were supposed to go to Atlanta, the day you burned the dress, I felt a pulling at your door. I mean, your daddy was so worried about you that night, and I…I was supposed to be talking with you, but I stopped when I heard you playing. Nicole, you've got to realize I had never heard playing like I heard that night. Even then, it almost felt like someone was taking my hand, trying to get me to open your door, but… the way you played that night. I couldn't ignore the possibilities. I even stopped your daddy from going to check on you because I just wanted to feel those possibilities. What you could do for us in the future?"

Mother's eyes began to water.

Normally, I didn't stare at Mother. I usually tried not to look into her eyes. She had always said it was like challenging her. But this time, she was rubbing her hands slowly on the table. I did the same thing while I stared. The table was soothing, allowing me to think.

God had heard my prayer all along. I wasn't—

"But you know," she said, interrupting my thoughts, "Ever since that night, it's been different in our family. I've been different. I knew things would level out, but as I think about it tonight, all I feel is regret. What I regret most is…"

Her words took off and flowed freely. She had changed overnight. There she was, opening up to me like I'd always wanted. As she talked, one of Daddy's stories came to me. It was a story about a man who'd spent his life building his dream mansion. Each brick, board, and nail he used cost something small: time from his wife, his child, trading a little of his health here or there. When he finished his mansion, the reporters all honored him, but when he walked into his mansion after all he had gained, he stood in the center of his success—alone. In the end, he realized what he'd really wanted were all the things he had traded away.

Mother stared at me.

"Nicole," she said, "I miss the old you. I saw that in your tapes earlier today. I must have spent hours looking at your tapes when you were a little girl. You were so beautiful and full of life. The laughter we used to share, the joy. The…"

I leaned back in my chair and took in all that she said. I realized what she was talking about. It wasn't the award, this moment, anything like that. I realized I was part of the mansion she had built, the wealth that Mother had poured into believing I would bring her satisfaction. She kept going on and on about how I used to be. The more I listened, the more I realized she had found no satisfaction in me at all.

"It's not that I'm...disappointed in you," Mother said. "It's that I can't read you. I mean, you..."

I listened as Mother told me about all my flaws. How I was like an actor pretending to be something I wasn't. I was a hollow shell. If all the things she was saying about me were true, then really, what good was I? I realized I was Picasso's first painting, not Le Picador but the one he'd thrown away.

And to think, if she had only opened my door four years ago, I would have told her everything. I would have told her about Charles and about all my fears. I would have willingly done anything for her. How I wanted so much to please her. She'd even said at the end of her acceptance speech tonight, "Words cannot express what I feel."

She paused for a moment, picked up my SAT results off the table, and studied them. I had done that myself. I'd wanted to show her that I could follow through. The SAT was the one thing I'd set out to accomplish on my own and surprise her with.

When she finished studying the results, she gently folded the letter and neatly placed it on the table.

"Perfect score."

"Yes, ma'am."

She actually looked down at the table and shook her head.

"Nicole...I was wrong."

"About what?"

"Everything. And you thought...never mind."

"Never mind? Never mind what?"

She said nothing else. We both sat in the silence of her weighted words. I stared at her and her award. My mind searched for the meaning of all this. I had done it all, completely surrendered my will, my emotions, my very life to each and every one of her whims, and she was telling me, 'I was wrong?' Not one word of congratulations? Like all that I had done meant nothing?

I stood up for the first time on my own, without her expectations and permission. "So basically," I said, "what you're saying is, you don't like nothing you see in me. Is that it?"

I wanted to hear plainly how she felt about me, but all I saw in her eyes was pity toward me.

"I don't get it," I said. "I aced all of my tests. I even got a perfect score on my SAT—something I did on my own. I made sure I could go to Ventura College just like you wanted. I flawlessly played all the piano pieces that you gave me. I learned every rule you made up, and I lived them every day. I'm someone you should be proud of."

Her lips moved. "Nicole, I just want you to be that girl who loved life, who laughed and played from her heart. That's all."

"That girl died four years ago, and I'm all that's left of her. Can't you just love what's left?"

"Nicole," she said.

Then, I saw it in her eyes; she was trying to get me to chase another empty promise. "No, Mother. Exactly the way I am now."

She lowered her head and didn't even try to say anything else. I didn't know what was worse, no words or a volume of words. At least with Mother and me, it was clear.

"I thought eventually you would love me," I said, "but I finally see that'll never happen."

"Please forgive me."

"It's all about you and only you. It was always just about you. You were the one who wanted the money, so Daddy went away for a year to make you happy, but nothing's ever good enough for you. Oh yeah, I won't say anything bad about your precious Charles as long as I'm in this house. Mother, I don't know how to forgive because you have to care first to do that…and I really don't care anymore."

Unexpected tears ran down my cheeks. I hated crying. I turned to leave.

"I never wanted you to be like this," she said.

I turned around. "Well, here I am…your creation. Come see the freak. Just wind her up and watch her play. Oh, she can entertain you and make you feel… so…good. Do anything you want to her. Call her anything, but she'll never mess up. Knock her down, choke her, slap her, but she gets right…back…up…and still…makes no mistakes. Use her, and use her, and use her, and use her until there's nothing left…But it doesn't matter…There are others who can replace her when she's all used up. See Mother. I learned well."

I turned around, walked up the stairs, and got on the phone.

Jeremy picked up on the first ring.

"I'll meet you at midnight at the corner of my street…Am I willing to what?"

I stood for a few moments, thinking about his request. It had come out of nowhere.

"Yes, I'm still here."

From the way he'd asked me, with such expectancy, it made me sense that maybe he was the ultimate dog, like everyone said, but I wanted to be held. I wanted to matter. If only for a moment, I could pretend he cared.

"Yes. Whatever you want."

CHAPTER FORTY-EIGHT

March 25, 1983 (Friday)

I used to dream of Mother helping me prepare for my first date, but it was just me now. Daddy had told me some things about boys, but that was a few years ago. I'd heard of date nights where your father took you out just to show you how someone should treat you. I wished we would have had a date like that one. I was sure sneaking out at midnight wasn't what Daddy would have expected.

There wasn't much to choose from in my closet, so I closed my eyes, reached out, and picked something. I cleaned my shoes again, placed them in the closet, took everything else I planned on wearing, and placed them in the back corner of my closet as well. I searched in my drawer and found a monogrammed silk scarf in a box, one that Grandma, Daddy's mother, had given me years ago before she'd passed away.

I snatched my towel and washcloth out of the linen closet. A few towels fell out. I threw them back in the closet and turned the shower knob to the spot that I had marked. It would take about two minutes to warm up just right.

I lingered in the shower way longer than usual, letting the water wash away any concern about Jeremy and what I was about to do. I dried off, put my pajamas on, and lay in bed, thinking of my boyfriend.

Mother came by and stood at the door, interrupting my thoughts. I closed my eyes and pretended to be asleep. I felt her lips press against my cheek, giving me a long, lingering kiss. I'd longed for any contact all this time, but now I knew she thought her kiss was supposed to fix everything. She ended the kiss and stood for a moment. Then she moved to leave. Once she shut my bedroom door, I rolled over to check the clock.

About forty-five minutes later, I was dressed and quietly walking out the back door, passing Mother's closed door. By the time I reached the corner, Jeremy's car was waiting.

"Hi Nicole," he said, but it was his eyes that did the talking. His eyes scanned my body as if taking inventory. I fought the memories of Charles when he scanned. I knew I was nowhere near any of the other girls, but when I looked at Jeremy, he smiled and nodded as if he approved.

He reached over and gently brushed my skin. I closed my eyes and breathed in deeply.

"Where are we going?" I asked, trying to gain my composure.

"Have you ever been to Bluffington's Point?"

"No." I had never been anywhere alone with a boy. He moved his hand to put the car in drive. I glanced in the back seat. There were a couple of blankets and pillows.

"Boyfriend and girlfriend?" he asked.

I nodded.

~

The road to Bluffington's Point was a dark, winding, two-lane highway heading up into the hills at the edge of town. The canopy of trees near the top formed a tunnel of darkness. As we drove under them, I moved closer to Jeremy, who put his arm around me. That was when I saw the beauty of the route.

Jeremy pointed to a slit in the trees to the right, where he guided his car through the dusty road; the narrow passage opened to a vast plateau showing an expansive view of the stars and sparse clouds that peppered the sky. Just that view alone made the long journey worth the ride.

The plateau was an open field with about fifteen to twenty cars parked in various locations, all having their own view of the city. Some of the cars had fogged-up windows, while other cars had couples sitting or lying on the hoods.

Our car slowed to a stop.

"Have you ever been out on a date before?"

I shook my head.

"You remembered?"

I pulled the silk scarf out of my purse and gave it to him.

"NRP? What's the R for?"

"Renee."

"Beautiful." He smiled and nodded. I even heard a sigh as he gently draped the scarf over his rearview mirror.

"Nicole, thank you. I want to show you so much. Just trust me and let me lead. There are many ways to date, and this is just one. What you see around you is the best part of dating. Don't let anybody fool you. This is what it's all about, sharing intimate times together."

The clouds gradually overtook the stars as Jeremy talked. His voice was tender. Then he stopped talking. The clouds continued rolling in, and I imagined how it would feel if a storm came through. I listened to the sound of the car as I lay in Jeremy's arms. I turned to him to comment on the beautiful night, and he kissed me on my cheek. Then he kissed my neck. I couldn't even explain the feeling. Once he stopped, he stepped out and walked around in front of the car. Then he opened the passenger door to let me out.

For a moment, we stood outside, looking up at the forming clouds and then out toward the city lights.

"I love this view." He turned to me. "I love this view too."

He placed his hand in mine and eased me toward his back door. The hinges were quiet as he opened the door. "After you."

It was all like a dance, so fluid in movement. I closed my eyes and then heard Desiree's voice out of nowhere. I tensed up and turned back to Jeremy. Desiree wanted me to stay away from him, but what else did I have or even feel? What else? At that moment, vulnerable was the right word.

He smiled, but I couldn't shake Desiree's voice.

"Jeremy…am I really special to you?" I asked, my voice unexpectedly trembling.

"Of course you are," he said. "I actually waited a whole week for this moment."

I moved toward the door. Then I thought of Mother and stopped. She couldn't love me just the way I was. If Jeremy could, then I would ignore Desiree's voice. "Jeremy, do you like me for who I am?"

"Of course."

"You don't understand," I said. "I'm frigid and lonely. I don't even know who I am anymore."

"I don't care about all that."

"What I'm saying is, what if I don't get in the backseat with you tonight? Will you wait longer?"

Jeremy fidgeted. "So, you're saying you want to be just friends?"

"I'm not saying that. I do like you. My daddy left. I had a bad argument with my mother, and I was hoping that maybe we could just talk first. I was hoping that's what boyfriends do. Maybe you can get to know the real me."

"But you don't like me that way," he said, leaning against the car.

"Yes, I do. I really do. I think I love you."

"Then what's the problem?"

This reminded me of Mother and Daddy and disagreements and having to be right. I didn't want to be like Mother, so I stayed vulnerable.

"I got so much on my mind," I said. "I don't know where to begin." I stared into his eyes, hoping he would see my need, put his arms around me, and just listen.

He smiled and let the seconds go by.

"Jeremy?"

His smile went away. "The truth of the matter is you don't know how many girls would love to be in your place right now, but I picked you. If you are with me, there will be other guys who will want to be with you. Girls will want to get to know you. You'll have more than just Desiree as a friend. Parents break up all the time, but life goes on."

He pressed against me.

"Come on, Nicole, I know this is something you want."

He touched my face. After his speech, his touch didn't have the same effect it had earlier. He'd almost sounded desperate. I gazed into his eyes this time, but as the moments passed, I hoped what I saw wasn't real. I couldn't have been that blind. He couldn't be that way.

"Jeremy," I said, holding his hand, "I'm not trying to be a tease. Can we talk for just one moment? That's all I want. I want you to wrap your arms around me and just talk to me. I promise, Jeremy, I'll do whatever you want me to do. I promise I will, but first, you have to talk to me. Help me. Please. Let's just talk."

To watch him struggle with speaking only reinforced what I felt. He smiled instead and caressed both my cheeks. He kissed me on my lips, yet all I thought was that he wouldn't even give me one word. I couldn't pretend anymore, so I slowly ended the kiss, pushed his hands away, and closed the back door.

Jeremy's expression changed before the door clicked. "What's that for?"

I just stared at him.

"I see where this is going," he said. "You think I want a girl to just talk to? A buddy? See, there are no free rides. It cost gas for me to pick you up and drive you out here."

He snatched open the back door again.

"Now, either get in that back seat and give me what I came out here for…or walk home. I ain't no counselor."

"Are you serious?"

"I don't mess with girls who don't put out. I know you know that."

I looked around.

"Oh yeah, it's a long walk home. That's why this is the perfect spot."

Not even thinking, I almost moved to get in. He was right behind me, pressing up against me, but when I glanced back at him, I stopped and searched his eyes again. As I watched, I knew without any doubt that he didn't care at all about me. He didn't care that I was afraid of the dark. He didn't care; I barely knew how to get home. He just didn't care, just like Charles.

I shook my head. "No. No. No," I said, pushing back. "No." I closed the door and backed away from the car. "I'll walk."

I felt a few drops of rain on my arm.

He caught the eye of the couple not fifteen feet away, grinned, and shook his head.

"So," he said, turning to me, "you're saying no to me?"

I didn't respond.

"Homely, quiet, stuck-up…Nicole Peterson is saying no…to Jeremy?" He grinned before going to the driver's side, got in the car, cranked up, and backed out. He turned the car around, stopped beside me, and rolled his window down.

"You know, you don't get it. Don't think this is some date gone bad. You were nothing but a bet, something on the side. Nadia came out of nowhere and bet me thirty dollars that I couldn't get you out by Friday at midnight. The bet was the only time I took a look at you. I made it sixty. Nicole, you're only good for one thing, and you probably can't even do that right. To tell you the truth, she should have paid me just for trying."

He wiped his mouth with the back of his hand and then snatched my grandma's scarf off his rearview mirror. "Thanks for the money." He threw it on the floor. "As far as you saying no? Just tell. Who's gonna believe you over me? They all saw you."

As he drove off, the sky opened up, turning the dust into mud before I could even make it to the narrow path between the trees. I turned around before walking through. The view was still beautiful. The couple that'd been closest to us were in their car now. A few other cars had already gone. Lightning burst across the sky, and it wasn't long before I was soaked.

I just put one foot in front of the other.

The walk home took over four hours. I made it home by 5:41 a.m. I went inside, took a shower, lay down, and fell asleep well after 6:29 a.m. Afterward, I buried myself in piano for the rest of the weekend.

CHAPTER FORTY-NINE

March 28 – 29, 1983 (Monday – Tuesday)

Homeroom on Monday morning was buzzing with conversations, but I tuned them all out. I sat staring at the wall mirrors, making the room seem much bigger than normal. My hair was unkempt, an embarrassment to Mother. I reached to straighten my glasses.

Who are you fooling, anyway? Nobody wants you.

"Cinderella."

I ignored Nadia.

"Cinderella, I know you hear me, or do you even clean your nasty ears?"

I didn't know why I looked up, but there she was with that evil smirk.

"Why don't you leave me alone?"

"Ahhh," Nadia said, "you finally found your tongue after all this time. Cinderella, how are the dinners at the mayor's mansion?"

"Mother wanted that life, not me."

"That's right. Blame it on your mother—Woman of the Year. Oh yeah, little Miss Innocent, I saw you outside with Jeremy all last week. Cinderella was on the prowl, trying to figure out how to use that tongue? I bet he showed you."

"Oooo," echoed throughout the class.

"Yeah," Nadia said, "you finally figured out there's only one way for you to get your prince."

"Yeah," Karen said, "the prince would come and sweep you off your feet."

Nadia laughed. "Oh yeah, with him, you would definitely be off your feet."

I got up to leave.

Nadia stood in front of me while Karen and the other girls moved in closer.

Nadia pulled something out of her pocket. "I believe you dropped this—NRP."

I tried to go around.

She blocked my way again and showed me the scarf I had given to Jeremy. Then she leaned forward and whispered, "So, tell me, Cinderella…how was your date?"

I slapped her just as the last word left her mouth. Nadia fell back against the chairs and then slid to the floor.

Karen rushed to her side.

Nadia lay still, holding her jaw in shock.

The other girls moved back. I glanced and saw Desiree rushing over to me.

Karen stepped away from Nadia.

I heard Nadia move to get up. I picked up my chemistry book from the table, raised it, and aimed it at her head.

Nadia fell back and covered herself.

I glanced at the mirror on the wall and saw enraged eyes like my mother's. When I looked down, Nadia lay cowering on the floor. I wanted her to move so badly.

"Nicole," Desiree said.

I felt a tug of the book.

"You could have hurt her bad with that book," Desiree said.

"That's exactly what I wanted to do."

I felt Desiree take the book. "It's me," she whispered. "Just let it go."

She placed my chemistry book on the desk. I reached down, snatched up my scarf beside Nadia, and leaned in close. "My name is not…Cinderella."

I sat down at my desk, leaving Nadia on the floor. She just sat there, but I didn't take my eyes off her.

"Nadia," Mrs. Jackson said, coming into the room, "what in the world are you doing on the floor?"

The room remained quiet.

"Nadia, get up from there. What happened to you?"

Nadia stood, brushed herself off, and pointed at me. "Nicole slapped me for no reason."

"Nicole?" Mrs. Jackson asked, staring at Nadia.

"She did," Nadia said, holding her jaw as she scanned her friends. "You saw it."

Nadia's friends stood frozen. Other girls shook their heads, but no one answered. Mrs. Jackson slowly shook her head as well. "Nicole," she said, "is that true?"

Mrs. Jackson had watched Nadia block my path many times. She had seen Nadia talk to me any kind of way she wanted and only listened as Nadia spread things about me the whole year, and now she stood there asking me?

I said nothing.

Mrs. Jackson sighed. "Then both of you go to the office."

"What!" Nadia said. "But I didn't hit Nicole."

"Desiree," Mrs. Jackson said, "please walk with Nicole to the office. I'll be up there with Nadia to get to the bottom of this."

Desiree and I headed toward the door.

"But I didn't do anything," Nadia continued.

"Uh-huh. So, Nicole would just walk up to you and slap you? That Nicole?"

"Ask her," Nadia said, pointing toward me.

"Nicole?"

I stopped and stared at Nadia, thought about this school, and then looked at Mrs. Jackson. "Whatever she says, Mrs. Jackson, just go with that. That's what normally happens around here anyway, isn't it?"

Mrs. Jackson shook her head as I walked out of the room with Desiree.

"Don't worry about that, Nicole," Desiree said. "Nobody's going to bother you after that."

I wasn't even worried about that. My mother had beaten me far worse than any of the girls in this school could have beaten me.

~

The office was a modern-day spectacle—a tall tan-desk barrier separating students, secretaries, assistants, and administrative offices. Each office had a vice principal or principal.

On duty today was the principal, Mr. Bronson, a tall, muscular man with broad shoulders. He came out of his office. Desiree and I arrived about a minute before Nadia and Mrs. Jackson.

Mr. Bronson asked the secretary, "Will you wait between the young ladies? I need to talk with Mrs. Jackson." He turned to Mrs. Jackson. "Please come in."

Time passed, the bell rang, and students filled the hallways.

Mr. Bronson stepped out of the office. "Desiree and Nadia," he said, "will you please come in?"

They were in the office for some time. From where I sat, I saw some cases filled with the trophies of various sports teams.

When mother arrived, her hair and makeup were perfect, like always. Nadia's mother came in afterward and was sent into the office with the others. About ten minutes later, Mr. Bronson called me into the office and excused Nadia, her mother, and Desiree.

"Nicole," he said, "it has come to my attention this morning all that you have gone through, not just this year, but for the past several years. Bullying beyond measure. I wish you would have said something earlier, but now we have this hitting matter. No hitting will be tolerated in this school under any circumstance."

"I understand, Mr. Bronson," I said.

In all cases, he was by the book, and I shouldn't have expected anything different. I knew I would be suspended for three days, and Mother would come up with some creative way to make life a living hell—no different from any other day.

"Nicole," he said, "you have always been an exceptional student. Even your SAT scores were something to behold. What I'm going to do is send you home for the rest of the day with an excused absence. Everyone needs a break. Nothing goes on your record. You're free to go."

My mother put her hand on my shoulder.

"Thank you, Mr. Bronson," she said. "Bye, Mrs. Jackson."

As we walked out of the office, Nadia and her mother passed us to go into his office. Mother didn't even look their way.

Once Desiree, Mother, and I were outside, Desiree was the first to stop.

"Mrs. Peterson," she said and waited.

Mother and I stopped and turned around.

"What are you going to do with Nicole?"

Mother shifted her stance.

Desiree stood between Mother and me and reached back to hold my hand.

Mother just stared, almost in amazement. I knew what Mother could do to her, but I didn't think Desiree cared.

"Nothing," Mother said, "nothing at all. Desiree…I see you're truly a real friend. Thank you for standing up for Nicole."

~

The next day at school was quiet, at least for me. I mean, Nadia didn't even look my way. Throughout the day, from class to class, I remained silent. I heard whispers and some laughter, but this time, things were different. I was Jeremy's latest conquest. I even saw Jeremy as he walked with a few boys. He winked, and the boys laughed.

By the end of the day, I sat outside, waiting for Mother. I had picked a different spot against the wall next to the school. Jeremy and Gloria strolled past me, casually holding hands. I couldn't turn away. Gloria rubbed her hand over Jeremy's arm as he whispered in her ear. She shook her head, covered her mouth, glanced at me, and giggled.

"Hey girl," Desiree said, coming up from my side. "You must have slapped Nadia so hard. I wish I could have been there to see that."

I stared at Jeremy and Gloria.

Desiree blocked my view. "Hey, I have a date tonight."

"With Timothy?"

"He's so nice. We're going to a movie."

"So, you haven't heard about Jeremy yet?" I asked.

"I don't believe it."

"Why?"

"I looked in his eyes when I asked. I know when he's lying. Gloria thinks she's special, but she's just like all these other girls, just plain stupid."

"Like me? You even warned me."

"No," Desiree said, putting her hand on my shoulder. "You said no."

"How do you know?"

"He came in slamming doors early Saturday morning. Now I know why."

My eyes followed another couple walking hand in hand. I wondered how it felt to really be in love, to have someone to love me just the way I was.

Desiree blocked my gaze.

"Be honest," I said. "Do you think anyone will ever want me?"

"Of course. I definitely think so, but you've got to let the guy get to know the real you. He'd find one of the sweetest girls."

Jeremy kissed Gloria at his car. I remembered the feel of his lips. "How am I supposed to know the next guy won't do the same?"

"Don't judge anything by a dog like Jeremy."

"You know you're right about one thing. No need to look at things I'll never have."

"You will someday."

"It's always someday for me. No more somedays. It was stupid to believe anyone would want me for who I was, just as I was."

"I'll get Jeremy to tell the truth."

"Does he even know how? You know, it doesn't matter. Who's going to believe me, anyway?"

Mother's car horn blew.

"I've got to go," I said.

"I'll see you later," she said.

I walked toward the car.

"Nicole…I'll see you later?"

I didn't want to lie to Desiree, so I didn't answer. When I got to the car and opened the door to get in, I asked Mother, "Did Daddy call for me?"

"No, he hasn't called yet."

I turned toward Desiree. "Bye, Desiree."

CHAPTER FIFTY

March 29, 1983 (Tuesday)

After school, while riding inside my Mother's Mercedes, Chopin played on the cassette tape, which meant something was on Mother's mind. She drove as if she were leaving church on a Sunday morning—no rush at all to get to the house. She took the back road that bypassed Mr. Raymond's pecan grove and meandered along the newly paved two-lane country road.

"Nicole," Mother said, "how do you feel about living with Grandmother?"

It had been a long time since she had asked me how I felt about anything, let alone Grandmother. I didn't know what she wanted me to say. I imagined, in a normal family, the question would have sparked nostalgic moments of laughter, fond memories, or good feelings, but that was in a normal family.

"Mother," I said, "do you really want to know how I feel?"

She peered in the rearview mirror and then nodded.

The fact was, I really didn't know Grandmother that well. I hadn't gotten to know much of Grandmother until Mother had reached out to her when I was nine and told Grandmother I was a prodigy. Since then, I'd known her as the epitome of perfection: the right clothes, the right words, and even the right stride. According to Mother, she was everything a woman should be, yet I couldn't remember hugging Grandmother even once.

Mother glanced in the rearview mirror.

What came to mind was a statue of a distant relative erected in the cemetery that sparked words of respect. Buried beneath those words, though, were an underlining history and a myriad of questions people my age wanted to ask but knew would never receive a response. Besides piano, my barometer was how Daddy and Grandmother would cordially, coldly greet each other. Grandmother would say with her chin up, "Glen." Daddy would say, staring directly into her eyes, "Gladys." And that was it. Daddy would find somewhere else to go after that.

"Mother, I don't want to live with her…ever."

I saw Mother biting the bottom of her lip. I didn't think I'd ever seen her do that.

"Nicole, I've been thinking about you since. Hmmm. Since, uh, since you said that you were my creation. Your words hurt. I have tried my best with you, yet, my best…my best is no good."

I was tired of all of her semantics. I'd told her I didn't want to live with Grandmother, but knowing Mother, she was again trying to convince me otherwise.

"What's wrong, Mother?"

"I just want to make things right with you."

"And how is that?"

Now it seemed like it was Mother's turn to escort the silence into the car. She took another turn away from where we lived as if avoiding the house. She then took that same deep breath she took to gather her composure.

"You have an opportunity," she said, "an opportunity for a better life. Things will be different for you."

"What are you talking about, Mother?"

It was frustrating trying to find the right words all the time—the beating around the bush, the questions. Oh, how I missed Daddy.

"Grandmother wants you to live with her for a short time, and I agreed. I just need some time to myself."

"What?"

"You know it's true. She won't mess up with you. You're so much more than I was. You see, Nicole—"

"Mother," I said, interrupting her, "does Daddy know about this?"

"He abandoned us."

"Now, you know that's not true. He just couldn't live with you anymore, but for me, I know he's coming back for me. I just know it."

"Well, believe that if you want. Men leave their families all the time."

Mother never talked like that.

"Nicole, I know you may not like it now, but you'll see. She will really like you. She'll be here to pick you up in a few hours."

For the first time in my life, I understood why people sometimes hated their mothers. She was giving me away because she didn't want to see the mistake she'd made with me. After all, my words had hurt, but I knew Daddy wouldn't stand by and let that happen.

When we got home, I rushed into the house and called Daddy's car phone.

"Nicole," Mother said behind me, "he's not going to answer."

"Yes, he will."

I kept trying, but I wasn't going to give up.

In between my dialing, the phone rang.

"Daddy?"

"Hi, sweetie," Grandmother said. "You're just the person I want to talk to."

This just wasn't the right time. I couldn't deal with this nonsense.

"Nicole," she said, "Aren't you going to say hello?"

"Hi, Grandma."

She cleared her throat on the other end.

"I'm sorry. Hi Grandmother."

"Nicole," she said, "how have you been?"

"Fine."

"No one-word answers with me. How have you been?"

"I have been just fine."

"Yes, I hear you have. And your mother had to go to the school the other day because you slapped a girl. So, I guess everything really is just fine."

I didn't really have a response. She heard what she wanted to hear. I had to hurry off the phone to keep trying to get Daddy.

"How would you feel if you came to visit me for just a little while, you know, get away for a short time? You wouldn't have to do chores, just keep your room clean, that's all. And for the time being, I would send you to one of the best and most expensive high schools in the nation—Brighton School for Girls. Oh, you will see, this is so wonderful."

She'd said, "Brighton School for Girls," like I would be visiting the White House and meeting the President of the United States.

"And Nicole, let me show you my heart. I have always wondered if it has been God's will for you to live with me, for a short time, of course. That's why I believe this is the perfect time for you to leave. I will show you a world that you could only imagine. I know your mother has tried, but with your talent and the connections that I have, oh, imagine little girls throughout this nation looking up to you. You think you have played for some dignitaries? Wait until you play for presidents and kings. This night is the beginning of the rest of your life."

Daddy had asked me to leave, and I couldn't believe I'd turned him down because I'd wanted Jeremy. I really thought Jeremy liked me, and I couldn't believe how wrong I'd been. I wasn't going to miss out on a third chance. I didn't care what Grandmother was offering. Daddy loved me, that I knew. No way was I turning that down to go with someone I barely knew.

Mother stood off to the side with bad posture and a depressed look.

"Again, Nicole," Grandmother said, "would you like to live with me?"

"No, ma'am. Never."

"Sweetie," Grandmother said, "I know you think the world of your father and believe he is going to show up at the last minute, but you need to know the truth about him."

"He is coming to get me."

"Nicole, sweetie."

"I am not your sweetie."

"Ok, Nicole Renee, your father is a runner, and he's not coming back. That's the Peterson men, bad judgment, blaming others, and running. Your Uncle Terrance abandoned his family by getting himself killed, all because of some stupid teenage vow. Now Glen is running. Oh yes, I really think he is next to end up just like Terrance and their father."

"No, he's not."

"Okay, you tell me what man who truly loves his daughter more than his own life would leave her as much as he did you?"

"He didn't leave me. He had to go."

"Semantics. He abandoned you."

"No, he didn't."

"I know it's hard to accept. I know you love your father but open your eyes.

Glen is no different than your Uncle Terrance. He's not coming back for you. Do not waste your tears and hopes on a man who cannot face the reality that he let a woman almost destroy his only daughter while he stood by and watched. After all this time, he can't stand up for you. He let your mother run over him… and you. He is a weak man. I am so sorry, Nicole, but somebody had to tell you."

I looked at Mother, who sat with her head down. It was almost like she heard and believed all of Grandmother's words.

"It's best you come back with me," Grandmother said. "I will straighten your life out. I will undo what Carla did and expose you to examples of what a man should be. I definitely can help you with that."

"Mother," I said, ignoring Grandmother's lies, "how was life with Grandmother?"

Mother took the phone from me. "Mother, I'll pick you up at the airport later tonight." She hung up.

"Mother," I said, "how was your life with Grandmother? And why do you call her Mother instead of Mama? What happened in that household?"

Mother closed her eyes. Her right fist clenched, and she breathed in deeply at the mention of the question, "what happened in that household?"

"Why can't you answer me? It's only me and you here, no one else. What about this school, Brighton? How did you like it?"

She almost looked like she was about to cry when she opened her eyes, but she refused. She just said, "You need to go pack."

"Mother, I'm asking as your daughter; is this the best thing for me?"

"You will grow as a woman."

"It feels like you're making a mistake."

"You will do better with your grandmother than I did. Things are different now. She will finally get what she wants. She always does."

"How long have you been planning this?"

"Your grandmother had asked me for a while, but your father has always been the last obstacle. I want to do right by you." Mother picked up her purse and keys. "I'm going to wait at the airport for a few hours for your grandmother. You really don't have to see me anymore. Please make sure you're packed neatly and be ready to leave. She will want to inspect your luggage, so please make sure it's neat. She doesn't like waiting."

I tried to call Daddy again, but there was no answer. I dialed again. No answer. Again. Mother left while I was trying for the fourth time, slowly closing the door to the house behind her. After she left, I called Desiree.

"Hello?" I asked.

"Hey Cindy," Jeremy said. "Or should I say, Cinderella? I just love that name."

I didn't have time for this. "May I speak to Desiree?"

"You don't know what you're missing. Besides, you owe me, so now, what are you gonna give me?"

"Nothing. Just please let me speak to Desiree. It's important."

"Tell me yes."

I heard Desiree in the background: "Whoever that is, don't believe anything he says."

"Jeremy, please."

"I love it when you beg."

"Don't do this."

"Girl, listen closely."

He hung up.

I quickly phoned her again.

"Oooh," Jeremy said, "I love it when you call back. I'll have you trained yet. All I want to hear is yes. I'll come pick you up tonight, or you'll never get through."

"Jeremy, don't…don't hang up."

"Tell me."

"You made your point. I won't tell anybody. I'll let them believe whatever they want. You can say whatever you want about me. Everybody believes you anyway. I know I'm not much to you, so why continue this? All I want to do is speak to Desiree. Please, Jeremy. Please let me speak to her."

"I can do this all night."

He hung up again.

I dialed again. Busy signal.

I waited for about a minute and dialed again.

"Hello, Cindy. Change your mind?"

I was tired of Jeremy. I was just plain tired. I didn't want to go with Grandmother.

It just felt bad. I didn't know anybody on Mother's side of the family—it was a shroud of secrecy.

"Cindy, you there?"

"Please, Jeremy. Let me speak to her. Don't be mean like this."

He laughed. "Nicole, you don't get it. You're a charity case. Desiree only keeps you around to ease her conscience. I know she hates the day she met you. So, let's cut to the chase. I want only one thing from you, and you know what it is, so if you're ready to say yes, then I'll let you speak to her. One thing I will have to give Desiree is she's faithful to her pets. So, Nicole, if speaking to her means so much to you, tell me, 'Please, Jeremy...have your way with me.'"

I hung up. If this was life, I didn't want it anymore. He was right. I realized Desiree had already given up too much for me. I knew she wanted peace and friends, just like everyone else. I knew she was tired of sticking up for me, constantly hearing all the bad about me. I hadn't even listened to her about Jeremy. I could only imagine what it felt like to be friends with someone like me.

"Yes," I said, "she would be better off without me."

I went back to my room, locked the door, and went to the piano. I could have been with my father right now, but I'd been stupid—stupid about Jeremy. Even now, come to think about it, Mother was probably just telling me goodbye in her own way, and I didn't see it.

She had failed with me, and now she was passing me over to Grandmother as an ultimate sacrifice to gain acceptance from a woman who only used. I was destined to become Carla Robinson the Second. Grandmother would remove whatever was left of the Nicole in me and then turn me into the vision that she and mother only dreamed of, but yet, I would be an empty, vast, desolate wasteland.

I sat at the piano, pushing the keys and the pain back, waiting for Grandmother and feeling like I was losing control of my life. Inevitably, I knew for sure that I would become my mother. I could fight it, but the more I thought of Mother's tears that had almost formed at the mention of how it was to live with Grandmother, the more I knew that whatever resistance I had would be destroyed.

If this was what my life was all about, then why should I hold on? Why should I prolong the inevitable? Why should I be like a person on death row with no more appeals and yet still hoping?

My thoughts painted a picture of being on the beach on an island, with pristine, clear water spraying gentle drops that were cool to the touch. There was no pain, no hurts, no tears. My hands moved and landed on the notes forming the sad A-minor chord. I started to make up something to capture how I felt. I wanted to find what was left of me through the music, through improvisation. I slowed down and kept time with the remnants of my emotions, letting images of the beauty of a place of no more pain wash over me. Then the image of Mother's face enveloped my mind, pushing everything of me away, and then "Moonlight Sonata" took over, brushing aside the freedom I had tried to regain.

Mother's voice rang in my ear, and then I knew I was destined to play the sonata I had come to hate. It wasn't Beethoven's fault. It was me—Mother's creation, programmed to play as I was told even when Mother wasn't around. I was just like Samson, who had been blinded, eyes gouged out, chained to a millstone, and then set walking an endless circle, grinding grain the same way I grinded notes.

I stopped playing and thought about the words "nothing left to take away" and the cost, and I had to accept that I had finally reached perfection. I should have been happy, but without all I had given up, I was dead. I was worthless. I was no better than a mannequin. I was sixteen, perfect, just like Mother made me, but all I thought about was dying. I wasn't Nicole anymore. I was an attraction designed to make others feel good. I played to the desires of the mayor, governors, and other dignitaries, to piano judges and audiences. I'd played at 307 weddings, events, competitions, and recitals over the past two years, sometimes three or four in a weekend.

The repetition of playing was all the same, note after note, taking me on the same familiar path to nowhere, through another round of a pointless song. The piano was supposed to be beautiful, just like Daddy used to tell me I was. I didn't believe Cristofori had envisioned this when he'd invented the piano, yet I'd learned it didn't matter how I felt. Feelings were a commodity I couldn't afford anymore.

Smile. Hold your head up. Cross your legs just right. Play another song. Play another. Then another. "Composure beyond her age," one interviewer had written.

Mother believed the sacrifices and the small attention to detail would pay off. Keep chasing. Take that extra step. We're almost there. All lies.

Did God even care? Did God listen to my prayers? How had I lost my dream?

Was I just a nameless face, a soulless doll? No matter what questions were in my mind, I knew I was nothing more than a container filled and emptied at my mother's whim.

Even my bedroom, once my refuge, now a showroom equipped with a Queen Anne upright piano, plush cream carpet swapped out yearly, walls painted and decorated with images of Beethoven, Chopin, and Bach in oak frames measured and leveled precisely, as Mother demanded. The lamps were centered on the bedside tables; the clothes in the closet were spaced, measured, and hung evenly throughout.

When I was turning twelve, all I wanted was to play in the swimming pool with the friends I once had. I wanted to laugh so hard that my stomach ached. I wanted to get butterflies when a boy I liked spoke and see Daddy's face the day that boy asked me out. I just wanted a simple life, but now I see Mother wanted more.

Daddy's gone now. No one wants me. No one will miss me. No one even cares.

A clear thought to end it all appeared in my mind as I turned to look at the closet: take the t-shirts of the competitions I'd won and tie them together, with one end around the rod in the closet and the other snuggly around my neck. Then I could sit on the soft carpet, and all I had to do was go to sleep. I wouldn't have to go through another day of knowing I was nothing.

I threw the clothes hanging in the closet aside. Would Mother first notice the clothes hanging in disarray or me?

I quickly tied one end of the tied shirts around the wooden clothes rod. I created a slipknot on the other end and placed it around my neck, leaving me just enough room to sit down. The carpet was so soft, almost like thick cotton.

I closed my eyes and let my mind drift, just like clouds.

CHAPTER FIFTY-ONE

March 29, 1983 (Tuesday)

Desiree sat in Timothy's Monte Carlo, quietly thinking about Nicole. Timothy flipped through the radio stations and found WGOV in Valdosta. Al Green's "How Can You Mend a Broken Heart" was playing. She didn't pay attention to the song; she was thinking about the pecan trees in her yard and picking up pecans to get money for the yearly Valdosta Fair. At the fair, she and Nicole had seen how guys would say, "See you later" instead of "goodbye." They'd liked it, so after that night they'd begun saying the phrase whenever they got ready to leave to go home. From that point on, they'd always said it.

Desiree thought about today after school with Nicole when Nicole refused to say, "See you later." Desiree squinted and realized that Nicole had mouthed, "Bye, Desiree," after getting into her mother's car.

"Stop!" Desiree said as Timothy backed out of their drive.

She jumped out of his car and ran toward the house. She knew everyone had a breaking point, and she knew deep down that Nicole had reached hers.

"What's wrong?" Timothy asked.

"I need to call Nicole before we go."

"Not her again. We're gonna be late!"

"Let me just call."

She ran up the steps to the porch and pulled at the screen door.

"Desiree, stop!"

She stopped immediately. She heard the leaves rustle in the bushes in her yard. Another car sped past her fence on the red clay road that ran by her house. Timothy had never raised his voice at her.

"Why are you so concerned about her anyway?" he said, coming up on the porch. "She's just another one of Jeremy's notches on his belt, but she's still all you talk about, especially today on our ride home and now on our date. I'm tired of hearing about her."

"You know what?" Desiree said as she turned around. "You can just go get in that Monte Carlo and don't come back."

His eyes widened, and his voice softened. "It's just I'm always hearing about her lately."

"You don't have to hear about her anymore. You can just go and lose my number."

"I thought you loved me?"

"I do. I really do, but I learned any boy or man who wants me to choose between him or what matters to me most loves himself more. So, I've made my choice."

"It's not like that."

"You can go. I'm going to check on my friend."

Desiree rushed into the house, slamming the door behind her. She ran through the kitchen.

"What's wrong, Desiree?" Mrs. Thomas said.

"I gotta call Nicole."

Desiree ran through the den to the hallway, where Jeremy was sitting by the phone.

"I need the phone to call Nicole."

"You gonna have to wait. I'm expecting a call."

"Give me the phone, Jeremy."

"I told you I'm expecting a call."

"I'm going to ask you kindly one more time," Desiree said. "Please…give me the phone."

"I'm…expecting…a call."

Desiree left and rushed to the laundry room next to the kitchen. Her mother sat at the kitchen table. Desiree took her mother's aluminum bat out of the laundry room.

"What are you doing with that?" Mrs. Thomas said.

"I just need it for a few seconds."

"Desiree?"

Desiree kept walking.

"Desiree!"

"All right," Desiree said, walking toward Jeremy. "We can call the ambulance after I call Nicole."

"You wouldn't dare."

Desiree raised the bat level to his head.

"Desiree!" Mrs. Thomas said, coming up from behind. "Stop! What is wrong with you?"

"I'm sorry, Mama, but I'm sick of him. He's like some dog in constant heat."

"Give me the bat," Mrs. Thomas said. "This is not you."

"I've had enough of him and the way he treats girls. I need to call Nicole."

"Now, what's really going on here?"

Mrs. Thomas' hands were used to hard work, but her eyes, windows to her soul, were filled with peace and beauty. Even through the peace, Desiree could also see her mother had grown tired of Jeremy's antics.

"Oh Mama," Jeremy said, handing the receiver to Desiree, "all she had to do was ask."

Mrs. Thomas shook her head. Desiree snatched the receiver as Mrs. Thomas and Jeremy walked toward the kitchen. She dialed Nicole's number and let the phone ring. She hated that smile Jeremy had given to their mother.

"Nicole," she whispered, "pick up. Please pick up."

After fifteen rings, Desiree hung up to make sure she dialed the right number. When she dialed again, she let it ring for another twenty rings.

Desiree hung up. She wanted to go to Nicole's house, which would take fifteen minutes. "Oh God, please let her pick up this time."

She settled herself by taking deep breaths. Then she dialed the correct number slowly.

~

I opened my eyes to find myself in the closet, leaning against the wall with the scarf tightening around my neck. I stood shaking just as a burst of air filled my lungs. I took the noose off and stood, although wobbly. My chest burning, I went and sat on my bed, staring at the makeshift noose.

The telephone kept ringing. It stopped for a few seconds and then rang some more. After seven more rings, I answered it. The ringing stopped just as I picked it up. I went back to my room, locked my door, and sat on my bed again, staring at the shirts and scarf hanging in my closet, and for a moment, I saw myself.

"That would have been it."

Was that really what I wanted? The phone started ringing again.

For the first time in a long time, I felt a calming, peaceful voice on the inside say, "Answer the phone."

I didn't want to play any more games. For all I knew, that could have been Jeremy on the phone. I thought of hanging the phone up and taking it off the hook, but the gentle voice said again, "Answer the phone."

I waited for the person on the other end of the line to give up, but the phone kept ringing. I unlocked the door, went to the phone, and picked it up.

"Nicole?"

"Daddy?"

"Finally," he said. "I've been calling. I had a bad feeling something was going on. My car phone has been acting up, so I won't beat around the bush. I really believe something is wrong with you. I know I messed up, and I've lost touch with a lot about you, but no matter, I want you to live with me. So, I'll ask one last time. Will you consider leaving with me…tonight?"

A coldness came over me as I imagined hanging in the closet. I always knew he loved me and knew Grandmother and Mother were lying about him not coming back.

"Nicole," he said, "does your silence mean you're happy where you are with your mother, and you don't want to come with me? Please don't worry about my feelings. I can always visit you. I just want you to be happy. I love you either way."

"Daddy, please come and get me."

"What? Are you sure?"

"Yes. Please hurry."

"What's wrong? Are you okay?"

"No. No. I just want to leave. Grandmother is coming to pick me up so I can live with her."

"No, that's definitely not going to happen. Where's your mother?"

"She went to the airport to pick Grandmother up."

"I'm on 75, about five miles from the exit. I'll be there in about fifteen minutes. Fifteen," he said. "Oh no. This phone is about to go out. Fifteen Nicole. You promise me you won't do anything. Please, Nicole, promise me."

"Okay, Daddy. I promise."

"Just pack your bags, and I'll take you with me tonight."

The phone went dead. Once I hung up, I threw some clothes in the suitcase and was done in a couple of minutes. I looked at the makeshift rope hanging in the closet. The phone rang again.

"Hello, Daddy?"

"Nicole," Desiree said, "I'm glad I finally caught you."

"I tried to call you a few times tonight, but Jeremy kept hanging up."

"Oh," she said, "I'm sick of him. He plays those stupid games, using that same old line of hanging by the phone or hanging up on girls. They all think they're special. Oh, I'm sorry, Nicole. It's him so callous about using girls. Throwing his charm around, but Nicole, you threw him off. It's so funny seeing him around the house now. I have never seen him act the way he's acting. You left a mark. Someone finally…finally didn't completely fall for his crap."

"I fell for his crap even after you warned me."

"You said no."

"Does it matter? Maybe that's all I'm good for, anyway."

"It does matter. It really does."

"Where's Timothy?"

"He's gone. I had to hear your voice."

I stopped talking and took in Desiree's desire to hear my voice, but then I realized that it had come at a price for her again.

"Desiree. I'm so sorry. See, that's probably something else I caused. To tell you the truth, I just thought it would be best if I wasn't around anymore. Jeremy was right. I am a charity case. Your life would be so much better without me around, you know?"

"No, I don't know. You listened to a liar like Jeremy and believed him over me? So, you think I stayed your friend because of some charity? You needed me. I saw the bruises on your back that day at school in the seventh grade. I never told you because I didn't want to embarrass you. I chose to take all this and don't regret it."

"I'm sorry," I said, "but I know it's hard having me as a friend. When is enough really enough? I am always happy hearing your voice, even tonight. I would have missed this call."

"What do you mean you would have missed this call?"

I sighed. I didn't know how to tell her.

"You're not talking about what I think you're talking about?" Desiree asked.

"I don't want to lie to you."

"Then don't. Nicole, I love you, and I don't think you realize how important you are to me. You think I don't cry when I still hear my mother's screams telling my daddy, 'Don't do this in front of her.' I grew to know exactly what he did to her after he dragged her into the room and slammed the door. I see my father's face every day when I see Jeremy, especially when he dogs out girls. Sometimes I want the voices and screams to end so bad, but you know what I do when things get really bad?"

"What?"

"I think of you and our friendship."

"Me?"

"Yeah, you. See, I always thought that you didn't need me. You had everything a person could dream of, friends, clothes, talent, great personality, and beauty, but you opened up your life to me and took me in just the way I was. Why do you think I ran cross country?"

"You're good."

"No, in elementary school, you know, the first time I raced, I came in last place in distant running. All that laughter, but you came up to me and said, 'If you like running, don't stop. Do it for yourself and just compete against your own time.' I ran again and came in last place, but you were there at the finish line with a stopwatch, showing me that I had improved. Since that day, I kept at it and found something I loved, and it makes me feel so good."

"I didn't know," Nicole said.

"Before I met you, we moved a lot, running from my daddy until he got killed by some jealous husband, but I didn't have any friends for long. I prayed and asked God for a friend, but after a while, trying to fit in and being pushed aside by all the girls I met—it was either my clothes or my hair. I just found it best to stay off to the side. We didn't have much, so my clothes weren't the best, but I remember the first time I saw you, you were so bubbly. There was something about you.

"You invited me to your birthday party. I still remember that shabby dress I wore compared to all your friends' beautiful dresses. Even back then, Nadia had something to say about me, but you put your arms around me so tight. You made me actually feel special that day. You stood back and let me share your friends. You were my friend that God gave me."

"I didn't know," I said.

"I just think you forgot. I'm not getting off this phone with you until somebody is there with you."

"My daddy just called, and he's on the way to take me with him."

"Then I'll wait with you."

I heard Timothy in the background on Desiree's end of the line. Jeremy's laughter carried.

"Hold on, Nicole," Desiree said. "What are you doing here? I'm not going out with you. I'm on the phone with my friend. Find some other girl if you want to dog someone and especially if you are into raising your voice. Jeremy can help you out, show you all his tricks."

"Don't go out like that," Jeremy said.

"Man, shut up," Timothy said. "I'm sorry, Desiree. She does seem nice."

"She's one of the sweetest girls you will ever know."

Jeremy laughed.

"You really mean that," I said, ignoring Jeremy's laughter.

"Of course, I do. Jeremy will regret this day. Mark my words. He will never find anyone as good as you. Excuse me, Nicole. Timothy," Desiree said, "you can go home or hang out with Jeremy. I'm done."

"I'm sorry," Timothy said. "I shouldn't have raised my voice. I should have listened more. I promise I won't do it again."

"Do what? Never mind. Just let it go. I don't have time for this now," Desiree said.

"I'm sixteen, and I say stupid stuff," Timothy said.

"Desiree," Nicole said, "you did that for me?"

"You got that right," Desiree said. "Never, ever let a man or, in this case, a boy make you choose him like he's some god or has you turn your back to someone dear in your life, and I'm talking about you. Mama taught me that."

"So, you love Timothy?"

"I sure do. And yeah, if I lost him, I would cry, but I would get over him because the one God gives me will not only love me but respect me and respect what I care about."

"Hey," Timothy said, "I'm right here, and I'm sorry."

Then I heard Jeremy's laughter in the background. "Tim, man, you went out like a punk."

Desiree sighed. "Okay, but we do need to talk. I'll call you later. I want to stay on the phone with Nicole."

"Tell Nicole hey," Timothy said.

"Man," Jeremy said, "I need to school you on how to handle women instead of turning into some little punk boy."

"Yeah," Timothy said, "you got it all figured out. Tell me; name one girl who loves you for you."

"Love?" Jeremy asked. "Who needs that? You sho' missing out. The field of girls and women is full, and you just want one? It's like having the same stale sandwich every day."

"I'll talk with you later, Desiree," Timothy said. "I love you."

"I love you too," Desiree said.

"Y'all make me sick," Jeremy said.

"One day," Desiree said, "all of this will come back on you, and you will regret hurting Nicole like you did. You really had a chance with her. Man, you're gonna definitely regret this."

"Not in a million years."

"You'll see," Desiree said. "Nicole, you're still there?"

"Yes," I said as I thought about the exchange of I love you. "Desiree, how does it feel to have a boyfriend?"

"Besides tonight, it's normally nice," she said, laughing. "And what I mean by nice…Hmmm. He not only loves me, but he likes me. It's like what just went on. He puts himself out there. He listens to me vent. Not all boys listen, and I know he gets tired, but he still tries. Even when he makes a mistake, he apologizes. No one's perfect. He walks me to my class, and sometimes we talk about nothing."

I thought about what it would feel like to run into someone else's arms. "You know," I said, "I don't know who I am anymore. I tried so hard to be perfect, but I have no idea how I feel or what's right. I couldn't even see it with Jeremy. To think someone would want me the way I am is almost impossible to believe."

"And for me to get a friend," Desiree said, "when I was moving constantly seemed almost impossible too…but God."

"But all I've been is trouble to you."

Desiree laughed.

"What's that for?" I asked.

"Your memory is bad. You've been worth it all. Now, tell me, why are you thinking of killing yourself? And don't lie to me."

"You're straight to the point."

"And the alternative is what?"

I thought about the shirts still hanging in the closet. I would have been dead by now. I wouldn't have heard how much Desiree loved me.

"Nicole?"

"I was just tired of the pain. I was tired of hurting. I was just plain tired."

"That's what I'm here for."

I heard the front door of the house downstairs. "Nicole!"

"Upstairs, Daddy!"

I heard his quick steps.

"Desiree, my daddy's here. Thank you for everything."

"Where's your suitcase," Daddy said.

"In the room."

"Where are you going?" Desiree asked.

"I'm leaving with Daddy tonight. I don't know where we're going, but we're leaving town tonight."

"I know I'm going to miss you," Desiree said, "but I feel strangely good about it. Just remember, when people get to know you, well, they'll see what I see."

"I love you, Nicole."

"I love you too. See you later."

When I hung up, I went to my room to find Daddy staring at the closet, his shoulders slumped, and head bowed. When he turned to me, he was crying. He came over and held me close. I heard his heart beating fast through his chest. I felt a tear hit my cheek.

"Nicole," he said, "I'm not going to lose you."

He immediately took me to his Cadillac, which was parked on the grass. There were skid marks where he'd stopped.

"You forgot my suitcase. Where are we going?"

"To the hospital. I'm admitting you tonight."

"But you promised you'd take me with you."

"It's obvious I failed before, and I'm willing to admit that now. I won't lose you no matter what, whatever I said, what promises I made. I don't care what these people in this town think. As long as you're alive, that's all I care about."

He ignored all my pleas as we headed to the South Georgia Medical Center emergency room in Valdosta.

CHAPTER FIFTY-TWO

March 29, 1983 (Tuesday)

An ambulance blared past us as Daddy pulled into the hospital emergency room parking lot. You could see the tall pine trees swaying back and forth. Daddy just sat for a moment, staring out the window.

"Daddy, please don't take me in there. School is already bad enough. Now they'll think I'm crazy."

"See, I had no idea that school was that bad. I was blind to everything. What else am I supposed to do? Just pretend everything is okay, smiling until one day you succeed at killing yourself?"

Daddy placed his elbows on the steering wheel and put his head in his hands. He kept shaking his head.

"But Daddy," I said, "I don't want to go."

I kept pleading with him, giving him all the reasons he shouldn't admit me, but none moved him. After a break in silence and another ambulance took off, lights flashing and horn blaring, he leaned back in his seat and whispered, "That could have been for you."

"Daddy, but it wasn't."

He turned to me. "When I was eighteen, I would sit in a park with my mom and pretend our family was normal. One day, I saw a man pushing a little girl in a swing. I don't know why, but I wanted to be like that man. No matter how bad things got in my house with your mother or my mother and father, that one moment stayed in my mind.

"Hope gave me a picture of my desire for something different, and faith held onto that picture. I had faith that one day, my dream would come to pass. Your mother had four miscarriages before you were born. Your grandmother, the doctors, and so many others told us to give up. We almost did, but God said, 'Give Me a chance,' so we did.

"Out of the billions of children who have been born throughout the centuries, God blessed me with you. You are my miracle from God, and I love you. I will never give up on you, and I will never give up on us."

He sighed. "I admit I messed up badly as a father and a husband, but that's over. I will not lose you. So tonight, you choose the hospital or opening up to me and talking everything out. Nicole, you promise that you will talk to me no matter how uncomfortable you feel."

Daddy waited as another car pulled into the parking lot. I thought about my options and knew he would give me time to choose. I knew I didn't want to go to the hospital, but unless I was ready to open up to him, I knew he'd carry me in if necessary.

"I slapped Nadia yesterday in school. There was way more to it than that, but for me, it was just the last straw."

He cranked the car up and drove away as I told him about my day. He turned left on Ashley Street, heading away from Valdosta. On the way home to get my bags, he listened patiently while I talked. Whatever came to mind, I said, but as we got closer to the house, I started getting anxious and wanted to leave town as soon as possible.

"Daddy, tonight Grandmother is coming to take me to live with her. She said it was for a short time, but I don't believe that."

He nodded his head. "I understand. Whose idea was it to live with your grandmother?"

"I don't know if it was Mother's or Grandmother's."

"I'm sure your grandmother had a lot to do with the decision."

"Why is that?"

"I just know her."

"Daddy, we can go ahead and get on the road right now and go wherever you want to go. I got a bad feeling something's gonna happen, and I don't think it's going to turn out right if we go to the house. You don't know what Mother is capable of. Let's just go."

"I'm not running anymore," he said. "When we get to the house, I'll put your stuff in the car, and we'll wait. We can't start a new life by running and looking over our shoulders. I won't do it, and I'm not going to let you do it either. I will let them know I'm taking you with me."

I shook my head and prayed, "God, please be with Daddy."

For the first time in a long time, I felt God listening.

CHAPTER FIFTY-THREE

March 29, 1983 (Tuesday)

We made it to the house before Grandmother and Mother arrived from the airport. I rushed upstairs, grabbed my suitcase, and headed back downstairs, hoping to be gone before they came in. I hoped Daddy would just leave a note. He and Mother had done that for several years.

I found him downstairs, sitting at the kitchen table, playing with a thick manila envelope, and sipping from a glass of water.

He took my suitcase and placed it in the trunk of his car. Then he came back into the house and continued drinking his water like it was a leisurely summer night. All I could think of was how close he'd come to beating Mother before.

"Daddy, I have a bad feeling about all of this. See, when I say you don't know what Mother is capable of, you really don't know."

"Then tell me."

"I was on punishment for a long time after you left, and I called Desiree when I wasn't supposed to. Mama had me lie down on her bed and—"

The front door opened interrupting our conversation. I could already see the effect of what I had just said to him. His eyes had tightened, and his breathing had deepened.

"No," I whispered. "Please, God. Help us."

Mother and Grandmother stepped in.

"Carla," Grandmother said. "What is he doing here? I thought you said all of this was set on the way over here?"

"I thought so too," Mother said.

She looked beaten down, even worse than before. I almost felt sorry for her.

Grandmother stood in her regal pose, perfect posture, head high, and even after her plane ride, her hair was immaculate as if she had stopped by the beauty shop.

"Young lady," Grandmother said, "go ahead and get your suitcase. I need to see what I'm working with."

"Carla," Daddy said, "her suitcase is in my car, and what in the world did you do to Nicole while I was away several years ago?"

I looked at Daddy.

"Carla," Grandmother said, "what's happening here?"

Mother's head was down like some beaten dog.

"Glen," Grandmother said, "you know she's not fit to be her mother. She knows that. I know that. We all know that. That's why she's looking like that."

"I wasn't talking to you," Daddy said.

"You forfeited your voice in this family," Grandmother said, "when you left to chase some pipe dream of starting over."

"Gladys. I was talking to Carla."

"Carla?" Grandmother said.

"Glen…I really don't think you want to hear what I did to her."

He closed his eyes and shook his head. "Just tell me. What happened the day she burned her dress?"

"That day, I did beat her because she wouldn't answer me about burning the dress, but I see now that was just an excuse for me. I didn't even wait for an answer." Mother turned to me. "Nicole," she said, "from the way you looked at me then, I knew something was wrong. Something was so wrong, but I didn't wait. Brenda had told me, but I missed it."

She lowered her head like she was actually ashamed. "I beat you," she continued, "slapped you, slammed you against the wall, and even hit you a few more times…because I thought…I thought you had scoffed at Charles, but now, thinking back, I knew it was nothing but a cough.

"And to think, ever since he left, he's never written or even called me once. I've heard it said you can tell if you've done a good job raising a child if that child comes back to visit after leaving. I must have been horrible. And I actually had truly chosen him over you."

Mother stopped talking.

"Daddy," I whispered, "please, let's just go."

It was like he didn't hear me. The muscles in his jaw tightened.

I stepped back and sat down on the loveseat.

Grandmother walked toward the kitchen. "What are you getting mad about? You asked to hear it, so be a man and listen, or will you run away again like some little boy?"

"Mother," Mother said, "Please stay out of it. It's me, all me. I need to tell my husband the truth."

"Have at it," Grandmother said and stepped back.

I got up to get Daddy to go.

By the time I got to the kitchen door, he'd walked over to the cabinets and grabbed a cup, but his cup hit another, which fell and broke on the counter. He stood staring at the shattered pieces. His hands shook as he turned around and threw the cup against the wall, just like he had thrown the phone.

"You acted like nothing was wrong," he said. "'Trust me this time,' you said. You promised me, but all you did was lie, and all of this started over Charles and some dress?"

He turned toward Mother, her head down.

"Look at me. Look at me!" He rushed back over to her and slammed his fist on the table. "What did she do that was so wrong?"

Mother wouldn't lift her head up.

Daddy stormed into the living room. "I don't believe this. I knew it. I knew it. I knew it! I knew something was wrong way back then. I knew it that night, but I trusted those tears, and you lied to me. You said you would take great care of her."

"You lied to yourself," Grandmother said. "If you knew it, why didn't you do something back then?"

Daddy stopped and stared at Grandmother, not in anger. Then he nodded.

"Gladys, you're right. You're actually right. I should have done something back then, but I wanted to believe your daughter's word. She can turn those tears on like a faucet to get what she wants, at least from me. She used my weakness of wanting to trust and believe her, but Gladys, you're right. I see Carla got her skills of taking advantage of weaknesses honestly through you."

"Really," Grandmother said. "Well, you are the one who let, and I repeat, who let Carla run the house. That's what weak men do."

"You're right again. I was a weak man but let me repeat…was."

Mother slowly looked up, but she stayed seated at the kitchen table while Daddy went and sat on the sofa. I watched both. I eventually sat on the loveseat adjacent to Daddy. Out of the corner of my eye, Grandmother approached Mother and whispered something in her ear. Mother nodded her head, got up, and walked toward Daddy.

"Mother," I said, "please leave him alone."

For the first time, I saw Daddy and Uncle Terrance as the same. They could be so quiet, but even Daddy's rage could flip in a moment, just like Uncle Terrance's.

"Mother," I said as I went to her. "Please, Mother, just leave him alone."

It was like Mother didn't even hear me. She stopped in front of Daddy.

"Glen, what I'm about to tell you, whatever you do to me next, it's okay. I deserve it. What I told you was just that day. There is so much more I've done to your daughter."

"Mother, please." I pulled at her, but she wouldn't stop. I just didn't want Daddy to end up like Uncle Terrance.

"Not now, Carla," Daddy said. "I get the picture. I don't need to hear it now."

"One school day—" Mother continued.

"Carla," Daddy said, "you don't understand. I get the picture. You just need to stop talking right now."

"On a rainy day at school, she wasn't where I told her to be, so I had her stand out in the backyard and get soaked. Then I had her lay down on the kitchen table, and I…I beat her again and again. That's not all. I purposely dressed her to be ridiculed at school, setting her apart from everyone else. Glen, I made your daughter's life a living hell because I wanted her to be strong. I wanted her to be the person I wished I could be."

Daddy stood and walked past Mother and me to the kitchen, where he paced back and forth.

"Glen," Mother said, pulling away from me as she followed him.

"Grandmother," I said, "do something."

"She asked me to stay out of it," Grandmother said calmly. "Besides, when he beats her, then you're definitely mine."

I rushed to Mother. "Mother, please leave him alone."

She looked at me. "Now that I think about it, she didn't do anything wrong at all, but that didn't matter."

"Look." Daddy turned around. "Don't say another word to me right now. Please, just get away from me."

"But Glen. I have slapped her, beat her, and so much more."

"Mother."

"Do you hear me?" he said. "Do not…speak to me right now."

"I killed…your daughter's…spirit."

Daddy grabbed Mother and slammed her against the pantry door. His fist rose as he pinned her with his forearm.

I ran toward them.

Mother held her chin up.

"Please," she whispered, "do it. Please."

She didn't struggle.

Daddy's fist stayed in the air.

I stared into Mother's eyes and saw her agony. She really wanted the pain to end.

Daddy stared at his fist in the air for a few seconds. "No," he said, slowly lowering his fist and letting Mother go.

Mother stood against the door as he walked back to the sofa.

I followed Daddy and sat by him.

I heard him whisper, "I'm no different than my father."

"Daddy," I whispered. "Daddy. Look at me, Daddy."

~

Glen felt Nicole sitting beside him—the only good thing left in his life. Glen's father had always said that life could change a man. His father died many years ago, frustrated and angry. Only three people were at the funeral: the preacher, Glen, and his mother. Terrance refused to go. At the gravesite, Glen shed no tears. He had stopped crying long ago. His mother, though, was broken by his father's death. Even at the gravesite, she still said he was a good man.

She died about nine years back. Some said they were surprised she had lived that long. All of Glen's penned-up anger over her life and death and the frustration and guilt of fighting and sometimes beating his own father to protect his mother, but then helplessly watching her go back time after time, all those years, had come pouring out in tears at his mother's funeral. Deep inside, he'd felt like a failure because he just hadn't been able to protect her enough.

The only person who'd comforted him that day had been Nicole when she'd climbed in his lap and hugged him. At that moment of Nicole's embrace, Glen renewed his vow that he would be a better man than his father and never beat a woman.

Yet today, Glen felt whatever had slowly and methodically taken over his father, and then his brother had now focused all of its attention on him. Violence had found a way into his family—a family he was supposed to protect—even if it costs him his life. All his superficial answers, his clever words of faith, were gone. "God will provide. God will sustain us. Our family will be different from what we saw. I believe, no matter what, God will be there for us." The only thing he could think about now was Nicole.

Daddy got up, walked over, and sat at the kitchen table across from where Mother sat. I followed. The clock above the sink clicked a steady rhythm. Even the refrigerator and fluorescent lights above made audible hums. There was really no such thing as silence.

Then Daddy said, "How do you quiet the voices of regret? How do you find your way off the wrong road?"

Daddy looked at Mother's lowered head.

"God," he said, "I don't know what else to do. I need your help. I should have seen how low I had gotten way before now, but I thought I could eventually work it all out. Then I broke the vow to be home on Nicole's sixteenth birthday.

"God, look at me. After all this time, my word means nothing, and without my word, I am nothing. If nothing changes in me, I will end up beating Carla. And then I know I will be staring down the barrel of a gun…just like my father and brother. My family is a mess. God, I've really tried. Lord, you know I have. I don't know what else to do."

He exhaled.

I closed my eyes to pray, wanting God to give me the words to say something that would make things better. One word, one idea, began to form in my mind. As it developed, Daddy spoke.

"God," he said, "I give up."

That was when I opened my eyes at the thought of forgiveness.

"We're not going to make it without you," Daddy said. "I'm not going to pretend anymore. You know everything. I'm done."

Daddy got up, gently took my hand, and quietly led me toward the door.

I didn't understand all of what was going on, but I forgave Daddy for all he laid claim to. I released him from all my expectations of a perfect father, a man who would do everything right. With each step to the door, I felt free, ready to start anew, wherever that would take us.

"Glen," Grandmother said as she grabbed my hand and yanked me away from Daddy. "She's supposed to come with me. Neither of you can raise Nicole."

There was no panic in Daddy's eyes. He casually walked to the kitchen table, took the manila envelope he had been playing with earlier, and laid it down on the coffee table.

"Carla," he said.

Mother got up and came into the living room.

"This is the envelope containing all the documents of our investment properties, stocks, bonds, and bank accounts. I have set up my own personal account and kept Nicole's education fund, but I left everything else in your name."

"Glen," Grandmother said, "you know you're going to waste her talent. You're going to waste her life. Why would God give someone so special to someone like you and her?" she said, pointing at Mother. "She's mine now!"

"No," Daddy said, as he held his hand out for me, "She has always been mine. Even before she was born, she was mine."

I pulled my hand away from hers and took Daddy's hand.

Daddy looked at me and smiled. "Let's go."

"Carla!" Grandmother said, "You're gonna just stand there!"

"This is not what I wanted, Mother. I didn't want to be like this. I just wanted to be loved just for me, that's it. I discovered I already had that, but it's too late now."

"So, you just whine and quit like you always do."

"Mama, I'm tired."

"It's Mother, damn it!" Grandmother said. "Glen!"

Daddy turned around.

Grandmother slapped him with all her might, but Daddy didn't budge. Mother and I, and especially Grandmother, were surprised.

Daddy held on tightly to my hand and lifted it. "She's all I want."

Mother said, "What about the dream God gave you about us?"

"It's not worth Nicole's life."

"What do you mean?" Mother said.

"Check her closet out."

Mother ran upstairs, and Daddy and I walked outside, heading toward the car.

"No!" is all I heard from inside the house.

We backed out of the driveway, leaving Grandmother on the front lawn and Mother crying inside the house.

I looked back at the window of my room, knowing I would never have to sleep there again. Daddy's car phone rang.

He unplugged the phone and patted me on my hand.

Daddy and I just rode as if going through Darlington one last time. We passed Jenson's Pool Supplies. We passed Moody Air Force Base, our church, and even the Skylark Drive-In Theatre. After a while, we hit North Valdosta Road, where I saw the sign to go to Interstate 75.

"North or south?" he asked.

This was finally happening. I thought about Nicolette Pearson, Piedmont High, and Atlanta.

"North."

CHAPTER FIFTY-FOUR

March 30, 1983 (Wednesday)

I imagined sections of Interstate 75 were originally a road cut through a dense forest. Although it was late when we left the house, the excitement of leaving kept me up during the trip. With each mile away from Darlington, fresh new feelings emerged, feelings that had been buried for so long. Hope, excitement, and peace all seemed to be new.

I sighed, thanked God, leaned back, and smiled as the car continued moving forward. I didn't know how far we'd go: would it be Virginia, North Carolina, or even New York? It didn't matter. I didn't want to mar our new life by telling Daddy where I wanted to be. I just wanted to be where God would have us be.

I let my eyes close, and I let sleep take over.

I felt the car come to a stop. Then he made a right into a neighborhood.

"Where are we going, Daddy?"

"It's a surprise."

We took winding turns through the hilly neighborhood, passing the beautiful two-story houses and big trees. I could actually see a lake in the distance. I was tired, but I didn't complain. Then we pulled into a long, circular driveway that led to a two-story red brick house trimmed in white. I especially liked the black shutters.

"Whose house is this?"

"Take a wild guess."

"Are you serious?"

"It's ours."

"When?"

"A few days ago."

I laughed. "Three-car garage?"

"It gives me a chance to buy that 69 Fastback Mustang I spotted a few blocks away, but more importantly, this was the only house available in the location I wanted for us."

"And where is that?"

"We're near Piedmont High. You always seemed to light up when we talked about it, just like you're doing now."

It had been years since my stomach felt light—joy bubbles. I smiled and then paid attention to the huge front yard.

"Daddy," I said, "I know where you'll be most of the time."

We walked through the front door, and immediately off to the right, in the family room, I saw a nine-foot grand piano in the corner of the room near the fireplace and sliding glass door. The door led to a wooden deck that surrounded the side and the back of the house.

I'm sure Daddy had thought of the cold days of winter when the fireplace would come in handy. I loved the natural heat from logs. Building a fire in the fireplace was something Daddy used to do years ago.

"Nicole," he said, pointing at the staircase in the hallway, "Run up to your room and take a look."

I hurried up the stairs, turned left at the top, and rushed toward a door with a powder-blue plaque stating "Nicole's Room" mounted eye level. I opened the door to a suite with powder-blue walls trimmed in white. To the left was a new queen-sized bed with a matching dresser, chest of drawers, and bedside tables. To the right was a sitting room with a baby grand next to the window. The room also opened to my own private bath.

I walked to a window that peered out over the wooded area, trails, and a lake off in the distance. My feet sank into the cream-colored carpet. I slid my hands over the baby grand piano next to the window.

"Check out your closet," he said, standing at the door.

I opened the French doors to an L-shaped closet. The closet had about ten dresses of an assortment of colors. I giggled and looked back at Daddy.

"I'm sorry. You'll have to help me with selections," he said. "You let me know when you want to go shopping. I just want to see what you come up with."

"I love it, Daddy." The dresses were mostly for a twelve- or thirteen-year-old, but it was just the way he saw me.

"Look in your bedside table drawer."

I opened it and pulled out a telephone.

"Just plug it in. I figured it would be a way to keep in contact with Desiree. Just don't make any calls to China or Africa."

"What about Japan?"

It had been a long time since we'd joked like that. Daddy walked out. I plugged up my phone, called Desiree, gave her the number, and we talked for a bit. She understood about me leaving and wanted to visit soon. It seemed my move was good for both of us. Then we hung up. I ventured around the house some more.

The second-floor private patio, only accessible from upstairs, had an overhang, which meant I could sit outside while it rained. I stood there for a while, looking out over the ledge. The backyard was outlined with trees and shrubs, a flowerbed, and the patio below. There was a walkway heading out toward a gazebo in the middle of the backyard. I went downstairs to find a glass solarium where I would be able to hear the rain.

Maybe that was Daddy's idea too. The back deck was raised slightly and had an overhang to provide shade from the sun. Sitting on the deck, Daddy joined me.

"Nicole, I found a job."

I turned my head quickly to him.

He grinned. "No, no, no. I start in two weeks. It's Monday through Friday. I drop you off at school and pick you up every day. There's no traveling. I don't work on weekends and holidays. You are my priority now."

I stared at him.

"Nicole, for real. You can call me anytime you need me. I let them know that before I took the job."

I leaned back with my eyes still on him. I didn't think he would go through all of this and go back to the way he used to be. I stared deep into his eyes for about fifteen seconds. I actually believed him.

I don't know how long we sat up outside, but I loved the night sky.

Eventually, we went to bed. I was especially happy with my bedroom set, with no more reminders of Charles or anything in Darlington. The view out the window revealed a clear sky and moon staring back at me. I relaxed—no multiplication tables, no piano, no counting, nothing but letting myself drift off to sleep.

"Goodnight, Nicole," Daddy said at my door, then turned to go to bed.

"Daddy."

"Yes," he said as he turned around and stood at my door.

"What if I had said south?"

He laughed and went to bed.

CHAPTER FIFTY-FIVE

March 30, 1983 (Wednesday)

The sun shone through my window, bouncing off the baby grand. I had been up in time to see the sunrise and watch the clear Atlanta sky. Daddy stood at the door.

"Nicole," he said with uncertainty in his voice. "It's time to go register for school. We don't want to be late."

"Good morning, Daddy. Are you okay?"

"I had two bad dreams about your mother, but they were only dreams. I'm good now."

"Is this a dream now?"

"Pinch yourself," he said.

"Ow."

"I guess not."

"You got everything?"

"It's by my wallet downstairs. I also read about the football team at Piedmont High; surprisingly, they're already beginning to be competitive."

"Daddy, I'm glad I'm here, regardless."

He nodded.

"Can you give me a few moments? I'll meet you downstairs."

I scanned my room. I thought of Daddy, Desiree, his prayer, and my prayer.

A reason to hope? "Yes."

I took one last look at my room, grinned, and went downstairs to go to Piedmont High. I enjoyed saying it.

Daddy turned onto the high school campus and passed the school sign with the words "Piedmont High" in dark blue letters outlined in silver. He pulled a brochure out of his pocket and gave it to me.

The campus sat on 117 acres, but to me, it was more like a little city of buildings, parks, and a few ponds, one with a water fountain in the center.

The large multi-colored brick and glass buildings were painted in rich colors that blended well with each other. The main building was dark blue and trimmed in silver. The science department was deep emerald green. The art wing was painted with primary colors.

The brochure mentioned the diversified student body from all parts of the country, even a few from other parts of the world.

We walked into the administration building, and Daddy pulled out my records.

"Excuse me," he asked the secretary, "where will her homeroom be?"

"Her last name and grade?" the secretary asked.

"Peterson, a sophomore."

"Mrs. Collison, room number 121, in the music wing. Follow the dark-blue arrow."

"Daddy, may I walk around a bit."

"Be back in fifteen minutes."

I made my way around the school, trying to find my homeroom. On the walls were brightly colored banners supporting the band, baseball, tennis, golf, chess, debate, and track teams.

Wow, what spirit.

I passed a well-lit display case filled with trophies, and I stopped to read a sign on the right that said "Under Construction. We are increasing the size to make room for more success."

I saw the first and second-place trophies from the competition a few years ago and a picture of Nicolette Pearson. I moved around the corner and down a long hallway toward my future homeroom. Just as I was about to step into the empty classroom, a faint sound of music caught my ear. The sound pulled me further into the music department.

Although there were many people in the other classrooms nearby, none of them were playing music. The piano in the distance sounded familiar, so I followed it away from the crowds and into a quiet hallway.

The closer I listened, the more I realized that the piano was played in a fresh new way, a way I had never heard before, but still, it seemed so familiar. I slowly opened the door with the words "CHOIR ROOM" written in a beautiful Old English script, and I didn't peek in but just listened.

I could tell three guys were playing, a small ensemble with a drummer, bass player, and pianist. There was something familiar about the pianist; he played with boundless freedom, breaking all the rules I had been taught. Almost in the same breath, he purposely played rich chords when the sound dictated simplicity.

I finally realized that was how I had played years ago. I could hear the innocence in his playing that wasn't tainted with compromise.

The group had superior timing and a smooth sound. They played unlike anyone I had ever heard. Still, they resembled a world that I always knew existed—a world beyond the restrictions of form.

I scanned my brochure and saw that the music department had an inspirational gospel choir, traditional choir, concert band, opera group, Chamber Singers, classical group, and at the very bottom of the page: Ensemble—TRIO (New). The brochure mentioned nothing about the style of this ensemble.

I didn't want to leave the peaceful atmosphere they created. It was filled with music and infectious laughter, but when I looked at my watch, I had to go. I finally worked up enough strength to pull myself away. I managed to take a few steps, and then I heard a piano solo that grabbed my heart and glued my feet to the floor.

I closed my eyes and opened my ears. The textures of the sound took my mind to a meadow of luscious green grass and beautiful roses of all colors. Off in the distance were snowcapped mountains.

Eventually, my feet could move again. The solo had ended too soon. I leaned against the wall, hearing the drums and bass and then the laughter that filled my heart. I knew from that moment forward that no matter what happened, I was where I was supposed to be.

As I strolled toward the office to meet Daddy, I realized I really didn't mind not knowing what tomorrow held.

I looked up and whispered, "Surprise me, God."

SPECIAL THANKS

To everyone who listened and gave of your time and patience, I am forever grateful to all of you. How do you thank so many people for all they have done? While looking at the many people who have helped me along the way, I realize God guided me through the process and blessed me with everyone who helped in their own way.

First, I want to thank God for being the ultimate orchestrator. Thank you to every person that came along on this journey. I don't know why it took so long, but that's just in my eyes. You answered my prayer of giving me what I need when I needed it. Throughout this process, you told me clearly what my purpose in life was, and although I didn't understand it at first, I was grateful that my lack of understanding didn't affect the truth of your words. Thank you for blessing me despite my anger toward the church when I told you, "Been there, done that, you're going to have to bless me where I'm at." I had no idea of the level of your mercy and grace when my foundation of church shifted.

Thank you for giving me a story that would take me on a therapeutic process of writing that helped me find the answers to my questions. Now that I look back, I see the world differently. I realize I should have never let anything or anyone affect my relationship with you. Thank you for helping me clear the fog and accept the many truths I once fought. I wanted to ensure everyone knew you were far greater than I had imagined.

My blood family. The blood that runs through our veins connects us. I may not know my entire heritage, but I am proud of the family I do know. Thank you for your love, patience, and willingness to accept me just as I am. I have seen God work in the midst of us all.

Jackson Street neighborhood in Valdosta, Georgia. Chapter 5 is dedicated to your spirit. A neighborhood where people could fight and then play like nothing ever happened. I grew to be comfortable in that environment mainly because of the love we had for each other and realizing it was like one big family. Still today, there was something about Jackson Street. I'm not saying our world was perfect.

I'm just saying it was our world, a world that formed us and a place where we accepted each person just as we were. We were truly a family.

Odell Griffin for being a great big brother. Thank you for showing me by your example that work ethic trumps all. You were the one who let me know that I had a love and talent for writing. Thank you for helping me see myself and understand who I was meant to be. I loved singing, but I had no idea how much I loved writing. Thank you for your lifelong example and for being an excellent big brother. Love you, Infinity Plus One.

Sonya Compton for years of encouragement of my artistic ventures from the talent show in 83 to this book. I thoroughly respect you as a Christian, a woman of God, and a lawyer who loves the law. You also helped me break through the wall I had hit while writing this story and trying to understand how an abused person could turn and abuse someone in the same manner. Your explanation freed me to write, and for that, I am forever grateful.

THE JOURNEY FROM IDEA TO FRUITION.

The unknown woman listener with the Jordan IVs in the 543 SPTS (August 2006). When I was on terminal leave, you patiently sat and listened to me tell this story that later turned into a series. Just by how you listened, let me know there was something to this story. Thank you so much for your kindness and your sacrifice of time.

Marvin and Ruby Barnes (2006), thank you for letting me tell you this story while I taped it. For 2 hours, both of you listened as if my story were a movie. What I appreciated most is that you remained engaged throughout the entire story. I am so grateful for our friendship, which was blessed by God.

Adrienne Williams, Le'Talia, Barnes, and Debbie Alamrew, thank you for reading the first 30 pages of my story, coming back for the rest, and finishing up the story on the way back to your homes. Your honest, heartfelt feedback helped me keep the first book's structure with minimal changes. I truly needed your words during my journey. Thank you for everything.

David Brinson and Tony Foster. My childhood friends. Thank you for being there for me and listening to Chapter 5, a tribute to Jackson Street, our old neighborhood. I wanted the spirit to be accurate, and I knew the chapter was done when it was real to both of you. It's weird. I loved the fact that our neighborhood held no grudges. Even today, looking back, some considered our neighborhood to be rough; I just didn't see it.

Nailah Brinson. Thank you for your help in the early edits and your willingness to share your editing and writing knowledge.

Ashley Hunt, thank you for coming along beside me so many years ago and patiently listening and sharing thoughts of the story. You were instrumental in me finding the benefits of reading aloud and eventually discovering the use of text to talk as an editing tool. Also, thank you for your constructive criticisms that made me revise some of the content that didn't add up. It's all about the story. You made this lonely journey of writing so much more enjoyable.

Sabrina Singleton, thank you for your educational feedback after reading my earlier drafts. You told me that the ending in the first book is like I just got tired. Your words forced me to get back to writing and treat the last chapter the same as the first. Thank you, Sabrina, for always being a person of integrity.

Prudence Griffin, thank you for your willingness to listen on many occasions throughout the years while I pursued this project. Thank you for your consistency in your support.

Erin Crawford, thank you for being a sounding board throughout the years. I loved the tradeoff. I shared my story, and you shared the Twilight and The Hunger Games book series.

33rd Network Warfare Squadron (2006 – 2020) for those who took even a moment to listen and support my goal of writing and publishing this book. Many of you in my work section gave input on which cover to select and why. Many of you have seen or heard of this book from its infancy until now. Thank you.

Christa Whelchel (2007), for your honest, straightforward criticism of my very early writings. I learned all my words had to stand on their own. Your words motivated me to write daily and take classes to ensure the words on the page fully reflected my intended story. In other words, learning to paint with words. Thank you.

Blaine Allen, for your straightforward feedback, saying, "Carla ought to get hit by a bus," let me know I hit the mark with the mother (antagonist of the story).

THE CHICKSANDS CONNECTION

God blessed me with some of my closest friends stationed at Chicksands, England, from 1989 to 1993. I definitely did not want to go to that place back then. I even whined while heading to the Atlanta airport, but I was so wrong. Chicksands was a place where I discovered that Christians could have fun. It was there my relationship with Christ grew, and my friendships flourished. Your encouragement also helped me drop my guard and find my passion for writing. More specifically, I'd like to thank you for letting God use you to bring my book to life.

Lisa "Sunshine" Kirk, my little sister, for being a constant supporter, true accountability, and a woman of strength. I thank God for our relationship. Thank you for being transparent and real with me at all times. You were there before the first word was typed and are still there even after the last word was written. Thank you.

Maurice and Patrina Hughes. Maurice, thank you for your words of encouragement throughout the entire writing process and for giving me a gauge for my growth as a writer. Your feedback has always been constructive. Thank you for being an example of a faithful man following God's plan for his life. I used that as a measuring stick for my writing.

Patrina, thank you for giving me insight into the mind of an avid reader and understanding how to communicate with that reader. Your invaluable words gave me the footing and knowledge to grow as a writer.

Harvey Catchings, for being that person on the side of the road during this marathon and giving me what I needed when needed. I have been blessed with all you have knowingly and unknowingly given me.

Frank Plummer, aka Deacon Plummer, for providing insight and conviction and being a true man of God. Thank you for the many conversations that helped me address the issues in my book. Thanks for referencing other helpful writings and being a true friend.

Michele Thomas, thank you for showing me the other side of Christianity through your faithful, down-to-earth approach to church and this Christian walk. You gave me counsel that helped us select our first church in San Antonio. Thank you for being an example. You have been a blessing to our family.

Shawn Braxton, for always being that consistent force needed to find ways to accomplish any task. You have remained consistent in your support and friendship.

GOD'S PROVISION OF AN EDITOR.

Pamela Keyes, thank you for helping me find my first editor. What timing. I had finished the massive book and needed an editor, and God used you to contact Alicia. Thank you for the handoff.

EDITOR (1)

Alicia Villanueva (2007 – 2009) for being my first editor and giving me a crash course in English and Novel writing. Your first corrections showed me that I should have paid attention in English. Thank you for helping me find the right place to separate one book into three books. You were a Godsend, and you helped me grow as a writer. Thank you for the well-needed foundation in writing in the first and third person and knowing when to break the rules. You are an excellent editor.

Readers (The Navigation system to my destination)

Chiquita Golden-Talbot, thank you for being an advocate for my book. You read the whole book before it was split into three books. Thank you for the insight, conversations, and support over the years. God truly sends the right person at the right time. Little did I know it would be years before I would publish, but you were there in the early part, and I am grateful for all that you provided.

Tonia Blakely, thank you for being transparent after reading my book and educating me about readers' likes and dislikes through your actions. Throughout the entire interaction, I was consistently looking to improve and finally get the story to stand alone. I've said it numerous times: I never want my words to get in the way of the story. You helped me with that process.

Alphanette Waters for building me up. I remember how shaky I was at the beginning. You explained the whys behind your feedback and compared my writing to other authors, giving me the confidence to write my way. Thank you for letting me know I was on the right path and giving me insight into the world of novels. Thank you so much for letting me be Karmen's Godfather. That alone has been a blessing. You raised a great daughter.

Karmen, thank you for supporting my love of writing and helping me find that my book can reach the young and the old. (My Aunt Florrie, 85, read all three books). If someone had asked me, "What is your target audience?" I wouldn't have had an answer because I was just trying to tell a story. You helped me realize that for my first book, I would let the discovery of my target audience happen organically. I guess you and my Aunt Florrie are the bookends of this story.

Shannon, for your early comments about one of the characters being like a blob. Your statement sent me on a journey to understand the true meaning of show, don't tell, and I'm glad your words challenged me to learn. I imagine it's hard to tell someone the truth, but I realize the need for honesty and constructive criticism is essential in growth. It's all about the story, not my feelings. Thank you.

Percy and Alicia Sonnier, Sharee Sullivan, Shana Phillips, and Kimberly. Percy and Alicia, thank you for setting up my first focus group with **Sharee, Shana**, and **Kimberly**. Here's the finalized story from way back. We lost contact after I retired, but thank you for the experience. Your group sacrificed their time to read and talk about the story. Oh, how far I have come, and yet, your words showed me what I needed when it came to storytelling. Thank you.

EDITORS (2)

Marcela Landres (2009 – 2010). Your words as an editor greatly impacted my growth as a writer. I went back to school and took UCLA online courses in writing. That decision helped me find a better way to capture and display the images and emotions in words.

Jefferson (Firstediting.com) (2017) for clear and effective feedback showing my strengths and the weaknesses in the story and how to resolve the issues. I also realized in my writing process that an editor is needed only when I've completely written the story down. It's hard to help someone get to a destination when that person doesn't know where he or she is going.

READERS

Heather Thompson (2017). You were a Godsend. Thank you for your love for the story. You freed me to pick up the series and finish them. Thank you so much for your time and your feedback.

Ken and Karen May (2017). **Ken,** for your friendship. We sang on the praise team and worked with a Children's choir. Those experiences expanded my understanding of the world of music and found their way into the novels. Thanks, Ken. **Karen.** Thank you for taking the challenge of reading all three novels with a partial goal of figuring out the outcome. I know you know that your opinion matters greatly. I appreciate your honesty and words of encouragement throughout this entire process. God has enriched my life with you and Ken. Thanks again.

Kensi May, thank you for helping me with the synopsis and giving your perspective on the story. You are an exceptional writer. It's a level that is inspiring. Keep up all the good work.

Janeen Harris (2018) for being a blessing in our lives. For having a solid relationship with God and always being an enthusiastic supporter. Thank you for all the conversations while you read the trilogy. The conversations helped me realize the story was complete. Your passion for dance and life was contagious. I am thankful you saw the photo for the cover of this book, but little did I know you wouldn't be here to see the book come to fruition, and still, you left a gift of assurance by living your life in such a way that I have no doubt that you are in the presence of God. I'm sure you're dancing in heaven with no more limitations. I miss you.

FINAL PUSH EDITOR (3)

Linda Miller (2018 – 2020), thank you for coming alongside me as my editor to enhance my writing process. God hooked me up with you. You have truly been a blessing and exactly what I needed. Thank you for your generosity of time, facial expressions, and conviction in the storyline when you told me, "Glen would not cuss in front of his daughter." The more I thought about it, the more I realized you were right. You are a blessing. It's about the story, and you have protected the integrity of the story I was trying to tell. You have listened and ensured the intent of my words came out on the page. The right editor means everything to writers, and God has blessed me with you.

FINAL PUSH READERS

Mitzi Singleton, for your insight and spiritual point of view of my story. I also love your angry phone call about Carla, the book's antagonist. After a few moments of talking with you, I realized you hadn't finished the book. You said you were going to finish that night. The next day, you were better. The story answered your questions, and I finished my storyline. You know I love you, my sister.

Jasmine Barnes, Nancy Serrano (Dr. McLendon's office). Thank you so much for reading and voluntarily promoting my book to others. I appreciate your honest feedback and support.

Candice Stephens (2019). I have come to trust your grounded, straightforward candor in such a short time. You are an avid reader with an innate ability to explain your feelings and give the why. Invaluable. Thank you for your willingness to give of your time.

Susi Barrera (2019). I was so encouraged when our discussions about the book turned into real-world situations. Imagine seeing the words you put down on the pages spark those conversations. Thank you for your transparency and viewpoint. I believe in you, and it has been a pleasure to see you with that spark of life and see how God is blessing you.

Aunt Florrie (2019) for believing in me and being the first purchaser of the books even before they were published. Thank you for your note and being the first to put in her preorder. I also laugh about your comment – someone ought to shoot Carla. You're not alone. I love you, and thank you again for everything. You are one of my book ends.

Maureen Patrick (2019), for your contagious laughter. You and Carol are so much alike. Thank you for reading and putting the books in Aunt Florrie's hand. I found my other bookend.

Regina Cody (2019). Thank you for taking the time to read and give your viewpoint of the story and letting me gauge the effectiveness of the final edits. Thank you again.

Sandra Edwards (2019), thank you for giving your drive-by words of encouragement after reading the book. You always had a smile while you maintained your positive disposition. Thank you.

Christa Smith (2020), thank you for reading and willingly refreshing my journey and letting me see the story through your eyes. From October 2019 to April 2020, I primarily focused on my screenwriting course. Your reading and sharing your thoughts gave me a chance to get back into the story and refocus on the final edits of the next two books. Thank you.

PUBLISHING THE BOOK

Nicole Thrash (2018) for providing the information for the Military Authors event, where I found Ms. Sharon to help publish my book. You are a hardworking woman who leads by example. Know you have been a blessing to me.

Ms. Sharon Jenkins (2018 – 2020). What can I say? You were a Godsend. I am so glad I met you. I saw your sign, and you were exactly what I needed. Then I saw your son and granddaughter, and their connection as father and daughter moved me. It reminded me of the relationship between Glen and Nicole in the book. They left a lasting impression.

Your accountability and words of encouragement helped me progress and overcome my shortcomings. I've enjoyed the ride and the opportunity to meet Walda, the Divas of San Antonio Book Club, Grady, Jade, Warren, and Jazmin. I can only imagine where I would be in the process of publishing had I not met you. Most importantly, thank you for your prayers and honesty. I have enjoyed working with you. You are a blessing.

Walda Collins, aka Chef Coco (2018). Thank you for opening up your place so Sharon and I could meet. Also, thank you for hosting the Focus group with the Divas of San Antonio Book Club. Everything was exceptional, especially the food. The atmosphere you've created is like a home away from home. I loved it when your vision and plan came together. May you be blessed with continued success.

Divas of San Antonio Book Club (2019). I was thoroughly impressed with your group. You embodied the phrase "dressed for success." Thank you so much for your insight, viewpoint, and discussion of my book (the title and cover have changed). I am forever grateful for the candid questions that allowed me to address my thought life and its representation within the story. Your discussion helped me conclude the matter of colorism, at least to me.

I admire strong women, and your group embodies that. You have definitely been a blessing to me. I love your vision, and I know it took a lot of hard work to create and maintain a dynamic, successful group. May you continue to grow and flourish.

COVER PHOTOSHOOT

Grady Carter Photography (2019). Thank you for listening to me. I was going to leave the photo shoot up to you, but you brought me back in, listened, and captured exactly what I was looking for. Grady, I have searched the internet, stock photos, and much more, so imagine seeing #55 in your proofs after my long search. That wouldn't have happened without your flexibility and guidance. Thanks again.

Jade Reign Jenkins and Warren D. Jenkins (2019). Jade. Thank you for modeling for the cover of this book. When my wife saw you the first time, she told me that you were the image of Nicole. That alone showed me that God was definitely in this. You did an exceptional job following the photographer and captured what I was looking for. Thank you so much. **Warren.** Thank you for letting Jade model for the cover and for your willingness to participate in the photo shoot. Thank you for having a wonderful father/daughter relationship. I could tell it the first time I saw both of you at that book show. I know that a father/daughter relationship doesn't just happen. It has been great to see it firsthand.

Jazmin Anderson (2019). Thank you for taking the time out to do Jade's hair. Her hair was perfect for the photoshoot, and I found that hair wasn't your primary business. You are definitely multi-faceted. Thank you again for your time and your professionalism.

EDITORS (4)

Dr. Shannicka Johnson, aka Dr. Shan (2021 – 2023). It has been a true blessing to work with you. You're a Godsend. Thank you for your insight, professionalism, and support throughout this process. You have far exceeded my expectations of an editor. Thank you for sharing your gift and experience. I have been tremendously blessed and will continue working with you as an editor. You're definitely up there!

ABOUT THE AUTHOR

Marcus Griffin was born and raised in Valdosta, Georgia. His books are steeped in faith and hope. He credits two experiences as significant factors in his walk with God and his writing.

The first experience occurred in the late 1970s. Marcus' favorite pastor, who made the bible more than just 'some old book,' was removed. In anger, he stood on his church steps and told God that he would rather be with people in the streets than in the church. In his first personal experience with God, he discovered he couldn't blame God for the actions of those in the church. This experience was foundational in his life, and his walk with God became personal.

Twenty years later, another experience in the church would impact his life, where he would go to God, telling Him, "Been there. Done that. You're going to have to bless me where I'm at." Shortly after, in August 2006, a story came to him and took him on a 17-year therapeutic journey to answering his many questions about God, church, and truth.

The 2006 story ignited his passion and dedication to writing. He committed to learning his craft of writing by attending UCLA Online, Gotham Writers Workshop, UCLA mentorship program, and many other venues, spending 10,000-plus hours in writing. His journey brought an appreciation of storytelling and communicating authentic living.

Out of that same journey came The Nicole Peterson Series. He published his first book, *Nothing Left to Give*, in 2020. In early 2024, the author plans to publish the series' second book, *Beyond Words*.

Marcus is a professed Christian of 40-plus years, retired from the Air Force after almost 22 years. Throughout his service at various bases, his love for music and people led him to men's singing groups, Children's Choir, and a Gospel praise team. He also served as a mentor, counselor, and confidant. Hearing about and experiencing the good and the bad of the Christian walk found its way into his stories, which he equates to the edgier side of Christianity. His flawed characters take the reader on a thought-provoking emotional roller coaster ride.

He lives with his wife of 34 years and their son in Schertz, Texas, just outside San Antonio.

Made in the USA
Columbia, SC
19 April 2024